THE FURYCK SAGA

WINTER'S FURY

THE BURNING SEA

NIGHT OF THE SHADOW MOON

HALLOW WOOD

THE RAVEN'S WARNING

VALE OF THE GODS

KINGS OF FATE
A Prequel Novella

THE LORDS OF ALEKKA

EYE OF THE WOLF

MARK OF THE HUNTER

Sign up to my newsletter, so you don't miss out
on new release information!

http://www.aerayne.com/sign-up

NIGHT OF THE
SHADOW MOON

THE FURYCK SAGA: BOOK 3

A.E. RAYNE

For more information about A.E. Rayne
and her upcoming books visit:

www.aerayne.com

 /aerayne

For Alfie

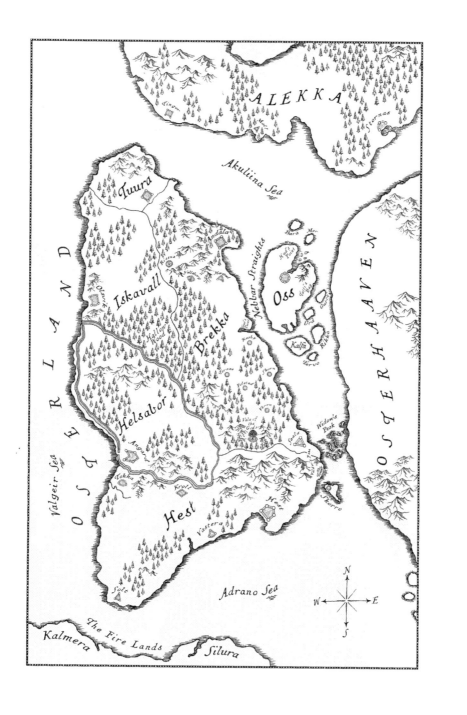

CHARACTERS

On the Island of Oss

Jael Furyck, Queen of Oss
Eadmund Skalleson, King of Oss
Aleksander Lehr
Thorgils Svanter
Eydis Skalleson
Brynna 'Biddy' Halvor
Gisila Furyck
Axl Furyck
Amma Furyck
Fyn Gallas
Evaine Gallas
Morac Gallas
Runa Gallas
Entorp Bray
Torstan Berg
Sevrin Jorri
Beorn Rignor
Tanja Tulo
Odda Svanter
Otto Arnwald

* * *

On the Island of Kalfa

Ivaar Skalleson, Lord of Kalfa
Isaura Skalleson, Lady of Kalfa
Ayla Adea
Bruno Adea

In the Kingdom of Hest

Haaron Dragos, King of Hest
Bayla Dragos, Queen of Hest
Haegen Dragos
Irenna Dragos
Karsten Dragos
Nicolene Dragos
Berard Dragos
Jaeger Dragos
Morana Gallas
Meena Gallas
Yorik Elstad
Egil Asgun

* * *

In Tuura

Marcus Volsen, Elderman of Tuura
Gerod Gott
Hanna Boelens
Kormac Byrn
Branwyn Byrn
Aedan Byrn
Kayla Byrn
Aron Byrn

On the Island of Bara

Frits Hallstein, Lord of Bara
Falla Hallstein, Lady of Bara
Borg Arnesson
Rolan Arnesson
Toki Arnesson

* * *

In Saala

Rexon Boas, Lord of Saala
Osbert Furyck, King of Brekka
Oleg Grenal

PROLOGUE

'You and I, my friend, we are as one. After all these years, it hurts me to do this to you. But I must, for they do not care about me. They disavow me. Disown me entirely! After all that I have done? For *their* cause? And yet, they have no need for me. They seek him. Only him.'

The woman with the black hair reached out her alabaster hand, barely weathered, even after all these years. She ran her fingers over the page, shivering at the familiar sensation of the fine vellum beneath her skin; even older than her and yet, still throbbing with life and power.

So much power.

Closing her eyes, she took a deep breath, gripped the top of the page and tore it from the book. 'There will *never* come a time when they don't need me!'

PART ONE

The Cave

CHAPTER ONE

'No!' Jael shook her head and slipped away, trying to hide her smile. The moon was bright, and she knew that he would see her face.

'No?' Eadmund followed her. 'Are you sure?'

The water was warm. There was still snow on the ground, but the water wrapped itself around their chilled bodies, cocooning them in liquid heat.

'Of course I'm sure,' she insisted, batting him away as he crept towards her.

'Then why are you smiling?' Eadmund laughed, forcing his way through her half-hearted attempts to stop him, kissing her pursed lips. 'If it's *no*, then why are you smiling?'

'I promise you, if I were pregnant I wouldn't be smiling!' Jael grumbled, letting him kiss her.

'No?'

'No! I couldn't think of anything worse!'

Eadmund sunk back, his smile vanishing. 'Really?'

Jael froze. She didn't know what to say without making it worse. 'I...'

Eadmund reached for her hands, his eyes down on the shimmering water. 'I understand but...' He looked up, and his smile came racing back. 'You'll change your mind when it happens. I know you will.'

Jael squirmed away from his gaze, frowning.

'I know you will, Jael Furyck. You love me. I know that too. We're meant to be, remember? You and me.'

'Jael!'

Jael turned away into the darkness.

She blinked, squinting. Shivering suddenly.

'Jaaaeeelll!'

'Grandmother?'

***

'Meena!' Berard tripped over a loose cobblestone as he ran after the woman whose red hair was streaming behind her as she scurried away. 'Meena!'

Meena sighed impatiently and stopped. She didn't know what he wanted, but she needed to leave. She had to go before Jaeger found her.

Before the sun set.

Berard stumbled to a halt. He had spied Meena from the first-floor balcony of the castle and he'd run all the way to try and reach her before she left. He looked down at her tiny sack. 'But where are you going?' he asked in surprise, trying to catch his breath.

Meena tapped her head with her free hand, staring at her boots, avoiding those concerned grey-blue eyes. She did not want to stop; did not want to stay. Berard Dragos had always been kind to her, but she would not let that influence her decision. 'I, I, I am leaving,' she said resolutely, looking up at last.

'But you can't!' Berard insisted.

'My grandmother is d-d-dead,' Meena sniffed. 'There is nothing here for me now. There is no one.' She shuddered, not wanting to think of Morana creeping around that horrible chamber, so gleeful that Varna was gone.

'This is your home, Meena,' Berard said kindly. 'You have no one else, do you? No one who will take you in?'

'I have an uncle. He lives on Oss. I will find my way there!' Meena turned to leave. She had to go. She couldn't stay.

Berard reached for her arm. 'Please, why don't you come back to the castle? Just for tonight. I know it's been a terrible shock, what happened to Varna, but you can't run off like this. You won't survive out there all alone.'

Meena's shoulders slumped as she turned around, her chest heaving. 'You don't understand. You don't...' she sobbed. '*She* let this happen. *She's* there. She'll kill me next!'

'Who?'

Meena shook her head, clamping her lips together, too scared to utter another word. She looked behind Berard, to the castle which towered above them both, to the tiny window on the very top floor. Shivering, she imagined the cold, dark chamber she would have to share with her evil aunt if she stayed.

The woman who had helped murder her grandmother.

Morana Gallas.

***

There was no pool. No Eadmund. No moon. Just darkness.

Heavy and cold.

Jael crept forward. 'Grandmother?' Her heart was thumping like a drum, her breath coming in short bursts. She listened but heard nothing. 'Grandmother?'

'Jael.'

It was faint now, so faint that Jael could barely make out which direction the voice was coming from.

And then light. Dull afternoon light.

An alley. A body.

Jael ran towards the crumpled figure sprawled in the dirt. 'Grandmother! No!'

Edela lay there covered in blood. Ashen-faced. Eyes closed. Chest still.

'Grandmother!'

'Jael?'

Jael opened her eyes, gasping for air, her head swivelling in confusion.

She was on *Sea Bear*.

Too far away.

Aleksander was by her side, gripping her hand; Axl behind him.

'Nooo!' she screamed uselessly. 'Nooo!'

'What's happened?' Aleksander squeezed Jael's hand, trying to get her to focus on him. 'What have you seen?'

Eydis' head went up on *Ice Breaker*. 'Jael?'

Eadmund was quickly at his sister's side. 'What is it? Has something happened?' He turned to his helmsman. 'Villas, bring us closer to *Sea Bear*.'

Gisila was there now, gripping her daughter's other hand, her throat tightening with every moment. 'Jael?'

But Jael was barely there. She was in the alley, desperately wanting to reach down and pick up her grandmother. To carry her back to the house. To Biddy. To Entorp.

To help.

Edela needed help.

Jael closed her eyes, shutting them all out again.

Edela needed help!

She couldn't be dead. She needed help.

Thorgils, Jael thought. Thorgils.

She saw the alley. Edela's body. Still. Lifeless.

She needed Thorgils.

Thorgils!

Jael was sobbing now. 'Thorgils!'

She saw him, holding a curl of hair in his hand, smiling to himself as he ambled towards the square.

In the wrong direction.

Thorgils!

Thorgils!

***

Thorgils tucked the soft, golden curl back inside his pouch.

There was a ray of hope now, and he wasn't going to shut it behind that door any longer. He strode away from the alley, imagining Isaura walking beside him. Listening to his growling stomach, his mind quickly focused on thoughts of Biddy's chicken and ale stew.

He stopped suddenly, frowning as the clouds darkened overhead, threatening a sudden downpour. Edela had not seemed well. She'd looked pale, unsteady on her feet.

Jael would never forgive him if something happened to her grandmother.

He turned back into the alley, deciding that it wouldn't hurt to make sure that Edela was alright. And, perhaps he could encourage her back to the house and see how far along that stew was?

***

Jael opened her eyes.

Gisila was staring at her, kneeling on the wooden boards of the deck, her one open eye pleading. 'Jael! What has happened?

Please!'

'Edela...' Jael shook her head, trying to wake herself up. 'I had a dream. She's hurt. Someone tried to kill her.'

Aleksander gasped.

Evaine.

'Is she...' Axl didn't want to go on. His sister's face was streaming with tears, her body visibly shaking. He'd never seen her like this. 'Is she... dead?'

Jael blinked. The dream had retreated now, but her ears were buzzing so loudly that she could barely hear her own thoughts. She pushed everyone's hands away and stood, limping quickly out of the wooden house towards Beorn. *Ice Breaker* was approaching; Eydis and Eadmund in the bow. 'Let them come closer, Beorn, and once I've spoken to Eadmund, get us back to Oss as fast as you can.'

Beorn nodded, disturbed by the look on Jael's tear-stained face. He jerked the tiller back and forth, trying to slow them down. 'Reef the sail!' he yelled to his men. 'Reef the sail!'

***

'Who is Morana?' Berard wondered.

Meena gulped as the black-and-white-haired woman shuffled across the square towards them, her stooped frame pointing ominously in their direction.

Berard turned to follow Meena's gaze. 'Is that her?' he asked, remembering something Jael Furyck had said about a black-and-white-haired dreamer. 'Is that Morana?'

Meena nodded, caught between an urgent need to run and the certainty that there was no point now.

Morana knew where she was.

'Is she a dreamer?' Berard whispered as Morana slithered

closer.

Meena nodded again, trembling all over, curling her shoulders into a defeated heap. 'She is my aunt. Varna's daughter.'

Berard was shocked. 'Varna had a *daughter*?' He turned towards the woman, swallowing, his face as anxious, his shoulders as curled as Meena's.

Morana glared down at Meena's sack, then back up to her niece's terrified face, peering at her blotchy cheeks, her red, bulging eyes. 'You're *leaving*?'

Berard was surprised by the venom in the woman's voice as it rasped out of her twisted mouth. She didn't acknowledge him, and although he was well used to being ignored by his father and disparaged by his brothers, he was not used to being so rudely disregarded by strangers. He coughed nervously. 'And who are you that is asking?'

Morana's eyes flared in annoyance, her head snapping to Berard who was barely taller than Meena and just as pathetic looking. 'Who am *I*?' she growled, her thick eyebrows sharpening as she intensified her dark-eyed gaze. 'I am Morana Gallas, your brother's new dreamer.'

Berard shook his head in confusion. 'My brother? You mean Jaeger?'

Morana laughed. 'Didn't he tell you?'

Berard grabbed Meena's hand down from her head. 'No, he didn't,' he said boldly, forcing his eyes towards Morana's. 'Perhaps I shall go and speak to him about that? Come along, Meena, you can accompany me.'

Meena blinked, sensing her aunt's need to claim her, her own desire to run for the mountains, and now, Berard's offer of help. She shivered, confused, desperate to tap her head, but now she had no hand free. 'I, I,' she started, then felt the warmth of Berard's hand, the strength in it as it squeezed hers. There was comfort there, much more than she would find in the mountains or with Morana. 'I... yes.' Meena ducked her head away from her aunt's scowl, allowing Berard to pull her towards the castle.

Morana frowned after them.

Meena was useless, she was sure. Useless for now, at least. And she just had to make sure she stayed that way.

Morana smiled. It was time to have a little talk with Jaeger.

***

It was cold in the alley.

Thorgils thought of Odda's cottage, which was always cold. He'd need to bring in some more wood for the night. His mother was still unable to get out of bed, and he had to make sure that she stayed warm while she recovered from her illness. And then he'd have to think about building a proper house; one with thick, plastered walls like Eadmund and Jael's. She would only get older and less inclined to cope with the challenges of winter on Oss.

He stopped suddenly, squinting at a basket that lay abandoned up ahead.

Edela had been carrying that basket.

Thorgils ran, holding his breath, not wanting to be right, but then he saw her boots. Her legs. 'Edela!' he cried, dropping down to the dirt beside her, instantly aware of the blood soaking through his trousers. He tore off his thick, bear-fur cloak, draping it over her body. 'Edela?'

Her face was snow-white. Cold to touch. Her eyes were closed. She was not moving. Thorgils dug his hands under her slight frame, scooping Edela into his arms.

Standing up, he held her tightly against his chest and ran.

***

'What's happened?' Eadmund called over the row of battered shields lining *Ice Breaker's* gunwale. Eydis was sobbing next to him, unable to speak. He couldn't get any sense out of her at all. And there was his wife, across the rolling waves, looking just as upset.

'It's Edela!' Jael called back, feeling the sting of tears in her eyes. 'We have to go to Oss! She's been attacked!'

'*Attacked?*'

'We have to go! You carry on to Saala!' Jael waved impatiently at him before walking over to Beorn, who bellowed at his men to shake out the sails.

The wind was stiffening.

They needed to fly.

***

Biddy hurried out of the house at the sound of her name, the puppies charging past her to see who was coming.

'Get Entorp!' Thorgils yelled to Askel as he rushed past the stables. 'Hurry!'

Askel took one look at the limp body in Thorgils' arms, dropped his shovel onto the manure pile and ran.

'Edela!' Biddy threw her hands over her mouth in horror as Thorgils hurried inside, blood dripping down his legs. 'Edela!' she cried, following after him.

Thorgils placed Edela onto one of the beds lining the walls of the main room. The fire was blazing, and the house felt warm. He unpinned her cloak, gulping at the sight of so much blood.

Edela's dress was stained a deep, dark red; her skin pale and mottled.

Shaking his head, still in shock, Thorgils stepped back to let Biddy through.

Biddy held her breath as she bent towards Edela, reaching for her wrist, searching for a pulse. 'Edela?'

***

Haaron Dragos looked morose as he slouched on his enormous dragon throne. His wife appeared hardly bothered, yawning as she stood next to him. In fact, she was almost cheerful. Amidst the devastating events of the past few days – the decimation of their entire fleet, the destruction of their piers, their sons' injuries – Varna Gallas had died.

And Haaron was bereft.

Bayla could not understand why. She had been a vile, odorous crone who had manipulated him since he was a boy, keeping him on an unambitious leash of her own making. He had been controlled by Varna, and now he was free.

Bayla was savouring the moment.

Haaron was not.

'I have spoken to Dragmall,' Haegen announced somberly as he limped up to his father's throne. 'He will speak at Varna's burial tomorrow. Sitha is helping to prepare her body. She will be laid next to her mother and grandmother, as she wished.'

Haaron looked up, barely listening. He nodded briefly, wondering what he was going to do now. Everything had fallen apart so suddenly. It was as though the gods had removed their favour.

All of it.

All at once.

And now they had taken Varna from him, just when he needed her advice more than ever.

How were they going to dig themselves out of the pit they were sinking into without her guidance?

Bayla placed one hand on his shoulder, and Haaron turned to her in surprise. 'It was well past time for you to have a new dreamer,' she said firmly. 'Varna held on for such a long time. For you. But the shock of what happened out on the square... it was obviously too much for her. The shame that she had not dreamed of what those Furycks would do...' Bayla smiled widely at Haegen, who frowned at his mother's gleeful expression. She was the only person in Hest who saw anything to smile about.

Haaron sighed as he watched Osbert Furyck enter the hall. *King* Osbert now, he reminded himself.

Another problem to deal with, amongst so many.

He stretched out his back, groaned irritably and stood.

'My lord.' Osbert limped forward, bowing briskly.

Haaron nodded disinterestedly, looking around for a slave. He was thirsty for wine and eager to be alone; wishing he could talk to Varna; already missing her advice. 'You are happy with your preparations, my lord?'

'I am,' Osbert said wearily. 'We will leave at first light. I must return my father's body to Brekka quickly.' He swallowed, feeling an unwelcome surge of emotion that he had no intention of acknowledging; not in front of Haaron and his family at least. 'I appreciate the loan of your cart.'

'Of course,' Haaron said with a dismissive wave of his hand. 'We are still allies. We still have Helsabor to conquer together.'

Haegen raised an eyebrow, thinking that after the loss of their ships and the deceit of the Islanders, there were more important things than Helsabor to turn their attention to now. But the eager look on Osbert's face reflected his father's.

He sighed.

'Indeed,' Osbert agreed. 'Once I have put the Islanders to the sword, and taken my revenge on my cousins, I will come back to claim it with you.'

'*If* you can put the Islanders to the sword,' Haegen suggested. 'Jael is a queen now, and with Eadmund Skalleson and her brother by her side, I think you might find it harder than you imagine. Especially having just seen what they can do.'

Haaron frowned at his eldest son, then smiled at the sight of wine being hastily delivered to him. He took his silver goblet, inhaling the fruity scent, which reminded him of Varna and their talks in his chamber. Instantly miserable again, he drank deeply. 'She is a queen, yes, but a murderous one now, and the gods will not look favourably upon her, will they? Beheading a king? Her own family? A Furyck?' He shook his head. 'Oh no, Furia will not be pleased with Jael Furyck at all.'

***

It was dark now, and most of the crew were inside the wooden house, grateful to be able to shelter from the biting wind. But as much as Jael wanted to dream and find Edela again, she couldn't sleep. Her mind was full of worry for her grandmother, and she felt far too tense to relax, so she limped around the deck instead, embracing the bitter cold as it numbed her face and froze her limbs.

Aleksander handed her a cloak. 'You might need another one if you're going to spend the night out here.'

Jael turned and took the thick, woollen cloak, wrapping it around her shaking shoulders. 'Thank you.' Her lips barely moved. She didn't want to speak at all.

Not even to him.

'Edela is strong,' Aleksander said softly. 'As strong as you.' He felt awkward, wanting to put his arms around Jael, to comfort her in some way. To be comforted by her in return.

But he knew her.

He didn't move.

Jael glanced at him, swallowing hard. The moon shone above him, highlighting his sharp cheekbones, his hollow eyes. 'It was bad.'

Aleksander reached out then and pulled her frozen body towards him, wrapping his arms tightly around her. His wounded shoulder was throbbing so much he wanted to scream, but all he could think about was Edela.

Evaine had done this, he knew. It had to be her.

He just hoped they could make it back to Oss before it was too late.

***

'Brother,' Jaeger sneered, looking from Berard to Meena and back again. He stood in the doorway of his chamber, not inviting them in.

He was furious.

Berard didn't blame him. Jaeger had just had his new wife stolen away while suffering through another humiliating defeat at the hands of Jael Furyck and her Islanders. 'Could we, perhaps, come in?' Berard wondered nervously, glancing at Meena who was jerking about beside him, trying to squirm her hand out of his.

Jaeger moved aside and ushered them in, noticing as he did so that Berard had hold of Meena's hand. 'Is there something you've come to say, Brother? Some news, perhaps?' Jaeger followed them into his chamber, not offering them a seat or a drink.

He was still too annoyed with Berard to be friendly.

Berard had let it slip that he'd encountered Jael Furyck as she was escaping the castle, but he'd been so drunk that he'd simply let her go.

No one was that interested in talking to him at the moment.

'News?' Berard looked confused, then followed Jaeger's gaze to his hand as it held Meena's. He dropped it quickly and moved away from Meena, who immediately started tapping her head. 'No, I've just stopped Meena from running away. From leaving Hest.'

Jaeger frowned at Meena, who was doing her very best to avoid his eyes. Whether from fear or displeasure, he couldn't tell. 'Leaving for where? Where were you going, Meena?'

Meena wanted to run out of the room. She couldn't breathe. The day had been long and upsetting. Her grandmother was dead, and now Morana loomed over her: a vicious, black-eyed threat.

And Jaeger. It was all his fault, she knew.

'You k-k-k-killed my grandmother!' she said boldly, lifting her eyes at last.

Berard gasped, horrified, turning to his brother.

'*Me*?' Jaeger was wide-eyed. 'Yes, I did. And she deserved it too, the stinking old bitch. And now we're all free of her and her scheming and plotting.' He stared at Meena, surprised by her anger. 'I thought you would've thanked me? You, who spent your life being terrorised by her!'

Berard was mortified. 'Jaeger!' he hissed. 'You killed a dreamer? *Father's* dreamer? But... but...'

'But what? And so what? Father will never know, not unless you tell him. Varna did nothing but turn him against me since I was a boy. Why wouldn't I kill her for all that she did to me? And you, Meena. How can you forget so quickly?' He grabbed Meena's hand, pulling it down from her head, staring into her frantic eyes. 'How can you forget so quickly?'

His eyes had more than anger in them now, and Meena blushed, remembering what he had done to her that night. That night that now felt so long ago. She looked away, hiding her face from them both.

Berard frowned, finding no satisfaction in anything his brother was saying. 'And what of this woman? Morana? She says that she's your dreamer.'

Meena shivered, shrinking away.

Jaeger peered at his brother, not noticing. 'Morana... mmm, yes she is, I suppose. Varna's daughter. A dreamer, just like her mother. She can read the Book of Darkness, and she's going to help me get everything I've ever wanted.'

Berard was unsettled by the disturbing look in his brother's amber eyes. He shuffled his feet, trying to think of what to say.

'You go, Brother,' Jaeger smiled, ignoring Berard entirely. 'Meena and I need to have a little talk.'

Meena gulped, tapping her worn boots on the dark flagstones.

Berard was hesitant. 'But –'

'I'm sure Father will be looking for you,' Jaeger said firmly. 'And you know how angry he gets when he can't find you, Berard.'

Berard thought of his purple-faced father and his ear-breaking curses. He looked at Meena, his face pink with guilt, then ducked his head and turned to the door.

'And send Egil up if you see him,' Jaeger added, not taking his eyes off Meena. 'I've run out of wine.'

Berard nodded briefly as he turned the door handle and slipped away.

Jaeger's smile vanished as the door closed. He grabbed Meena's arms, trying to wake her up. 'We must talk, you and I. About what will happen now, with Varna gone and your aunt here.'

Meena shivered, not looking up.

'You're truly *mad* at me for killing Varna?' Jaeger laughed incredulously as he led Meena towards the bed and pulled her down to sit beside him. '*Varna?*'

Meena's body tingled from his touch, but still, he was a murderer. She did not feel safe. 'You shouldn't have hurt her. She was o-o-o-old.'

'*Old?*' Jaeger snorted. 'You think the old shouldn't be punished? Even when they do terrible things? To you, Meena. Think of all that she did to you!' He stroked his hand down her shuddering arm. 'Think of all that she *didn't* do. How she didn't care for you. Didn't show you any warmth or affection. None! Not in all the years you were with her.' He leaned forward, turning Meena's face towards his. 'Tell me you aren't glad she's dead. Grateful that I ended her.'

Meena blinked as he bent forward and kissed her cheek. She fought the urge to move, caught between the danger she knew he posed and the desire she could feel weakening her limbs. 'I...'

She closed her eyes and saw Varna. She heard Varna screeching at her, beating her, starving her, bullying her, hating her. 'I am glad she's dead,' she whispered, at last, opening her eyes.

Jaeger smiled and kissed her roughly, feeling Meena relent as she came towards him, willingly now, kissing him back. 'Good. Because I need you, Meena,' he breathed, his stubble scratching her lips. 'I don't trust Morana, but I do trust you, and you are going to keep a very close eye on her for me.'

***

'She is coming.'

Evaine glanced at her mother, wringing her hands as they walked along the beach. 'Will she know it was me?'

'Know?' Morana laughed. 'She will know. Of course! They will all know, but there will be nothing they can do, not with Eadmund here to protect you.'

Evaine looked relieved. She was desperate to see Eadmund, to feel safe in his arms again.

'But you must make sure that he stays yours. They cannot be together. Ever.' Morana stopped and grabbed Evaine's wrists, pulling apart her nervous, twisting hands. 'Do you understand me, girl? A candle will not do. Not for what we need. Not after what you did to Edela Saeveld. Trying to kill a dreamer?' Morana frowned in annoyance at the mess Evaine had made. 'You must go to my book.' She shook her head, dismissing Evaine's protests. 'Not *that* book! Before Morac left Rikka, I gave him another book to keep for you. As soon as you wake from this dream, you must go to him and get that book. You will find the spell you need on the very last page.'

Evaine smiled, suddenly hopeful, closing her eyes, imagining Eadmund.

And when she opened them, Morana had gone.

CHAPTER TWO

Jael splashed down into the water, not waiting for *Sea Bear* to make land. She waded through the frothing waves towards the beach, Axl and Aleksander surging through the icy water behind her.

The afternoon sky was grim and foreboding, drizzle misting over them as they reached the foreshore and ran, not caring for the slickness of the stones or anyone else left behind. They ran towards the hill that led to the stone fort, where Jael could see Thorgils, his bright-red hair bouncing in the wind as he waited by the gates.

Swallowing, Jael limped closer, trying to ignore the nagging pain in her leg; almost wanting to stop and turn around; afraid to hear the truth.

Afraid that they were too late.

'Thorgils!' she called, cresting the hill.

Thorgils walked quickly towards her, his usually cheerful eyes hooded, his shoulders up around his ears in tightly bound knots.

'Thorgils!' Jael reached him, grabbing his forearms, pleading with her eyes. 'Is she alive?'

Thorgils sighed heavily as Axl and Aleksander joined them, breathless after the climb. 'Yes. She's at the house.' He noticed Fyn crossing the stones with Jael's mother, and a girl he didn't recognise. 'You go. I'll bring your mother.'

But Jael wasn't listening as she ran past him, desperate to get to the house.

***

Isaura changed her mind and turned away, crumpling the scroll, shoving it back into her purse. She shook her head, cross with herself but undecided as to why. Because she had written the note in the first place? Dared to think of giving it? Or for not having the courage to do so at all?

Her body was tense. She was desperate to do something, but so used to being afraid.

'Isaura?'

Isaura swallowed and turned around. 'Bram,' she smiled nervously. 'It's been a long time since we saw you on Kalfa. I thought you must have given up on trading?'

Bram's small, blue eyes were suddenly sad, but he blinked, and they quickly twinkled again. 'Well, you can't keep a man like me shackled to the land for long. Not when there's breath in this old body and men thirsty for adventure and gold.' The old trader sighed wearily, pushing his boots against the stones, trying to still the roll of his body. 'We've been at sea for the past few months. Down in Kalmera, Silura, up past Helsabor and Iskavall, even Tuura, although we didn't have much joy in that miserable shit-heap. We're ready to head back to Moll, but first, we thought we'd round the islands.' Bram yawned, one eye on his men. 'Hopefully, I can find some takers for the last of my furs.'

'I'm sure you will. From what I hear, the Islanders have a lot of gold to spend these days.'

Bram narrowed his eyes, lowering his voice. 'I hear the same, but perhaps not the Kalfans?'

Isaura looked uncomfortable, glancing back to the fort, sensing the guards' eyes following her. They stood on the beach, watching Bram's crew unload armfuls of furs and hides. 'No, it appears that my husband left Skorro before he could claim his share. Perhaps his guilt finally got the better of him?' She swallowed, regretting speaking so boldly.

'Mmmm, well I hear many things on my travels, but none so unpleasant as that. To kill a king? Your own father?' Bram's voice was hoarse, his eyes darting about, but his men appeared too busy to pay much attention to them. 'Eirik was a fine man. An even better king. The islands will take time to recover from such a loss.'

'Yes, but Eadmund will make a good king.'

'And his wife?' Bram asked eagerly. 'You've met her?'

Isaura blinked. 'Jael? Yes, I have. She is... strong. Fiercesome. Eirik chose her to be his heir with good reason. She earned it. I saw that with my own eyes.'

'Well, anyone who could get rid of Tarak Soren is worthy of a crown, and more! I shall look forward to meeting her, although perhaps I need to polish up my sword skills first?' He winked at Isaura and turned to leave.

Isaura ducked her head and reached into her purse, pulling out the crumpled scroll. She hid it in her palm and gripped Bram's hand as if in friendship, staring desperately into his kind eyes. 'For Thorgils. And only him. If Ivaar were to find out...' she whispered.

Bram saw the terror in Isaura's eyes before they raced away from his. He had known her as a girl, and he'd always had a soft spot for her. But Ivaar Skalleson? It was a foolish man who'd make trouble with a lord intent on becoming a king.

He smiled to himself, shoving the scroll into his pouch, quite happy to be considered a foolish man.

***

'Grandmother!'

Jael rushed to the bed, dropping to the floor, gripping Edela's limp hand.

It was warm.

Her body heaved in relief.

Aleksander was quickly beside her, Axl behind him.

Biddy hovered nearby with Entorp as Ido and Vella raced inside, jumping up on Jael, wailing, excited to have her home.

'How is she?' Jael asked breathlessly, pushing the puppies away.

Biddy's eyes were swollen. She had barely slept since Thorgils had carried Edela into the cottage, working desperately to keep her alive until Jael returned. Her shoulders loosened as she realised that she had.

With Entorp's help.

'She's hanging on,' Biddy whispered, her voice breaking. 'But fading fast.'

Aleksander turned to Biddy, his eyes full of tears. 'Hanging on?'

Entorp stepped forward into the light, sensing Biddy's distress. Sharing in her exhaustion. 'She was stabbed in the stomach. Thorgils found her lying in an alley, and he brought her home.'

Jael's head snapped around.

Thorgils.

'She lost a lot of blood but we sewed her up, and Entorp made a salve that we can only hope will do something.' Biddy smiled at Entorp who looked uncomfortable as everyone turned to stare at him. 'It appears to be healing the wound. She is still here. Still fighting.'

Jael squeezed Edela's hand, then moved out of the way to

let Axl through.

'Grandmother,' Axl sobbed, bending his head to hers, kissing her forehead, smoothing away her hair. 'Who would do this? To an old woman?' He shook his head in disbelief, rubbing his eyes. 'Why? Who?'

Biddy glanced at Aleksander and Jael.

They all knew who.

***

'Evaine!' Morac slammed the door and raced past Runa, up the stairs to the mezzanine.

His daughter sat calmly on her luxurious bed, playing with her baby son, who gurgled happily, his chubby legs curling in the air. She turned to her father, barely acknowledging him.

'She's here,' Morac breathed heavily, surprised by Evaine's calmness.

'And Eadmund?' There was a hint of desperation now; an edge to the picture of serenity that Evaine was so carefully portraying.

Morac shook his head. 'Not Eadmund.'

Evaine looked puzzled as Morac sat down on the bed, ignoring his grandson.

'He will be home in a day or so, from what I hear.'

Taking a deep breath, Evaine nodded slowly. 'Well, I shall prepare myself, then.'

'For Eadmund?'

Evaine smiled. 'For his wife.'

***

'Mother!' Gisila threw her arms around Edela's still body, bursting into tears.

It was simply too much: the pain of what Lothar had done to her; the fear and terror of their escape from Hest; the exhausting journey; her worry for Edela. Gisila sobbed without restraint. She needed her mother so desperately, now more than ever.

She couldn't lose her.

Amma stood next to Axl, both of them crying. After what they had just been through, it was too much for all of them.

Not Edela.

Biddy looked at all their broken-hearted faces and realised that she had to do something. 'Why don't I pour us some small ale and we can sit around the fire? I'll have Askel bring in some more logs, and we can get those flames going. You're all shivering! And Entorp, perhaps you have something for Gisila's face? Those are some terrible bruises.' She bustled into the kitchen, frowning. 'Aleksander, what has happened to your shoulder, and Jael... your leg?'

They all turned to Biddy, relieved for some guidance.

Some sense of direction.

'Lothar did it,' Jael said mutely. 'He attacked Mother, so Axl cut off his head, and we had to leave Hest in a hurry.'

Biddy wondered for a moment if Jael was teasing her as she liked to do, but no one was smiling. 'Well, perhaps we are going to need something stronger than small ale, then?' She hurried outside to look for Askel, leaving Entorp to search through his leather satchel for a jar of salve.

Jael hobbled towards Thorgils, who was lingering awkwardly near the end of Edela's bed with Fyn. 'Where's Evaine?' Jael could feel her shoulders tightening, her jaw clenching. She squeezed her hands into white-knuckled balls. 'I need to see her.'

Thorgils swallowed, glancing at Aleksander, but his eyes were just as angry as Jael's as he came to join them. 'Well, I, ahhh, I don't think you should do that, Jael. Not yet. Not without

Eadmund.'

'Eadmund?' Jael was furious. '*Eadmund*? Eadmund's the reason Evaine is here in the first place! The reason Edela is lying there! Eadmund brought her back here!' She was shaking from head to toe and not inclined to listen to anything but her throbbing need to see Evaine.

Thorgils reached out to calm Jael down, to get her to focus on him, to see sense, but she shrugged him off and headed for the door, disappearing through it before anyone could move to stop her.

***

Haaron studied the strange looking woman who perched on a stool opposite him. He was transfixed by her similarity to Varna. She was angular and awkward as she hunched over; as though her limbs were wooden, unused to movement; as though she was ready to launch herself at him.

Just like Varna.

He smiled wistfully, remembering their talks in his chamber; her rasping words of advice. His own mother had died when he was too young to remember her, and he had grown up with Varna as a constant presence in his life. And now, here was her daughter, who no one had known anything about.

Not even him.

'Your arrival is timely, it seems,' Haaron said sharply, his dark-blue eyes narrowed into accusatory slits. 'How is it that you dreamed of your mother's death, but then didn't choose to save her?'

Morana looked annoyed as she peered at him from beneath her wiry mane. '*Save* her? When death was all she wanted? To be free? At peace? With the gods themselves? No, my lord, death is no punishment, and my mother would never have seen it like that. She was eager to die. A woman of her age?' Morana laughed, and it was shrill like a raven's warning. 'There is little peace in living when you are nothing but a shrivelled up, broken down reminder of who you used to be.'

Haaron sipped his wine, feeling more broken down and shrivelled up than he had in his entire life. His kingdom had never been in such disarray. Never so vulnerable. So crippled. 'Well, as you say, Varna was a woman who had given so much, right until the end. For Hest. For me.'

Morana swallowed, ignoring the silver goblet of wine that remained untouched in her hands. 'She spoke with great pride of her life spent looking after you and Hest.' It was an effort, and her lips twitched with displeasure.

'She did?' Haaron was surprised, not imagining Varna feeling anything but anger and disappointment.

Morana nodded, bored, wanting the pretence over with. 'Yes, she spoke of her desire that I would carry on her work. That I would help you when she no longer could. When I dreamed that she was weak and would not last long, I came to ensure that her wishes were carried out.'

'And you were in contact with Varna all these years? How?'

Morana's face revealed nothing. 'Dreamers communicate in ways that others cannot.'

'I see,' Haaron murmured, not really seeing at all. 'Well, it is no secret that I am now without a dreamer at the very moment when I have an urgent need for one.' He sighed, glancing at the door, wondering who Bayla had sent to eavesdrop on their conversation. 'You are willing to stay, then? In Hest? In Varna's old chamber? To dream for me?'

Morana tried not to smile. 'I will do anything I can to help you, my lord, for as you say, it appears that your kingdom is in great peril. I have seen that, and more besides. Your enemies are rising against you. All around you. You must act quickly if you are to save Hest. And yourself.'

Haaron swallowed, leaning forward. 'Tell me... what do you advise?'

***

Jael didn't knock.

She simply threw open the door and strode into the house, Aleksander and Thorgils trailing behind her.

Evaine sat in a chair by the fire, cradling her son in her arms, Morac standing behind them. Runa perched nervously on a bed in the far corner of the main room, wishing she was anywhere else.

Jael's eyes flicked to the baby. 'Runa!' she called. 'Come and take the child!'

Evaine gripped Sigmund tightly as Runa rose from the bed and crept anxiously towards her. 'You will not take him! He is Eadmund's son!' Evaine cried defiantly.

'Stand up and give the child to Runa,' Jael said coldly. 'You are coming with me.'

Morac looked horrified. 'What do you think you're doing?' he demanded crossly, moving to step in front of Evaine. 'You cannot barge into my house and try to take my daughter! For what reason?'

Jael ignored Morac and walked towards Evaine. 'Take the child, Runa.'

Evaine relented and handed Sigmund to Runa, who hurried him upstairs.

Aleksander could feel the throbbing pain in his shoulder, but it was not as demanding as the throbbing anger pulsing in his body at the thought of what Evaine had done to Edela.

He did not doubt that it was her.

'You cannot hurt me!' Evaine insisted, stepping forward to

meet Jael. She was small and delicately framed, and Jael towered over her, her shoulders broad and straight, her face emotionless and hard. 'Eadmund will never forgive you!'

Jael's face contorted. *'Eadmund?'* She felt a twinge in her heart at the truth in those words, but it did little to stem the flow of her anger. 'The Eadmund you put a spell on? The one who loves you so much you had to use dark magic to claim him? Because he *doesn't* love you! Because he *didn't* choose you! Not even when you had his child! That Eadmund? My husband? Is that the Eadmund you mean?'

Evaine's eyes sparked with rage. 'He will *never* be yours!' she screeched. 'He is lost to you now, and if you try to hurt me, he will spend the rest of his life mourning me and hating you!'

Jael frowned. 'Edela broke your spell once and she will again when she recovers. And if not her, then I will, or Biddy, or Entorp. You will never have him,' she growled. 'And you will pay for what you did to my grandmother. *I* will make you pay!' She snatched at Evaine's wrist, yanking her forward.

'You cannot do this! When Eadmund returns, he will stop you!' Morac bellowed, rushing towards Jael.

Thorgils reached out one of his giant-sized arms, blocking Morac from coming any closer.

Jael squeezed Evaine's wrist tightly as she tried to escape her hold. 'Morac Gallas,' she smiled coldly, her eyes snapping to his pinched face. 'Once I have finished with your *daughter*, I shall have to think about what to do with you. After what you did to Fyn?' She shook her head, turning to leave, pulling Evaine along behind her.

Evaine panicked, trying to wriggle away from Jael, her boots scuffing uselessly against the floorboards. 'If you hurt me Eadmund will be lost to you, don't you understand?' she wailed desperately. 'He is bound to me now! Forever!'

Jael didn't turn around as she dragged Evaine towards the door.

'His soul is bound to my soul!'

Jael stopped, glancing at Aleksander who blinked at her, his face mirroring the confusion on hers. 'Your *soul*?'

***

Biddy busied herself in the kitchen, too worried to even think, but knowing that she must. She needed to make something for supper, and there were now many more mouths than she had planned for. She watched them all sitting around the fire, staring mournfully at one another, glancing at Edela, holding cups in their hands that none of them ever looked at.

Entorp's forehead wrinkled as he approached, his blue eyes squinting anxiously. He inclined his head towards the back room. Biddy looked intrigued as she wiped her hands on her apron and followed him.

'What is it?' she whispered, sensing his desire for privacy as he closed the door behind them. 'What's wrong?'

'Evaine did this,' he began. 'We both know that.'

Biddy sighed impatiently.

'But I can't stop thinking about *why* she did it? To take a knife and try to murder an old woman? It must have been because of Morana. Morana is in this, I'm sure,' he shuddered. It was cold and dark in the storage room to keep their food stores as fresh as possible, and Entorp was already missing the warmth of the fire. 'If Edela can dream walk, then someone as powerful as Morana certainly can, and she wouldn't have hesitated to do so. She must have come to Evaine. Told her what to do. Edela said that Eadmund had gone again, which means that Evaine did something to reclaim him. And getting rid of Edela would mean that she would remain unchallenged. There would be no one to stop her.'

Biddy frowned. 'And?'

'We don't have Edela anymore.'

'Don't you say that!'

Entorp ducked his head. 'No, I mean that we don't have her to help us save Eadmund. To see for us. To show us how to help her either. We're blind. We cannot see, so we need someone who can.' He looked up as an idea sparked, quickly skipping to another.

'What is it?' Even in the darkness, Biddy could sense that he was working on a plan.

'Eydis will be here soon, but I'm not sure we have the time to wait.'

Biddy nodded, agreeing.

'There *is* Jael...'

'Jael?'

'Edela said she was a dreamer. That it was in her.' Entorp looked down at Biddy, desperate for some hope.

'Yes, but...'

'Jael might be able to help her,' Entorp insisted, his eyes suddenly bright. 'I have an idea.'

***

'What do you mean, your *soul*?' Aleksander asked furiously. 'What have you done?' He grabbed Evaine's other arm, just as wild as Jael now.

Evaine grimaced, trying to pull away from them both.

Jael released her hold on Evaine's arm and stepped back. 'And?'

'If you kill me, Eadmund will be trapped forever. You cannot break the spell, not if I'm dead at least. You need me if you ever want to reclaim him!'

Aleksander dropped Evaine's arm, and she pulled down

her rumpled sleeves, pushing her shoulders back as she glared up at Jael. 'You may be the queen for now, but you do not have Eadmund, I do! So leave my house, and take your men with you!'

Jael bit her teeth together and narrowed her eyes, considering things. She believed Evaine. Or that Evaine, at least, believed what she was saying. Morana was her mother, so what she was suggesting was entirely possible. There was no reason not to believe her. And yet...

Jael turned to Thorgils. 'Get Sevrin. I'll need some shackles.' And nodding at Aleksander, they lunged for Evaine, grabbing one arm each.

'You cannot do this!' Morac cried hopelessly as they dragged Evaine to the door. 'You heard what she said! It's true! You cannot hurt her without losing Eadmund forever!'

Jael ignored him. She ignored Evaine's furious squawking, and Thorgils' anxious grimacing as she pulled Evaine through the door and out into the rain.

Sigmund, lying in Runa's arms, suddenly burst into tears.

***

Sevrin stood on the hall steps, waiting in the drizzle as Thorgils hurried towards him, some way ahead of Jael and Aleksander, who were dragging an uncooperative Evaine between them.

'Bring the shackles!' Thorgils called, almost reluctantly.

Sevrin stared at Thorgils' red face, then looked back to Jael who was lugging Evaine to the Wailing Post: the old, worn, muck-covered post that stood in the middle of the square. 'For *Evaine*?' He was shocked. 'Are you sure?'

Thorgils nodded, his mind scattered as Sevrin disappeared back into the hall. He knew from his conversations with

Biddy that it was likely Evaine who had attacked Edela. But he also knew that Eadmund was going to be furious, and that would have repercussions for them all. He turned back to Jael and Aleksander, neither of whom even raised an eyebrow in acknowledgement as he approached.

'You think you can try to kill an old woman and get away with it?' Aleksander spat. 'That you should suffer no punishment because you are the mother of Eadmund's child? That he will *protect* you?'

'Who are you to know anything about Eadmund?' Evaine screamed. 'Get your fucking hands off me! Morana will kill you! She will kill you all!'

Jael said nothing. She was too busy fighting the urge to gut the screeching girl; trying to shut out the booming voice of her father who was crossly reminding her that she was a queen now. 'You hold her,' she muttered to Aleksander, striding past him towards the hall, needing a moment to think.

'Are you sure about this?' Thorgils asked gingerly as Jael stopped before him.

'*This*?' she snapped. 'This is not what I'd do at all, but it is something. After what she has done? To Eadmund? To Edela?' Jael shook her head, on the verge of tears, but not wanting them to dilute her anger. She frowned instead, turning to Sevrin as he came through the door with shackles in his arms. 'There is not much to her so you'll need to make sure they're tight. I don't want her slipping away in the night.'

Thorgils swallowed, imagining the look on Eadmund's face when he saw Evaine.

Jael glanced up at the clouds which were darkening dramatically overhead. 'Looks like more rain. Maybe a storm.' She took a deep breath and strode back towards Aleksander, who was working hard to keep Evaine still while Sevrin clamped the shackles around her ankle and the post.

'So, now you are safe, Evaine Gallas, and you can't run away. Eadmund will return soon, and we'll see what happens next. But for now, you are *my* prisoner. Murder is a very serious charge...' Jael's voice caught. 'I'll return tomorrow,' she said stiffly, ignoring Evaine's screams. 'And perhaps you'll be ready to confess by then?' She turned to Aleksander, and they walked away, both of them desperate to get back to the house.

'Noooo!' Evaine cried, wide-eyed with madness, lunging after them; screaming in pain as the iron clamp bit into her ankle, her feet slipping in the thick mud that had already covered her boots.

Crying even more as the drizzle turned to hard rain.

CHAPTER THREE

Biddy smoothed a fragrant salve around Gisila's swollen eyes. Made from arnica and chamomile, its calming scent helped them both start to relax.

Entorp sat with Edela, his hand on her chest, his fingers around her thin wrist. He dropped his head and turned back to the waiting crowd. 'She is getting weaker. Her wound is not leaking anymore, but I fear that the damage might have been too great, or perhaps Edela is simply not strong enough to survive such an injury? The dream walking weakened her. And she had her illness as well. Her body and spirit have gone through so much lately.'

Jael put her hands over her face, rubbing her eyes.

Angry, tired, helpless. Worried.

She turned to Thorgils. 'Has there been any sign of Ivaar?'

Thorgils looked surprised. 'Ivaar? No. No sign at all.'

'Good,' Jael murmured, trying to think of everything she had to deal with. As much as she just wanted to stay with her grandmother, she was in charge of the island – at least until Eadmund's return. 'Best you take Fyn to Runa. She'll be desperate to see him. And make sure that Morac understands how serious this is... what Evaine did.' Jael shook her head, wanting to scream; fighting the urge to run out into the square and finish Evaine. But she thought of the baby, of Eadmund, and of Edela, who was certainly more merciful than she was.

None of them would want such a thing.

'And talk to Sevrin. Make sure he keeps a watch on her all night. I can't leave. Not yet. I don't want to be gone when Edela...' Jael blinked, stopping herself. 'I need to stay here.'

Thorgils nodded. 'Come on, Fyn. Let's take your chest back to Odda's, then we can go and see your parents.'

Fyn, who had not uttered a word since they'd arrived, looked up from his stool in horror, but he smiled sympathetically at Jael and followed Thorgils out of the house.

'Is there nothing we can do?' Axl asked desperately as Entorp stood, stretching his back and moving away so that Aleksander and Jael could sit by Edela. 'Nothing that you know of? Or you, Biddy?'

'Well, there is one idea,' Entorp mumbled into his chest. 'It's something I've only seen done once. And that was with an experienced dreamer. We don't have one of those, unfortunately.'

'We don't have a dreamer at all,' Axl sighed, walking to his grandmother's bed. 'Not one who can help us.'

'We have Jael,' Biddy said softly.

Everyone turned to Jael, who frowned at Biddy.

'Jael?' Gisila looked confused. 'She's not a dreamer.'

'Jael dreamed of this,' Aleksander reminded her. 'She dreamed of Ranuf's death too.'

'But that is not the same as *being* a dreamer, surely?' Axl wondered as he clasped Edela's limp hand, willing her to wake up.

'You need to spend years at the temple to become a true dreamer,' Gisila added. 'To be trained by the elders.'

'But what choice do we have?' Aleksander insisted. 'We must do anything we can to help Edela. We cannot wait!'

They grumbled amongst themselves, arguing over Jael's lack of experience and ability as a dreamer.

'What would I have to do?' Jael asked Entorp, silencing them all.

***

'You can't sleep in the stables!' Berard laughed, making Meena jump. 'You're not a horse!'

Meena didn't know what to make of Berard Dragos. He kept following her around like a friendly dog. She felt embarrassed and uncomfortable around him; half of her wishing he would go away; half of her grateful for his concern. She had crept away from Jaeger as he slept, eager to find somewhere to be alone so that she might think. 'I will not go back to that chamber. With Morana?' She shuddered. 'And there is... nowhere else.'

They were walking towards the stables as the sky turned a deep blue above them. The temperature had cooled, but it was still warm enough for neither to need a cloak. But the night would turn things colder yet, and Berard was certain that Meena would not be so enamoured with the breezy stables then. 'We have so many chambers in the castle. Most of them are empty. I will have a servant prepare you one tomorrow.'

Meena stopped and turned to Berard, tapping her head. 'Why would you d-d-d-do that?' she asked. 'Why do you care if I stay here at all? I am nothing without my grandmother. I may as well be a slave.'

Berard sighed, pulling Meena to one side as the blacksmith and his apprentices walked past, having locked up the smithy for the night. 'But you could be,' Berard insisted. 'You could work in the kitchens, or for my mother or sisters-in-law? You could help with the children? Or you could be your aunt's assistant? It is what you know how to do after all.'

Meena shook her head violently, her whole body quivering in terror. 'I could never. Never! She's a witch!'

Berard frowned, not prepared to let Meena just disappear. In the days since the disaster in the square, his entire family had shunned him, making him eager to forge a friendship with the one person who seemed as much of an outcast as he was. 'Well, what about me, then? I have no servant, no one to care for my things as Jaeger does. Haegen and Karsten have handfuls of slaves and servants looking after their every need. Perhaps it's time that I had someone too?'

Meena's eyes rolled down to the cobblestones. It was the most appealing idea he had proposed but still... what would Jaeger say?

'There are a few empty chambers next to mine,' Berard went on, gently ushering Meena back towards the castle. 'Mostly small, but nearby. There will be much to do as my chamber is in a terrible mess, and I never remember to set a fire or send my clothes to be washed. I'm afraid you'll be quite busy.' He smiled, watching Meena's shoulders easing away from her ears; her eyes lifting towards him now. 'I shall pay you, of course. Provide you with meals too.'

'But, but your brother...'

'My brother?' Berard looked confused, then slightly annoyed. He had seen the way Jaeger leered at Meena, as though she was a possession; something he desired to own. Frowning, he pushed back his rounded shoulders and lifted his chin. 'This would be no concern of my brother's, Meena. What we choose to do is no business of his at all!'

***

Morac looked from Thorgils to Fyn and back again. 'Has our new queen sent you for the baby now? Does she plan to throw *him* out into the freezing rain too?' he growled, leaving them standing in the doorway, despite the deluge of foul weather drenching them both.

'Evaine has been accused of a crime, Morac,' Thorgils began

calmly as Runa ran to the door, pushing past her husband and scooping Fyn into her arms. 'And she will be judged fairly, as is our way, but for now, she is the queen's prisoner.'

Morac scowled at his wife's weeping as she looked Fyn over and hugged him again. 'But not for long,' he said sharply, his long nose in the air. 'Eadmund will return soon, won't he?'

Thorgils took a deep breath. He was not looking forward to that. 'He will. And he will support his wife's actions, I'm sure,' he said firmly, clenching his teeth to remove the hesitation in his words.

Morac laughed. 'I only hope for your sake that he doesn't view your part in proceedings too harshly. It's hard to remain friends with a man whose loyalty you cannot trust.'

Thorgils frowned irritably and turned to Runa. 'Fyn will be staying with me until things... resolve. You'll find him there. But for now, we must go and speak to Sevrin. And check on Evaine.'

Morac looked anxious. 'Here,' he said, pulling his cloak off its peg. 'Take this to her. I will come again later with another. Tell her that she will not have to endure this much longer. Eadmund will be home soon. Tell her that everything will be different then.'

Thorgils took the cloak, uncomfortable with the whole situation, but most of all at that moment, uncomfortable with Morac's certainty that Evaine was the injured party. 'I remember passing you in the alley that day, Morac,' he said quietly, his eyes sharp. 'Perhaps Jael is wrong, and it's not Evaine who did this? Maybe she's punishing the wrong Gallas?'

Morac baulked, stepping back, suddenly aware of how precarious their situation was without Eadmund to protect them. 'I... I did see you in the alley, yes. I saw many others too. Why not chain us all to the Wailing Post if that is your wish?' he challenged boldly. 'Not the sort of kingdom Eirik imagined Oss becoming without him, I'm sure.'

'Come on, Fyn,' Thorgils grumbled, glaring at Morac. 'We

shall leave your father to his nice house and his warm fire. Both of which he got off the back of Eirik Skalleson. Before he then abandoned him. Loyalty... it's hard to come by these days, wouldn't you say?' And with one final, sneering look at Morac, he pulled Fyn away into the pouring rain.

***

Jael glanced at the door, stroking Vella, who had relaxed into a warm, furry lump over her knee as she sat before the fire.

'Entorp won't be much longer,' Biddy smiled wearily from Eadmund's chair. She had a cup of passionflower tea in her hands, trying to calm her nerves. Edela had weakened even further. Her breathing was laboured now, and Biddy couldn't stop looking at her chest every few heartbeats to ensure that she was still with them. 'He just had to find the last things we need. We have most of them left from last time but never enough mugwort!'

Gisila sat next to Edela, with Axl and Amma perched nearby on stools.

Aleksander paced around them all, too anxious to sit still.

'You've seen this dream walking, then?' Gisila asked Biddy.

'Yes, once,' Biddy said. 'When Edela went to warn Jael. It worked, didn't it?'

Jael nodded. 'She told me about Morana. How she was in Hest.' She frowned, remembering her encounter with the strange woman, whose black eyes had been so desperate to claim her.

Evaine's mother. Morana Gallas.

She thought of Evaine, chained to the post in the square. Morana was not an enemy to be trifled with, but whether she actually cared for her daughter was another matter altogether.

'And the book,' Biddy added.

'The Book of Darkness?' Jael looked confused, shaking her head. 'Edela didn't say anything about the book.'

'No,' Biddy remembered. 'She said that you disappeared before she could warn you.'

'About the book?'

'Jaeger Dragos has it.'

Jael's mouth dropped open.

'It's been *found*?' Aleksander stopped moving and stared at Jael.

'By Jaeger Dragos?'

Amma shuddered at the sound of that name, shrinking away from the memories that came surging back: of his hands, his voice, the smell of his breath...

The pain.

Axl reached out and clasped her hand.

The fire was suddenly loud, rain splashing onto the flames as they hissed and crackled in protest.

The book. Jaeger had the Book of Darkness.

Jael did not have the room inside her head to think of the ramifications of that. Not yet, not without Edela to help them understand what to do.

***

'Berard?' Jaeger was surprised to see his brother wandering down the corridor, and even more surprised to see Meena appear from behind him. She had been in his bed when he'd fallen asleep, but he hadn't given a thought to where she had disappeared to. He cocked his head to one side. 'You're not going down to the hall for supper?' He stared at Meena, who blushed immediately and hid beneath her hair.

Berard was at once both nervous and annoyed. He didn't want Jaeger staring at Meena at all. 'I'm going to show Meena around my chamber. I'll probably miss supper tonight as we have much to discuss.'

Jaeger's injured ankle gave way, and he wobbled, reaching out for the wall. '*Your* chamber?' His amber eyes sharpened, not leaving Meena's face.

'Meena is my servant now. She will care for my chamber, my clothes, my meals.'

Jaeger's eyebrows rose, irritated by his brother's attitude. 'Your *servant*?'

'Yes, with Varna gone, Meena needs a new purpose here, and you've been telling me to employ a servant for years. So, it couldn't have worked out better.' Berard turned and pulled Meena's hand down from her head. 'Come along, Meena.'

Jaeger watched as Berard and Meena scurried away together. He was incensed. Why had Berard made this sudden move towards her? He had always liked to care for helpless things, Jaeger knew. But Meena? Meena was not some motherless animal. She was not his to care for.

Not her.

He watched them turn at the end of the corridor, heading towards Berard's chamber. His stomach rumbled loudly, but he suddenly had no appetite at all.

***

Entorp read aloud from the book, squinting to make out the words by the flames.

Jael repeated them back to him. The Tuuran phrases felt unfamiliar as she twisted them around her tongue. She tried to focus her mind as she knelt before the fire, clearing away all distractions: her tired and grainy eyes, the discomfort in her leg, the sudden ache in the arm Tarak had broken.

Evaine.

Finally, she closed her eyes as Entorp went silent, keeping the words in her mind, repeating them over and over in a rhythmic pattern.

Everyone else was sitting on stools by Edela's bed, except for Entorp who knelt on the floor near Jael, the drum leaning against his leg.

Jael opened her eyes and took a deep breath, readying herself. She glanced at the small circle that Entorp had painted around her in blood. Stones joined the dark-red lines to each other; a Tuuran symbol painted onto each one, turned up, illuminated by the flames.

Jael was plagued by doubts as she stared at Entorp's calm face. She was not afraid of the dream walk, but she was afraid that she wasn't a dreamer at all; that she wouldn't be able to do anything to help and that, ultimately, it was pointless to even try. 'Are you sure we shouldn't wait for Eydis?'

Entorp shook his bushy mop of orange hair. 'Eydis is too young for such a load. It requires immense focus and strength of mind to enter a trance. To be able to hold it and dig deep inside a dream. To lose yourself and drift away while remaining tethered here.' He handed Jael the bundle of herbs he had gathered. 'If anyone is going to be strong enough, it will be you.' He could sense Jael's uncertainty, and he quickly sought to reassure her. 'Edela believed in you. She was convinced that you were a dreamer. And the dreamers in the temple said that Edela must save you. But perhaps they saw it the wrong way around? Perhaps it is *you* who must save her?'

Jael glanced at Aleksander, who smiled encouragingly at her from his stool. She wished that Eadmund were here, then thought of Evaine wailing in the rain, and was glad he wasn't.

'Just start chanting, and once you throw the herbs onto the fire, close your eyes and inhale the smoke. Deeply. Take it right down into your lungs. Slow, slow breathing. And think of Edela. She is dreaming. She is alive. Think of her waiting for you to come, just as she came to you. Imagine yourself finding her, how that would feel. To be able to see her, talk to her again.'

'And if I do? How can I possibly save her? In a dream? It's not real.'

Entorp swallowed, wondering the exact same thing. 'Sometimes, we need a reminder of what holds us here in this world. What is important. Edela is strong. Like you. She would never leave you without a fight. You must remind her to fight. Remind her that you need her, that she is supposed to save you. Her body will respond to her mind. So, you must get into her mind.'

Jael took a deep breath, adjusting her position.

'Here,' Biddy murmured, handing her a cup of water. 'You may need this.' She smiled, then retreated into the dark shadows of the room to join everyone else.

The only light came from the subtle glow of the fire.

Jael could hear the rain, lighter now, falling on the roof.

She felt the different types of herbs in her hands: some damp, others dry. They were fragrant, almost familiar, and she inhaled slowly, trying to calm her racing heart.

With one last glance at Entorp, who had started thumping on his drum, she threw the herbs onto the flames and closed her eyes, searching for her grandmother's face in the darkness.

***

'At least she's quiet now,' Sevrin sighed, pushing away his empty cup; groaning as he stretched out his legs.

'Well, after all that whining and wailing, I expect she's lost her voice,' Thorgils muttered, not feeling good at all.

About anything.

Fyn looked from one to the other and said nothing.

Sevrin leaned forward. Do you think she did it, then? A little girl like that? Tried to kill a dreamer?' He glanced behind himself. They were at the high table, and he could see servants bringing food out of the kitchen, but there were not many in the hall tonight, and no one was even looking their way. 'Doesn't make any sense to me.'

'I don't think it needs to, you not being the queen,' Thorgils suggested, draining his cup and wiping a hand over his damp beard.

'Jael's a dreamer,' Fyn said quietly.

Sevrin blinked.

'She saw what happened to Edela,' Fyn went on. 'She sees things. If she thinks Evaine did it, we should believe her.'

'A dreamer?' Thorgils was surprised by that news. 'A warrior dreamer?'

Fyn nodded earnestly.

'Well, it seems that I missed out on a lot not going to Hest. Like, for instance, why is her family here? And where are Lothar and his weasly son?' Sevrin lowered his voice, refilling Fyn's cup. 'Perhaps you should tell us what happened?'

Fyn gulped, still seeing Gisila's back, covered in cuts from Lothar's belt; remembering the moment when Axl had taken off Lothar's head with one swing of his sword. He had not imagined that something like that could be done so easily. So cleanly. Axl looked no stronger than him, but something had snapped, and he had reacted on pure instinct.

It had been the right thing to do, Fyn was sure.

Just as it was the right thing to keep Evaine out there, shackled in the rain.

Fyn knew that not everyone would agree, but he trusted Jael. Jael had saved him. He just hoped that she could save her grandmother in time or there would be nothing to stop her from cutting Evaine's throat, no matter what Eadmund thought.

***

Jael's eyes flickered open. Her head felt foggy, her tongue thick and huge inside her mouth. She took a sip of water, desperate to swallow.

'Try again,' Entorp urged gently.

His voice sounded so far away.

The beat of his drumming rolled over Jael like crashing waves, her body rolling with it. She blinked away from him, back to the flames. Blurred ribbons of yellow and orange entwined around each other; Entorp's voice echoing in her head.

'Try again.'

Closing her eyes, Jael inhaled the fragrant smoke, every part of her tingling in the darkness. She started chanting, stumbling over the words, tasting them in her mouth, dry and burned by the harsh smoke; losing track of them, muddling them, forgetting them, thinking only of Edela.

She needed to see Edela.

Edela...

'Well, this is a surprise. A gift! A treat beyond my wildest dreams. Jael Furyck has come to *me*!'

Jael saw nothing but darkness. The hawkish voice was loud, echoing around her as though she was in a large cave. It felt damp. She shivered, but from the voice or the cold, she couldn't tell.

'You think that you can save her? *You?*' the voice laughed, cackling with menace. 'A dreamer you may be, at last, but you are too late. She is mine now! You may as well go back. There is nothing for you here... dreamer.'

Jael tried to catch her breath. She tried to see anything at all.

Pushing her boots down, she could feel rock beneath them.

Then a light ahead. Flames?

Running towards the light, Jael could feel the sharp edges

of the rocks piercing her boots, jabbing into the soles of her feet. But she was not limping.

There was no wound in her leg. Not in here.

'Grandmother?'

'She is not yours, Jael Furyck! She is mine!' the voice cried in warning.

It was so loud, deafening, invasive. Jael wanted to put her hands over her ears, but then she heard a trickle of water and saw a stream. 'Grandmother?' She ran on, breathless, her legs suddenly heavy now.

There was a raft; wooden planks made into a raft, tied across a stream. Jael blinked harder. She noticed a twisting flame in the distance, certain she could see Edela now.

'Grandmother!' Jael jumped into the icy water which quickly numbed her legs, rising over her knees. She felt around, wishing there was more light. Edela was tied to the raft, her arms splayed, her body still, eyes closed.

But she was breathing.

Jael fumbled with the ropes around Edela's wrists, but she couldn't find any knots. No way to undo them at all. She growled, frustrated, wading towards the poles the ropes were tied to. Jael felt around.

No knots there either.

Reaching for *Toothpick*, she could hear the sharp intake of breath as the voice hissed, trembling around her. Jael slashed through the ropes, and they fell away. She sheathed *Toothpick* and scooped Edela into her arms, walking carefully back to the rocks. Laying her limp body on the cave floor, Jael leaned over, feeling the coolness of Edela's cheek against hers. 'Grandmother?' she whispered in her ear. 'I've come to take you home. Back to me. Back to all of us. We're there, on Oss, waiting for you.' She paused, taking a deep breath. The air was so thick and heavy. Her chest heaved, her lungs working hard. 'Grandmother,' she breathed. 'You have to come back. You can't leave me. Not yet. Not when you're supposed to save me.

Remember? You must come back. You must save me!' Jael sat back on her heels, suddenly dizzy, feeling as though she was slipping away.

'Hahaha!' the voice crowed. 'You may have your sword, Furia's daughter, but what else do you have? Your husband? Your grandmother? There is more you need... so much you don't know!'

Jael stilled, searching the darkness for the source of that grating voice but there was nothing to see.

No one was there.

'Your husband is lost to you now. Forever! And Edela? The one who is supposed to save you? I don't need to tell you how that will go,' she laughed.

Jael gripped Edela's hand and leaned forward to whisper in her ear again.

'She is mine now! You cannot claim her! She is mine!' the voice cried, angrier, harder, more threatening now as it slithered around Jael's body like a venomous snake.

Jael tried to ignore it, tried to shut it out of her head as she focused on Edela. Reaching into her pouch, Jael pulled out a stone – the one Edela had given her before she left for Saala. She pressed it into Edela's palm, rolling her fingers closed over it, feeling herself slipping further away. Leaning down quickly, she lay her head on Edela's chest, desperate to cling on. 'Don't give up, Grandmother! You're the strongest person I know. And I need you! Without you, what hope do we have? Come back to me, please!' Jael gritted her teeth, feeling Edela slip away from her. She trembled with the effort of holding the trance; the tiny flames fading as darkness enclosed her.

And as everything spun, and Edela slid away, Jael thought she heard a voice. 'Grandmother?' She listened, trying to hold on. And then she heard it, the faintest whisper. But she knew that voice.

It was Edela's.

'Tuura.'

CHAPTER FOUR

Osbert closed his eyes, wishing that sleep would come, but as weary as he felt from two days of trekking over the steep mountains of Hest, his body would not unwind. He had barely slept since his father's death.

Since that night.

He shuddered, remembering the stench of the chamber, the mess of Lothar's headless body, the humiliation he had endured as the Brekkan army ignored his orders, refusing to attack Jael and her Islanders.

His army, who, for a time, refused to follow him at all.

Yet, here he was, King of Brekka at last. But his sister had escaped too, and now they would all plot to remove him. All of them. Perhaps even Haaron and his sons? Osbert was relieved that they had been too distracted by the chaos in their own kingdom to think about taking his head as well.

For now.

He glanced around his tent, certain he'd heard a noise. Paranoid.

Loyalty was not something that could be beaten into a person, he knew. Not unless they were a slave. He shook his head.

Not even then.

And those men out there, sleeping in the dirt? Those men had all appeared loyal to his father. They had chosen Lothar over Axl three years ago. But now? His father had been a foolish, vain king, driven by greed to make reckless decisions that had ultimately led to his death. Osbert sighed, troubled by the doubts that whirled around his head; weighed down by them; desperate for some respite from them.

He needed to get home, back to Andala. He had to prepare for what would come next. Unless Jael and Axl were already there? Unless they were waiting for him in Saala?

***

Jael couldn't stop coughing. The smoke was still tickling her throat after three cups of water. She left Biddy to air out the house and headed to the stables to check on Tig and Leada.

Aleksander followed her. 'You're sure it was Edela's voice?' he asked once they were inside.

Jael nodded, trying to swallow. She ran her hand down Tig's face, comforted by the familiar feel of him; enjoying the warmth of his breath as he snorted and blew at her. He was grumpy, she could tell, but pleased to see her as well. Night had fallen, and she was ready to sleep, but just as eager to ride into the wind and let it blow the smoke from her muddled mind.

Aleksander frowned. 'They sent her here to save you. Everything Edela learned about that prophecy, which wasn't much, came from Tuura.'

Jael turned around, narrowing her eyes. 'Do you think they knew what would happen to her? That the elders wanted her out of the way? Convinced her that she was coming here to save me when they knew she would only be putting herself in danger?'

Aleksander thought of Tuura, shivering as the wind wailed through the stable doors, spooking both Tig and Leada who shuffled about uneasily. He hadn't trusted anyone there. And the whispers about Marcus Volsen, the elderman, had painted him as a shadowy character.

Edela had not trusted him at all.

'I don't know. I don't know whose side they're on. What happened in Tuura all those years ago...' He stopped, not wanting to think about what had happened in Tuura all those years ago. 'Someone wants you dead. More than someone. But who? Maybe them. Maybe just Evaine and her mother.'

Jael stepped away from Tig. Her head felt clear enough to go back inside now, and she was eager to check on Edela. 'So, is she telling us to go to Tuura or that Tuura is the reason this happened?'

Aleksander shrugged. 'I don't know, but I think that after what you just managed to do, you really are a dreamer now, so perhaps you need to dream on it?' He smiled crookedly, suddenly overcome with tiredness; wondering how long it had been since he had slept in more than snatches.

Jael was surprised to realise that he was right. But a real dreamer knew how to bring dreams to her. And despite all the years of watching and listening to Edela as she tried to encourage her gift, Jael had absolutely no idea how to do that at all.

***

Nicolene had grown bored of caring for Karsten and his injuries.

The wound in his side had bled so much at first that they had wondered if he would, in fact, die. But there was no way that Karsten was about to let Jael Furyck end him. So, he had rallied quickly and had spent the past few days in a foul mood, moaning, groaning, and demanding to be let out of bed.

Deciding that even Haaron and Bayla would make better

company than her irritating husband, Nicolene had spent most of her time in the hall, as far away from him as possible.

'Sitha seems to think that Karsten should be up and about tomorrow,' Bayla said happily, swallowing a honey-glazed baby turnip.

Nicolene ignored her mother-in-law as she watched Jaeger pick through his meal, distractedly pushing a sausage around with his knife. 'Not hungry, Jaeger?' she asked softly, nudging her knee into his. 'No appetite tonight?'

Jaeger didn't even look up. He was thinking of Berard. Of Meena. Of the book and Morana. But mostly then, of Meena.

Why had Berard sought to claim her?

What did he want her for?

Bayla quickly became annoyed that no one was listening to her. She turned to Haaron, who had cheered somewhat since his talk with Morana. There was comfort to be found in having a dreamer in the castle. And he was relieved to have someone who could help him decide what to do about Jaeger.

'Have you seen Berard today?' Bayla wondered, trying a new subject. 'Is he still skulking about, avoiding everyone?' She glanced over at Jaeger, who, irritated by the mention of his brother's name, finally looked up.

'Berard?' he muttered. 'Berard is busy organising his new servant.'

Haegen looked at Irenna, bemused. 'A servant? Berard? Well, perhaps he realises that having someone to wake him up would be a good thing, especially when we're under attack!'

'I think it's nice that Berard has finally found someone to care for him,' Irenna said, catching Bayla's eyes as they glared fiercely at her. 'To care for his things, I mean.'

Bayla turned back around, not looking any less displeased. 'How did he find this servant?' she grumbled. 'On his own? That doesn't sound like him at all. He is always so utterly hopeless.'

'He has struck up a friendship with Meena Gallas,' Jaeger almost spat. 'He has taken her on.'

Haaron was surprised. He had forgotten the girl entirely. 'I thought she would have stayed with her aunt. Now that Morana is here, why wouldn't she just carry on as she was, doing whatever she was doing?'

'Whatever that was,' Nicolene snorted, trying to meet Jaeger's eyes, but although he was staring at her, he appeared far away.

'Well, I suppose it is good for him to have found someone to put his things in order,' Bayla murmured, sipping from her goblet.

Jaeger felt a burst of rage rush through his arms and legs, rising up to his chest. He remembered Amma Furyck, his wife, as she lay weeping beneath him, limp and broken. But despite his fervent desire to reclaim her for his pride, and to rehabilitate his ruined reputation, he couldn't stop his mind from twisting back to Meena.

Always her.

Jaeger frowned, shaking away his dark mood, suddenly aware of the pressure from Nicolene's thigh as she leaned it against his. He turned to his pretty sister-in-law, his eyes narrowing into slits. 'Perhaps I should come with you to visit Karsten after supper? He might enjoy some company.'

Nicolene smiled, happy to have claimed his attention at last. 'I'm sure he would,' she breathed.

***

'You need to get some sleep,' Axl insisted gently as Amma tossed and turned. He had been trying to sleep on the floor beside the bed, but her restlessness meant that both of them were still wide awake. 'It won't help Edela if we're too tired to think tomorrow.' He ran his hand over her salty, brown hair, trying to soothe her.

She looked so terrified.

Still.

There had been no time to talk yet. Not alone. No time for Amma to tell him what had happened. What Jaeger had done to her.

If she ever would.

Axl was instantly wild, feeling his anger burn like sea-fire across the water. He thought of Lothar, remembering the sound of his uncle's head as it hit the flagstones. He blinked, unsure what his father would have made of that. Would he have been proud that he had protected his mother? Disappointed by his lack of self-control?

Turning away from the memories of that night, Axl leaned over and kissed Amma's forehead. 'Sleep,' he murmured.

Gisila sat on a stool next to her mother's bed with no intention of sleeping at all. Entorp had gone home, and Biddy was in the kitchen, tirelessly preparing herbs for a tea to encourage her to sleep.

Axl's head was swimming. The smoke had been intense, suffocating him, undoing his senses. And now he felt confused. Displaced. He didn't know what to do with himself in this strange, new world, where Edela lay dying, and Osbert was king. And Amma was his again. And his mother was free.

And he was a murderer.

***

'Will you stay with me?' Evaine pleaded as Morac wrapped another cloak around her shoulders. She was soaked through, and the rain was only getting heavier as the wind picked it up and threw it into her face.

Morac cringed under its freezing onslaught, worried for his daughter, but less than keen at the thought of joining her for the night in the mud. 'Well... I will stay until you fall asleep, yes,' Morac said, already thinking of his warm bed, and Runa, who would hopefully be waiting in it for him.

Evaine saw the truth in his eyes as they tried to avoid hers. 'She will pay for this, you know!'

Morac spun around, but the square was empty. There was not a soul in sight on this foul evening. 'Of course she will. Morana will see to it.'

'Why wait?' Evaine insisted desperately, tugging at the heavy, iron clamp around her ankle. 'Why wait for Morana?' She lowered her voice to a whisper, her wide, blue eyes jumping everywhere. 'You didn't need *her* to kill Eirik Skalleson, did you? You didn't need magic for that!'

Morac put a finger to his thin lips, his eyes panicked as he glanced around, but they were still alone. He sighed, feeling a tightness in his chest, a guilty twinge at the reminder of his crime. For all that he had resented Eirik, he had still been his friend – almost a brother – for most of his life. It was strange to be without him; to know that it was he who had killed him. There were moments when he realised that there was no one left who understood him as Eirik had; no one he could talk to in the same way. There was Morana, Evaine, even Runa, now that she had warmed to him again. But Eirik had been his closest friend since he was a boy. And despite all that had happened – all that he had done – he missed him. 'Edela Saeveld is dying. And Jael knows that you stabbed her,' he whispered hoarsely. 'What Eadmund will believe when he returns, I don't know. Jael is his wife. She is queen here.' He held up a hand to stop Evaine's protests. 'If we kill her, there will be no doubt of your guilt any longer. There will be no sympathy around here, I promise you that.'

Evaine looked horrified, sodden, humiliated. She was numb to her very core, desperate for the warmth of a fire. 'You would just let her get away with this?' she seethed, her teeth chattering uncontrollably. 'What she has d-d-done to me?'

Morac grabbed her hand before she could slam it against his chest. '*You* are the one who did this, Evaine,' he reminded her firmly, more confident now that she was chained to a post. 'It was not in our plans to kill the old woman, so you must accept the consequences. For now. Eadmund is not far away. He will save you.'

Evaine bit her numb lip, ready to protest, but he was right. She could feel it. Morana's new spell had changed everything inside her. It was as though there was a direct connection to Eadmund now.

She could feel him getting closer.

Evaine shut her eyes, trying to ignore the discomfort of the iron clamp, the chill of the rain as it streamed down her back. The shame of it all.

Eadmund was coming home.

***

Jael lay on the floor beside her grandmother's bed.

She had not wanted to be away from her. Not even in the next room. She tried to imagine where Eadmund was, hoping that he would return soon but, remembering Evaine, Jael wondered what would happen next. If Evaine was right and Eadmund was bound to her soul, what could they do? How could they undo the spell without Edela's help?

And then there was Morana, who would be telling Evaine what to do, surely? It was better for everyone that Evaine was restrained, she insisted to herself, taking a deep breath and rubbing her hand down Vella's back as she snuffled alongside her.

Closing her eyes, at last, Jael thought about Jaeger Dragos and the Book of Darkness. Did Berard know? He must have, she realised. He had been so defensive of his brother, but hesitant, as though he was holding something back. Perhaps now she knew what.

Jael's eyes flew open.

Morana Gallas was there, in Hest, within reach of that book.

***

Meena didn't know what to do, but Jaeger wasn't waiting for her to stutter and tap her way to a decision. He barged through the doorway, pushing past her, his giant frame dominating Meena's slight, shaking one.

'Better than Varna's chamber,' he noted gruffly, staring around the simple, barely furnished room that Berard had found for Meena. There was one tiny window, a few struggling flames in a stone fireplace, a single bed with a fur and pillow. A chair and table. There was even a rug.

Meena blinked, brushing hair out of her eyes, trying not to tap her head. Jaeger reeked of wine, and he looked furious. She shuffled about nervously, her eyes fixed on the door she had just closed, suddenly wishing that she was sleeping in Berard's chamber. That would have kept Jaeger away.

If that was what she truly wanted.

'I'm surprised Berard's not here, waiting in your bed,' Jaeger growled, gripping Meena's arm, forcing her eyes towards his. 'That seems to be what he wants.'

Meena tapped her toes, her heart pounding. Jaeger suddenly jerked her towards him, pulling her into his arms.

She squeaked.

'Is that what you want?' he glowered.

Meena stumbled, conscious of his breath as it blew warmly all over her, muddling her mind. She didn't know what to think.

With Jaeger, she never felt safe.

But her body stirred as she sensed the anger in him cool and change. 'No,' she almost whispered, shaking her head. 'No.'

Jaeger lifted her chin, staring down at her, confused by his feelings. Why did he care so much about this strange little mouse?

She was no beauty. No lady.

She was nothing.

Nicolene had been an entertaining plaything, but he had barely noticed she was even there, writhing beneath him, so eager to please.

And when he'd closed his eyes, he'd seen Meena.

Placing his hands on either side of her face, he kissed her passionately. 'You're not Berard's, do you understand me, Meena?' he grunted. 'You're not Berard's. You're mine. You belong to me.'

Meena, her body limp, her lips as desperate as his, could only mumble back. 'Yours.'

***

'You *killed* him?'

Jael nodded, ignoring the displeasure in her father's voice. She pushed her shoulders back and stared up at him.

'And you think that was the right thing to do? Over a *dog*?' Ranuf's face was unreadable, but his voice was not.

'She was *my* dog. You gave her to me!'

'You think I don't know that?' he growled, his green eyes darkening as he glared down at her. 'But I also know that Ronal was the son of *my* man. My man, who has now lost his last son!'

'He was a useless pig. And a dog murderer!' Jael jutted out her chin, furious at the reminder of what had happened; haunted by the last, pitiful sounds her dog, Asta, had made when Ronal slit her throat. He had waited until Jael was there, making her watch.

The twisted bastard.

Ranuf gripped Jael's arm, pulling her closer. They were in the stables, but he could hear people approaching. 'And you thought that it was *your* place to punish him?' he hissed.

'She was *my* dog!' Jael was defiant. 'He deserved it.'

Ranuf sighed, his anger dissipating. His daughter's temper was worse than his, he knew. And it would not serve her well if she allowed herself to be ruled by it. 'Yes, she was,' he said, more sympathetically now. 'But it was *my* place to decide what to do about Ronal. Not yours. Not until you are queen here will you make those decisions yourself.'

Her father had spoken so matter-of-factly that Jael had barely heard him, but her body quickly stilled in shock.

Ranuf raised a dark eyebrow. 'That's a surprise to you? That you're my heir?' He laughed at the look on her face. 'Well, who else would it be, Jael?' Dropping her arm, he stepped back, studying his only daughter. She was tall and strong, with broad, straight shoulders and a permanent scowl on a face that was otherwise pleasing to look at. She had a sharp jaw, a pair of defiant green eyes – much like his – and a mouth that rarely curled into a smile.

She was fiercesome.

Fifteen years old and ready for battle, he was sure.

But that temper...

'And when you're queen, you will need to take hold of your tongue and keep a grip on your sword arm because a queen's decisions must be made without anger. Everyone will be looking for you to be fair. Decisive but fair. No one should be led by a man or a woman who puts their own interests above everyone else's.'

Jael was still too stunned to speak. Her anger had been entirely swallowed by surprise.

'So, yes, as a man, I would have killed the little bastard for what he did to Asta,' Ranuf growled, his hairy lips pursing in anger. 'But as a king, I cannot dispense justice for personal revenge. And nor will you be able to. Not if you are to rule for a long time, Jael. Kings and queens are disposable. There is only so much your people will tolerate before you wake up in the night with a knife at your throat. Just ask the many dead kings of Iskavall.'

But Jael wasn't listening.

Her father's heir? Queen of Brekka?

She couldn't stop smiling.

CHAPTER FIVE

Edela was still there.

Still hanging on.

Biddy felt her body relax, then tense again quickly. She was still there, but for how long?

Entorp was listening to Edela's chest, feeling the pulse in her wrist. 'She's stronger,' he announced, at last, standing up with a growing smile. 'Most definitely stronger.'

The sigh of relief that weaved its way around the room was weary and deep.

'What does that mean?' Gisila asked, her eyes aching with the strain of holding them open. 'Will she recover?'

'I'm not sure.' Entorp glanced at Biddy, who appeared just as uncertain as he did. He turned to Jael. 'And she said Tuura? You're sure that it was her, not that voice?'

'It was Edela's voice. The other voice was loud and screeching, but this was faint. Weak. Afraid.'

'There is a book in Tuura that Edela mentioned,' Entorp started, looking at Aleksander. 'A book the elderman gave her. She left it behind, didn't she?'

Aleksander nodded. 'It was supposed to help her save Jael.' He frowned, poking the fire with a long, iron rod, trying to awaken the flames. 'Well, at least, that's what they told her.'

'Do you think she wants us to take her back there?' Axl wondered, not liking the sound of that idea. 'To Tuura?'

'Either that or she's saying that Tuura did this to her somehow,' Aleksander suggested.

Biddy walked past Jael on her way to the kitchen, deciding that it was well past time to organise some breakfast. 'Which one do you think it was, then? You heard her say it. Perhaps you got a sense of her meaning?'

They all looked at Jael, and her mind went completely blank.

***

Thorgils had dragged Fyn down to the beach at first sight of the ship. He needed to prepare Eadmund for what he would find when he walked into the fort. He'd been lying awake for much of the night, imagining how he would react.

How Jael would react in turn.

Evaine against Jael was only ever going to go one way.

Until Evaine had Eadmund on her side. And if she truly had bound him to her soul, Thorgils had no idea how Eadmund would react at all.

But not well seemed a good bet.

Eadmund, hanging onto *Ice Breaker's* dragon prow, sighed in relief at the familiar sight of mist and gloom that greeted his homecoming. He was uneasy, though. Oss didn't feel like home without his father waiting for him, and his shoulders felt heavy with the sudden weight of responsibility. He was king now. A king who had made an enemy of the two biggest kingdoms in Osterland.

And then there was the nagging problem of his brother.

Eadmund yawned, reaching down to grip his sister's hand. 'I'm going to lift you over the side, Eydis,' he said. 'Thorgils and Fyn are there, waiting for us.'

Eydis' milky eyes widened. She was anxious and had been

since they'd left Jael behind on the sea. Her dreams had been confusing, and she felt an urgent need to see Edela; hoping that she was still alive. She swallowed nervously as Eadmund hoisted her into the air, feeling Thorgils' firm grip around her waist as he eased her down onto the sandy foreshore.

'Eydis!' Thorgils boomed. 'Let's get you up to the fort before the rain comes down again!'

Eydis frowned. Thorgils sounded strange.

'Hello, Eydis!' Fyn said quickly.

Fyn sounded strange too. Both of them seemed awkward. Oddly loud.

Eydis turned, listening for Eadmund, wanting to know what was happening. 'Is it Edela? Is she dead?' she asked frantically.

'No, no!' Thorgils shook his head, staring at Eadmund as he joined them. He looked tired. Irritable even.

That was not a good start.

'What happened to Edela?' Eadmund wondered, taking Eydis' hand and helping her across the beach, his eyes focused on the familiar shape of the fort struggling out of the heavy morning clouds. His legs wobbled, and he thought of his father's fur-lined throne. His throne now. 'Jael had a dream that she'd been attacked. So did Eydis.'

Fyn's eyes dropped to the stones; Thorgils' quickly following.

Neither of them spoke.

'Evaine did it,' Eydis said, feeling the tension in Eadmund's hand as it tightened around hers.

Eadmund stopped, turning to her. 'What do you mean, Evaine did it? Why would *she* do such a thing?' Just the feel of her name on his tongue had his whole body tingling. She was close. He could feel it. He ached with need to see her. To see their son.

Thorgils and Fyn looked from Eydis to Eadmund.

'Evaine did it,' Eydis insisted again. 'She hurt Edela. She wanted to kill her!'

Eadmund narrowed his eyes into moody slits, staring at his sister who could not see how truly angry he was. 'You *dreamed* it?'

Eydis shook her head, her black braids swishing across her light-blue cloak. 'No,' she said, at last. 'But I know she did!'

Eadmund grunted and started walking again, irritated and confused as he hurried his sister along. 'You can't accuse her, Eydis. Not without proof. You have no proof! You should keep your accusations to yourself,' he grumbled. 'Evaine would never try to murder someone. Why would she?' He stared at Thorgils, who appeared to be paying particular attention to the stones as he walked. 'Why would she?'

Thorgils sucked in a deep breath. 'Well, Eydis *is* a dreamer. She has a strong sense of things. You should listen to her, perhaps? And then there's Biddy and Entorp... and Jael...'

'What?' Eadmund stopped again, his hazel eyes flaring as they fixed on his friend. 'Jael? Jael thinks Evaine did this? Hurt Edela?'

'Jael is a real dreamer!' Fyn blurted out, unable to keep quiet any longer. 'She knows it was Evaine!'

Eadmund glared at Fyn, whose eyes quickly retreated beneath his floppy fringe of auburn hair. 'She *saw* Evaine do it?'

'Well, no,' Fyn admitted meekly.

'A *real* dreamer?' Eadmund was confused. '*Jael?*' He shook his head. 'But if that were true, then two dreamers didn't actually see Evaine do it. So, as it stands, there is no proof!'

'No,' Thorgils admitted. 'But...'

'But?'

'Jael doesn't appear to be looking for any. Not at the moment.' Thorgils didn't know how to say it. 'She has...'

'She has what?'

'She has taken measures to ensure that Evaine doesn't hurt anyone else.'

Eadmund's eyes popped open. He let go of Eydis' hand and ran. 'Take Eydis up to the house!' he called over his shoulder as he headed for the hill, his bear-fur cloak flapping angrily behind him.

'Well, that didn't go quite as I'd hoped,' Thorgils said awkwardly as he clasped Eydis' hand and hurried her across the stones after their quickly disappearing king.

***

Morana was distracted. Yorik smelled like valerian.

She loved the smell of valerian.

He barely knew that she was there, though, as he muttered to himself, checking over his shoulder, peering amongst the bushes as they walked higher and higher up the path that led away from the castle and into the winding gardens her mother had been so fond of.

'You cannot *take* it from him,' Yorik murmured, his hands busy as he walked. He was trying not to appear as impatient as he felt. They had come so far and were so close now. But he was also conscious of the need to take their time, to ensure that everything fell into place as it was meant to. Yorik was usually a measured man, but the sudden appearance of the Book of Darkness had unsettled him greatly. They were within reach of all they sought, but one false step... 'We need *him*, not just the book, remember? And he must be filled with need for what only we can offer.'

Morana glared at him, thoroughly frustrated by his constancy.

Yorik had not changed much in the years since she had last seen him. He was a slight, sallow-skinned man of average height, nearing old age. His short, light-grey hair was tinged with the faint reminder that he had been red-haired once. His thin lips were now hidden beneath a generous amount of white stubble. There had never been anything remarkable about him at all, apart from his eyes, which were different colours: one pale blue, one dark green. They were so distinct from each other that most people found it unsettling to look at him directly.

Morana did not.

She sighed, quickly bored with talk of Jaeger. They had done nothing but speak of the Bear and how they would use him since her mother's death. 'His focus is on what the book can do to remove his father and brothers. He cares nothing for the gods, old or new. He cares only for himself! He wants to be a king, to crush his enemies. Nothing more. He is a thick-headed fool.' She frowned, too warm in her woollen cloak; weary now from the steepness of the path. 'And he does not trust me. He barely lets me look at the book! The ritual spell is difficult, and so far, I have not been able to translate it. Not with him over my shoulder, breathing on me! He will not even let me write anything down. So, even if I did manage to translate it, what could I do about any of it?'

Yorik stopped and turned to Morana as she unpinned her cloak, her fiery red face scowling at him. He smiled, nostalgic for her ornery temper and how it was for them all those years ago when they had made their daughter. Perhaps they had been in love once? He couldn't remember now. 'Morana,' he said softly. 'When you show him what that book can do, he will trust you. How could he not? The power it can wield will intoxicate him, as it must.'

Morana draped her cloak over her arm, glaring at Yorik through sheets of matted hair.

'Make sure his mind remains on the book. That it is always near him,' Yorik urged, brushing her hair away from her eyes before reaching down to kiss her cheek, his stubble brushing against her creased skin. 'For, the closer he is to the book, the more of his soul it will claim. Like a desperate thirst, he will need to be with it, to be at one with it. The book revealed itself to Jaeger. It is meant for him, so we must clear his mind to all other thoughts.'

Morana stared into Yorik's uneven eyes. 'I can do that,' she smiled.

***

'Are you sure you don't want some company?' Aleksander asked as Jael grabbed Tig's reins and led him out of the stables.

Both horses had been kept inside by Askel under Biddy's firm instruction since the attack on Edela, and Jael could tell that Tig was as desperate to clear his head as she was. He nickered impatiently next to her, swishing his tail in anticipation of a long-overdue ride.

Jael shook her head. 'I need to think. I can't in there. I have to find a way back into that dream to see what Edela was really saying. Maybe riding will help? It always has in the past.'

Aleksander nodded, his dark eyes tight with tension. 'Well, don't be long. We need to decide what to do. I'm not sure there's time for much thinking.'

Jael turned back to him, her face as tense as his. 'I know. I won't.'

Aleksander watched her go, feeling the familiar ache in his chest. She was so far away from him now that he wondered if there was any way back?

Putting all thoughts of Jael out of his mind, he sighed and headed towards the house, desperately worried about Edela.

She meant so much to all of them.

She couldn't die.

***

'Evaine!' Eadmund ran towards the slumped figure chained to the Wailing Post.

Evaine, sodden and miserable, pushed away her father who had been comforting her and stood, turning towards his voice. 'Eadmund! Eadmund!'

Morac stepped away from his daughter as Eadmund reached her, pulling her into his arms. He smiled smugly, watching Jael approach with her horse.

Now they would all see who the true ruler of Oss was.

Evaine shivered and sobbed against Eadmund's chest, certain she had never endured a more horrific night in her life. Her ankle was aching where she was shackled. Her body, numb from the cold and rain, shook uncontrollably. She was desperate to escape the humiliation. Eager to sit in front of a fire.

Thorgils and Fyn hurried through the square after Eadmund, Eydis between them. Thorgils' eyes went immediately to Jael who was standing there, holding Tig's reins, her face unreadable.

Eadmund's wasn't, though, as he caught sight of his wife. 'Morac,' he said coldly. 'Stay with Evaine.'

'Eadmund, no!' Evaine begged, gripping his hand. 'Please, release me! Don't leave me here like this. I did nothing! Nothing! You can't leave me here!'

But Eadmund wasn't listening or even looking at Evaine now. His eyes were fixed on Jael, and they were burning with anger. 'Morac,' he said again, nodding to the old man as he pulled Evaine out of his arms and strode towards Jael.

'Thorgils?' Eydis asked, wanting to know what was happening.

Fyn sensed her confusion. 'Eadmund is going to speak to Jael. About Evaine, I suppose.' He shuddered, as he always did when he saw his sister. He had been hoping she would remain chained up, but the look on Eadmund's face told him that there wasn't much hope of that.

Eydis sighed. 'Oh. Poor Jael.'

Thorgils frowned, thinking how right Eydis was. He

squeezed her cold hand. 'How about we take you to see Edela? I'm sure Biddy will make you a hot cup of something to warm you up.'

Eydis nodded reluctantly, allowing them to lead her away, past Jael and Eadmund who were silently eyeing each other up.

Thorgils smiled encouragingly at Jael, but she didn't notice. She was still reeling from the sight of Eadmund as he raced to comfort Evaine.

Blinking suddenly, Jael thought of her father; her father, who had tried to teach her how to rule. And there she was, standing in the middle of the square, in the centre of a growing crowd of curious onlookers.

And now she was a queen.

A queen with a very bad temper.

'Why don't you get Leada?' she suggested quickly as Eadmund approached, her fury simmering at a steady heat, just below the surface. 'The things we need to say should remain between us, don't you think?'

Eadmund felt ready to burst, but he had enough sense left to see the wisdom in that idea. 'Alright. Wait here for me.'

Jael tightened her grip on Tig's reins, her eyes snapping to Evaine as she wailed, comforted by her sneering father. Jael didn't care that she was shaking and wet through. She didn't care that she was the mother of Eadmund's son. Evaine had stabbed Edela. She had tried to kill her, no doubt at Morana's insistence.

Jael frowned, remembering her talk with Eirik.

Morana had hated Eirik. If she had taken her revenge on him somehow, knowing that Eadmund would then become king...

A king under their control.

Jael felt Morac's eyes on her.

The pointy faced man. Morana's brother.

***

Jaeger ran his hand over the book.

Its soft, leather cover was as dark as a starless night. He was enamoured with the feel of it; the fine texture of its surface, always so cool to touch. Somehow, it soothed him.

Just being near the book made him feel calmer.

He slowly turned the delicate vellum pages; each one filled with spidery scrawls and magical symbols that made no sense to him at all.

Morana Gallas could read some of it, he knew. But what did she want in return for her assistance? A woman like that? A woman happy to watch someone murder her mother? To encourage it, even? That was a woman who was sure to betray him for her own ends.

But what were they?

Egil had seen her with Yorik Elstad, leader of The Following. And The Following would want the book. They wouldn't care how they got it.

Jaeger frowned, running his fingers around the intricate symbols, wishing he didn't need Morana. If only Meena could read it for him instead.

Then they wouldn't need anyone at all.

He thought of Berard and tightened his hand into a fist. Once he had felt as though they were in this together, on a path of mutually desired revenge against their tyrannical father. But Berard had befriended Jael Furyck – perhaps even plotted with her – then tried to take Meena away from him.

Soon, he would want to take the book away from him too.

They all would.

***

They rode until Eadmund's anger had built to such a heat that he could no longer keep it in. He yanked harshly on the reins, pulling Leada to a skittering stop. Jael, following behind on Tig, came to a halt beside them.

Eadmund dismounted and quickly strode to the edge of the lake. Its smooth water was as grey and dismal as the sky above them. Light rain washed over him, and he remembered how cold Evaine had felt in his arms. How wet and miserable.

And his anger grew.

Spinning around, he glared at his wife. 'What were you *thinking*?'

Jael clamped her lips together, fighting to control her tongue.

This was not Eadmund.

'Evaine tried to kill Edela,' she said slowly. 'She may well have succeeded. Do you think we should keep our criminals roaming freely around Oss? That they shouldn't be punished for the crimes they commit?'

Eadmund's eyes flared. '*Criminal*? How is she a criminal? What proof do you have?' He shook his head, his sandy hair curling damply around his face. 'You, who are so fond of proof when it comes to Ivaar! You, who kept me from killing him when he *actually* murdered my father! Demanding I find proof! But now you've decided that Evaine committed a crime, just because you don't like her? Because you're jealous of her?'

Jael's temper exploded like a bonfire. 'Come back to me, Eadmund!' she screamed. 'Stop this and come back to me!' She lunged at him, but he caught her arms. 'How can you not even remember Hest? It was only days ago!' Jael's face twisted in pain. She was desperate to see something in his eyes that was familiar, that told her he was still in there.

That there was still hope.

Eadmund pushed her away, scrubbing angrily at his beard. 'What are you talking about?' he yelled. 'You think that Evaine is some witch who put a *spell* on me? As though I'm not in control of my mind or body? That what I think and feel is somehow not of my own choosing?' He laughed but it was hollow and bitter, and he shuddered, momentarily lost in those green eyes, so full of fire.

Jael watched Tig's ears flatten back. He knew that something was wrong.

So did she.

'Edela broke the spell –' Jael started.

'Evaine is not a *witch*! What are you thinking? Spells? Magic? Evaine is not a witch!'

'No, perhaps, but her mother is!'

Eadmund frowned, watching Jael's dark braids flap across her face. The wind was becoming as angry as they were. 'Runa?'

'Runa is not Evaine's mother. Your father told me that Morana was her real mother. She gave Evaine to Morac and Runa to raise as their own when she was born.'

Eadmund was horrified. Morana's daughter? He hated that bitch. 'Eirik told you this?'

'Yes, he did, just before we left for Saala. He regretted he ever allowed it to happen. He told me that.'

'And Evaine knows this?'

Jael shrugged. 'What do I care if Evaine knows who her mother is, Eadmund? I care that Evaine tried to murder my grandmother! I am the Queen of Oss now. Do you think I should just let her get away with it? What sort of queen would that make me?'

Eadmund was suddenly hesitant. Morana *was* a witch, but Evaine... he couldn't stop thinking about her. He felt sick with worry, his body vibrating with an overwhelming urge to see her, to comfort her.

She needed him.

He glared at Jael. His usually kind eyes were harsh and unforgiving. 'Find me proof that she did it or leave her be. Until you show me anything to the contrary, Evaine is not your prisoner, nor mine. Stay away from her, Jael, I warn you!'

Jael cocked her head to one side, pushing her boots onto the grass. 'You *warn* me?

They eyed each other furiously, shoulders taut, jaws clenching.

Neither one saying a word.

Then the rain came down.

***

Eydis burst into tears at the sound of Biddy's voice.

'Oh, Eydis,' Biddy soothed gently, pulling her into her arms. 'There, there, my poor girl.'

The puppies were jumping up Eydis' legs, desperate for her to notice them too. Entorp was there, tears in his eyes at the sight of his dear little friend, who was now an orphan.

'How is Edela?' Eydis sniffed, trying to get a sense of who was in the house, of what was happening.

'She is stronger,' Entorp said kindly, reaching for her hand. 'Here, come and sit by her. She will hear your voice, I'm sure. And maybe you'll feel how she is.' He led Eydis to the bed as Amma hopped out of the way.

'Stronger?' Eydis asked. 'Does that mean she will live?'

Entorp glanced at Biddy, who looked ready to cry. 'Well, she is very weak. Can you feel it? When you touch her?' Rada had been able to tell so much by touch, and, being blind, Eydis' senses were even stronger than her mother's.

Eydis nodded as she held Edela's hand. It was limp, and, although warm, it felt almost lifeless. She could barely sense any energy in Edela at all. Just darkness. Eydis turned around, listening, less nervous than she usually would have been. Everyone in here loved Edela, she knew.

She felt safe.

'I dreamed about Edela,' she began softly. 'I know of something that might help her.'

***

Jael and Eadmund didn't move as great sheets of icy rain slammed down on top of them. But the horses did.

Tig and Leada reared up, galloping away as a bolt of lightning shot through the dark clouds, landing amongst a cluster of moss-covered boulders nearby.

Jael blinked in shock. 'Tig!' she screamed, running after the horses who were quickly heading home without them. 'Leada!'

Thunder boomed all around them.

Eadmund chased after her, putting his fingers to his lips, whistling furiously but the storm was so loud that any hope he had of attracting the horses' attention was lost in all its noise.

They were just as annoying as the puppies, Jael grumbled as she ran, hood pulled low, eyes half closed against the teeming rain. 'Tig!' He looked as though he was slowing down, but then another shard of lightning struck and after that, there was nothing slow about him as he disappeared into the distance, Leada right behind him.

Eadmund stopped, realising the futility of chasing them any longer. The horses were, at least, heading in the direction of the fort. He grabbed Jael's hand. 'Come on!' he cried. 'Over here!'

Thunder rumbled ominously above them as Jael followed Eadmund towards a tiny cave tucked beneath an overhanging ledge of rock. Not big, but big enough for two soaked, storm-chased bodies to shelter in; although neither was in the mood to be in such close proximity to the other.

Jael felt uptight, annoyed, desperate to get back to Edela. She was wet through, worried about the horses. She shuffled about, crouching beneath the roof of the cramped cave, grateful to be out of the rain as it lashed the ground outside their shelter, quickly flooding it.

'You may as well get comfortable!' Eadmund shouted, trying to make himself heard over the roar of the storm. He sat on a large rock, trying to calm down, worrying about Evaine, wishing he'd had her released before he'd left with Jael.

Jael peered around the cave, then took a rock near her husband, biting her fingernails, not letting her eyes stray near Eadmund for a moment.

She couldn't stop thinking about Hest.

How every part of her had felt right again, having him back. All of him.

There had to be some way they could set him free. Edela had done it once before. Surely she could do it again?

If she had that book, maybe...

CHAPTER SIX

Eydis hesitated, suddenly overcome with nerves. The house was so quiet that she couldn't even hear Edela's breathing. She could feel the beat of her heart, though, throbbing steadily in her wrist.

That was a good sign, she thought.

'I saw a book in my dreams,' Eydis began. 'An important book. A man has the book. He keeps it hidden. He has dark hair. He is a powerful man but not a dreamer.'

Aleksander's eyes widened. 'And can you see where this book is? Where the man is, Eydis?' he asked gently.

Eydis turned towards Aleksander's deep voice. He was standing somewhere behind her. 'He is in Tuura. He wants Edela to come. He wants Jael to come too.'

Aleksander frowned, the hairs on the back of his neck rising. He glanced at Axl, who looked just as disturbed.

Gisila visibly shuddered.

They couldn't go back to Tuura.

'But what about the journey?' Amma wondered. 'Wouldn't that be too much for Edela?'

Biddy shrugged. 'I don't think there is much choice, is there?' She turned to Entorp, seeking his opinion.

'Well, it appears that Eydis and Edela are of the same mind,' Entorp said, kneeling next to Eydis. 'And yes, of course, it would not be the wisest thing to take her on a ship. But perhaps she will die here if we don't? And we cannot hope to save Eadmund without Edela.'

Thorgils burst in through the door, wide-eyed and panting. 'Jael and Eadmund went for a ride, and only their horses came back!'

***

The storm was blowing its way across the island, away from the cave, and they could finally hear themselves think. The rain was still heavy, but Jael didn't want to wait. 'Let's go,' she said, standing, shaking her wet clothes away from her body, resettling her sodden fur cloak. 'I need to get back to Edela. I want to make sure the horses got home safely too.' Pulling up her hood, she edged towards the mouth of the cave.

'Wait!' Eadmund grabbed Jael's arm, turning her towards him, blinking at the fire in her eyes that had not dampened one bit. 'We can't go back to the fort like this. Our people need us to show them that the kingdom is safe. They've just lost their king. All those years of stability with Eirik in the hall? We can't put them in the middle of a war between their new king and queen.'

Jael sighed moodily, not wanting to agree with him at all. 'Of course.' She wanted to reach up and brush his wet hair out of his eyes, but she looked away instead. 'What are you suggesting?'

'We need to focus on what's important. Forget about everything else.' His own anger was still there, but fighting with Jael was not going to help them protect Oss. 'For now. Just for now,' Eadmund insisted. 'We can talk about Evaine and what I will do with Ivaar at another time. A *better* time. But for now, we have made more enemies than I can count, and we need to think about how to make us safe and quickly, before they're in our harbour, trying to take our fort.'

Jael frowned. He was right, annoyingly, and Eirik would have felt proud to hear him talk so; perhaps even surprised. But Evaine? 'It makes sense,' she admitted reluctantly, her teeth barely opening. 'A truce.'

'A truce,' Eadmund agreed.

'But don't expect me to apologise to her,' Jael grumbled, ducking her head on her way out of the cave.

Eadmund ducked his own head, a wry smile on his face as he followed her. 'I would never expect that,' he snorted. 'Not ever!'

'Good, because you're *my* husband!' Jael said fiercely, turning back to him. 'No matter what she says or does, or how you think you feel right now, you're *my* husband, Eadmund Skalleson, and I'm not letting you go! Not without a fight!' And, not waiting for him, Jael strode off. 'And I'll have you know that I'm very good in a fight!' she bellowed into the wind.

Eadmund stared after her, confused. He felt as though he was in the middle of a tug o' war; Evaine and Jael pulling him from either side. And as much as Evaine pulled, he still found himself drawn to his wife's demanding eyes.

Shaking his head, Eadmund hurried after her.

***

'I thought you could read it? *All* of it?' Jaeger sneered, watching Morana frown her way down the page.

'*All* of it?' she sneered back. 'Of course not! I'm not a god! A god wrote this book. *The* god! He has secrets in here. Secrets he doesn't want the likes of you or me to know.'

Jaeger leaned over her shoulder. He hated other people touching the book. It was not Morana's, not The Following's, not Berard's book. He felt his blood heating, pulsing in his veins. 'Well, who is going to help me uncover those?'

Morana spun and glared at him, willing him to back away from her. He was always so close. She couldn't stand the smell of him. 'You think you can find another dreamer? Someone who will keep this book a secret?' She stood up, her body a hands-breadth from Jaeger's. He jerked away at last. 'You're a naive fool not to see that another dreamer would just take it for themselves! The power in this book...' she shook her head, batting him with her hair. 'It is without equal. It is *all* that is desired by people with a mind to do what *you* want.'

'And why are you so noble, then? A woman who happily stood by as her mother was killed?' Jaeger growled. 'Why should I trust you? You, who appears to be such good friends with Yorik Elstad?'

Morana laughed throatily, not revealing her surprise that he had uncovered that. 'Well, do or don't. Your choice entirely.' And she crept towards the door.

Jaeger frowned. 'Where are you going?' he panicked. 'You haven't told me anything at all! Again!'

'No, and I won't,' Morana said firmly, not bothering to turn around as Egil scrambled to open the door for her. 'Not today. I promised to meet with your father. You keep the book safe, and I may return tomorrow with some answers.'

Jaeger sighed irritably as Morana slithered through the door. She had told him nothing. After all these days. She kept promising things, touching the book, running her hands over its delicate pages, her dark eyes widening and narrowing, but she never revealed anything that would help him.

'My lord?' Egil murmured. 'Shall I put the book away now?'

Jaeger spun around, his eyes aflame. 'No! You shall not. But you shall bring me some wine, Egil. And quickly!'

***

'I won't be long,' Meena smiled, closing Berard's door, feeling unusually content. She was away from Morana, in her own private, almost-warm chamber. Soon she would be earning her own keep too, caring for Berard who was being so kind to her.

And then there was Jaeger.

She felt sparks of desire bursting inside her body at the thought of him. It was not a feeling of safety, but it was as though she belonged with him. That he understood her. That they were the same in some strange way.

She shivered, desperate to see him again.

'And where have *you* been hiding, little mouse?' Morana hissed as she crept up behind Meena, who jumped, biting her tongue. 'Not running away from me, are you?'

As much as Morana terrified her, Meena knew that Jaeger cared for her. How much, she didn't know, but enough to hope that he would keep her out of Morana's grasp.

And Morana needed Jaeger.

For now.

'I have a job.'

Morana recoiled. Confused. '*Job?*' she snorted, wrinkling her face in disgust.

'I am in the employ of Berard Dragos now,' Meena said nervously, tapping her leg; fighting the overwhelming urge to tap her head as well. 'I have my own chamber too.'

'Is that so?' Morana murmured, creeping closer. 'Hmmm....' She closed her eyes, inhaling as though she was breathing in Meena's very soul. Opening her eyes, she sighed contentedly. 'Well, do enjoy yourself, girl, for he won't be around to protect you much longer. His brother will see to that.' And running her tongue over her teeth, she slunk away.

***

Aleksander guided Tig down the steep hill behind Thorgils, who was bouncing along on Leada, scanning the vast expanse of barren land that lay to the south of the fort. The rain was almost horizontal, and the wind was attempting to blow his cloak right off him.

The horses had not been impressed to be taken out in it again.

Thorgils pointed suddenly, turning around with a toothy grin. 'Over there!'

Aleksander squinted, following the line of Thorgils' arm to a couple of dark shapes moving slowly towards them beneath the moody sky. He sighed in relief, but his body did little to unwind. It was permanently tightened by thick knots of pain and worry; much of it about Edela, but Jael was always on his mind too. He had not felt like himself since she'd left Andala, and he wondered if he ever would again. The memory of his visit to the Widow and the visions he'd had at God's Point taunted him. The idea that they would be together again one day seemed like a joke that the Widow had played on him now. Yet, there was still a part of him that wondered if they had been real dreams of a future where Jael was his; dreams of a time when she wouldn't love Eadmund anymore.

'Come on!' Thorgils called, nudging Leada forward.

Aleksander sighed, blinking the rain out of his eyes as he urged Tig down the hill after him.

***

'And what should I do about my son?' Haaron frowned at Morana. 'My youngest?' He nodded to two of his shipbuilders as they passed on the road away from the castle. Haaron glanced around, but there was no sign of Jaeger.

It was a warm day, and he had not wanted to stay inside the castle, imprisoned by his embarrassment any longer. He was ready to get out and remind himself of all that he still had. His fleet was being rebuilt to an even greater size. His new piers would be longer to welcome more merchants to his harbour. Men were already at the Tower, putting it to right, and he had paid a Kalmeran lord for the use of two ships to ferry his men to Skorro to begin repairs there too.

He would rebuild all that had been burned down, and then he would reclaim his reputation. At least he had managed to escape with his head and the opportunity to do so, unlike Lothar Furyck and Eirik Skalleson.

'Jaeger?' Morana appeared bored, barely listening as she shuffled along beside him. 'His mind is occupied elsewhere.'

They reached the arched entrance to the winding gardens, and Haaron ushered Morana ahead of him.

'Elsewhere?'

'He has lost his wife,' Morana said, her eyes on the steep path ahead. 'And his reputation. He has lost the respect that anyone may have had for him. His brothers. His men. He has even lost his strength. All that smoke? His festering ankles?' She shook her wiry hair. 'He is weak and is no longer thinking of destroying you, so much as he is thinking of rebuilding himself.'

Haaron was surprised by that. It made sense, though, and he was quickly comforted by Morana's words. 'But eventually, he will turn his attention back to me, surely?'

'Well, if one of your other sons hasn't by then,' Morana panted as they climbed the path, desperate to find some shade; determined never to come this way again. 'I would think that you have far more to worry about from his brothers. The one-eyed man? Your eldest son? They will rise against you soon.

Even the hunchback. I see their eyes in my dreams, and they all burn with the fire of ambition. After how Hest was humiliated? They are all coming for you now, especially the one-eyed man. I see him most of all.'

'But Karsten is barely out of bed! He was badly injured,' Haaron scoffed. 'Weaker than any of them now.'

'A man may be weak in body but strong of mind,' Morana muttered. 'In the end, they will all come. You are old, and they are not. Your time is done. They all dream of being king here. Have since they were boys. They are your sons and enemies both. And you must decide what to do about each one of them.'

Haaron sighed. Morana reminded him of Varna, but she did not care for him in the way Varna had. She had no loyalty to Hest or him at all. She spat words from her mouth with distaste and disinterest. There appeared to be no thought or consideration behind anything she said. But, she was a dreamer, Varna's daughter, and he saw no reason to doubt her.

And if that were so, then his sons were coming for his throne. And if he were not careful, then just like Eirik Skalleson and Lothar Furyck, he would soon be nothing but ash on the wind.

***

'Eydis!' Jael pulled Eydis into her arms, happy to see her; relieved to have made it out of the rain at last.

'You're so wet!' Eydis cringed, backing away from her dripping sister-in-law.

'Yes, you both are,' Biddy grumbled, glaring at Aleksander as he shut the door behind him. 'And no doubt you'll be sniffing soon, which will do none of us any good. Get those clothes off right away, then you can have a bowl of soup by the fire to warm you through.'

'I will,' Jael shivered, 'but not until I've seen Edela.' She took Eydis' hand and led her to the bed where Entorp sat, his hand on his patient's chest. 'How is she?'

'Steady,' he said softly. 'Very steady.'

'Steady enough for a sea journey?' Jael wondered, looking at the anxious faces as they crowded around her. Biddy was hovering nearby, trying to unpin Jael's cloak, and she let her, eager to get out of her wet clothes. 'Do you think she will survive the Nebbar Straights?'

'I think she may not survive here,' Entorp said carefully. 'She is stable now, but for how long, I don't know. You must decide whether to take the risk.'

'Eydis dreamed about taking Edela to Tuura,' Gisila said quietly. 'She saw a book in her dreams. The book Edela was given by the elderman.' She swallowed, worn down by the constant worry. Axl gripped his mother's hand, sharing her fears, her memories. 'I think everything is pointing us towards Tuura, isn't it? As much as we don't want to go.'

Jael took a deep breath. She glanced at Aleksander and saw the anxiety in his eyes. They were evasive, hurrying away every time hers approached. 'We go,' she said. 'As soon as possible. Tomorrow morning.'

'I want to come,' Eydis said immediately. 'I want to come with you, Jael!'

'We'll need to think about who can go, Eydis. Who needs to stay behind. There is much to talk about, but for now, I think, Aleksander and I had better get changed before we freeze to death!' Jael smiled wearily at Aleksander who looked away, his eyes refusing to meet hers again. She frowned, walking to the bedchamber, the puppies following eagerly in her wake.

It was time Aleksander told her what really happened in Tuura.

***

'You must *do* something!' Evaine urged into Eadmund's chest. 'You can't allow what she did to me to stand!'

Morac cringed at the sound of Evaine's screeching as he sat in front of the fire, glancing at Runa, who looked just as uncomfortable.

'It's not as simple as that, Evaine,' Eadmund soothed patiently, smoothing his hand over her damp, blonde hair. 'Jael is the queen. She believes that you tried to murder her grandmother. There is nothing I can do to change that. You must stay here, in the house, while we wait to see what happens with Edela.'

Eadmund was wet through, eager to remove his clothes and sit by a fire, but as uncomfortable as he felt, he didn't want to let go of Evaine. It was as though no other thought could enter his head while she was there, pressed against him. He could feel every part of her, and every part of him responded in turn.

He wanted to be alone with her, desperately.

'Evaine!' Runa called. 'You must let Eadmund go so he can change out of his wet clothes. I'm sure you don't want him to fall ill.'

Evaine stepped back, at last, and Eadmund felt the loss of her, his body suddenly cold.

'Yes, you must go and change,' Evaine smiled tightly. 'I will come to you in the hall as soon as Sigmund wakes. He'll be hungry before long, I'm sure. I will bring him to see you.'

Eadmund's face brightened. 'I'd like that,' he shivered, looking up to the mezzanine where Sigmund slept; excited by the prospect of being with his son again.

'I won't be long, I promise,' Evaine purred, walking Eadmund to the door. 'And then we can talk. Perhaps we can discuss Sigmund and me moving into the hall? It would be much better if we were close to you, don't you think?'

Runa gaped at them, horrified that Evaine was being so bold; mortified that Eadmund was so lost in her spell that he didn't say a word to dissuade her.

After all that they had tried... and failed.

Eadmund kissed the top of Evaine's head, fighting the urge to do more. He noticed Runa staring at him and quickly ducked his eyes away from the horror on her face; discomfort stirring amidst his desire now. 'I'll be waiting,' he mumbled awkwardly.

Evaine sighed with pleasure as Eadmund opened the door and left, raising a hand in farewell. She held up her own hand, watching him hurry away into the rain. Turning around, her smile vanished. 'What?' she growled at Runa, her eyes quickly sharp with displeasure. 'What are *you* looking at?'

Morac frowned. 'Evaine, that is no way to speak to Runa. After all she has done for you? Raised you? Cared for you as though you were her own all these years? She is my wife. She deserves your respect.'

Runa was surprised but relieved to hear Morac hurry to her defense.

Evaine was far less pleased. '*Respect*? For working with those old women to try and break my spell? For trying to come between Eadmund and me? *Respect*?' she snarled. 'There are many things I would be happy to give you, Runa, but respect is not one of them!' And storming past them both, she headed upstairs, deciding to wake Sigmund, certain that he had slept enough already.

***

'Tell me,' Jael said bluntly. 'What happened in Tuura?' She shook her head. 'I mean, I know what happened all those years ago. We both know that. But what happened on your visit with Edela over the winter?' She walked towards Aleksander as he stood, feeding Leada an apple. The strong smell of damp horses was in her nostrils, but the stables themselves were dry, and Jael smiled sadly, remembering how quickly Eirik had had them built to please her.

How strange it felt not being able to talk to him about Eadmund.

There was nothing Jael could say about it to Aleksander.

She wouldn't.

But she did need to know what had happened in Tuura before they went back there. And Jael could tell that he was hiding something.

Aleksander shuffled his feet in the freshly changed straw. He hoped that Sky was being well cared for in Andala. She would enjoy the warmer weather: being outside, at last, free of the snow, free to roam. But missing him, no doubt.

Thinking of Sky reminded Aleksander of Tuura and his trek with Edela. 'It's not easy to talk about,' he said haltingly. 'It's about my mother.'

Jael frowned. 'Fianna? What about her?' She felt odd. The pained look on Aleksander's face unsettled her. Jael had loved Fianna like a mother. Gisila had been distant after the loss of her two eldest sons, but Fianna had always been there, she remembered.

A smiling face, an encouraging voice.

Aleksander leaned his back against the wall. 'Edela uncovered some things in her dreams,' he began, his eyes on his boots. 'And... eventually, so did I.'

Jael looked on encouragingly as Aleksander took a deep breath and slowly told her about Edela's dreams. About the note Fianna had written, telling someone that they were going to Tuura and that Jael would be there. He told her about the Widow too; how his family's connection to her had seen his grandmother banished from the temple as a young dreamer.

How the elderman had sent his soldiers after him.

How he had run for his life, chased down, forced to kill to escape.

'So, I don't expect they'll welcome you back, then?' Jael tried to smile, but her face was tense. She didn't want to believe that Fianna was responsible for what had happened to them.

They had all lost something that night.

Something that none of them could get back.

'No,' Aleksander agreed. 'I can't go back to Tuura.' It was hard to say because he didn't want to abandon Jael and Edela. Not now. But his presence would only make it worse for everyone. He blinked, thinking of Hanna for the first time in weeks; hoping he hadn't caused trouble for her, leaving the way he had.

'No, you can't. Which is a good thing, perhaps? The elderman might have sent Edela here to die, and if that's the case, we might need rescuing.' Jael had a sudden vision of the man, a sense of his darkness, as though there was a cloud cloaking him.

Hiding him from her.

Was it safe to go to Tuura? To walk towards the possible danger that lurked there? Or, where Oss was concerned, away from it? To just leave everyone vulnerable and in Eadmund's spellbound hands?

Jael remembered how Eadmund had saved them in Hest. Yes, Oss would be safe in his hands, she was sure. Evaine may have twisted herself around his heart, but his leadership did not appear in doubt.

Not yet, anyway.

***

Fyn and Thorgils had barely worked their way through one cup of ale. Torstan, hunched over opposite them, was halfway through his fourth.

'Well, things are about to go from bad to even worse, I think,' Torstan sighed morosely as Evaine strode into the hall, a grizzling baby in her arms.

Eadmund's baby.

The hall hushed immediately, a whisper of shock creeping around the tables.

Thorgils swallowed, glancing towards the green curtain that Eadmund had just disappeared behind. 'I think you're right,' he whispered.

Fyn gulped. 'At least Jael's not here.'

'No, and I doubt she will be, not with Edela in such a bad way,' Thorgils agreed, his voice low, his eyes never leaving Evaine, who, after spending a torrid night wailing in the mud as an accused criminal, looked a picture of serene elegance. 'Not until they know what is happening with her.'

'You think she'll die?' Torstan wondered.

Thorgils shrugged. He didn't want to imagine such a thing. He thought of Eirik, remembering his dead body as it slumped in that chair, wine all over him like blood.

Someone had murdered him.

Someone had tried to murder Edela too.

'She's strong,' Thorgils said at last. 'Just like her granddaughter. And if anyone is going to save her, it's Jael.'

Fyn nodded in agreement, his eyes rounding in horror as Evaine slipped behind the curtain. He could imagine the smug smile on her face; the glow of satisfaction as she dug her claws deeper into Eadmund's heart.

But who could stop her now? From all accounts, Edela had tried and look at what had happened to her.

CHAPTER SEVEN

Jael's voice rang inside her head like chimes blowing about in a furious wind. She thought of her tiny cottage in Andala and felt an ache; a deep longing to be safe again.

To feel free.

The cave was a prison, and there was nothing she could do except relive the moment when Evaine had stabbed her. Over and over again, she watched helplessly as the darkness crept towards her, claiming her piece by piece.

And all she could hear was that voice, laughing as she lay there, bound and helpless.

So old.

But Jael had come for her. A dreamer, at last!

Jael had come for her. And she had managed to give her a clue.

Not enough.

But a clue. And Jael was clever enough to know what to do.

Jael was hers. Her favourite. Her heart. Jael would know.

The answers were in Tuura.

She closed her eyes, desperate to find Jael; wanting to hear her voice, to feel her touch again.

She felt so alone. So cold.

So scared.

***

'Eadmund will not want you to come,' Jael said carefully as she hurried Eydis back to the hall. It was still raining, and she was quickly wet through again; her long, dark hair sticking to her neck as she pulled on the door. 'But I will ask him. Although,' she murmured, 'perhaps he needs you here now? Perhaps this is where you can do the most good?' Jael frowned. Evaine was out to hurt anyone who stood in her way, and therefore, Eydis was in danger. She felt that. Especially after what had happened to Edela. They both had tattoos to ward off any spells that Evaine or Morana attempted to cast, but Evaine obviously did not need spells to hurt anyone.

Not when she had a knife.

Eydis squeezed Jael's hand. 'Eadmund will have Thorgils, though, won't he? Torstan and Sevrin too,' she suggested, caught between the overwhelming pull of Tuura and worry for her brother.

Tuura was all Eydis had dreamed about since her mother had died. There were answers there, she knew, to both her past and future. And now, without her father, she felt an urgency to grow stronger.

To become more in control of her gifts. To become a real dreamer.

'He will, yes,' Jael agreed, ushering Eydis into the hall. She stopped as soon as they were inside, listening to the soft thud as the door swung closed. It was oddly quiet. Jael shivered, her eyes immediately seeking out a fire. 'Here, Eydis, let's take off your cloak,' she said, spying Thorgils, Fyn, and Torstan who sat watching her from the table closest to the fire. Unpinning Eydis' wet cloak, she led her towards them. 'Why don't you sit here by Thorgils for a moment to warm up. I'll go and find Eadmund.'

Thorgils was up, stumbling off his bench, hurrying to stop

Jael as she headed towards the green curtain that separated the hall from the bedchambers. 'Jael!' he cried loudly. 'My queen!'

Everyone in the hall, already hushed and panicked in their conversations, suddenly stopped talking, all eyes fixed on Jael as she slowly turned towards Thorgils.

She frowned, her body shaking with something other than cold now as she watched Thorgils' face contort itself into strange shapes. Fyn had joined them, his expression as odd as Thorgils'.

The crack of the fire was suddenly loud.

Everyone was staring at her.

'Hello, Eydis,' Fyn said quickly before turning to Jael, trying to get her attention. 'How is Edela?' He licked his lips. His mouth had gone so dry that he couldn't speak properly.

Jael looked from Fyn to Thorgils. She felt the pressure of Eydis' hand as she came to stand beside her; the sense of unease that dried her own throat. Then she saw Evaine emerge from behind the curtain, pinning her cloak to her shoulder.

Evaine smiled at Jael, running her hands through her long, blonde hair, draping it over her chest. Eadmund was behind her, holding their son. He caught sight of Jael and felt a sharp pain in his chest, as though he had been stabbed. His eyes retreated, and he swallowed, quickly handing Sigmund to Evaine.

Jael didn't move. She could sense tiny, white holes in the darkness; eyes flicking around the hall, jumping between her and Eadmund.

Watching their king and queen.

And Evaine, who stood between them.

Jael blinked, trying to remove the excruciating pain from her eyes. Her hands shook by her sides; her body trapped somewhere between agony and anger. She imagined Eirik on his throne, remembering his fears for Eadmund, for the trouble Morana's daughter would cause; hearing her own promise not to let anything happen to Eadmund or Oss.

Jael clenched her jaw so hard that she was sure her teeth would crack. She pushed her boots onto the floorboards and lifted her chest, feeling the cool wetness of her hair as it clung to her neck. It reminded her of Eirik's hot pool, and she remembered all those nights she had spent sneaking into it with Eadmund.

When he was hers.

Eadmund.

If he had a choice, he would choose to be hers.

He loved her.

Jael fought against the pulsing, beating rhythm of rage as it sought to destroy her self-control. She squeezed Eydis' hand and led her towards her husband and his...

'Evaine,' she said loudly, the sound of that name jabbing into her heart. 'You seem to have recovered from your ordeal. But, let it be known that if Edela dies, I shall come to your door again and we shall have a *very* different conversation than this.' Jael let go of Eydis' hand. 'Here, let me see that baby of yours. After all, I am his step-mother, am I not?' Jael smiled as her eyes did everything they could to avoid Eadmund's embarrassed face. Her stomach flipped, bile rushing into her throat.

She knew what they had done. Could almost see it in her mind.

'What is his name?' Jael asked, her arms still outstretched. She hoped nobody could see that they were shaking.

Evaine froze.

Eadmund nodded at her, urging her to do as Jael had asked.

Evaine sighed petulantly and held out her son. 'His name is Sigmund.'

'Sigmund,' Jael said with a smile. A fake smile. There was nothing about her that wanted to smile at that moment. She cradled the baby as though she had been holding children all her life, but in truth, she was terrified, afraid that she would drop him. His head lolled about awkwardly as he gurgled at her. 'Sigmund,' she repeated, looking at his face for the first time, feeling a surge of something that was deeper and stronger than she had expected. He looked like Eadmund. Like Eirik. 'I think you and I are going to be friends,' she said quietly. 'One day. You are Eadmund's son, so you will always be mine too.'

Evaine was livid; desperate to reclaim the moment she had been so certain would be hers to own. She reached out to snatch back her baby, but Thorgils stopped her.

'Your queen wishes to get to know her stepson,' Thorgils said coldly. 'Best you let her unless you want her to put you back outside. It is still raining, I believe.'

Eadmund didn't move; caught in a thickening mire of guilt and more guilt.

'It's alright, Thorgils,' Jael said, handing the baby back to his mother. 'He's not mine. Not yet.'

Evaine glared at Jael but her face was a mask of strength, and she saw no fear in her eyes. No hurt. No surprise. Nothing but her certainty in that statement.

She shuddered.

Eadmund found his voice at last. 'You should be going, Evaine,' he said, clearing his throat. 'Fyn, please see your sister home. Take something to cover her and the baby, so they don't get wet.'

Fyn looked disturbed by the request, but he nodded and hurried to find his cloak.

Evaine frowned at Eadmund, wanting more than to be dismissed; sent away like a servant. She screwed up her eyes into small, blue beads, feeling her chest tighten with anger. 'You will come to see us tomorrow?' she asked sharply, demanding Eadmund's attention which was being solely claimed by Jael now. 'You will come to the house?'

'I will, Evaine,' Eadmund said hurriedly, motioning for Fyn to take his sister away.

Evaine smiled at him, glowered at Fyn, and allowed him to hurry her through the crowd of silent onlookers, towards the doors.

Jael said nothing. She stared at Eadmund, forcing her anger back behind a heavy door. Anger wasn't the answer. Not here.

Not now. She kept seeing her father's face, hearing his gruff voice in her head, demanding that she remember who she was.

A Furyck.

Above all, she was a Furyck. She would not be cowed by anyone.

She was Furia's daughter.

Eadmund's wife.

Queen of Oss.

Jael heard the door thud shut. She glared at Eadmund. 'We need to talk.'

***

Meena stared at the rafters, running over the things she needed to do for Berard. She didn't want to forget anything. She felt an immediate sense of responsibility for him that was both welcome and overwhelming; for as much as Meena longed to be cared for, she was just as desperate to have someone to look after. Jaeger did not need her at all. He seemed eager to take her to his bed, but quite happy to dismiss her entirely when he was done.

'I must find a way to get my wife back,' Jaeger mumbled, rolling away, his voice a hoarse, sleepy whisper. 'I can't let the Furycks think they can take everything from us. From me.'

Meena lay in his bed, uncomfortable.

Naked.

Her body was fizzing with desire, but he had simply finished and left her. Not even glancing her way. She shivered, pulling the furs over her chilled breasts. It was dark now, and she wondered if she had brought in enough wood to see Berard through the night. He would likely not notice such a thing until he was lumping the last log into the fireplace. She started twisting her fingers into knots, not wanting to wake Jaeger up by tapping her head.

He hated it when she tapped herself.

'I must get her back, Meena,' he yawned. 'And you will help me.'

It was not what she wanted to hear. Not at all.

Meena imagined Morana's gleeful face. Her aunt would be spying on her in her dreams, she knew; watching her make a fool of herself, over and over again.

Meena rolled away. As desperate as she was to leave, she was just as eager to crawl over Jaeger's slumberous body and claim her own pleasure. But, she shuddered, she would never think to do such a thing.

Sliding quietly out of bed, she looked around in the candlelight for her clothes.

'Meena?' Jaeger murmured. 'Where are you going?'

She froze. Confused. He sounded so sleepy.

Meena stayed still, waiting, and eventually, he started snoring, and she crept away into the shadows.

***

They sat opposite each other in Eirik's private chamber.

Jael could barely breathe.

Eadmund didn't know what to say.

'I'm leaving,' Jael stated matter-of-factly. 'In the morning.'

Eadmund's eyes bulged. He leaned forward, studying his wife, who sat rigidly before him, her eyes hard and fixed on his. He suddenly wanted a drink of ale. 'Leaving for where?'

'Tuura.' Jael felt a burst of anger. She wanted to punch him in the face. She bit her lip and looked down instead, towards the fire that burned brightly between them. 'We're taking Edela there.'

'*We*?' Now Eadmund was unsettled.

'Aleksander and I,' Jael said, happy to unsettle him. 'My mother, Biddy, Entorp. I plan to take everyone.'

'What does that mean?'

'It means that no one is safe here. Not after what Evaine did to Edela,' Jael said, working hard to remove all feeling from her voice. 'I won't be leaving anyone or anything behind that I care about. I'll be taking Tig and the puppies too.'

'The puppies?' Eadmund shook his head. 'On a ship?'

'You think I shouldn't be worried about them? That I should leave them here? When I left my grandmother behind, and look at what happened to her!'

'They're my dogs too, Jael,' Eadmund insisted. 'I would never let anything happen to them. Never!'

'No, you wouldn't, Eadmund,' Jael said. 'But nor would you have done what you just did with her. Not if you were free. Not if you had a choice in the matter. So, no, I won't leave them. And I'll be taking Eydis too.'

Eadmund was quickly furious. 'No!'

Jael leaned forward. 'Eydis wants to come. *I* want her to come,' she said firmly. 'You really think you can keep her safe? Safer than I could?'

Eadmund felt caught, overwhelmed by opposing feelings of guilt and shame, desire and regret. He wanted a reprieve from those judgmental eyes. 'Eydis is my sister,' he tried.

'Eydis is *my* sister too,' Jael insisted. 'And she will come with me. You are far too occupied to keep her safe. Oss is a kingdom in great need of its king, don't you think, Eadmund? With Ivaar in the wind? With Haaron and his sons coming for us?' She clenched her hands over the ends of the chair. 'But I must save Edela's life first. And there is no time to waste. Eydis is a dreamer, promised to Tuura. You owe her that. Eirik reneged on his promise. You cannot stand in her way as he did. I will keep her safe.' She stared at him with a confidence she suddenly did not feel.

Eadmund swallowed, words and images jangling around inside his head.

Evaine. Naked and perfect. Everything he wanted.

And now, Jael. So strong and determined.

Jael...

She smelled damp, like wet wool and horses. He inhaled her, and he remembered: the evil tincture, the Contest, Tarak, Hest.

All those nights in Eirik's pool.

Closing his eyes, Eadmund tried to escape the oddly torturous memories.

'Eadmund?' Jael was worried by the strange look on his face.

He opened his eyes. 'Yes, take her. Take everyone. You shouldn't be here,' he said hoarsely.

Jael blinked. She had seen him. Just for a moment. She had seen him, and she wanted to cry and scream to bring him back. He was in there! Lost, but in there.

If she could just find that book in Tuura.

Perhaps the answers to everything they sought lay hidden inside?

***

Morana wriggled about, wishing she had a more comfortable pillow; a mattress with some padding.

How could her mother have survived for so many years in such pitiful deprivation? Impoverished, yet working for the King of Hest, ruler of the richest kingdom in Osterland? She growled, wistful for the soft silence of wool stuffing; irritated by the incessant rustling of straw beneath her ear.

Morana felt trapped in this irritating place. The Following needed her. They needed Jaeger. And he needed to use the book, so somehow, she would have to become a bridge from one to the other, keeping everyone happy, which was not something that interested her at all. Other people's happiness had never been a concern of Morana's.

And then there was Haaron.

He was smart enough to know that his part in proceedings was coming to an end, surely? Yet she needed to keep him calm; oblivious to and unthreatened by the emergence of his youngest son.

Because he *was* coming. Morana had seen it.

Soon Jaeger Dragos would burst from the shadows and crush them all.

***

Thorgils walked Jael back to the house.

She barely looked at him, shattered by what she knew had happened, desperate to be alone. The triumphant sneer on Evaine's face, the heated shame on Eadmund's: those images were carved into her memory.

They were all that she could see.

It was too real, too painful to even acknowledge. She could only try to exist outside it all; not opening her heart or mind to any of it.

It didn't matter.

It couldn't matter.

It mattered to bring Eadmund back. Nothing would be real until then.

'You must keep him safe,' she said mutely as they stopped before the door.

'Safe?' Thorgils looked confused. 'Eadmund? From Evaine, you mean?'

Jael nodded. 'From Ivaar too. From Haaron. From Jaeger. From all of them. I won't be here.' Her voice drifted away into sadness.

'What he did...'

'He's her prisoner, Thorgils. Hers and Morana's. And when I save Edela, she'll find a way to free him. We will leave in the morning. You will keep Eadmund safe until we return.' Jael gripped the door handle. 'Promise me,' she urged, looking up at his worried face. 'Promise me, Thorgils. I would kill him if I knew he could help it. I would kill her if I could set him free.'

Thorgils could feel her pain, and he wanted to say something to make her smile so they could laugh it off, but what? Jael had given up Brekka for Eadmund. And now he was lost to her. Thorgils grabbed Jael's free hand. 'I promise. You save Edela, and I'll keep him safe for your return.'

Jael turned and opened the door, not wanting him to embrace her.

Not wanting tears to come.

She shut the door quickly, and Thorgils stared at it for some time. He thought of Edela. He hadn't been sure that she was even alive when he'd found her, but something had driven him to turn back into that alley just in time.

And perhaps that something could save both her and Eadmund.

***

They were all asleep, Jael could see, even Ido and Vella who lay on either side of Edela.

Keeping her safe.

Jael smiled sadly and turned towards the bedchamber. The door was open, the warm glow of a lamp inviting her in. She thought of that first night in the house, when Thorgils had deposited Eadmund onto the floor; a great snoring lump who had disappeared in the night.

And she had saved him.

Or had she?

Had he simply always loved Evaine?

Jael noticed Aleksander watching her, the faint flames of the fire glinting in his eyes. She stared at him, oddly wistful for his comforting arms and soothing voice. She watched Edela's chest moving slowly up and down, remembering her cottage and the chair where all advice sought would miraculously elicit the right answer; even if that answer was not always welcome.

Jael walked into the bedchamber alone, thinking about Tuura.

Where everything had fallen apart. Where people had died.

Where her life had both ended and begun.

She squeezed her hands into tight balls and trudged towards her empty bed.

Evaine had tried to kill her grandmother.

Evaine had taken her husband.

It was time to get them back.

PART TWO

The Room

CHAPTER EIGHT

Amma's sobs woke him.

Axl scrambled off the floor where he'd fallen asleep on a rug next to the fire. He could see Gisila stirring, already moving to check on Edela. Aleksander was sitting up, yawning. Biddy wasn't there, but the chickens, cows, and goats were full of dawn noise, and he guessed that she was outside, organising them all.

The door to the bedchamber was still closed.

'Sssshhh,' Axl soothed, stroking Amma's hair as she lay there, sobbing in her sleep.

Amma suddenly jerked awake, away from him, her eyes bursting with fear, her body recoiling, then slowly relaxing.

'You were having a dream,' Axl whispered gently. 'A nightmare.'

Amma sighed, wiping her eyes, feeling the wet tears on her cheeks.

'Was it him?'

Amma couldn't look at Axl. She was still there, trapped in that bed.

With Jaeger Dragos.

She nodded, shivering. 'He hurt me,' she mumbled.

Axl pulled the furs over her, feeling his body throb with fury. But his anger would not help, nor heal her. He saw Lothar's severed head in his own nightmares, but he had saved his mother, he knew. And, although Amma was with him now, he had not saved her in time. She was Jaeger's wife, and in the brief moment they'd been together, he had scarred her.

Amma could feel Axl's tension, and she panicked. 'You won't do anything silly, will you?' She reached for his hand. 'I'm here now. We're together. Safe.'

'Safe?' Axl frowned. 'We're about to leave for Tuura, hunted by everyone in Osterland soon, I'm sure. I don't imagine that Getta is going to be very happy when she finds out what happened either.' He didn't sound reassuring, and he could see the fear in Amma's eyes grow, but it was better to be honest. Amma wasn't a child. 'Sometimes, you have to fight to make yourself safe. You have to fight for your freedom.'

Amma didn't like the sound of that at all, but she knew Axl was right. While Jaeger lived, she was bound to him as his wife, and in her nightmares, by the things he had done to her.

She was desperate to be set free.

***

Jaeger wondered what trouble he had gotten himself into with Nicolene. The sun was barely up and there she was, at his door, pushing past Egil, sliding into his bed.

He had woken up, surprised to see that Meena wasn't there.

He wondered where she had gone.

'I think,' Jaeger began as he hurried out of bed, wrapping a fur around his waist, leaving Nicolene sitting there undressing. 'I think it's best if we don't play this game anymore. Not with Karsten almost recovered. Not with so many things I must attend to.'

Nicolene looked embarrassed, her face flushing pink. She stopped removing her dress and started covering herself back up. 'Attend to?' she sneered. 'What are you talking about, Jaeger? What must you *attend* to? This early? What's so urgent that you must leave your bed at dawn?'

Jaeger's mind went blank. He had drunk too much wine again, and his head was a thick tangle of half-grasped words. 'I am... training. Trying to recover my strength. We must go to war again soon. After what the Islanders did? What Jael Furyck did? We have to prepare for what will come.'

Nicolene's anger overrode her embarrassment, and dressed now, she stood. 'And how will you go to war against a group of islands when you have no ships?' she asked coldly. 'No ships at all! And why would you even want to try, when they can just throw more fire balls at you? Why make a war you don't need? So more men can burn? More ships can be lost? So Hest can become even more of a joke?'

Jaeger was annoyed by her attitude; enraged by the reminder of his failures. 'Is that what Karsten says?' he demanded, striding around the bed. 'That we shouldn't even try? That we should admit defeat?'

Nicolene's laugh was bitter. '*Karsten?*' She turned away from him, too livid to stay any longer. She had lain awake for hours, dreaming of him, eager to escape her marriage bed; concocting a story that Karsten would find believable, but Karsten hadn't even been awake when she'd slipped away.

Nicolene was annoyed that it had all been for nothing; that she would simply have to return to Karsten. Moaning, limping, pathetic, one-eyed Karsten. 'What do *I* care what he thinks? Or you? Fools!' she spat angrily, reaching for the door handle. 'Fools who will get us all killed!'

Jaeger rushed towards her, grabbing her hand. 'Or fools who will make Hest the greatest kingdom in this land! You would do well to hold your tongue around the man who intends to make that happen, Nicolene. Wives are easily replaced, you know. And widows are completely irrelevant. It's best not to make enemies with the one man who could save you from either fate.'

He was hurting her, squeezing her fingers, but her anger was burning with such intensity that Nicolene barely noticed. Ripping her hand out of his grasp, she glared at him before yanking open the door and slamming it behind her.

Meena's head went up at the sound of the door, and she looked down the corridor to see Nicolene stalking away from Jaeger's chamber. She felt a pain somewhere deep inside; a hot rush of jealousy. Ducking her head away, she swallowed, reaching for Berard's door handle, trying not to drop the logs she was carrying, determined to shut Jaeger out of her head once and for all.

***

Eadmund did not want to leave the bed.

It was his father's bed, which felt strange. Evaine had been in it with him, and that felt stranger still. He had dreamed of her, vividly, as though she was still there, wrapping herself around him like water. His body stirred, and he had a sudden urge for ale.

Eadmund frowned. That desire felt oddly familiar, and yet, it was a thirst he had not experienced in a long time.

Had the tincture stopped working?

Jael had been so cold and calm, but he knew that he'd hurt her. She was his wife and his queen, but she was not the woman he loved, and for so long he had been blind to that.

It had always been Evaine. He knew that now. He had fought his way through the murky clouds of his mind and found Evaine, waiting there for him.

If only he could decide what to do about Jael. What *could* he do? She was his wife. His father had wanted her for him. Eydis, too. And Jael had saved him, but perhaps that was all she was supposed to do? To save him in time so that he could become king.

But as for love?

Eadmund closed his eyes and remembered the feel of Evaine; the softness in her eyes, the urgent desire in her tiny body. She was his again.

And together, they had a son.

That was what his father had wanted most of all. For him to have heirs, to be happy. And now there was a chance he could be.

If only he could think of what to do about Jael.

***

Marcus Volsen, Elderman of Tuura, sat by the fire, warming his feet.

The tiny enclave of Tuura clung to the very tip of Osterland's northern reach, and it was rarely warm. Even during high summer, Tuurans wore thickly woven cloaks, for when the sun disappeared behind the clouds, they all shivered, deprived of its benevolent warmth.

'When?' he asked the woman who sat opposite him.

Her name was Ada. She was a dreamer.

'Within days,' Ada murmured.

Marcus narrowed his gaze, watching her shy and shrink away from him. 'You are certain? There can be no mistake?' It was pointless asking a dreamer such a thing, he knew, especially Ada. She was Tuura's most experienced. Old now, but her dreams had only become more accurate as her wrinkles had deepened.

She nodded.

He frowned.

'Well then, leave me. I must prepare myself to welcome our visitors.' His dark eyebrows knitted together, his jaw working away furiously as Ada creaked up from her stool and padded to the door.

Marcus' eyes moved to the fire.

Jael Furyck. At last. He ran a hand over his short, dark beard.

He did not have long to make sure that everything was ready.

***

'Is everything ready?' Jael asked Thorgils, who looked flustered as he raced around in circles on the foreshore. 'Thorgils?' she grumbled, reaching for his arm, demanding his attention. 'Is the ship ready? We need to bring Edela down.'

They were taking *Sea Bear* to Tuura, and Beorn had been at work all morning preparing a secure bed for Edela; building wooden guardrails they would wrap with furs to lessen the impact of the waves on her weak body. *Sea Bear's* house was still intact, but her catapult was being removed to leave room for Tig.

Jael was not leaving Tig behind.

Or the puppies.

If she had her way, she'd take them all. Thorgils and Eadmund too.

But Eadmund was no longer hers, and Thorgils needed to stay and keep him safe. But the rest of them?

They were all going.

'No, not yet, but soon,' Thorgils said. 'Beorn's still fussing. Fyn and Axl are in there, helping him. Amma's making it comfortable. She's taken most of the bedding from your house, I think! Beorn's trying to build a box for the puppies too.' Thorgils frowned, feeling odd. He would miss those puppies.

It felt as though they weren't coming back.

'Give me some of your hair,' Jael said quietly.

'My hair?' Thorgils looked horrified, then realisation dawned. 'Oh, for dreaming! I thought you wanted a keepsake to remember me by.'

Jael couldn't help but laugh. 'I'm not *that* fond of you!'

'Well, Jael, I'm not sure that's true,' he winked. 'There are not many who can resist my charms, you know. Even a woman as stubborn as you.'

Jael smiled, enjoying the sensation before it was quickly replaced with a frown. 'You will keep Leada safe?'

'With my life,' Thorgils promised. 'I will.' He glanced around. 'She's Eadmund's horse, so I can't imagine Evaine having a problem with her.'

'Well, don't give her reason to have a problem with you,' Jael insisted. 'Stay on her good side. And Morac's. They're working together with Morana to control Eadmund. I don't want them working against you.'

'I think I'll be safe now that Entorp has had his way with my arms,' Thorgils grimaced, reminded of the pain that still lingered from his recent tattooing.

'Edela wasn't,' Jael said in warning. 'If you try to come between Evaine and Eadmund, you'll not be safe. And if you want Isaura back, you have to look after yourself.'

That straightened Thorgils' spine. There was nothing he wouldn't do to have Isaura back again.

***

Osbert's shoulders slumped in relief at the sight of Saala's gates.

The sun, though new, was already scorching. Sweat dripped down his back, streaming past his temples into his eyes. He was looking forward to shelter, a seat that wasn't a saddle, and a cool drink of ale.

But more than anything at that moment, he was desperate to set fire to his father.

He had not thought it right for a Furyck to be cremated in Hest. A noble Brekkan king should not have his pyre in Haaron's kingdom. So, they had borrowed a cart and a pair of horses, wrapped Lothar's stiff, stinking, headless corpse – and his head – and brought him with them.

And the flies had followed.

And now, after three days of steaming under the sun, their old king was stinking like an overflowing midden. And worse. Osbert had never smelled anything so stomach-churningly awful. He was desperate to turn his father's corpse to ash just to be rid of the vile stench.

Osbert held up a hand and his man, Oleg, rode up to join him.

'My lord?' Oleg panted, just as hot and nauseated by the stink as his new king.

'We cannot be sure what trouble my cousins may have stirred up on their return to the islands,' Osbert said quietly, batting away a persistent fly. 'Rexon never appeared particularly loyal to my father, did he?'

'Well...' Oleg mused, then quickly realising that it was pointless to have an opinion that wasn't Osbert's, he coughed, dropping his head. 'No, lord.'

'So, perhaps Jael is waiting for us? Perhaps they have set an ambush?' It was a thought Osbert had chewed over the entire journey. He saw betrayal in every shadow, in every pair of eyes around him.

Two kings had died. Each one cruelly murdered.

He did not feel safe.

'They would not have the men, my lord,' Oleg reminded

him. 'We have the Saalans with us. They would only have Rexon's garrison to turn to their favour. And I doubt there was time to organise any reinforcements from the islands.'

He didn't look certain, though, and Osbert's fears were not eased. 'Send your men in first. You lead them in. The rest of us will remain here until you give me the signal.' He felt his shoulders tighten again, his nostrils flaring as a warm breeze wafted another wave of his father's fly-blown corpse towards him. 'And make it quick!'

***

'It's best that you stay away, Evaine,' Eadmund urged, watching the fire build in her eyes; feeling his body respond to it. He blinked, trying to force himself away from her, but it was not easy. 'They will be gone soon. Very soon. Just stay here. Jael and I must talk. There are things we need to discuss. About the island.'

Evaine pouted, enraged by the idea of Eadmund being anywhere near his wife. 'She chained me to the Wailing Post!' she grumbled, annoyed that he had done nothing to make that right.

Eadmund brought his hands up to her face, ignoring her petulance. 'Stay here with Morac, please,' he soothed, kissing her. 'She'll be gone soon.'

Evaine sighed, impatient but accepting. Jael leaving so soon was more than she had hoped for. But what if she were to find a cure for Edela in Tuura? What if Edela were to wake and tell Eadmund what she had done? Would his connection to her and her control over him be strong enough to withstand that? Evaine stood on her tiptoes and stared into Eadmund's eyes. 'Don't be long. I just want us to be together. All of us. Now.'

Eadmund smiled before turning away. 'Soon,' he promised over his shoulder. 'We will be. Soon.'

Morac crept up behind Evaine. 'What did I tell you?' he whispered. 'He's yours now, isn't he?'

Evaine watched Eadmund striding away. Yes, he was. At last. But now she just needed to find a way to stop Jael from ever coming back to Oss.

She needed to speak to Morana.

***

'And?' Jaeger hovered impatiently behind Morana as she sat at his table, poring over the book.

Morana spun around, whipping him with her hair. 'You must decide what you want. This book is powerful, and with it, you can create true destruction. But what is it that you wish to achieve first?'

Jaeger had thought that it would be obvious, but her question gave him pause. He walked towards the window, peering down to Hest's charred harbour. The harbour with no ships. No piers.

He thought of his father. His brothers.

His wife.

'I want to be king here,' he said, turning around. 'I cannot do anything until I am.'

'You want to kill your father? Kill your brothers?' Morana laughed. 'You do not need this book for such insignificance. You can do that in many ways that require no magic at all.'

Jaeger frowned, walking back towards the table, leaning over the book.

'You must desire more than that? Surely? This book did not seek you out because you are a man of small ambition. A man meant to become just another forgotten Dragos prince. This book was meant for one worthy of its true, horrible darkness.'

Jaeger felt a violent throbbing in his chest, jerking in his limbs. The book was calling to him, drawing him in, demanding more of him.

Challenging him.

He cocked his head to one side. 'What are you suggesting?'

'You can become king here easily enough, but you must seek more for yourself and this kingdom. You must seek the destruction of all others so that Hest becomes the *only* kingdom in this land.' Morana's eyes were dark as she inhaled the ancient power of the book herself. 'You have enemies, the ones who stole your wife, who humiliated you, burned your ships, cut your ankles, hurt your brothers. You must crush them all. But especially...' Morana stopped and stared at Jaeger, ensuring he heard this most of all.

He wasn't even breathing as he lost himself in her hypnotic eyes. 'Especially?'

'Especially, Jael Furyck. She is the one who will stand between you and all that you dream of. *She* is the one you must kill. For if she lives, you will not.'

***

'My lord?' Meena mumbled again, desperate to tap her head. The sun was up and warm now, and she wanted to wash Berard's bedsheet and clothes and have them drying in the sun.

She needed to get down to the stream quickly.

Berard wasn't listening, though, as he stared out the window. He was thinking about Jael. She had warned him about Jaeger, urged him to protect Amma, and he would have, he was certain. He was glad they had taken her with them, imagining what might have happened if she'd been left behind. 'I'm sorry,' he said, turning to Meena. 'What did you say?'

'I must go,' she said, nodding to the bundle in her arms. 'To wash.'

'Oh,' Berard smiled. 'Yes, you go. You don't need to ask my permission, Meena. I'm happy for you to do whatever you think is needed. And please, you must call me Berard.'

Meena blushed, easing herself out of the chamber. Smiling awkwardly, she shut the door and scurried away.

Berard turned back to the window, frowning suddenly. He had to keep Meena away from his brother. Jaeger was changing so quickly. It may have been too subtle a difference for anyone else to notice, but Berard could see it.

For the first time in his life, he didn't feel safe around Jaeger.

He wondered if any of them were.

***

Aleksander helped Jael manoeuvre Tig onto the ship.

Tig knew Aleksander. He trusted him. And Aleksander's soothing voice helped him focus on Jael and the carrots she was holding on board *Sea Bear*. Aleksander coaxed him up onto the platform they had pushed alongside the ship, and from there it was a quick jump over the gunwale.

Jael smiled in relief, working quickly to secure Tig to the pole Beorn had attached from the prow to the roof of the house. She hoped the weather would treat them fairly as she'd likely need to keep Tig company for the entire journey.

Holding out her last carrot to Tig, Jael's eyes rested on Eadmund who stood on the stones saying goodbye to Eydis.

He did not look happy.

'Jael will take good care of me,' Eydis insisted firmly, not about to have her mind changed.

'Yes, I know she will,' Eadmund muttered. 'But, Eydis, you're my sister. I'm responsible for you.'

'But Jael is my sister too,' Eydis reminded him. 'She'll keep me safe.'

Eadmund wrapped his arms around her delicate frame, holding her tight against his chest. He felt muddled again, his mind swirling with memories.

'Ivaar will come,' Eydis said suddenly, pushing herself away from him. 'He is making plans. You must prepare for that, Eadmund. He won't give up until he destroys you.'

Eadmund looked surprised. He hoped that she was right, but at the same time, he felt anxious that they would not be ready. 'I will. Thorgils will help. Don't worry, we'll be here when you return.'

Eydis was suddenly terrified. The idea of leaving him with Evaine...

But they couldn't help Edela or Eadmund if they didn't go to Tuura.

'We must hurry, Eydis,' Biddy said gently as she walked up behind her, watching Beorn eyeing them irritably over the gunwale. Edela was on board, secured into her specially made bed. The puppies were in their box. Everyone was ready to leave.

Except for Eydis and Fyn. Biddy looked across to where Fyn stood, saying goodbye to Runa.

'I wish you would come, Mother,' Fyn whispered anxiously, gripping his mother's gloved hands. 'You're not safe here.'

Runa tried to look more confident than she felt. 'I have to stay,' she said firmly. 'That poor baby needs me. Evaine does not care for him. And Eadmund. Someone must be here to help Thorgils with Eadmund. Morac will keep me safe from Evaine, don't worry.'

It was brave of his mother, Fyn decided. The easiest option was to escape with them; to be safely away from Evaine. He felt proud that she was trying to do the right thing.

If it was the right thing.

He hugged Runa, then turned and hurried towards the ship, fighting back the tears he could feel burning the corners of his eyes.

Jael jumped down onto the foreshore. 'You get on board,' she said to Biddy as Eadmund gripped Eydis around the waist and hoisted her up to Aleksander.

It was not easy to let her go and Eadmund didn't look away as Aleksander placed Eydis gently on the deck and led her towards Amma.

'We'll return when Edela is well again,' Jael said coldly, trying her best to meet Eadmund's eyes. She kept seeing Evaine's triumphant face and had to fight the desire to erupt in anger or dissolve in tears.

Neither felt right.

The truth lay somewhere in between, and Jael knew that she was better to leave it all alone for now.

'I hope she will recover,' Eadmund tried. He looked away, awkward and embarrassed. 'And that you find the answers you seek.'

Jael watched him trying so desperately to avoid her eyes. 'I'm still queen here,' she said hoarsely. She could see the Osslanders on the beach, some way behind them, and up on the hill. 'No matter what you think of me, you and I are bound by your father's wishes. He chose us both. Not just you, not just me. And I promised him that I would keep Oss safe. So, you can expect my return, Eadmund, because this is my home now.' She turned away, hurrying across the foreshore to *Sea Bear*, ignoring the urge to look behind herself one last time.

Eadmund didn't know what to think as feelings rose and fought against each other inside his heart. He frowned, watching Jael clamber on board. It had only been days since she had rested her head on his chest, and he had held her in his arms, but she was a stranger now.

And he didn't want her anymore.

CHAPTER NINE

The signal came from the fort quickly enough, and Osbert was pleased for it. He was sweltering, desperate to escape the flies.

Eager to rest in comfort and plot his next move.

He would have to face Jael eventually, but *he* would choose the time and place for that battle. He thought of his sister; enjoying the fleeting image of dragging her back to her husband one day soon.

The disloyal bitch.

'Rexon!' Osbert dismounted, wanting to fall into a sweaty heap, but remembering his new position as King of Brekka, he remained erect and strode towards Rexon Boas, Lord of Saala.

His man now.

'My lord,' Rexon said, his face troubled. 'I have heard the news from Oleg. I'm very sorry about your father.' He bowed his head, attempting to show respect, although he didn't feel any. Nor any sorrow. Lothar had been the worst king in Brekka's history, he was sure.

'You heard it from Oleg, did you?' Osbert scowled. 'Did you, Rexon? Or did you, in fact, hear it from Jael on her way back to Oss?'

'Jael?' Rexon looked confused.

Osbert waved his hand at Rexon's face, not wanting to continue their conversation in the scorching heat. 'I need something to drink.' He turned to Oleg. 'See to my horse, and the men as well. When you've done that, come to me in the hall. There is much we have to discuss.'

***

Thorgils felt terrible. Biddy, Edela, and Entorp had left, and his mother had promptly taken a turn for the worst. In his desperation, he'd turned to Runa who had found someone to help: a mousey, young woman called Elona. She was not known for any great skill with herbs, but there was little choice now.

They had shooed him out while they discussed what could be done for Odda, and Thorgils had headed straight to the hall, horrified to find Evaine prancing about, making herself at home.

Barely a murmur escaped the few occupied tables of equally horrified Osslanders. The hall had emptied quickly when it became apparent that Evaine had come to stay.

They had seen her tied to the Wailing Post.

They knew what it meant.

She was a witch, they whispered to each other. And a murderous one at that.

Thorgils frowned, his eyes meeting Torstan's. 'I imagine we'll be the last ones left in here soon,' he mumbled, reaching for his ale.

They both peered around.

There was Gurin, now Eadmund's steward, who was preparing the high table for the evening meal. Sevrin was there, talking to Eadmund as he sat on his throne, listening to all the things they still needed to do to prepare the fort for Ivaar's expected attack. And Morac, running around behind Evaine as she made suggestions for improving the hall, which had, up until now, suited them all just fine.

Torstan finished his cup and plonked it down on the table.

'Well, I don't know about you,' he muttered, 'but I'd rather be standing out in the rain than sitting in here watching this. Jael's barely left.' He shook his head and stood. 'Come on, let's get out of here.'

Thorgils couldn't help but agree. He felt old and weary, weighed down by the load of caring for his mother and his best friend. Both of whom looked in dire straits.

One of the hall doors burst open, ushering in a gust of wind and with it a gaggle of strangers. Thorgils squinted: not strangers.

He smiled so widely you could see his gums.

'Thorgils! Torstan!' Bram strode towards the two men, his arms out wide. 'How big you've grown! Yet still punier than me!'

'Uncle!' Thorgils was overcome with pleasure as Bram pulled him into a hug.

His father's youngest brother, Bram Svanter, had grown up with itchy feet, and a giant-sized thirst for women and adventure. A man too big for Oss, he had left to pursue both at a young age. He would return every few years with tales of the far-flung places he had reached and the strange people he had encountered; showing off his ever-increasing collection of scars and tattoos; enthralling them with stories of how he had acquired his newest arm rings and his shipload of booty. And they would all be enamoured. Eadmund, Thorgils, Torstan, and their friends had looked at Bram as though he was a walking god. A man so mighty that they all wanted to be just like him when they grew up.

But eventually, at a very late age, he had fallen in love and turned into a man mostly content with a plot of land in Moll – a small village in Alekka – and a house filled with squawking children. He had continued to trade and travel but only in the pursuit of supporting his family.

They had scarcely seen him since.

'Bram!' Eadmund and Sevrin hurried forward, embracing

the long-seen stranger with smiling faces.

Morac lurked in the shadows. He had never liked Bram Svanter.

'I was sorry to hear about Eirik,' Bram said soberly as they led him to a table by the fire. 'I wanted to come and pay my respects to you, Eadmund. He was the finest king. A good man.'

Eadmund felt the depth of feeling in those words. Eirik had loved Bram, always trying to convince him to return to Oss to fight for him. But for Bram, the call of the sea had always been louder than that of his king.

Bram looked barely older than the last time he'd visited, though his red hair had long since become a salt-and-peppery mix of wiry waves, and his bushy, grey beard was growing whiter with every year. He appeared strong and powerful still, with a broad, barrel-like chest, and arms big enough to lug a sea chest with little trouble. But something about him was different.

There was no light in his crisp, blue eyes anymore.

'He was,' Eadmund said sadly as he sat down. 'He would've liked to see you again. To hear where you've been. What you've seen. What treasure you have to tempt him with. It's been too long.'

'It has,' Bram agreed. 'We've had a hard few years.' He nodded at Gurin as he handed around cups of freshly poured ale. 'A hard few years indeed.' Inhaling deeply, Bram considered the ale, his body still rocking from side to side as if he were at sea.

No one spoke. There was an unfamiliar sadness about Bram that troubled them.

'And your family?' Thorgils asked hesitantly. 'How are my little cousins?'

'Dead.' It was hard to say, and Bram quickly dropped his eyes to the table, studying his cup.

'Dead?' Thorgils was shocked. 'All of them?' From memory, Bram had two daughters around Eydis' age and twin boys a few years younger.

Bram supped deeply, wanting to avoid any more questions, though he knew he could not. 'An illness swept through Moll over a year ago. Never seen anything like it. Our healer was the first to die. I went to the next village for help, but their healer was dead too, and the next.'

Eadmund looked puzzled. 'Just the healers?'

Bram shook his head. 'No, more besides, but it's a strange thing when a healer dies. Doesn't give you much faith that you're going to survive, does it?'

The fire popped, and Thorgils jumped. 'So, this sickness, it killed your children?'

Bram nodded, clearing his throat, trying not to bring the haunting pictures to mind. 'And then my wife. That was the most heartbreaking thing of all. I tried to get her to hold on, but once the children were gone, she lost the will.'

'But you didn't get sick?' Torstan wondered.

'No,' Bram sighed. 'Which makes the whole thing even harder. It seemed to strike the women and children. Suddenly we were a village of men, mostly alone.'

Thorgils didn't know what to say. He couldn't imagine the gods could be so cruel.

'But enough about me,' Bram smiled, eager to escape the dark shadows clouding his heart. 'Enough about me! You must tell me how it is for all of you. My boys, so big now! Grown up and causing trouble still, I'm sure!' He tried to sound jovial, but the pain was still in his eyes, and their sympathy for him was still on their faces. Finishing his cup, he quickly looked around for another. 'So, come on then, tell me, how are things on Oss?'

***

'As I said, it would make no sense to attack them immediately, my lord,' Rexon said wearily, having talked in circles for hours, trying to lead Osbert away from the idea of heading straight for the islands to take his revenge upon his cousins. 'Besides, Edela Saeveld knows how to make that sea-fire, doesn't she?'

Osbert, after four cups of ale and three goblets of wine, was less inclined to feel as fearful of the sea-fire as he knew he should. 'Perhaps. But she is not in Andala. It will not be so easy to find what she needs on Oss, I'm sure.'

Rexon glanced at Oleg, who he knew well. They had both been in Ranuf Furyck's household once. Oleg looked as bored with the conversation as he was. 'It may not, but surely, lord, we must take our time to think this through –'

'What we must *do*,' Osbert growled, interrupting him, 'is listen to me, wouldn't you say, Rexon? *Me* being the man who cares if *you* are here or not. And if I don't...' Osbert snapped his fingers and shrunk back into the comforting furs of Rexon's chair. It was cooler in the hall. A breeze blew welcomingly towards him, and his stomach rumbled. 'I require food.'

Rexon swallowed, irritated by Osbert's manner, which was even coarser than his headless father's, and stood. 'I shall see to it, my lord,' he said through gritted teeth.

Osbert frowned. 'And be quick about it!' He turned to Oleg, lowering his voice. 'Do you trust him?' he asked, inclining his head towards Rexon, who was talking to a servant.

Oleg looked surprised. 'Rexon? I don't see why we wouldn't. He has always been loyal to Brekka. Ranuf taught him to put the kingdom above everything. If that had changed, it would be a surprise to me.'

Osbert was not convinced. 'Go with him,' he ordered. 'Watch him. The last king who stayed here ended up dead, and I don't intend to follow in his footsteps.' He leaned forward, reaching for his goblet, which he noted, was nearly empty. Feeling a surge of nausea, he belched.

Sleep deprived, uncomfortable, injured... and suddenly a king.

It was all he had ever dreamed of, yet Osbert had never felt more unsettled in his life. He needed to destroy his enemies, to exact revenge for the murder of his father. There was no time to delay. He would have to conquer the islands fast.

He could not allow Jael to live.

***

Jael watched Edela as she lay in her narrow bed, swaying gently with each roll of the ship. She couldn't stop thinking about the cave, seeing her grandmother trapped on that raft. Did Edela know where she was, or what was happening to her? Did she have the strength to escape?

Not without help, perhaps...

Momentarily assured by Edela's steady breathing, Jael closed her eyes, resting her head against the wall of the house. Riddled with holes, it was breezy but better than nothing.

She was a dreamer, she reminded herself, yawning. It didn't feel right, but Jael could no longer deny it. She was a dreamer.

And she had to find some answers.

***

'I can stay in the hall,' Bram insisted for the third time as they walked across the muddy square. Tired and weary after so many stories and too many cups of ale, he stumbled along beside his nephew with barely one eye open.

Thorgils batted away his offer for the third time. 'There's room at Odda's now that Fyn's gone. And besides, if you can stand it, I'd be glad of the company. After today, I was starting to feel a little lonely.'

'So I hear,' Bram yawned, looking up at his nephew. They had once been the same height, but Bram, despite his towering frame, had shrunk a bit over the years. 'But maybe not for long.' He pulled the crumpled scroll from his pouch and handed it to Thorgils. 'Maybe not for long,' he smiled.

Thorgils felt his heartbeat thundering like an angry horse in his chest. It was as though everything else had blurred around him except that scroll.

He gulped, staring down at it.

Bram squeezed Thorgils' arm. 'We're not far from the house. I can find my way from here, so you take your time.'

'You saw her?' Thorgils asked throatily.

'I did,' Bram grinned. 'And she was well. Blooming. Surprising for a woman with so many children! Read your note, Nephew.' And he turned away into the night.

Thorgils looked at the scroll again, then hurried to find a patch of moonlight before unravelling it. Isaura's hand, he was sure. It was not so long since he had seen it. Not in his mind at least.

He held his breath as he read:

Ivaar has gone. He left five days after he returned from Skorro, taking both ships. A garrison of twenty-five men guards the fort. He promised to come back for us when it was time. Come now, please. We will be waiting.

Thorgils couldn't breathe.

He rolled up the scroll, placed it gently into his pouch, and ran for home.

***

There was blood everywhere. Screams of horror and pain echoed around the hall.

Jael jerked awake, shaking, her body vibrating with the vivid intensity of the fading dream. She wanted to vomit.

'Jael?' Aleksander was at her side, holding her shoulder. 'Are you alright?'

It was dark now, and she could only see shadows on Aleksander's face.

She tried to blink him into focus. Her head hurt. She could hear the whistling wail of the wind through the holes in the walls, the rush of waves as they jerked the ship about. And she remembered where she was. 'I had a dream,' Jael murmured, feeling oddly uncomfortable with that statement. It was Edela who was supposed to say that. Not her.

'About what?'

But Jael wasn't listening. She was reliving the dream, seeing the blood as it splattered across the flagstones, seeping into the grouting, dying everything a dark, ominous red.

Berard Dragos' blood.

CHAPTER TEN

'Runa?' Bram blinked, trying to adjust his eyes to the dull orange firelight as he stood in the doorway of Odda's cottage.

Runa spilled her tea over her knees. It was hot, and she jumped up, yelping in discomfort, stumbling near the flames.

Bram sprinted into the room and lunged for her, steadying her arm, removing the cup. 'Here, you look as though you're all at sea!' he laughed, and it was throaty and hoarse. He stared into her eyes.

She looked sad, he thought.

Older. Much like him.

Runa turned away, shaking in surprise. It had been years since Bram Svanter had last been seen on Oss, but he appeared much the same: huge and smiling, too much hair, leathery face.

But older. Greyer.

They both were.

'You look well. Unlike poor Odda over there.' He'd seen Odda tucked into her bed, eyes closed, fur up to her nose. 'Is she sleeping?' he asked gently.

Runa forced herself to focus. 'She is... sleeping deeply. I had Elona Nelberg here checking on her for Thorgils, but I don't put much faith in anything she said. She didn't appear to know what she was talking about.'

Bram frowned. He had never liked his sister-in-law who had driven his brother into an early grave, but she was family and Thorgils' mother. And she had most certainly raised a good son. 'Elona? When did she become a healer?'

'When her mother died,' Runa sighed. 'But I'm afraid that she has no gift for it at all.' She turned to the door. 'Where is Thorgils? I must be going. Morac will be wondering where I am.'

Bram shook off his furry cloak, following her gaze. He smiled. 'I imagine that's him now.'

Runa looked confused, but the very next moment, the door burst open and in rushed Thorgils, face flushed, eyes wide, hair standing up all over the place. He looked from Runa to Bram and back again. 'I, I...' Then he saw his mother and his face dropped. She did not look any better at all. He shook his head.

'Your mother will be fine,' Bram said firmly, his eyes twinkling. 'And if she isn't, then that was meant to be. You know that. You can't keep someone from the gods when it's their time.'

Runa looked confused.

'Isaura,' Thorgils started, then stopped, feeling as though he shouldn't even consider the idea with so many other things to worry about. 'Ivaar has left Kalfa. She wants me to come for her. But...' He almost cried, because, after eight lonely years of being without her, it didn't feel real.

Could it really happen? As easily as that?

He shook his head, dropping his shoulders.

'I'll help you, Nephew,' Bram said encouragingly. 'I have a ship. We only need another two to take that fort and hold it, I'd say. I had a good look around, just in case. It can be done.'

'And I can stay with Odda while you're gone,' Runa added. 'I would be happy to.'

They turned to her. She seemed so eager to help.

'You're sure?' Thorgils asked.

'Your husband won't mind?' Bram wondered, remembering what a miserable man she had married.

Runa pursed her lips, remembering what a miserable man

she had married. 'I don't mind if he does.'

Bram grinned, happy to hear it. 'Well, hopefully, we'll leave tomorrow, once we've had a think about how it will go, so best get your things and be here in the morning. Thorgils and I will have to organise ourselves and speak to the king.'

Runa smiled, happy to have a purpose and a reason to escape Morac; one he could hardly argue against. 'I'll be here,' she said as Bram showed her to the door. 'Elona left a tincture on the table. You should try and give Odda some if she wakes. One spoonful is all she needs.'

Thorgils nodded, easing himself down onto the tiny bed, which groaned in protest, gently taking Odda's cold hand in his.

Life was a gift from the gods, and here was an opportunity for him to start living again before it was too late and he was lying in his own bed, waiting for the gods to come for him.

Isaura. He closed his eyes, still vibrating in surprise and shock and most of all... hope.

***

'What do you see?'

They were alone in Ayla's cottage, sitting on stools on opposite sides of the fire. Making plans. Nervous and excited.

But mostly nervous.

'I...' Ayla stared into the flames. 'I see fire.'

'Truly?' Isaura laughed, uncertain if Ayla was teasing her.

'I see darkness and fire and storms and death,' Ayla went on. 'So much death.'

'Well, that's not a great portent, is it?' Isaura whispered, glancing at the door. 'Not for what I hope we're about to do.' She shuddered. Ayla looked only half there. Her eyes appeared glazed, transfixed by the twirling flames.

Ayla swallowed, trying to bring herself back into the room. 'But I do think Thorgils is coming. I feel that.'

'You do?'

Ayla smiled reassuringly. 'How could he not?'

Isaura was suddenly terrified. 'But will there be time? What if Ivaar comes back? What if...'

'Isaura, you asked him to come, so he is coming. Whether Ivaar is here or not, Thorgils is coming. We just need to prepare ourselves to do what we can to help him.'

'Help him?' Isaura was confused. 'How can *we* help him?'

'There are things we can do, so put on your cloak and grab that basket by the door. I must find my other knife.'

***

Osbert had drunk too much and yet, not enough.

His throat had been dust-clogged, still filled with the smoke of the sea-fire Jael had destroyed Haaron's piers with. He shook his head at the memory of that night. Once he was back in Andala, he would have to find Edela's recipe.

If he could.

Laying his head against the soft fur of the chair, Osbert closed his eyes, then sat upright, worried that he was sitting in the very chair Eirik Skalleson had died in. His eyes darted around the softly lit bedchamber, but he was alone.

Still...

A king was never safe.

Both his father and Eirik had proved that.

Osbert suddenly panicked about the wine he'd drunk but then he remembered that Oleg had drunk it too, and Oleg had still been standing when he'd bid him goodnight.

He thought wistfully of Keyta, whose silky body had been a delight; her nightly company making his time in Hest oddly pleasant. Turning his head towards the bed, he felt a sense of emptiness that there was no one to share it with.

There was no one to talk to at all. No one he could trust at least.

His parents were both gone; Amma was now with his enemies; Getta had her own kingdom to worry about.

He was completely alone.

Osbert yawned, ready for bed now. In the morning, they would burn Lothar's bloated corpse, and he would take a ship back to Andala.

He couldn't wait.

He had a war to wage.

***

Berard was sitting by the fire, half asleep, a goblet of wine in his hand, his toes warming too close to the flames.

'I will see you in the morning,' Meena said shyly, tapping her toes as she waited to be dismissed.

Berard scrambled to his feet, blinking himself out of his post-supper doze. He had eaten so much that he felt ready for his bed; his bed, which looked clean and more inviting than he remembered it ever looking before. Meena had already worked wonders with his dark and dingy chamber; disorganised and dusty as it had been.

It even smelled better.

'Yes, alright then, tomorrow,' he smiled, walking her to the door.

'Do you have enough wine?' Meena wondered, suddenly anxious.

Berard laughed. 'I have enough wine,' he assured her. 'I'm more interested in my bed than wine, I promise.'

'You had a long day.'

'Yes,' he yawned. 'My father is desperate to get the piers rebuilt quickly, for without them we'll struggle to accommodate the merchants, and if we're not careful, they'll drift away and find other ports and new markets to trade in. It makes it difficult for them to unload their cargo without the piers. He wants to fortify the castle too. After what happened...' Berard frowned, not really sure what had happened. He couldn't imagine that Jael would have killed Lothar Furyck without reason. She was not that sort of person, he was sure.

Yet, now they were enemies again.

'Well, I only hope that we'll be safe from the Islanders. I don't want them to come back with that fire,' Meena said, shuddering at the memory of that night as she opened the door.

Berard patted her arm. 'I don't think you have to worry about that. They didn't try to attack us. They just wanted to leave.'

Meena didn't look so certain. 'Jaeger said they want to kill us all.'

'Jaeger?' Berard's eyes flared in annoyance. His brother had become a stranger in the days since the battle for Skorro. The humiliation of his constant failures had made him retreat even further from his family, pushing even Berard away.

But not Meena, it seemed.

'Jaeger talks a lot,' Berard grumbled. 'Best not to listen to most of what he says. He's an angry man. Too angry these days.' He stopped himself from going any further, surprised by his own bitterness, or perhaps it was just that the truth was finally stirring in him now that he was no longer blinded by loyalty.

'But the book?' Meena whispered, glancing up and down the corridor. 'The book will give him unlimited power.'

Berard froze. 'Will it?' He looked worried.

Meena nodded. 'Especially now that he has Morana's help.

She can read it.' And tapping her head, she dropped her eyes to the floor and disappeared through the door.

Berard was suddenly wide awake. He stepped out into the corridor, watching Meena hurry away from her own chamber.

Towards Jaeger's.

***

It was Fyn's turn with Tig and Jael was glad for a chance to get out of the wind.

She couldn't stop shaking as she sat down next to Edela's bed, enjoying the protection of the walls; listening as the wind picked up even more.

Her grandmother's hand was warm.

Hers was not.

Edela lay wrapped in layers of thick furs, tucked into Beorn's makeshift bed. The rolling movement of the ship appeared to have little effect on her frail body. She simply lay there, her eyes closed, utterly still, apart from the slow rise and fall of her chest as she swayed from side to side.

They kept checking on her, terrified that she would die at any moment. But there was nothing anyone could do except keep her comfortable and warm and wait to see what help they could find in Tuura.

Jael shivered, memories of that night surging back with force. She glanced at her mother, who was sleeping next to Biddy and Amma on the opposite side of the house. Gisila had barely spoken to anyone since Hest. She was traumatised by what Lothar had done to her, desperately worried for Edela, and now having to face Tuura and the nightmares they had all sought to bury in a deep, deep grave.

Jael closed her eyes and tried to think of something else

instead.

Eadmund.

That was even worse.

She opened her eyes, blinking away the memory of Eadmund with Evaine, desperate to hold onto the thought that he was a prisoner and not a willing participant; that he hadn't simply chosen to be with Evaine and love her instead.

Jael squeezed Edela's hand again. There had to be some way she could rescue her grandmother from that cave and bring her back to them.

They all needed her.

***

'You are mine!' the voice crowed, almost singing with happiness. 'Mine, mine, mine! And you cannot help her. And she cannot help you. You are here with me now, and you cannot help her, Edela!' she laughed, and it sounded as though a flock of birds was racing around the walls of the cave, angrily batting their wings, screeching far into the darkness. 'You think that someone in Tuura can help her? Can help you? Oh, Edela, have you learned nothing about Tuura?'

The echo of her question disappeared slowly into the silence.

'Tuura is where you will all die!'

***

Meena could barely breathe.

One of Jaeger's hands was between her thighs, the other

was winding its way up, over her stomach, towards her breasts.

She arched her back, her body exploding with pleasure. Her head was swimming with waves of desire, her limbs throbbing and heavy.

Jaeger ran his tongue up to her neck, kissing her jaw; finding her lips, kissing her so hard that she lost all feeling in her mouth. He rose up on an elbow, peering at her. 'You don't need to work for Berard,' he growled deeply. 'You don't need to take care of *him.*'

Meena squirmed, not wanting to talk at all; uncomfortable that he was speaking of Berard. She stiffened, embarrassed, trying to ignore the vision of Berard as he smiled goodbye to her.

'You can stay here,' Jaeger went on, oblivious to her sudden discomfort. 'With me.' Bringing his hand up to Meena's face, he stared into her eyes, trying to see what she was thinking in the flickering glow of the candles that were dripping wax over the tables on either side of the bed.

Jaeger's stare was so intense that Meena felt her stomach clench. She swallowed, the familiar voice, loud in her ears, urging her to tap her head so she could feel safe again. Furrowing her brow, she tried to ignore it. 'What about Nicolene?' she asked, clicking her toes instead.

Jaeger's serious face broke into a smile, and he laughed loudly. 'Nicolene? Ha! What do you know about Nicolene?' He watched Meena's face twist and turn itself away from him as he started rubbing his finger around her nipple. Slowly. 'Nicolene is bored and doesn't like her husband. I was bored and thought it would be... fun.' His eyes were hard and cold; there was nothing fun about him.

Meena looked doubtful. 'But what about your b-b-b-brother?' She closed her eyes, trying not to notice the way his finger was making her feel.

'Karsten? Karsten is irrelevant to her and me. And soon to Hest as well. There will only be one heir when my father dies,

Meena, and that will be me.'

Meena shivered as Jaeger bent over her, his lips on her nipple now. She couldn't help the moan of pleasure that escaped her mouth as she felt his teeth, but the voice in her head was growing louder and louder, warning of the danger she was placing herself in. 'What about Berard?' she asked suddenly, regretting the words the moment they escaped her lips.

Jaeger froze.

Meena froze too, furious with herself. Swallowing.

'Berard?' Jaeger said slowly, his lips barely moving now. 'Berard has no ambition to be king, unlike Karsten or Haegen. If Berard keeps out of my way, he shouldn't have any problems at all.' He didn't move, though. His lips remained poised over Meena's firm nipple.

Desperate to feel safe, to feel Jaeger relax again, Meena nervously reached out and touched his head. He flinched, but she kept going, stroking his blonde hair, so straight and smooth beneath her hand.

Jaeger moved, leaning towards her face now, his eyes open, studying her as his lips brushed against hers. 'You are not Berard's, Meena,' he moaned, sliding over her body, pressing himself against her. 'And tomorrow you will bring your things here. No more Berard, do you understand? I need you here with me. I need your help with Morana. And the book. She is not as much use as I'd hoped. I need you here, with me, Meena. We must do this together.'

Meena shivered, her ears ringing with danger, but her body craving his; all thoughts of Berard drifting slowly away on a tide of ecstasy.

***

'Hello, Osbert.'

Osbert's eyes flew open. It was so dark in the bedchamber that for a moment he didn't know where he was.

But he knew that voice.

Gant.

CHAPTER ELEVEN

Gant's back ached.

He had been crouching in the shadows for too long. Hiding behind the curtain that draped across the only window in the chamber, waiting for Osbert to finish drinking. Waiting for him to get into bed. To fall asleep.

And now?

'What are you doing here?' Osbert demanded, hurrying to sit up, trying to see.

Gant's hand was suddenly over his mouth, roughly slamming his head back onto the pillow.

Osbert's heart raced in panic. The room was starting to come into focus now, but it was still so dark. He wanted to see Gant's eyes, to see what he was thinking, but he didn't need to. He jerked and thrashed about with his legs, desperate to remove the hand so he could scream.

He couldn't breathe! He couldn't breathe!

But Gant didn't stop. He didn't remove his hand. 'Best say your prayers, Osbert,' he whispered hoarsely. 'Vidar is not coming for you. You're going to meet your father in the Nothing instead. And when the sun comes up, we'll burn your body along with his and scatter your ashes in the midden. Your sister wanted me to tell you that. She wanted that to be the last thing you heard.'

He pushed his hand down harder, sensing Osbert weaken.

His chest wasn't rising so high now; his legs weren't flying about so wildly.

His head slowly became still.

It didn't feel right to end a man's life in such a way – neither of them with a sword in their hands – but they had all talked about it.

Agreed to it.

No loose ends.

Axl was going to be the King of Brekka now.

***

'It's a chance to take back Kalfa,' Bram suggested encouragingly, sensing Eadmund's hesitation. 'To install a new lord.'

They were sitting around a table in the hall, chewing over Thorgils and Bram's plan. They'd both been working on it for much of the night and were bleary-eyed and yawning, but eager to be gone.

'It could be a trap,' Eadmund frowned. 'To lure you away from Oss, just as he's about to attack us.' He looked at Torstan and their friend Klaufi, who had joined them. They both shrugged.

Thorgils chewed noisily on an apple.

He couldn't keep his fingers still; couldn't sit still at all. He'd left Odda in Runa's hands and was worried about her too, but most of all, he couldn't stop thinking about Isaura.

She was waiting for him. He didn't want to let her down or leave her vulnerable to Ivaar. Perhaps this was the only opportunity he would have to bring her home?

'I don't think it's a trap,' Bram insisted. 'Or else Isaura is the best liar I've ever met. And who would Ivaar come here with? Do you really think any of the lords would have sided with him? My bet is he's skulking around Alekka, looking for someone desperate enough to help him.'

Eadmund was suddenly distracted by Evaine as she walked out from behind the curtain, issuing orders to her wet nurse. He smiled, watching Tanja cradling their tiny son.

'Eadmund?' Thorgils nudged him impatiently. 'It's likely not a trap. Not yet, anyway. We need to go.' He jiggled about on the bench.

'And if you do? Who will be my new Lord of Kalfa?' Eadmund wondered, turning to Thorgils. 'You?'

Thorgils shook his head firmly. 'No. Isaura wouldn't want to stay there. And I need to be here with you.'

Eadmund frowned, wondering what that meant. 'Klaufi, how about you, then? I'm sure Ilina wouldn't argue about becoming the Lady of Kalfa.'

Klaufi laughed. 'Well, you're not wrong there. She's always had an eye on dressing like a lady, at least. As long as we get to take Ivaar's share of the gold back to Kalfa!'

Torstan looked slightly put out that Eadmund hadn't asked him, but no one noticed as they continued trying to decide on a plan.

'If you do bring Isaura and the children back here, Ivaar will come,' Eadmund mused, suddenly keener. 'There's no doubt about that.'

'True. And although it doesn't feel right to steal away another man's children, I suppose Ivaar won't be alive for long anyway. Not once you get your hands on him!' Thorgils tried to raise a smile, but despite it being Ivaar, it still didn't sit well with him. Jael was certain that Ivaar was innocent of Melaena's and Eirik's deaths. And now that she appeared to be a real dreamer, he had a lot more faith in what she believed was true. It was hard to think of killing a man who had committed no crimes.

But then he thought of Isaura, and all arguments fell away.

He would leave Eadmund to worry about Ivaar.

***

Breakfast was over, and barely anyone had spoken.

Berard occasionally glanced at Jaeger, who glared back at him. Nicolene eyed Jaeger, ignoring Karsten, who was being fawned over by Bayla as he sat down to eat with his family for the first time since he was injured. Haegen and Irenna could sense the tension in the hall and were quiet because of it.

And Haaron...

He was busy trying to think of what to do to keep himself safe from all of them.

The slaves shuffled about, their shaved heads bent, eyes to the floor as they cleared plates and refilled cups, just as uncomfortable as everyone else.

There was a loud cough, and all eyes snapped to the entrance of the hall where Morana Gallas stooped, waiting.

Bayla sighed. Another strange dreamer to contend with.

She couldn't believe how quickly Haaron had replaced Varna. She'd barely seen him since he'd started skulking around, plotting with that evil-eyed, wild-haired woman.

Bayla didn't trust her.

'Morana?' Haaron put down his cup of buttermilk and narrowed his eyes. 'What is it?'

Jaeger's eyebrows were up, his eyes fixed on the creeping figure as she edged towards the high table.

'My lord,' Morana croaked, clearing her throat. 'My lord!' she said more dramatically. 'I come with news!'

Bayla rolled her eyes. Just like Varna, she thought irritably, glancing at Haaron who appeared transfixed.

'What news?' Haaron asked eagerly.

'There is a new King of Brekka!' Morana announced. 'Osbert Furyck has been murdered!'

That had everyone's attention. Even the slaves stopped to

join in a communal gasp of surprise.

'*Murdered*?' Haaron shook his head in disbelief, glancing at his sons.

'Who is the King of Brekka now?' Jaeger asked, his teeth clamped together, knowing he would dislike any answer Morana gave him. 'Who killed Osbert?'

'Axl Furyck is king,' Morana said, trying not to smile. 'He ordered Osbert's death, and now he is the King of Brekka, and your wife is beside him. And soon, he will come. He wants to make her *his* wife, but first, he must get rid of you.'

Bayla looked horrified, turning towards her youngest son, who suddenly appeared vulnerable. She did not feel confident in his ability to survive another battle. Not with the Furycks at least.

'*He* wants revenge?' Jaeger snorted, standing up, ignoring the sudden pain in his ankle. '*He* wants revenge? After he stole *my* wife?' He glared down at his brothers and his father, who all remained seated. 'Well, come on! What are you waiting for? We must go and plan what we're going to do about this! What we're going to do to destroy Axl Furyck and take back my wife!' And flapping his arms around in a wild-eyed fury, he knocked over his cup, flooding milk across the table.

Berard squirmed. Jaeger's rage was burning with such intensity that everyone around him froze, uncertain how to react. He looked to reliable, calm Haegen who appeared just as surprised by their brother's outburst as the rest of them.

'We'll get your wife back, don't worry, Brother,' Haegen said as he stood, placing his hand on Jaeger's arm, hoping to cool his fire.

Jaeger shook him off. 'Don't worry?' he growled, screwing up his face in disgust. 'We have quickly become the joke of Osterland! All of us! Our kingdom will be overrun by our enemies if we do not do something now! Axl Furyck and his sister will come and take everything we have if we don't *do* something! Can't you see? Can't anyone see?' he yelled, his eyes bulging. Pushing past Haegen, Jaeger stalked away to the map table in the opposite corner of the hall. 'We have to *do* something!'

No one said a word.

Haaron, who was used to having the loudest voice in his hall, was completely unsettled by his son's explosive outburst.

Morana watched the Dragos', their faces painted with shock and confusion.

They would turn against each other now.

She had seen that too.

***

Gant stared into the flames, his elbows on the table, his weight resting heavily on them.

He was unsettled, wondering if he had displeased the gods by murdering Osbert. Would Furia take revenge upon him? Punish him somehow? Then he thought of Gisila and Axl. And Ranuf.

He had done the right thing.

He had put Axl on the throne, at last.

Gant smiled wearily. Axl could be hammered into shape, he was sure.

Over time.

'Here,' Rexon grinned, handing him a cup of ale. 'You might need something to drink after your busy night.'

Gant took the cup, nodding distractedly. His stomach was churning, though, and he had no interest in drinking. 'I need to get the men organised. We have to head back to Andala. Axl will be waiting for word.'

Rexon shook his head, reaching for a flatbread. 'It's a real bitch out there this morning. Nothing but storm as far as I can see. You won't be going anywhere for a while, my friend. Might as well make yourself comfortable. I'm sure you could do with some sleep?'

Rexon wasn't wrong, Gant thought to himself, and it wasn't just last night either. Everything had been a disturbed mess for weeks, and now, with Edela to worry about and a kingless kingdom to get his new king to, he didn't see a lot of sleep coming anyone's way for a while.

But the quicker he got to Axl, the quicker they could secure Brekka. He was certain that the Dragos' would be at their door, demanding Amma back before long.

***

Beorn had beached *Sea Bear* in a small cove some way from Andala. They did not want to be discovered; not until they knew what had happened with Osbert.

Jael frowned, glancing at the familiar moss-covered cliffs and the black sand beach; listening to the chirping golden plovers circling above them.

It felt strange to be back in Brekka.

It didn't feel like home. Not anymore. Not to Jael, at least. She missed Oss and couldn't stop wondering what was happening there without her.

It was hard not to think about Eadmund.

Or Evaine.

'You're sure you won't come ashore with us?' Axl asked, wrapping his arm around Amma's waist.

Jael shook her head. 'We don't have time. I want to get to Tuura tomorrow if I can.' She shivered, not wanting to get to Tuura at all. Her stomach clenched at the thought of seeing that place again.

Aleksander nodded, glancing up at the sky which remained gloomy, but the worst of the weather had left them as they'd approached Andala. 'Jael's right. Edela needs to get off the ship soon.'

Axl hugged Gisila. 'Take care, Mother. I wish I could go with you.' He had said goodbye to Edela and was ready to leave now. Now, before he didn't want to leave at all.

He wondered if he would ever see his grandmother again.

Amma squeezed Axl's hand, watching his eyes fill with tears. 'Perhaps you will stop on your way back to Oss?' she asked. 'When Edela is well again?'

Gisila started to cry. 'What if Gant didn't kill him? What if...'

'Gisila,' Aleksander said softly, putting his arm around her shoulder. 'We'll know soon enough. And in the meantime, we'll stay out of sight, well away from Andala, I promise. If all went well, Gant will come as soon as he can. He knows where we'll be, and if not, we'll come to Tuura and figure out our next move.'

'They'll have plenty of food,' Jael assured her, handing over the sack Biddy had put together before they left Oss. 'It will be fine.' She hoped that she was right. There wasn't time for anything more than that. 'Don't worry, Mother.'

But Gisila couldn't stop worrying. Her ears still echoed with the terrible noise of Lothar's headless corpse flopping to the floor; her face and back still ached where he had beaten her.

And more than anything, she did not want to go back to Tuura.

***

They stood around the long map table, Karsten leaning his

weight against it, taking the pressure off his injured knee.

Haaron felt odd. Strangely displaced. Not himself.

This was his chance to fight for Hest.

For his family.

But he couldn't think at all as he stood there, sensing the eager eyes of his four sons as they waited for him to begin. All he could think about was Morana's warning that they all wanted him dead. It wasn't a surprise, of course, but with everything that had happened, Haaron had the uncomfortable feeling that he had simply run out of luck and that it was only a matter of time before he followed Eirik, Lothar, and Osbert onto a pyre.

Lifting a hand to his pock-marked face, he could still smell the smoke from the fire that had destroyed so much. So much he needed to rebuild.

Impatient with his father's mournful silence, Jaeger burst into action. 'We must strike now while Axl Furyck is still finding his feet! He will be in Saala or, at least, nearby. We can attack them there. We don't need ships for that. We have the men! We defeated them last time!' His eyes were frantic as they sought his brothers' support.

Not even Karsten looked as desperate as he did.

Jaeger caught Nicolene's eye as she walked out of the hall with Irenna. She glared at him, lifting her nose in the air as she stalked away. He looked back to the table, to his father, who seemed as though he wasn't there at all.

'They have their weapons back,' Haegen tried. 'They will not let us defeat them so easily again.'

'*Let* us?' Jaeger snorted. 'What choice will they have? We must attack Saala now! My wife is there! The Furycks are there! King murderers, both of them!'

Haaron had finally had enough of listening to the mindless ranting of his largest son. He banged his fist down onto the map table, scattering the wooden figures. 'You will be quiet!' he bellowed, his lips curling savagely. 'This is not *your* kingdom, Jaeger! You are not the king of this land, and you will not stand in my hall, around my table, screaming your orders at *me!*'

His sons were silenced, and happily so; glad to see their father return with his familiar roar. All, that is, except Jaeger who looked anything but.

'You want to attack Brekka? Reclaim your wife? Commit my army to support your cause? You? You who lost my fleet? My men? Your wife?' Haaron growled. 'And why should anyone help *you*? Why should anyone follow you anywhere? What have you proven to all of us except how accomplished you are at failing? We are in this position solely *because* of you!'

Berard gulped, turning from his father to Jaeger, wishing he could just slide away. He would much rather be sitting by his fire, talking to Meena, watching her tidy his chamber. He liked the way she frowned at his messy habits, scolding him with her kind eyes. She didn't tap her head much when she was busy, taking care of him.

Jaeger's face contorted into an intense scowl as he rose up on his toes, shadowing his father with rage. 'You think we should do *nothing*? Sit here and do *nothing*?'

Haaron took a deep breath, ignoring the discomfort he felt standing in that threatening shadow. 'We need to rebuild our kingdom before we try to destroy anyone else's!' He looked at Haegen who was busy rubbing a hand through his beard, his eyes troubled, showing no sign of support for his father at all. 'You don't agree?' he demanded crossly.

'Well,' Haegen began. 'I think you're right in that we are weak, but perhaps Jaeger's right also. Axl Furyck is no king. Not as it stands. He's barely a man. We could take advantage of that now.'

Berard's eyes widened. Haegen, siding with Jaeger?

Karsten looked surprised, sensing the rage building in his father. He sought to calm him. 'Axl Furyck might not be used to being a king, but his sister is there, isn't she? She must be there,' he spat. 'And *she* certainly has no problem taking charge of things. With the experienced men she has around her?

Gant Olborn? Aleksander Lehr? And her husband?' He shook his head, desperate to sit down. The wound in his side was throbbing, but he was determined not to appear as weak as he felt. 'I want to gut the bitch and her brother, but I agree with Father. We're not ready.'

Two against two.

They all turned to Berard, who didn't know where to look.

***

'Calm down, calm down!' Bram laughed, watching his nephew rush around *Ice Breaker*, checking they had enough of everything.

Shields, swords, spears, food.

Furs!

'We need furs for the children! For Isaura!' Thorgils exclaimed. 'Somewhere comfortable for them to sleep, wouldn't you say?' He was already striding towards the gunwale, ready to clamber down onto the beach and head back to the fort for the third time. 'Maybe a pillow or two?'

'A good idea,' Bram nodded. 'I still have a few furs on my ship that I haven't sold. You can use those.'

Thorgils stopped and turned around, his eyes skipping about frantically. 'You're sure?'

'I am. Now think of anything else quickly because my stomach is telling me it's well past time for another breakfast!'

Thorgils laughed, relaxing for a moment. It was his uncle who had taught him about the joys of eating more than one breakfast, much to the horror of his mother who had already been struggling to feed him three giant-sized meals a day. His face fell as he thought of Odda. She looked worse than ever and had not opened her eyes for some time.

Bram reached out and gripped Thorgils' arm. 'Your mother

would be happy for you.'

Thorgils snorted. 'It's been a long time since you were on Oss, Uncle. You have forgotten Odda entirely!'

Bram smiled. 'Oh no, my memories of your mother are burned into my soul, I'm sure. But I know how much she loves you. As she did your father. She just hides it very well!'

Thorgils laughed, nodding at Torstan who had clambered on board to say his goodbyes.

Torstan glanced around the ship, then back at Thorgils. 'You need anything else?'

Thorgils shook his head. 'No, once I get a few furs I think we'll have everything. Except sea-fire. It would be good to have some of that.'

Bram looked confused. 'Sea-fire?'

Thorgils winked at Torstan. 'We'll tell you all about it some time. Hopefully, when we're back in the fort, sharing a cup of ale with Isaura.' He couldn't believe he was saying that; wondering if he was cursing himself by daring to mention such a thing out loud.

Bram shrugged. 'Well, I look forward to hearing all about it. Now, if you two ladies don't mind, I'm going to head up to the fort and grab something hot from Ketil before we leave. Your grandfather always told me that you should never head to battle on an empty stomach!'

They watched him go, skipping across the stones, sprightlier than most men his age.

'How old do you think he is now?' Torstan wondered.

Thorgils shrugged, smiling, happy to have his uncle back again, especially now, without Eirik, when everything on Oss seemed to be falling apart. There was comfort to be found in Bram's experience, and his calm certainty that everything would be alright. 'I don't know, but it doesn't look like he cares if you ask me.'

Torstan peered around the ship. 'You're sure you don't want me to come?'

'No, I need you here, looking after Eadmund.'

'And how am I supposed to do that?' Torstan muttered. 'Evaine has him all to herself now. She never leaves the hall. There's no way anyone's getting near Eadmund.'

Thorgils frowned. It was true. Evaine's claws were so deep into Eadmund now that he could barely breathe without her rushing to his side, scowling at anyone who tried to talk to him.

But he had to believe that the real Eadmund was still in there somewhere; that there was a chance Jael could help Edela, and together they could break the hold Evaine had on him.

***

Berard swallowed, unsettled by the deafening silence in the hall.

He couldn't hear a thing except the sound of his heartbeat throbbing loudly inside his head. His palms felt sweaty as he rested them on the table. 'I think,' he said at last. 'I think Father and Karsten are right. We must focus on Hest first. We open ourselves up to an attack if we leave for Saala now. We should build up our fleet again. Construct defenses. If we are to attack Brekka, and then hold it for ourselves, we'll need more than men or horses. We'll need ships and those ships will need piers and crews.'

Jaeger's eyes flared, but Berard ignored him as he edged closer to his father.

Haaron was pleased, but not triumphant. It was a finely balanced situation, and he did not intend to tip the scales in Jaeger's favour by being overconfident. 'Good,' he said simply. 'We will rebuild the fleet. And in the meantime, you will all recover from your injuries, and we will construct a plan. We have no allies anymore, so dreams of Helsabor are gone for now. And Aris Viteri is barely on speaking terms with me after the disaster you led him into on the Adrano, Jaeger. So, there will be much to occupy us all for the next few months and little time for thinking about Brekka or Axl Furyck. Not yet, anyway.' Haaron nodded curtly to his sons, his eyes softening as they lingered briefly on Berard. He gave him a slight smile, then turned and strode out of the hall.

Haegen was not particularly bothered, content to follow his father's plan, even if it was not his preferred choice of action.

Karsten patted Berard on the back, pleased with his support.

Jaeger simmered furiously.

He had to find Morana.

CHAPTER TWELVE

Tig was unsettled. Jael could hear Fyn struggling with him. He'd had quite enough of the sea now.

They all had.

After they had left Axl, Amma, and Aleksander behind in Brekka and headed up the Nebbar Straights, the wind had picked up again, and their stomachs were desperate for some respite from the constant roll of the waves. But as much as they weren't enjoying their journey, they were all just as reluctant to be on land.

Because land meant Tuura.

Jael held Edela's hand and glanced at Entorp, who nodded nervously at her. Biddy had told her about The Following, who Entorp suspected had murdered his wife and children. That was much worse than any nightmare she had to face. Jael smiled encouragingly at him as he approached. 'Still hanging on,' she murmured, peering at her grandmother's ghostly face.

Entorp bent over, squinting in the grey morning light, happy to see that Edela's fur-wrapped chest was still moving up and down in a steady rhythm. 'She is. For you.'

Jael blinked. 'You think it made a difference? The dream walk?'

'Oh yes,' Entorp insisted, stumbling as *Sea Bear* reared up. He reached for the swinging pole that still hung down from the archer's flaps. 'She has come back since then. She feels much stronger. Your grandmother would do anything for you. To help you, she will fight.'

Jael stared at Edela, wishing she would open her eyes again. 'Well, good, because we all need her.' She glanced at Gisila and Biddy who huddled against the walls of the house, their faces pale with worry and anticipation. 'And now, for the first time, she needs us too.'

***

'Good luck.' Eadmund was pensive as he clapped Thorgils on the back. He didn't feel confident at all. The plan itself made sense, but where Ivaar was concerned, he was always left with the feeling that something bad was about to happen.

Thorgils jiggled about next to him, eager to be gone. The sun had started to shine, glittering off the calm harbour, and he felt a burst of optimism because of it. He wrapped his fingers around the wolf amulet which swung across his green tunic. Vidar's symbol. Bram had given it to him as a boy, and despite not being overly superstitious, he'd never taken it off. The gods, Odda had drummed into him, would either grant him their favour or they wouldn't. Thorgils had always thought that there wasn't much he could do about that, but he'd kept the amulet in the hope that one day it would grant him some luck. 'And you.'

'Me?' Eadmund looked confused for a moment. 'Oh, you mean Ivaar?'

Thorgils wasn't sure that he did, but he nodded anyway. 'I think we both need to keep an eye out for that vengeful cunt.'

Eadmund laughed as Bram joined them. 'I'm sure he'll be on his way as soon as he hears that you've taken his wife and children!'

Bram smiled. 'Mmmm, I should like to see what he does

about that. Slippery bastard. If we happen to come across him, we'll take care of him. Unless you'd prefer to do it yourself?'

'Well, I can't say that I wouldn't, but I'm more concerned about getting rid of him for good than any revenge, so take whatever chance you get,' Eadmund said, thinking of Jael. It felt odd not having her here. He was not unhappy to think that Evaine was waiting for him in the hall with Sigmund, but with Jael, he could discuss the island, the fort, Ivaar.

Their kingdom.

'Eadmund?' Thorgils grabbed his shoulder. 'Are you still in there?'

Eadmund shook his head. 'Just thinking about Jael. I hope Edela made it to Tuura. It's not an easy trip on a good day.'

Thorgils felt both sad and cross. He knew Eadmund couldn't help it, but he would have loved to slap him across the face; to make him wake up and see what he was doing.

He shrugged. That was for another day.

It was time to get going.

***

Jael swallowed, watching Gisila twist her fingers into strange shapes as she walked beside her. She knew how her mother was feeling as the memories of their last visit caught in her throat.

They had arrived by ship then too.

Her mother had always preferred to travel that way. She was not overly fond of horses.

Tuura looked nothing like the place they had left, though. Aleksander had warned them, but it was still a surprise to see how the once sprawling village had transformed into a towering fortress of wood and stone.

The Tuurans were a people who had lived as one with

the land, and the gods had walked freely amongst them once. They had not believed in walls. Prisons, they had called them. Barriers meant to keep them from their gods.

Yet, over time, their lack of walls had made them easy targets for the Osslanders, who had taken away their land, piece by piece. Nearly all of it. And now, when it was almost too late, the Tuurans were finally surrounded by impenetrable walls.

It looked like a hard place to attack, Jael thought as she dragged Tig down the pier. He was disturbed by the unfamiliar smells and sounds and, as usual, was not making it easy for her. The puppies, happy to feel solid footing again, revelled in their escape from confinement, racing around everyone's feet, charging up the pier, barking at the seabirds as they swooped down, searching for scraps.

Jael frowned. There were few people about. She saw three other ships tied along the small pier, but no one looked their way; no one seemed surprised by their presence at all, which was odd, she thought.

It was as though they were expected.

Turning back to Fyn, she smiled encouragingly. He was walking next to Eydis, who held Biddy's hand, vibrating with excitement. Entorp had remained on *Sea Bear* with Beorn and the crew to watch over Edela. They would need a cart to bring her into the fort.

If that was indeed what they were going to do.

Jael closed her eyes, desperate to turn around and head back to the ship. Back to Oss, to Eadmund.

But there was no Eadmund waiting for her on Oss.

Just a man she didn't know, who didn't love her anymore.

***

Ayla felt a lift as she walked towards the prison, wondering if it was truly possible. She knew that Thorgils was coming. She had seen him on a ship, standing with the man Isaura had given the note to.

But could he really save them?

Ivaar felt so close that Ayla kept stopping, glancing around. Or was that just fear stalking her, she wondered anxiously, smoothing down her hair. It was a damp day, and her long, brown curls tended to frizz in the misty weather.

Straightening her cloak and rolling back her shoulders, she nodded to the guard, who unlocked the gate and led her down the muddy path towards Bruno's hole.

The prison compound was a sorry sight: a barricaded slop of boulder-riddled earth containing four large mounds which Ivaar had burrowed into, creating... burrows. And into those airless, earthen holes he threw his prisoners, locking them behind iron-strong doors.

The guard knew her.

He felt sorry for her.

She would come every month, for that one moment when she was allowed to be with her husband. He could barely look her in the eye as he led her towards the prison holes, imagining how difficult it was for her. He had a new wife and felt the pull of needing to be with her, so it was easy to sympathise with the sad dreamer.

The guard never hurried her. He always let her take as long as she wanted.

Ayla wrinkled her nose at the decaying stink of the men who bent and stooped and slumped in the mucky holes, waiting in the hope that they would be freed by their merciful lord.

Most just died there.

Their lord was not that merciful.

None had been there as long as Bruno Adea, though. His bones clicked as he tried to stand. He was stiff and weary from doing nothing; weak from barely eating or drinking. From no light. No warmth. No companionship, love, or care. Nothing at all but this bleak, dark, reeking hole that Ivaar Skalleson had thrown him into.

Before he had taken his wife.

At first, Bruno had spent his days dreaming of all the ways he would kill Ivaar. Now, he dreamed of all the ways he would kill himself.

'Bruno,' Ayla whispered, tears in her eyes. He looked frailer than ever. His kind, brown eyes were lifeless, hollowed out, filled with despair. His black hair had become a birds nest of coarse, grey curls. His dark-skinned face was almost entirely covered in dirty-white whiskers. He was 53-years-old, but he looked as worn as an old man on his deathbed.

Her heart broke.

Ayla reached through the tiny window in the cell door. It was small enough so that food or cups of water could be passed through. It allowed light to filter in, but also wind and cold, and when Veiga, the Tuuran Goddess of Weather, was feeling ornery, rain and snow too.

But once a month it allowed Bruno to touch and glimpse his beautiful wife. And as desperate as he was to shy away from her, ashamed of the shadow of a man he had become, he was just as eager to inhale the life in her.

Reaching up, he clasped her soft, warm hand. 'Ayla.'

***

Their tiny party did not have to wait in line at the gates. They were quickly ushered into the fort, the puppies charging off ahead of them before creeping back, suddenly filled with trepidation.

Tuura was a dark place.

A faintly familiar place.

The walls were so high that the shadows they threw onto the ground stretched far, covering the Tuurans who stopped and stared at them with narrowed eyes and pursed lips. Jael watched her mother stiffen. Gisila's most recent memories of Tuura were mixed up with a childhood which had been happily spent here.

When it was a different place.

A different time.

Jael stopped, wondering where to go before a familiar voice rose above the low hum of curiosity. 'Gisila! Gisila!'

Gisila turned, relieved to see her sister and brother-in-law pushing their way through the crowd. 'Branwyn! Kormac!' She sunk into her younger sister's welcoming arms. 'Branwyn!' she sobbed desperately against her shoulder. 'Oh, Branwyn!'

'Whatever has happened?' Branwyn wondered, stepping back and staring with concern at her sister whose gaunt face was pale and bruised. 'Why have you come? And what has happened to your face?' Her eyes snapped suddenly to Jael. 'Jael? Is that you?' Tears came quickly as she thought of her own daughter, Evva, who would have been the same age as Jael now. A woman. She shuddered as memories of that night burst out of the shadows.

'Branwyn,' Jael said awkwardly, allowing herself to be embraced. 'It's been a long time.'

'Yes, it has, and you are quite different from the little girl I remember.' Looking Jael up and down, Branwyn noticed her trousers, the sword poking out of her cloak. 'Quite different!' Blinking away her tears, she turned to Kormac. 'You remember Jael?'

Their reunion was suddenly interrupted by a flurry of activity at the rear of the crowd, and they watched as four guards in dark-red tunics pushed their way towards them.

'My lady,' the first guard to arrive said roughly. 'The Elderman of Tuura requests that you accompany us to the temple to meet with him.'

Branwyn and Kormac blinked at Jael in surprise.

Jael nodded. 'Of course.' And handing Tig's reins to Fyn, she turned to her aunt. 'I won't be long. I'll find my way to your house when I'm done.' She followed the guards, who were forcing their way back through the crowd, not afraid to shove anyone who didn't hop out of their way quickly enough.

Jael kept her eyes fixed straight ahead as she hurried to keep up with them. She didn't want to recognise anything that might stir a memory. Her body was tense, holding her tightly.

Holding her together.

Tuura was a door she had shut and locked. A door she hoped never to open again. A scab of a place that existed only in her nightmares, but despite her best efforts, she could feel it being slowly ripped away.

Yet the wound was still there.

Festering.

The guards pushed open the giant temple doors and left Jael with a shrunken elder woman who led her across the grand chamber. The ceiling of the ancient temple stretched so far above her head that it reminded Jael of the limitless cave in Edela's dream, yet nothing echoed. Thick columns of stone rose up around her, marked with symbols she didn't recognise. It was a dark, cloying place, and despite being only mid-morning, it felt as though she had stepped into the night. The only light in the cavernous chamber came from a row of angry, sparking flames running through its centre, leading towards one large, blazing fire.

The Fire of Light.

Edela had told Jael stories about that fire when she was a little girl, before she had ever visited Tuura. Supposedly, it had burned from the time of Dala. Through centuries of destruction, through storms and famine and terror, legend had it that its flames, guarded by the elders, and above all, by the elderman, had never gone out.

Finally, the grand chamber ended, and they turned down a narrow corridor. It was even darker down here, with only a few torches to light their way; colder too, Jael thought as she walked past door after door. All of them closed. Another twist, a turn, and the woman stopped outside a door that looked just like all the others. She rapped loudly on its wooden panels, nodded curtly to Jael, and left.

Jael waited impatiently, trying to remind herself that she was a queen. A warrior. But at that moment, shivering in the dark, she felt ten-years-old again.

The door opened suddenly, and a tall man stood there, frowning so intensely at her that the lines between his eyes stood out like great posts. Jael eyed him back, not feeling very welcome at all.

Sighing, Marcus attempted a smile and motioned for her to come inside.

***

'Is everything alright?' Gant asked as Rexon approached his column.

Rexon scratched his beard, his brow furrowed. 'More sickness. More dead men,' he sighed wearily. 'It's spreading like weeds. No matter how quickly we isolate the ill, it's not fast enough.'

Gant felt anxious, dismounting immediately.

'What are you doing?'

'I don't want to take the sickness back to Andala,' he grumbled, listening to his impatient men shuffling in their ragged lines, eager to go home. The sun was already older than he would have liked, and although he felt tired and not at all keen for another long march, he knew he had to get to Axl and set his mind at ease. 'Let's just go through the columns. Isak! Rag!' he called before turning back to Rexon. 'Whatever this sickness is, I hope you can stop it soon. I just can't take it back to Andala.'

Rexon nodded. 'Agreed. I'll take your last column and meet you in the middle.'

Gant worked his jaw as he looked over his men, one by one. But as much as he didn't need the delay, he knew that his new king would not appreciate a bunch of shitting, half-dead men delivered to his door.

That would be no way to start his reign.

***

Branwyn and Kormac's house smelled of spices.

Something was steeping in the cauldron that hung over the meal fire, and it reminded Eydis of Vesta. She inhaled deeply, enjoying the rich, festive smells as they awakened her senses, then giggled as Fyn's stomach gurgled loudly beside her.

'I shall put Berta to work on a hearty stew!' Branwyn declared after she had found everyone a seat around the fire. 'After being at sea, there's nothing as comforting as a bowl of hot stew!' She smiled at Fyn, who looked gratefully at her. He reminded her of her sons, Aedan and Aron. The house had felt empty since Aedan had married and left home, taking his younger brother with him. It was so nice to have people to care for again that she didn't stop to wonder where she would put them all.

'You don't think we should go and get Edela?' Kormac wondered. 'I have carts in my workshop. We can take some furs from here. Lay her on them.'

'It's best that we wait for Jael,' Gisila insisted, her stomach growling as loudly as Fyn's. Now that her body had come to rest in a safe place, her constant nausea was dissipating, replaced by the realisation that she had barely eaten in days. 'We need to see what will happen in the temple. With the elderman.'

Branwyn and Kormac glanced at each other.

'What is it?' Gisila wondered, taking a cup of small ale from Branwyn's servant, Berta. 'Should we be worried?'

'About the elderman?' Kormac certainly felt worried as he tried to reassure his sister-in-law. 'I don't imagine he'll have any problems with Jael. But if he did, it looks as though she could handle herself.'

Biddy nodded, picking up Vella who had finished sniffing the floor with her brother and was ready for some affection. 'Yes, Jael can handle herself, although I'm not sure her sword is going to do her any good in the temple.'

'No,' Branwyn mumbled, counting the beds, suddenly realising that there were not enough of them. 'The temple is not what it once was. But that could be said of most things around here. Even the people. Some we considered friends not so long ago, now feel like strangers. Something is wrong here, but we don't know what.'

***

'Queen of Oss, Queen of the Slave Islands, and now, sister to the King of Brekka,' Marcus mused as he led Jael to a small chair by a large fireplace. 'Do you think your gods will look kindly on your family for such actions? Two murders to reclaim a throne?' He shook his head gravely, clicking his tongue.

Jael was quickly irritated by the dour man, whose superior way of talking scratched at her temper like a cat at the door. He took his own seat and stared down his long nose at her. The room was dimly lit, but she could make out his features, which were heavy-set, and his eyes, which were too small for his face. Lightly coloured. Perhaps blue.

She didn't like him at all.

'I think our gods would thank us,' Jael said, just as coldly. 'Especially Furia.'

The corners of Marcus' lips barely moved, but his eyes narrowed even further. After all these years of hearing about Jael Furyck, it was surreal to have her here at last. There was so much he wanted to say. He rolled his large hands over the ends of his chair, trying to restrain himself. Other than that, he didn't move. And nor did Jael, and so they sat like that for a while, listening to the hiss and spit of the flames, their eyes fixed on each other.

'You sent my grandmother to Oss,' Jael said, breaking the awkward silence. 'Why?'

Marcus' thick eyebrows rose at that. '*Why*?'

Jael leaned forward. 'I don't have time to waste dancing around each other like newlyweds. Let us speak plainly. Why did you send Edela to Oss?'

'To save you. As I told her. She was supposed to save you.'

'Yet *she* is the one about to die, not me. The one who is barely hanging onto life, not me. So why didn't your dreamers see that *that* would happen? Or perhaps they did, which is why you really sent her there?' Jael suddenly felt hungry and sick all at the same time. It made her even more irritable and desperate to hurry through their conversation.

Marcus looked offended. His nostrils flared as though he had inhaled a midden heap. 'My dreamers advised me that Edela was needed on Oss, because of the threat Evaine and her mother posed to you,' he said slowly, deliberately. 'They all saw that. The fact that Edela then went and put herself in such danger by... taunting that girl. By speaking when she should have remained silent.' He looked down at his hands, clasped in his lap. 'She didn't make the right choices.'

'What does *that* mean?'

Marcus sighed, realising that it would simply be easier if he told her what he knew. He looked up. 'It means that Morac Gallas killed Eirik Skalleson. Your grandmother realised it and confronted Evaine, who tried to kill her to protect him. If Edela had simply kept her mouth shut...'

Jael was both surprised and incensed by that. 'Morac Gallas?' She shook her head, unsure why she was surprised at all. She'd had a bad feeling about him since they'd met. 'You're saying that it was her own fault that Evaine tried to kill her?'

'Edela had one thing to do on Oss. To keep you safe. And now you are not even *on* Oss with your husband as you are meant to be, and she is dying, so, perhaps I am saying that, yes, it is her fault.' Marcus sat up taller in his chair, his body rigid.

Jael felt ready to lose control of her tongue, but she thought of how desperately weak Edela was and took a deep breath. 'I don't imagine she was expecting to be stabbed, no matter what she said to Evaine.'

'No,' Marcus conceded. 'I don't expect she was.'

'And, if she could have, she may have done things differently. But I'm not as concerned with *how* she was injured as I am about how to help her. Now. That is why we've come, which I'm sure you already know. I need your help.'

Marcus clenched his hands into fists and glared at Jael. 'You want *my* help bringing your grandmother back from the dead?'

'She's not dead yet!' Jael was almost out of her chair, fighting against the urge to hold her knife to his throat until he gave her the damn book. 'And I know there is a book here that can help her. She knows it too, which is why she sent us here.'

'The book you speak of,' Marcus said, discomfort flickering in his eyes. 'It is a book to counter dark magic, written when there was... trouble in Tuura. A time when dreamers and elders both abused their gifts. When some had their heads turned from the gods.' His voice was softer now, watching the pain in Jael Furyck's green eyes. 'It is not a book of healing. It breaks spells.

Wards against them. But it does not heal. And I no longer have that book. I gave it to your grandmother, but when she left, it was not found. I assumed that she had taken it with her.'

Jael felt all the air leave her body, taking any last vestige of hope with it. She looked down at her hands, twisting her wedding band.

Without that book, how was she going to save Edela?

How was she going to get Eadmund back?

'You have healers here,' she said quietly, looking up. 'The best healers in the land, supposedly.'

'We do.'

'Then, please, send someone to my aunt's house. I will have my grandmother brought there.' And standing up, trying to ignore the crushing pain of defeat, Jael strode to the door.

She couldn't let Edela die.

She must have sent them here for a reason.

Eydis had seen it too.

'There is still much we have to discuss,' Marcus said irritably, following her. 'Much more. About the prophecy –'

Jael spun around, glaring at him. 'You think I care about your prophecy when my grandmother is about to die? When I came here for a cure, and you tell me there is none? Do you think I want to sit by your fire and talk about *that* while you stare at me? Look down your nose at me? Dismiss me as a murderous, nothing queen?' She looked disgusted and turned to grab the door handle.

Marcus reached out for it at the same time, fighting her for control. Jael frowned at him, confused and irritated. He was a most unpleasant man.

Then she stopped fighting him and stared into his eyes.

They were cold, emotionless. He didn't blink as he stared back at her. 'I am sorry that I cannot offer the help you seek. And I do appreciate that you must care for your grandmother now. But we *will* need to discuss the prophecy before you leave.'

'You're right, we must. And more. I want to hear all about

why you tried to kill my friend, Aleksander Lehr too.' She scowled at Marcus and pulled open the door. 'But for now, let me just focus on saving my grandmother.' And with one last, scathing look, Jael turned and disappeared down the corridor.

Marcus stood in the doorway for a moment, watching her go before turning back into his chamber and closing the door.

CHAPTER THIRTEEN

Morana was proving to be almost entirely useless.

She disappeared for days at a time, and when Jaeger did manage to find her, she was always with his father. He could barely contain his rage when he finally managed to force her into his chamber. 'Where have you *been*? We cannot delay any longer! We have to do something! Kill Axl Furyck! Get my wife back! Now!' He paced up and down behind Morana, who sat, curled over the book.

Meena lingered uncomfortably by the window, not wanting to be near her terrifying aunt at all.

Morana didn't even look around as she ran her hands over the jagged edge of the missing last page.

Torn out.

She smiled wryly. The woman who had ripped out that page had made herself indispensable. As was Jaeger, she knew. The book had revealed itself to him, chosen him, so she needed to keep him onside, and yet, to create chaos now... she could almost see what her mother had been trying to achieve.

Almost.

'You wish to kill Axl Furyck?' Morana growled. 'But I thought it was his sister you had decided to destroy?'

'And you don't think I can do *both*?' Jaeger spat as he stopped, slamming his hands on the table. 'With the power of that book, we should be able to kill anyone we choose. Surely?

What is the point of it, if not?'

Morana was slowly growing frustrated with the book.

She had discovered many spells that were both intriguing and useful – so many that she could not wait to try – but what she really needed was a way to translate the ritual spell. That was the first step to bringing Raemus back from the oblivion of the Dolma: the black prison hole where discarded men and gods were thrown. Dead, forgotten, but not without hope.

Not when they had the book.

For The Following believed that they could bring Raemus back, and with his return, the Darkness would reign again.

'I think you can do many things with this book, but it is best to be cautious to begin with. It holds great power within its pages, so you should test it like a hot tub of water. One toe at a time. You want your wife back?' Morana asked, turning away from the book, her eyes meeting Meena's; enjoying her niece's sudden, head-tapping discomfort. 'Is that the most important thing to you now? That Axl Furyck dies so you can bring back your wife? Return her to your bed? Reclaim what is yours? Take his kingdom?' Morana kept going, enjoying every twitch of Meena's face. She could feel the pain in her heart at the thought that Jaeger was still so desperate for his wife.

Jaeger frowned, forgetting that Meena was even in his chamber. The idea that his stolen wife was lying beside the new King of Brekka incensed him. Nothing else compared to the white heat of his rage at that picture. For all that he hated his father and imagined himself on the dragon throne of Hest, he couldn't stop thinking about ripping Amma out of Axl Furyck's arms, right before she watched him die.

'Yes.'

Morana smiled. 'Well, then...' And she trailed a yellow fingernail down the almost-translucent vellum page. 'Let's see what we can do to make that happen.'

***

'How long will we have to wait here?' Amma sighed, already longing for a proper bed.

They were sheltering in one of Aleksander's favourite caves, half a day's ride from Andala. They had agreed to wait there for Gant, deciding that it was best not to take any risks until they were sure that the Brekkans were ready to support Axl as their king.

Until they knew that Osbert was dead.

Amma shuddered. It was strange to think that her father and brother might both be dead now. A year ago she would have mourned them.

Well, perhaps not Osbert.

They had both betrayed her for their own ends, gleefully handing her off to a dangerous monster who had killed his first wife and child. Neither one had given it a second thought. Her happiness and safety had been completely irrelevant to whatever they were hoping to gain for themselves.

And if Osbert was, in fact, dead, Amma was determined to feel no guilt at all. Her marriage to Jaeger Dragos had been her scheming brother's idea. He was responsible for what Jaeger had done to her. It was still uncomfortable to walk and sit. She burned and ached, feeling dirty and humiliated.

Osbert deserved to die for that. And more.

The Nothing was where he belonged now.

Amma turned to Axl, waiting for an answer. He'd barely spoken since they left Oss. She knew that he was worried about Edela and was struggling with the notion that he might be a king.

King of Brekka.

Axl wasn't listening, though. All of his attention was on the fire. The wet logs had made for spluttering flames, constantly on the verge of going out altogether. 'It's a six-day ride,' he mumbled at last. 'Gant would have left quickly once it was done, I hope.' He looked up as Aleksander came back into the cave with a rabbit on a spear.

Supper.

'It won't be so bad,' Aleksander reassured Amma with a smile. 'We'll be dry in here, and there'll be plenty to eat. It won't be long before Gant arrives.' His insides were churning, though. He wanted to be in Tuura, as much as he didn't. It was not a place where anyone was safe.

Not with those dreamers, those elders.

Always plotting, secret keeping.

***

Kormac laid Edela on the bed she had slept in over the winter. It felt like only weeks ago, but it had been months now; months since she had run away in the early hours of the morning, determined to get Aleksander safely back to Andala.

To get them both out of Tuura alive.

Branwyn sobbed as she tucked the bed furs around her mother's tiny frame. Edela had wasted away so dramatically that she almost disappeared into the mattress. There was barely anything to her.

'Where is this healer?' Gisila muttered impatiently, looking at the door again. 'Perhaps you need to go back to the temple?' She directed this at Jael, whose eyes were also focused on the door.

And then a knock.

Berta, aware of the tension in the house, was at the door in a heartbeat, ushering the old healer inside. Branwyn sighed in relief, wiping her eyes. Marcus had sent Derwa, Tuura's most experienced healer. She was a tiny, hunchbacked, white-haired woman with a sharp tongue, but a comforting ability to find a cure when it appeared that none existed.

Derwa peered around at all the pensive faces, then grunted and shuffled towards the low bed where Edela lay. 'There are too many in here!' she rasped irritably. 'I am here to see my patient, not all of you!'

Branwyn stood, helping to usher everyone out. She hovered in the doorway with Gisila, both of them wanting to remain. Someone needed to stay with Edela.

Derwa turned, squinting at Eydis who was being led through the door by Jael. 'The blind girl will stay!' She turned back to Edela, her long, white braid hanging down past her thick waist, flapping as she moved.

Eydis froze, gripping Jael's hand as she took her towards Edela's bed.

'Shall I stay with you, Eydis?' Jael asked.

Derwa was just about to growl, but she peered at Jael and harrumphed instead. 'Yes, you will stay too, Queen of Oss. Two dreamers will be better than one, I'm sure.'

***

The sun was sinking low in the sky as they pulled down the sails and slotted in the oars.

It was worth being cautious as they approached Kalfa. If it was a trap, Ivaar could be lurking anywhere.

Thorgils stood on the precipice of everything he had dreamed of for so long. Isaura was within reach; almost his again. Well, she had never stopped being his, he smiled to himself. But he would finally be able to hold her again and keep her safe with him.

He blinked away tears as Villas walked up to the bow to join him. 'What do you think?' he croaked, tasting the salt of the sea on his tongue.

Villas wiped his dripping, red nose on the back of his hand and squinted. His eyes were old now, but he was certain he could actually see further than he used to. 'I think we have no reason to wait.' He winked at Thorgils. 'Unless you want to go and comb your hair first?'

Thorgils laughed, slapping him on the back. 'You don't think I've spent all day doing that already?' He took a deep breath, walking around the wooden house, back to the stern, waving at Bram to follow them in. 'Let's go to Kalfa!' he cried, before heading back to Villas. 'Let Bram go first. We'll beach before we get anywhere near the harbour. We need to stay out of sight till nightfall.'

Villas hurried back to the tiller, shooing away his second in command. 'Let's just hope that old goat remembers how to use his sword!' he smiled. It had been some time since he'd fought alongside Bram Svanter, but he'd always been a fine warrior. And he knew that they were going to need every bit of wit and skill they could muster to get off Kalfa in one piece.

***

Derwa had her eyes closed as she hunched forward, moving her hands in circular motions above Edela's body, her tiny, gnarled fingers never touching her patient as they skimmed expertly over her. Edela was stripped of her furs now, but she did not shiver as she lay there exposed in her simple, grey night dress.

She did not move at all.

Derwa inhaled throatily, then belched. Sitting down with a thump on the side of the bed, she peered up at Eydis who sat quietly on a bench beside Jael. 'So, Eydis Skalleson, what colours do you see when you look at Edela?'

Jael was puzzled by the question; surprised that the healer knew who Eydis was.

Eydis was not. She didn't hesitate. 'Black. Mostly black. Some blue. But all very faint. Like smoke. Misty and dirty.'

Derwa nodded, grunting. 'I brought your mother into the world, you know. Rada Lund, she was then. A quiet little blue-faced baby, I remember. Cord around her neck. She couldn't breathe. But I saved her. And now, here you are. A dreamer like her. A good dreamer too, if you can already see colours.'

Eydis' small mouth fell open.

'And what about you?' Derwa grumbled at Jael. 'Close your eyes. Tell me what colours you see.'

Jael swallowed. 'I don't see colours. I'm... not really a dreamer.'

Derwa peered at her impatiently, her head cocked to one side. 'Your grandmother is my friend,' she said quietly, looking back to Edela. 'She was not much of a healer once, but I taught her many things. She was a better dreamer than me, and I was a better healer than her. But we both learned. Helped each other. Talked a lot. About you.'

Jael froze.

'Everyone talks a lot about you, of course. But not many talk about you being a dreamer. But Edela did, to me.' Her sharp eyes softened in sadness. 'So, Queen of Oss, close your eyes and breathe in your grandmother. Tell me what colours you see.'

Jael clenched her jaw, ready to protest, but she closed her eyes instead and took a deep breath. She could hear Derwa talking to her as she tried to concentrate, as she tried to find Edela in the darkness, lying on the raft in the cave.

The cold, dark cave.

Jael tried to see anything unusual. Any colours at all. She crept closer in her mind, remembering rushing to Edela's side, helping her off the raft, laying her down. Her body was dark.

Black shadows. She saw nothing but black.

Then...

'I see yellow!' Jael exclaimed, surprising herself. She opened her eyes. 'There's yellow. Almost gold.'

'Where?' Derwa asked quickly. 'Come, show me.'

Jael walked over to the bed and bent down towards Edela, pointing to her head.

'Good,' Derwa smiled. 'Now, we can begin.'

Jael took her seat next to Eydis. 'Can you save her?'

Derwa was barely listening as she stood, breathing heavily. 'Save Edela? Oh no, it's only Edela who can save herself. But now we know that she's still there, so I can open the door. It's up to her if she wants to walk through it.'

***

Amma had fallen asleep, and Axl and Aleksander were sitting around their still spluttering fire, trying not to wake her. It was early, and although dark, neither of them were ready for their uncomfortable beds of dirt yet.

'What if Osbert didn't even get to Saala?' Axl whispered. 'What if Haaron just killed him and now he's marching his Hestians upon Rexon and Gant?'

Aleksander had considered that. 'He very well may have, but it would've been a bold move, and I don't think Haaron was in the position to do anything bold after what we did to him. We'll find out soon, though, won't we?' he yawned. 'And until then, there's no point worrying. Whatever we have to do, you'll be King of Brekka. We'll see to it.'

Axl poked at the flames with his stick. 'And when I am, I have to kill Jaeger Dragos. I have to set Amma free, so we can be married.' He glanced at Amma, who seemed restless as she lay underneath her cloak nearby. 'So she can be free from what he did to her.'

Aleksander thought of Jael and what had happened to her in Tuura. 'She'll never be free from what he did to her. But she will be happier, being with you. So you need to stay alive for her. Keep Brekka safe for her. And I don't think you have to worry about getting to Jaeger Dragos. I've a feeling he's busy thinking about how he can come and kill you!'

***

Morana's ragged cloak slithered behind her, sweeping across the red dust as she crept through the torch-lit catacombs that wound their way under the castle.

She walked past wall after wall of skulls; hollowed-out empty masks of the very men, women, and children who had lost their lives digging the ancient tunnels for their demanding Dragos kings.

She could almost feel their spirits following her.

Morana smiled, closing her eyes for a moment, inhaling the intoxicating scent of death that pervaded the hidden passageway; this secret, terrible place of darkness and sacrifice and most of all... magic.

It was here that The Following had survived and grown, spreading their message underground until there were members of their covert sect in every kingdom.

And now, at last, they had the book.

Or, at least, Jaeger did.

For now. His usefulness to them was temporary, she knew. There would come a time when there was nothing more they required from him at all.

But until then...

She sighed, irritated by the thought of having to placate and manage him as though he was a giant, angry child.

Morana's ears pricked up. She could hear Yorik talking in the distance, and she hurried forward, eager to tell him what she and Jaeger had planned.

***

Derwa had spent some time with her eyes closed as she leaned forward, her hands splayed above Edela's middle. She had grunted, moaned, belched a lot and now seemed suddenly spent. 'She has one foot here, maybe just a few toes,' Derwa sighed, collapsing onto the bed again. 'But that is enough for now. The damage to her body is deep. It is working to kill her from the outside in. And I must meet it from the inside out. You two can leave now. Send in Entorp Bray, and I will see if he can work his own sort of magic to help her.'

Jael wrapped Eydis' cloak around her shoulders, then grabbed her own as they headed for the door, leaving Derwa to catch her breath.

'What's happening in there?' Branwyn asked eagerly, her sister peering over her shoulder as Jael opened the door. They had waited outside as the day turned to night and the air chilled even further, not wanting to go anywhere until they knew what Derwa had to say.

'Is she any better?' Gisila wondered, her face pale and anxious, her faded bruises visible around her puffy eyes.

'No, not that I could see. But, the healer...'

'Derwa?' Entorp spoke up shyly. 'I know her.'

'Yes, she asked for you,' Jael said. 'She wants your help.'

Entorp blinked at Biddy, surprised by that. He appeared hesitant and nervous.

Biddy pushed him forward. 'Go on, then. Get in there.'

Kormac glanced at all the cold, worried faces around him. 'Why don't we go to Aedan's house? I can hear more than one rumbling belly, and we might need something to hold us over until we can get back inside to Berta's stew.'

'That sounds like a good idea,' Jael agreed. 'I'll just go and check on Tig and the men first. Can you take Eydis, Fyn?'

Fyn looked pleased to finally have something to do as he came forward to take Eydis' hand.

'I'll come to the stables with you if you like?' Kormac suggested. 'Then I can show you the way to Aedan's.'

Jael shook her head. 'No, you go. I'll find my way there.' And without waiting to hear any arguments, she wrapped her cloak around her shoulders and headed off into the darkness, hoping she could remember her way to the stables.

***

Bram and his men were feasting in Kalfa's hall, hungry after a long day at sea, although their appetites were tempered slightly by the nervous anticipation they felt stirring in their bellies.

Isaura and Ayla watched them from the high table, neither of them able to eat a thing. They barely moved as they aimlessly pushed rolls of herring around their plates, wondering what was going to happen.

Bram had stared at Isaura when he entered the hall earlier. A stare she was certain conveyed what she had hoped for, but still, where was Thorgils? She only saw Bram's men. Alekkans. There were no Osslanders.

No one who looked familiar at all.

Ayla felt slightly calmer but still concerned, wondering how long it would take. She could hear rain falling now, and she thought of Bruno, whose hole would flood quickly.

How long would it take?

'My lady,' Bram said, coughing loudly as he stood. 'We shall sleep on our ship tonight so you may keep the peace of your hall. I thank you for your kind hospitality, though. As always, you Kalfans have the best herring I've ever tasted!'

Isaura nodded, her neck stiff, her back rigid as she watched him turn to leave. His men, pushing away their own plates and moving slowly, followed him.

And then the first man fell.

One of Ivaar's men.

His head dropped straight onto his almost-empty plate; the knife he had been holding, clattering to the floor.

Ayla swallowed, gripping the table.

Bram froze, turning back to look at the man.

And then another.

And all around them, Ivaar's garrison dropped to the ground or slumped over at their tables.

Bram turned to his nearest man. 'Signal Thorgils!' he urged. 'It's time!' He drew his sword, his men fanning out around him, rushing to secure the doors, swords quickly in their hands.

Bram nodded at Isaura, who blinked rapidly and scrambled to her feet.

It was time.

***

Tig was unsettled.

Missing Leada, Jael decided. Missing the familiar smells of home. And Oss was now home for both of them. Although, when she thought of Oss, she thought of Eadmund, and didn't want to. She didn't want to imagine what he was doing in her absence.

With Evaine.

The stables were dry and smelled fresh enough for her to feel satisfied with her decision not to leave Tig behind in the vicinity of Evaine and her knife.

Running a hand down his smooth, black cheek, she pulled a stale flatbread from her pouch. 'I'll see you in the morning,' she whispered as he noisily gobbled it up. 'Perhaps, I'll even take you for a ride? Anything to get away from this place.' Then she thought of Edela and wondered if she would feel comfortable leaving at all.

Tig seemed happy enough with the flatbread not to protest as she crept away. She hadn't heard anyone but snorting, nickering horses and murmuring Osslanders who were busy making themselves comfortable for the night, but she felt on edge, wondering if someone had crept in to spy on her.

Jael hurried to the rear of the stables towards a door, almost hidden in the darkness, just past the last stall. Once there, she looked around again, then knocked three times. She waited a heartbeat, then knocked three times more.

The door opened quickly, and there, waiting for her, stood Marcus.

CHAPTER FOURTEEN

Varna had been right, after all, Morana decided as she listened to the grating screeches of the black-robed Followers who crowded Yorik to argue against her plan.

She was unused to people. More comfortable in her own company.

And although Morana had welcomed being with Yorik again, she was not enjoying sharing him with the mad-eyed bunch of Followers who had taken an instant dislike to her; Morana being Varna Gallas' daughter.

They had not liked Varna.

'We need Jaeger!' Yorik insisted, his hands raised. 'If Morana doesn't show him what the book can do soon... if he doesn't see its true power, he will take matters into his own hands. And as we all know, those hands of his are disaster prone. So it's up to Morana to guide him towards the place we need him to be. Ready for us. And if we do what she is suggesting, we will have him right where we want him. Begging for more. Willing to do whatever we ask.'

Yorik stood in front of a crumbling statue of Raemus, wearing the same black robe as the Followers who surrounded him, sighing at the scowling faces of those who would not be convinced. Their desires and ambitions had been harmonious once, flowing together like a rushing stream towards the same goal. But when Morana had arrived, and the book's presence was revealed, everything had fallen apart, and Yorik had struggled to forge them back into a cohesive force.

Here, in the antechamber of the catacombs, they could be as loud and indiscreet as they liked. And so, the arguing had continued for some time. But he could tell that Morana had grown impatient.

They did not have access to the book. Or Jaeger.

She did.

'We will work *this* spell!' she growled loudly. 'We all need to be together, united, to make it work as intended. But if not, then I will find a way to do it on my own!' She glared at Yorik, urging him to take control.

'Morana is right. We must act now! We need to show Jaeger that we are not impotent dreamers. We must show him that we are a dark force to be reckoned with!'

They were silent now, eager to begin, even if they didn't agree on the path Morana and Yorik had decided to take. After all this time, just being able to use the book was too tempting an idea to resist for long.

'We will meet at the Crown of Stones, just before dawn,' Yorik said with feeling. 'It is time for us to send a message. The end of this world, as it has become, is near. Soon they will all know that the Darkness is coming!'

***

'Why are we here?' Jael asked impatiently, trying to adjust her eyes. There were no windows in the tiny room. It was almost too dark to see anything at all, but for the faint light seeping under the doors – the one Jael had come in through, and another to the rear.

'Do you have the stone?' Marcus asked quickly.

'Yes,' Jael nodded, revealing the stone he had given her when he'd pressed a note into her hand as they'd fought over the door handle in his chamber.

'This room is safe,' Marcus said. 'Safer,' he corrected himself. 'Protected against the dreamers.'

Jael frowned. 'Protected? Why?'

Marcus felt impatient. They didn't have long, yet there was so much he was desperate to say; so much she needed to understand. 'You have heard of The Following?'

'Yes. Some.'

Marcus sighed, his shoulders tense with the weight he had been carrying for so long. 'They have spread like a disease over the years, throughout Tuura and beyond. There have been purges. Good has risen against evil, and the temple has been purified, time after time, but never fully. The evil that lurked in the shadows simply threw a cloak over itself, becoming almost invisible in order to survive and rise again. And now... now the opposite is true. The temple is almost entirely corrupt. The Following has control of Tuura.'

Jael was puzzled. 'You're not in The Following, then?'

'No. Never. My last ally, Neva, was killed recently. She was an elder, a friend of your mother's. There's no one left in the temple I can trust anymore. I'm not sure how long I have before they come for me too.'

'But you sent my grandmother to Oss. Why should I believe anything you say? I know Edela didn't trust you. From what I hear, no one around here does.'

'No, I expect not, but I had to become what was necessary to protect Tuura.' Marcus felt around for a hay bale and took a seat. 'Although, now that the Book of Darkness has revealed itself, I'm not sure what I can do. With that book, there is no reason for The Following to hide any longer. It is everything they want and need. They will come for me, for you, for Tuura. Destroying everything, until nothing exists. Just darkness.'

'But the prophecy? Do you know what it says? What I'm

supposed to do? How we can stop it?'

'The actual prophecy was stolen from the temple centuries ago. Memories were recorded at the time of its theft, then they were stolen as well. But, yes, I know some of it.'

Jael felt her way to a hay bale near him. 'Tell me.'

***

Thorgils saw the signal, and with his heart in his mouth, he turned to Klaufi and his men, motioning for them to follow him.

Gripping his sword, he ran silently along the stones towards the fort. They had beached *Ice Breaker* around the headland, out of sight, and once night had fallen, they had started creeping slowly along the beach, hugging the tussocked banks.

Despite the cold, Thorgils' palms were sweaty, slipping on the leather grip of his sword. He swallowed, trying to see Isaura in his mind, knowing he needed a calm head to keep her safe. Wind billowed his cloak away from him, blowing hair across his face. Annoyed, he brushed it away as he approached the fort. The salty sea had dried his throat, and he was desperate for a drink of ale.

'Nephew!' came the call and Thorgils froze, squinting in the fleeting glimpses of moonlight as Bram hurried towards him.

He was alone.

And smiling.

***

'The prophecy warns of a return to the Darkness. The time of endless night and burning fire. Of life without death. The fall of the gods and the humans and the return of Raemus. The end of the world as we know it,' Marcus said bleakly.

'The prophecy *says* that will happen?'

'The prophecy *warns* that it will happen. It tells of the fire and the darkness and the monsters that will return if you fail to stop it.'

'Monsters?'

Marcus shivered. 'The gods and goddesses tried to please Raemus for a time. To tempt him out of his shadowy gloom. They thought to impress him by creating creatures he could admire in a way that he could never admire the humans Dala had made. So, they created monsters. Aros, God of Fire, made the powerful dragon, Thrula, for his father. But Raemus used her to burn villages to the ground. Mirea, Goddess of the Sea, made the sea serpent, Sabba, but Raemus used her to sink ships and drown men. He turned all of their creations into weapons, forging an army of monsters to help him destroy the world.

'And what happened to them?'

'The time of monsters was ended by Dala. She saw to it that when the Great Uprising was overcome, the monsters were vanquished, along with Raemus and many of his Followers. They were killed, their souls imprisoned in the Dolma, which your people call The Nothing.'

'And that is what the prophecy is about? That Raemus and his monsters will return?'

Marcus frowned. 'Partly.'

'Partly?' Now Jael was confused.

'That is all implied. But the actual prophecy is about someone else entirely.'

Jael was intrigued but conscious of how long they had been. As was Marcus, she could tell, as he rustled around, unable to sit still on his hay bale. 'Who?' she asked. 'Who is the prophecy about?'

'A woman. I don't know who she was. It may have been

recorded at the time, but it was lost when the prophecy was stolen.'

Jael stilled, uncomfortable with the idea that she was involved in such a thing. That a dreamer had seen her all those years ago and imagined what she would need to do. A dreamer who had believed that she was capable of doing it. 'And what did it say?'

'That you had to kill this woman. With your sword. With Eadmund's help.'

Jael stilled. The memory of leaving Eadmund was still fresh. The loss of him nagged at her like a new scar. There were so many things tumbling around her head, but her heart was always full of Eadmund.

She missed him with every breath she took.

'Well, that's not looking so likely, is it?' she said haltingly.

'This is the book I gave to Edela. The one you came for.' Marcus lifted a thick, leather-bound book from the hay bale next to him and handed it to Jael. 'As I said before, it will not save Edela. Derwa is the best healer in Tuura. If Edela can be saved, she will find a way. What is in here, I hope, is the answer to breaking the hold The Following has over all of us, including Eadmund.' He stood, swallowing, anxious to leave. 'I'm no dreamer. The answers in here are not meant for me. Whatever you do, don't take the book out of this room. They will know you have it if you do. Keep it here. There is a chest in the corner by those tools.' He dug into his pouch and held up two iron keys. 'This key opens the chest, and this one the doors. Make sure you keep them locked.'

'You're leaving?'

'I have been too long already,' he murmured, handing her the keys. 'We can meet here tomorrow, at noon. But, for now, I cannot just disappear. And nor can you. They are always watching. Keep the stone with you at all times. It will hide you from the dreamers. Do not speak of this to anyone. It is not safe.'

Jael needed to get back to Edela, she knew, yet here was

a man who had so much knowledge. She stood up, almost reluctantly. 'But the prophecy... did it say that I defeated this woman? That I stopped the Darkness coming?'

Marcus shook his head. 'The end of the prophecy was lost, almost from the beginning. Long before it was ever stolen. So, I do not know.'

Jael looked up at the shadow of Marcus' face. He was an exceptionally tall man, awkwardly so, and he stooped before her, almost shaking, desperate to leave. 'But?'

'But if you do not, she will bring back Raemus. And Raemus will destroy us all.'

***

Aleksander yawned, feeling around for the least unpleasant place to lie. It took a while, but finally, he shuffled into a spot that was uncomfortable but hopefully, sleep-worthy. Laying his head back on the dirt, he closed his eyes, pulling his cloak up to his chin as he listened to the fire's last breaths and Axl's light snoring. It was cold in the cave, and it had cooled down even further since nightfall, but they didn't want a bright fire to draw wolves and all number of beasts and bugs to them while they slept. So, they would shiver through the night and hopefully, wake in the morning unharmed.

Aleksander's mind immediately wandered to Jael. He knew how she would be feeling in Tuura. How shocking it was to face your worst nightmare again; to walk through the streets, see the buildings. All of them were markers of the darkest moment in their lives.

Nothing about Tuura had felt as though it was a good place to be. And Edela had not trusted that elderman, he knew.

Or, perhaps it was that the elderman had not trusted them?

Yet, who was to say who was right where the Widow was concerned?

He closed his eyes, not wanting to think of her because thoughts of the Widow always led to his mother, and Aleksander still couldn't face the truth of what she had done to hurt them all.

***

'Come on!' Bram yelled to the Osslanders who were hurrying towards him.

The stones were slippery, wet from the gusting rain, so they were careful, tip-toeing along, squinting as the sliver of moon slid in and out of the rain clouds.

Thorgils was at the front, leading his men, not even sure that he was breathing.

And then Isaura was there, standing before the open gates with a handful of women and children.

Isaura was there!

Thorgils ran, losing his balance, slipping and stumbling but not caring in the slightest.

He raced towards her, pulling her into his arms, holding her close, touching her damp hair, inhaling her sweetness. 'What's happening?' he called over Isaura's shoulder as he hung onto her, fighting back the tears he had kept inside for eight long years.

'Ivaar's men are mostly asleep! We've locked them in the hall!' Bram cried over the howling wind.

'*Asleep?*' Thorgils was confused, glancing back at Klaufi, who was ready to assume lordship of the tiny island. He looked just as puzzled as Thorgils.

'That was Ayla,' Isaura said, blinking the rain out of her

eyes as she looked up at him, relieved to be in his big arms again. She had missed the feeling of safety they provided. 'We picked some herbs and made a tonic to add to the mead bucket.'

'It will not last long, though,' Ayla warned. 'We must leave now!'

Thorgils turned to Klaufi, his arms still around Isaura, not wanting to let her go. 'I'll take everyone to *Ice Breaker*, and then let's secure the fort, although I don't see why they would want to fight us. Not when they can have a much better lord than Ivaar!'

Klaufi smiled, imagining his wife's face when she arrived to take her seat as Lady of Kalfa, but it faded quickly when he realised that Ivaar would likely come to try and take back the island. How could he not?

Thorgils looked down at Isaura. 'You're sure, then? You want to come home?' His voice broke. They were the words he had been saying to himself for what felt like a lifetime. It felt strange to finally utter them out loud. To her. 'Home with me?'

Tears were running down Isaura's face now as she gripped his hand. 'Yes. Please. Yes.' She looked at her children who were half asleep and wide-eyed with confusion as they stood around in the darkness. 'Please. Before Ivaar comes.'

'You think he'll come?' Thorgils wondered, staring at her worried face.

'I think you can never be sure what he's planning or when,' Isaura said anxiously, desperate to be gone. She ran her eyes over the men who were gathered around Thorgils. She recognised some and their presence was reassuring.

She hoped there were enough of them to keep Ivaar at bay.

***

Jael stepped out into the street, leaving the stables behind.

There was not much to see of the moon, and she felt almost hidden because of it. Lost. Set adrift from everything and everyone.

Alone.

It was as though every part of her was being pulled in different directions.

Pulled apart.

She wanted to drop to her knees in the street; the muck-filled, stinking street. All the things Marcus had said. All that he hadn't... it was like a crushing weight, and she couldn't breathe.

Yet, somehow, it still felt as though she knew nothing.

Jael fingered *Toothpick's* moonstone pommel and felt some certainty, but it was fleeting as her mind wandered quickly to Eadmund and Evaine. Evaine was surely in Eadmund's bed now; in his heart, his head, winding herself around him as though she was his wife.

But she wasn't.

And the prophecy said that Jael needed Eadmund.

And the prophecy said that they all needed Jael.

So, somehow, Jael had to get back to Oss and save Eadmund.

***

'A hot pool!' Evaine was beside herself with glee as she hurried to remove her dress, inclining her head for Eadmund to join her.

But Eadmund hesitated.

He frowned, watching as Evaine threw her clothes to the ground as she rushed towards the inviting, warm water, her lithe body disappearing quickly into the pool.

'Eadmund,' Evaine purred. 'Come... it's so warm!'

But Eadmund didn't move. He felt as though he was

somewhere else entirely. He could almost feel his hand reaching back to grab Jael's, leading her towards the pool.

Her smile.

Her eyes.

Her lips as he skirted them. As they pursed and protested. As he fought his way towards her, never giving up.

As she relented.

Jael.

His wife.

'Eadmund!' Evaine called, smiling. 'Come!'

He blinked and Jael was gone; just a memory drifting away, and he was removing his clothes and hurrying into the water to join Evaine; all thoughts of his wife vanishing into the night air as though she had never been there at all.

***

'He can't walk on his own!' Ayla called. 'You need to carry him! He does not have the strength!'

She waited while Thorgils' men broke down the doors, releasing Ivaar's prisoners.

Releasing Bruno.

Ayla could barely breathe as they carried him out.

'Bruno!' she cried desperately, reaching for his hand as he tried to blink away the rain that fell into his eyes. 'I'm here! I'm coming with you! You're coming with me!'

Ayla followed the men as they carried him slowly through the fort, across the beach, down to the ship.

The ship that would take them to their new home.

Thorgils watched as they worked to get Bruno on board Bram's ship. He turned to his uncle. 'What do you think?'

Bram yawned, suddenly ready for his bed. He thought of

his dead wife and was quickly not so enamoured with the idea of bed at all. 'I think we go now. No reason not to. Let's get Isaura and the children away from here. That's all that matters. Leave Klaufi to sort out the fort. He's got enough men to deal with those sleeping babies when they wake up!'

'You think he can convince them to follow him instead of Ivaar?'

'I think he has gold and Ivaar doesn't, so I hope so. At least until Ivaar returns!'

Thorgils felt a chill seep into his bones.

No one knew where Ivaar was, but Ivaar would not let this stand.

His wife and children taken?

Ivaar would not let this stand.

'Get to your ship!' Bram insisted, watching Thorgils dither. 'I'll follow!' And clapping his nephew on the back, he turned away into the rain which had started teeming down now, icy and sharp against their faces.

Thorgils stood for a moment, watching his uncle gather his men together before turning towards the headland where *Ice Breaker* waited with his new family on board.

PART THREE

The Storm

CHAPTER FIFTEEN

She opened her eyes.

Still in the cave.

But her eyes were open, and she'd had a dream.

She sighed, but her chest was so tight that it barely rose or fell. But she'd had a dream, and her eyes were open.

Derwa could heal her, she knew.

But she had led them all to Tuura.

And now they were trapped.

And danger was coming.

She felt so weak, so weary.

Her eyelids fluttered closed, and she drifted away again.

***

Ayla covered Bruno's cold hands with her own as she knelt beside him. His lips were cracked and bleeding. It hurt for him to say much.

But he tried.

And she tried to stop him. 'Sleep,' she kept saying. 'Just close your eyes, my love. We will be safe soon.' And, eventually, he did fall asleep, tucked into the side of the ship, covered in a mound of furs. There was barely any meat on his bones at all, and despite the layers of warmth, he shivered uncontrollably.

'How is he?' Bram asked as Ayla walked to the stern, eager to stretch her legs after crouching over Bruno for the past few hours.

Ayla frowned. As relieved as she was to be away from Kalfa and to have Bruno back, she could barely hear a thing over the building storm of fears in her head. 'He is... he needs to be cared for. Fed. Healed. He is half dead.' She bit her lip, not wanting to cry here, in front of these strangers. She didn't know them. She could only hope that they were better men than Ivaar and his Kalfans.

They were. She could feel it.

This big, old man was kind. He looked at her with sympathy and respect. Even in the faint beams of moonlight, Ayla could see what sort of man he was: strong but gentle, like Isaura's Thorgils.

'Well, soon he'll have that, don't you worry. In this sort of weather, we'll be blown back to Oss in no time!' Bram cried as the ship rose up on a curling, white-capped wave, slamming down onto the angry sea with a thump. Reaching out, Bram caught Ayla before she lost her footing. 'Best you grab hold over here!' he said, pushing her further into the stern, where ropes flapped about in the wind, tied around the smaller dragon prow. 'Sit down on my chest and hold on tight!'

Ayla was ready to protest, but she could see that Bruno was as secure as he could be – men were hunkering down all around him – and she was suddenly so tired. She nodded gratefully, taking a seat on Bram's wooden chest which carried the contents of his entire life now. Ayla could feel the sadness emanating from it as she slid around, trying to blink it all away, not wanting to intrude on his pain.

She reached back, gripping hold of a rope as the ship rose up again, watching as Bram steadied himself, before going to check on Bruno. He turned back to her, satisfied that he was alright, and gave her a wink.

Ayla smiled, trying to ignore the sudden urge to vomit as she closed her eyes.

She needed a moment to think.

***

'You must go! Go! Leave! You are all in danger! You must leave for Tuura! Now! Jael needs you! Do not delay!'

Aleksander rolled over, unsettled by the urgent voice. The ground of the cave was so uncomfortable, and his mind was so troubled that he had taken a long time to fall asleep. And now, as turbulent as his dreams were, he wouldn't allow himself to wake. He didn't want to even think about moving.

Aleksander listened and ignored the voice in equal measure; mumbling, protesting against it, tossing and turning, but never waking, never letting the dream grab hold of him.

It was only a nightmare, he told himself.

Just a nightmare.

***

Branwyn and Kormac's house was large and comfortable but not big enough for their influx of visitors, so Fyn and Entorp had been sent to stay with Aedan, his wife, Kayla, and his brother, Aron.

Gisila and Biddy had managed to find a bed each. Jael and Eydis were sharing another bed opposite Edela. Eydis had finally drifted off to sleep, but Jael was wide awake, still thinking about her conversation with Marcus.

A prophecy had been written about her. Hundreds of years ago. A prophecy about Furia's daughter.

Furia was the Goddess of War.

And she was a warrior.

A warrior who had lost her way in a mire of dreamers and danger and dark magic. But she was a warrior. The gods had spoken to her when she was a child; she remembered that now. A warrior dreamer, they had said. The one who would save them all.

Save them all?

Jael couldn't move. The bed was narrow, and Eydis had curled into her, and she didn't want to wake her.

Save them all?

She pushed her head back onto the pillow, trying to remember Eadmund. Trying not to think about Evaine.

She saw a vision of Berard and remembered the dream she'd had of Hest.

Save them all?

All of Osterland?

Jael sighed. Not a dreamer, she thought, closing her eyes.

Not a dreamer at all...

***

Fianna Lehr put down her quill and picked up the scroll, shaking it distractedly, trying to dry the ink before reading:

We will be in Tuura in ten days time. Jael will be there. We will stay for five nights only. You must not delay.

'Mother!' Aleksander raced into the house, making her jump. 'Mother! Mother, come! The fight is about to start! You must come!'

Fianna looked at her son as though he was a stranger. She rolled the scroll and slipped it into the small leather purse that hung from her belt, then eased herself up from the stool. 'Why your father thinks he can beat Gant Olborn, I'll never know,' she smiled, although there was nothing about her face that looked happy. Her eyes were completely blank as she rubbed one hand over her rounded belly, certain she could feel a leg moving about in there. 'After what Gant did to him last time? And the time before that, and that...'

Aleksander was already racing ahead of her, though, disappearing to find Jael, she knew. Fianna grabbed her cloak, turning to her servant. 'Find Rollo for me. I need him to deliver a message. Tell him it's urgent.' And leaving her nodding servant, she walked out through the house after Aleksander, towards the training ground.

'Fianna! Fianna!' came the excited cry from the dark-haired little girl. Not so little anymore, Fianna realised as Jael grabbed her hand and pulled her towards the ring. She was getting so tall, just like her father. 'The fight is about to start! Come on!'

Aleksander gripped her other hand, and Fianna allowed herself to be dragged to the railings, watching as her husband, Harald, and Gant stalked each other, swords resting on top of shields, unblinking eyes peering over iron rims.

Aleksander and Jael clambered onto the rails, Jael turning back to smile at her. Fianna stared into those green eyes, shivering all over.

She remembered those eyes.

And for a moment her head cleared.

She remembered that little girl.

Jael turned back around to watch the fight and Fianna shook her head.

'My lady?' It was her man, Rollo.

Fianna ushered him away from the crowd, pulling the scroll from her purse. 'Take this to Tuura, to Gerod in the temple,' she whispered in his ear. 'Make sure no one sees you, whatever you do. Tell no one about this. Don't allow yourself to be followed. And quickly. You must go quickly.'

Rollo nodded and left immediately as Fianna heard a cheer go up.

'Mother! Mother! It's Father! Gant is down!'

But Fianna was barely listening as she watched Rollo hurry away to the stables.

***

Ivaar's children were not happy.

Pulled from their beds in the middle of the night; carried to a strange ship; sailing away to a strange place, with a strange man, and his strange crew.

They were not happy at all.

Mads had thankfully wailed himself to sleep, and Leya, who was not much older than her little brother, had curled up next to him, closing her eyes. But the two eldest girls, Selene and Annet, clung to their mother, utterly bereft and confused, unwilling to let her go or allow themselves to fall asleep.

Isaura hadn't wanted to warn them of what might happen because she hadn't been certain that Thorgils would even come. But now, the shock was simply too much for them. They wanted their father and being around Thorgils was only making things worse.

As much as Isaura wanted him near her, never leaving her side again, she frowned, shooing him away whenever he tried to approach. The sea was rough, and Isaura and her two servants had sheltered inside the wooden house with the children, wrapping themselves in furs that, despite the rain sprinkling in through the holes in the walls, were keeping them dry.

But it was bitterly cold.

Thorgils watched Isaura murmuring to her girls, feeling oddly conflicted. These children loved their father. What was he thinking, imagining that they would want to be his?

Selene and Annet glared at him as though he was about to run at them with a knife and murder them all.

He didn't know where to look.

Isaura smiled sympathetically at him, stroking Annet's long, golden braids, trying to soothe her to sleep.

If they could just get to Oss.

Everything would be alright if they could just get to Oss.

***

Jael hopped out of bed to check on Edela, relieving to see that her grandmother's chest was still rising and falling. Yawning, she padded back across the room. She hadn't been able to get back to sleep since her dream about Fianna. It was still the middle of the night, she was sure, and the house was filled with snorting, snoring, breathing noises. All of them too loud.

It didn't feel familiar at all.

Heading back to her bed, she reached around in the darkness for Ido and Vella, who, she discovered, had quickly claimed her spot next to Eydis. Smiling wearily, she sat down on the floor instead, leaning her back against the bed frame. It was not comfortable, but it was, at least, a warm house; the house of a successful blacksmith, with a lucky wife. Although, when she thought of Evva, Branwyn's daughter, who had been murdered that fateful night, eighteen years ago, she realised that, like many mothers, Branwyn was not lucky at all. Just like her own mother, who had lost two of her sons before they had become men. Nothing could erase the pain of losing a child, she supposed. Gisila had certainly never been the same. Every loss had dulled her eyes, breaking off another piece of her heart.

Jael thought back to her dream. She had been shocked by Aleksander's revelation that Fianna had killed herself; in front of him too. She sighed sadly, not understanding it at all.

The moment she had decided to let the dreams come, they had come like a frantic blizzard, and now she couldn't stop them. But as much as she wanted to be free of them, Jael knew that there were clues in each one; as unpleasant as those clues might be. But Fianna? She simply couldn't imagine what had led her to do such a thing. To write that note? Send those men to kill her?

That was not the Fianna she had known.

Jael closed her eyes, yawning, knowing that sleep would help her see things more clearly when the sun came up. If only she could stop thinking and dreaming.

Fianna, Eadmund, it was too much.

Fianna.

Eadmund.

Jael sat up, blinking rapidly. Fianna had looked the same as Eadmund. The same appearance of disinterest, as though she was floating outside the world that everyone else existed in. No longer herself. No sparkle in her eyes. No sense of humour. No warmth.

Just like Eadmund.

She had changed.

Just like Eadmund.

Jael was suddenly wide awake.

***

Meena had not arrived by the time Berard left to breakfast in the hall, and when he returned to his chamber, there was still no sign of her. His bed remained unmade; his fireplace was still full of cold ash.

Berard hurried along the corridor to find out what had happened, but when Meena opened the door to her chamber, she would not even meet his eyes. He hovered in the doorway, trying to get her to talk to him.

Meena felt strange. Uncomfortable. She had enjoyed the privacy of having her own chamber, and she had welcomed taking care of Berard, but Jaeger had demanded that she leave both of them behind and move into his.

And she didn't know what to say.

Nor did Berard. 'I don't understand,' he said again. 'You were not happy? Did I do something wrong?'

Meena, tapping her head violently, tried to shake it at the same time, her hair shuddering around her in a confused mess. 'No, no, no,' she stammered. 'Your br-br-brother, he... he insisted.'

Berard felt a burst of rage. It was obvious that Jaeger had a hold on Meena that he could not break through; that he could not understand at all.

But there it was.

Women had always been captivated by Jaeger; willing to abandon all sense and reason to simply do his bidding in the hope of gaining his attention.

But Meena?

It didn't make sense. Why did Jaeger want Meena? She was not someone he would be attracted to. She was not glamorous or elegant, or a lady at all. She had no noble breeding, no wealth, no connections. She was a timid, shy creature with strange habits; so desperate to hide away from everyone that you barely knew she was even there.

Apart from the tapping.

Berard couldn't understand it. He had thought that at least Meena would have been safe from his brother. Perhaps that was why he found himself drawn to her in the first place?

Meena appeared to be growing more uncomfortable by the moment, and he didn't want to do that to her. 'Well, as you wish. I only wanted to help you, Meena, so that you weren't alone. So that you would stay here, in the castle. As long as you're happy to be with Jaeger?' He looked at her, hoping for some sign as to the truth, but her eyes dropped to the flagstones and he could barely hear her mumbled, 'yes.'

Berard sighed.

Meena felt ready to cry.

She had to keep Berard far away from Jaeger. He had become so angry and bitter about his brother, and she was afraid he would do something to hurt Berard if he saw them together again.

Berard turned to leave. 'If you change your mind. If you ever need my help...' He stared at her, then lowered his voice. 'If you ever feel... unsafe, I will help you, Meena. Just ask.'

Meena watched him disappear down the corridor, feeling guilty for his sadness, then, twitching all over at the thought of being with Jaeger again, she raced inside to prepare her things.

***

'Do you see any colours today?' Eydis wondered shyly. Gisila and Biddy had left to walk to Aedan's with Branwyn, leaving Jael and Eydis behind with Edela.

Entorp had arrived earlier, dropping Fyn off at the stables to check on Beorn and the men.

Jael shook her head. 'No, not today. Not yet, at least.'

'Do you?' Entorp wondered, bending over to touch Edela's forehead. She had pink cheeks, and he was worried that she was feverish, but she felt fine. He uncorked the small jar he was holding and placed it on the bed. Dipping his finger into the jar, he started rubbing a salve onto Edela's temples in gentle, circular motions.

Eydis nodded, wrinkling her nose at the unpleasant smell. 'Still black, but it's different today. It feels clearer. Sharper,' she smiled nervously. 'Better somehow.'

Jael looked hopeful, then her face contorted. 'Entorp!' she cried. 'That smells terrible!' And she rushed through the door before he could even open his mouth to defend his salve, which was indeed eye-watering.

They could hear Jael retching outside.

'Are you alright?' Entorp wondered as Jael stepped back into the house, wiping a hand over her mouth, looking around for something to drink.

'No,' Jael spluttered. 'If you can watch Eydis, I think I'll take Tig for a ride. I can't sit in here and smell that!'

Entorp felt almost embarrassed, but his patient didn't seem to mind, and neither did Eydis, so he continued to rub the salve on Edela's temples. 'You go. Eydis will be fine with me. Derwa will be here soon. No need to hurry back.'

Taking one last look at Eydis, who seemed content to sit by Entorp, Jael grabbed her cloak, trying to stop herself from vomiting again.

***

'Tomorrow?' Jaeger looked pleased as he paced in front of the empty fireplace, wondering where Egil had gotten to. After days of warm, humid weather, a storm was battering Hest, bringing a sudden drop in temperature, so he'd sent Egil off to bring in some logs. 'Where? I shall be there.'

Morana hadn't thought of that. She hesitated, turning towards him. 'Well...'

'The book is not leaving my sight, Morana,' Jaeger said firmly, sensing her desire to simply take the book and leave. Her hands were all over it, and his veins pulsed with jealous fervour. 'It is not leaving this room. Not without me! If you need it, I will bring it, or you'll simply memorise the spell while you're here. Write down what you need and then go. I have ink, quills, vellum.'

Morana hesitated. Irritated.

Beyond irritated.

She tried to remind herself why they needed this thick-headed fool at all, taking a quick breath and grabbing hold of her tongue, which she could feel twitching inside her mouth.

The spell they had decided upon would be a call to The Following all over Osterland. A signal that the return to the Darkness had begun.

This would be the first true announcement of their intention.

The beginning of the end.

She didn't want Jaeger to be a distraction, but perhaps it was a good idea for him to actually witness what they could do with the book. To be a part of it himself.

A crash of thunder rattled the window.

'You may come, of course. Bring the book. I must have it with me. It has the power of Raemus in it still. I feel that. It must be there. I will come for you before dawn –'

There was a knock at the door.

Jaeger frowned, then realising there was no Egil, he stalked towards the door, opening it to a smiling Meena. She shook, shy, but pleased to see him. He glared down at her and didn't move.

Meena blinked, feeling awkward as she stood there, sack in hand, not knowing where to look.

'What is it, Meena?' Jaeger asked impatiently.

'I...' Meena tapped her head with her free hand, crouching over. 'I have come, as you asked. I've left Berard.'

Jaeger sighed, annoyed, stepping aside. 'Well, come in,

then.'

Meena hesitated, but he only glared more furiously at her, so she shook herself upright and scrambled under his arm into the chamber.

'Ahhh, my niece!' Morana smiled as Meena came to a shuddering halt. 'What a surprise to see you.'

Lightning burst outside the window and Meena jumped, looking quickly back to the door which Jaeger had now closed and stood in front of, then back to Morana, who sat there with her long, curling fingernails gripping the Book of Darkness.

She felt as though she had just walked into a trap; certain she could hear her grandmother's cackling laughter ringing in her ears.

CHAPTER SIXTEEN

Jael watched the storm clouds gather in the distance. They seemed to be heading for Tuura, and she was eager to get Tig back to the stables before the rain started falling. He had been unsettled by the occasional burst of thunder on their ride, and she was having a hard time convincing him to go in the same direction as her.

She was concentrating so hard on Tig that she nearly ran down an old man. 'Are you alright?' she asked, reaching out to help the small man, who stumbled backwards, red-faced and cross as Tig blew and snorted all over him.

'Luckily, yes,' he grumbled, smoothing down his ragged, brown cloak. 'No thanks to you and that horse!'

Jael frowned. Old and small, but rude. 'Well, I apologise,' she said shortly. 'I'm not used to people wandering across the street without looking where they're going. In Oss, we keep our eyes open, no matter how old we get.' She had barely slept, felt like vomiting again, and was more irritable than she could remember.

The old man froze, his curiosity quickly overriding his annoyance. 'You're from Oss?'

'Yes. I am the... Queen of Oss.'

His eyes widened as his body retreated. He bobbed his head quickly. 'Oh, my lady, I am so sorry,' he said, dropping his eyes briefly towards the muddy street, before looking up.

'You're Edela's granddaughter. Jael?'

'I am. And who are you?'

'I am Alaric Fraed,' he smiled. 'Edela's friend. Perhaps she mentioned me?'

Jael shook her head. 'No.' She was impatient, watching Tig's ears twitch.

'Oh.' Alaric looked disappointed, but not for long. 'How is Edela? Did she come to see you on Oss?'

'She did, but she was stabbed, left for dead. We have brought her here to try and heal her. Derwa is trying to save her.'

Alaric gulped in shock, his eyes wide, his mouth opening and closing as he sought to find any words.

'Are you alright?' Jael wondered, trying to control Tig, who heard thunder again and decided that he would like to go to the stables after all.

'Will she... live?'

Ido and Vella came rushing up to Jael and Tig, welcoming them back. Jael tried to push them away as they jumped up on Alaric, who stumbled again. 'I don't know,' she said quickly. 'Ido! Vella! Get down! Edela is at Branwyn's. Why don't you go and see her? Perhaps she can hear us talking to her, and if she can, I'm sure she would be happy to have some new company.'

Alaric hesitated, not wishing to intrude, but then he nodded, eager to see Edela. 'I will. Yes, I will. Thank you.'

Turning Tig away, Jael pulled him towards the stables, remembering her talk with Marcus. The Following was everywhere, he'd warned. He couldn't trust anyone.

She glanced over her shoulder, hoping she hadn't just sent a Follower to her grandmother's bedside.

***

Jaeger wondered what he'd been thinking, inviting Meena to stay in his chamber. He could barely remember asking her, but there she was, looking as uncomfortable as ever as she hovered by the fire Egil was setting.

Morana had left, thankfully, and he was eager to get downstairs and find Haegen. They had started training every day; both determined to strengthen their injured bodies; preparing for their next assault on the Brekkans. The storm was still lingering above the castle, but they could train in a ship shed as most were still empty.

'I'll be back later,' he grumbled, reaching for the door handle.

Egil turned around. 'Will you be eating your supper in the hall, my lord?'

'I suppose I will, Egil,' Jaeger muttered, and without looking back, he pulled the door closed behind him.

Meena sighed as the flames sparked to life beside her.

Egil glared at her as he struggled to his feet and waddled to the table, picking up the empty wine goblet and heading towards his corner of the chamber without saying a word.

Meena peered around the sparsely furnished room but didn't move. She thought of her own little chamber, then glanced down at the pitiful sack she was still holding, filled with nothing more than a comb and her cloak.

She had nothing else. Nothing she wasn't wearing.

Dropping it to the floor, she started tapping her head.

***

Aleksander was distracted as they fished.

They had all left the cave, eager to inhale some fresh air; wanting to feel the warmth of the sun as it popped out from behind the clouds from time to time. And they were hoping to find something tasty for supper. But Aleksander hadn't caught a thing. He stood, spear in hand over the stream, barely concentrating.

'Aleksander!' Amma scolded as another fish slipped away. 'You could have got that one!' She smiled at him, then frowned. 'Are you alright?'

Aleksander shook himself awake. He'd had such a disturbed night with that voice drumming inside his head. It was familiar, he knew, but he didn't want to listen to it.

It was too confusing. Too troubling.

What did it want? To trick him?

To lure them all into a trap?

Yet, if he didn't listen...

'I think I could do with a mattress and a pillow!' he yawned. 'I'm not sure I slept at all last night.'

Amma looked sympathetic. 'Well, hopefully, it won't be long before Gant arrives.' She turned to Axl as he drove his spear into the water, straight through an escaping trout. 'Well done!'

Aleksander's smile disappeared, the voice echoing in his head again.

'Danger!' it cried. 'You are all in danger!'

***

Jaeger glared at Berard as he walked into the hall with Haegen. He turned away quickly, following his eldest brother over to Irenna and Bayla, who were sitting at the high table with Nicolene.

'You seem to have made an enemy there,' Karsten said quietly to Berard as they stood around the map table, observing the strange tension that had built up between his two youngest brothers. He lifted an eyebrow, noticing how Nicolene was glowering at Jaeger as well.

Everyone, it seemed, was starting to lose patience with the Bear.

Except, oddly enough, Haegen. But he'd always been overly tolerant and weak, Karsten thought to himself. A weak man who'd make a weak king, if he were ever lucky enough to find himself in that position.

If...

Berard sipped his wine and frowned. He'd been frowning ever since Meena had told him that she couldn't work for him anymore.

Because of Jaeger.

'Well, I think the opposite is true,' Berard murmured, almost to himself. 'I think our brother has made an enemy of me.'

Karsten's instinct was to laugh out loud, but as he looked at his normally shy, bumbling brother, he was surprised to see a fiery determination in his placid eyes. His back even looked straighter as he stared Jaeger down from across the hall.

There was no smile on his face.

Karsten shrugged. 'I guess it's going to shit all over the castle, then. Inside and out.' He looked at his wife, watching the way her eyes kept flicking towards Jaeger. No matter how disinterested she was trying to appear, she couldn't stop looking his way.

They were all used to that, he supposed: the way women admired Jaeger.

But Nicolene? Karsten chewed on a toothpick, rolling it around his mouth.

That was new.

'My sons!' Bayla smiled as Karsten and Berard wandered over to join them. Once they had sent the children off with their servants, Bayla had started enjoying the company of her family as they sat around drinking wine and picking from a tray of sweetmeats. There was nothing to celebrate, but Bayla had sent her servant to buy a selection of her favourite treats that morning, eager for a little something to help pass the time while the storm rattled the castle.

Berard tried to smile back, but his eyes were cold and fixed on Jaeger.

Bayla didn't notice. 'And how is your new servant?' she wondered, winking at Nicolene, who rolled her eyes. 'I think, perhaps, you do look a little tidier today. Cleaner, even.'

Berard frowned at his mother's tittering, and the full-throated laughter of Haegen, Karsten, and Nicolene. Only Irenna and Jaeger stayed quiet, but for very different reasons. Irenna had always felt sorry for Berard and the way the entire Dragos family made him the butt of their jokes.

Jaeger was still furious that Berard had tried to steal Meena away from him; Meena, who was not Berard's at all. He smiled at his brother, remembering that she was waiting in *his* chamber now.

'Well, it did not last long,' Berard said curtly. 'I shall be back to my messy self by tomorrow.' He grabbed a sweetmeat from the tray, not caring that it was the last one.

Bayla was intrigued. 'And why is that? What has happened to your little *helper*?' She sipped on her wine, considering her moody son with interest.

'Why not ask Jaeger,' Berard grumbled. 'He is the one who took her away from me. Apparently, he needs two servants now!'

They all turned to Jaeger who simmered, irritated by Berard, and not keen to encourage anyone's interest in what he chose to do. 'Well, Brother, if you couldn't keep your servant happy, don't blame me. I can't help it if Meena prefers to work for me instead.'

'*Work* for you?' Berard snorted. 'Is that what you call it?' Despite the intimidating size of his brother, he leaned towards him, puffing out his chest.

Haegen stepped in between his brothers, pulling them quickly apart. 'This weather has made everyone turn one-eyed with madness!' he laughed, trying to sound light-hearted, though nobody was smiling, especially Karsten, who didn't appreciate any reference to his one eye. 'Perhaps we'll have to send you away to join the children? They couldn't stop fighting either!'

Bayla watched Berard and Jaeger eyeing each other up. She noticed the way that Karsten was glaring at Haegen, and Nicolene was frowning at Jaeger.

She had the uneasy feeling that everything was slowly coming apart at the seams.

**

Alaric felt sick.

It wasn't just the terrible stink of the salve that Entorp kept rubbing on Edela. It was the jarring sight of his dear friend in such a state of decline. She looked barely present. More of a spirit than a person.

He glanced around at Branwyn, who was talking to Gisila and Biddy by the fire, the three of them sipping tea, enjoying the poppy seed cake that Berta had recently made.

'Do you think she'll recover?' Alaric asked Entorp. They had known each other years ago, although Alaric had always found Entorp a little strange and reclusive. Still, if his foul-smelling salve could save Edela...

'Derwa seems to think that it's up to Edela,' Entorp said quietly. 'Although, we are hoping this will give her a little push in the right direction.'

Alaric wrinkled his nose. 'Well, I think if anything could wake her up, it would be that salve!' His eyes started watering.

'Alaric, come and have a piece of cake,' Branwyn smiled kindly. 'It's still warm. And it certainly smells better over here!' She was feeling encouraged after Derwa's recent visit and although there was no obvious improvement in Edela, just knowing that Derwa and Entorp were working so hard made her rest a little easier.

Alaric eyed the cake, and squeezing Edela's hand, he left her to sit on a stool near the ladies. Nodding at Biddy, who he had been introduced to earlier, he eagerly took the plate she offered him.

'I wonder if Jael is out in that storm?' Gisila asked, unusually worried about her daughter. She felt so unsettled being in Tuura; haunted by the reminder of how she hadn't been able to protect Jael all those years ago. 'It sounds as though it's getting heavy out there.'

'No, she's in the fort,' Alaric said through a mouthful of cake. 'She nearly knocked me over with her giant horse, which is how I came to find out about Edela.'

'Oh.' Gisila looked relieved. 'That's good. And Fyn and Eydis? What has happened to them?'

Biddy sat forward, reaching for her cup of fennel tea. 'Fyn took Eydis to Aedan's after Derwa left. I think everyone wanted to escape that stink!' She smiled at Entorp, who dipped into his jar of salve and started applying it to Edela's chest.

'I think Mother will raise herself off that bed soon just to make you stop covering her in that salve!' Branwyn laughed.

Alaric chuckled, trying not to inhale. 'I wouldn't blame her!'

Branwyn leaned towards Alaric. 'Have you heard anything about Marcus? What he wants with Jael, perhaps? She wouldn't say much, just that he was unhelpful and rude, which, of course, is unsurprising.'

Alaric looked uncomfortable. 'Me?' He shook his head firmly. 'No, no. I don't know a thing.' But his eyes darted to the right, and he started blinking rapidly.

'Alaric?' Branwyn narrowed her gaze. 'If you know

something...'

***

Jael had brought a torch into the secret room. It revealed more than she had seen the day before. Symbols were carved into the wooden walls, around the door frames, on the backs of both doors.

Over the chest.

Symbols to keep out the dreamers.

Jael held onto the torch with one hand, unlocking the chest with the other. There was nothing inside it, apart from the book. She took it out, laying it open on a hay bale, gagging at the strong, musty odour that escaped its crackling pages. It was filled with symbols, scrawls, and sketches; many of them crossed out, then rewritten. Notes, scribbles, splotches of ink.

Jael had no idea what she was looking for, though.

She couldn't understand any of it.

Slipping the book back into the chest, she locked it, standing up as thunder boomed overhead. Oss' stormy weather appeared to have followed them to Tuura. The spring sun, which had offered so much promise only weeks ago, had gone into hiding.

Her hand jerked suddenly to *Toothpick* as she heard a key in the door behind her. Spinning around, she was relieved to see that it was only Marcus. Her shoulders relaxed, her hand resting by her side.

Marcus smiled awkwardly at her.

Jael peered at his grim face in the torchlight, wondering if she could trust him. She didn't know, but in order to help Edela, she had to trust someone.

'How is your grandmother?' Marcus asked, shaking the rain from his cloak.

'The same. That I can see, at least.'

'And have you had any dreams?'

'Not about anything to do with my grandmother.'

She was not forthcoming, and Marcus didn't push her. 'You need to find a way to save your husband,' he said. 'He is important.'

'So you said,' Jael muttered. She kept seeing images of Evaine, naked, writhing over Eadmund, hoping that it was just her imagination rather than some sort of dreamer's vision about what was happening on Oss. 'Although, you didn't say why.'

'You are Furia's daughter,' Marcus said. 'The only female born in the Furyck line.'

Jael wrinkled her forehead. 'No, I have two cousins. Lothar's daughters, Amma and Getta.'

Marcus smiled knowingly. 'Well, Lothar wasn't actually a Furyck,' he murmured, walking towards the hay bales.

Jael's eyes widened as she followed him. '*What?*'

'His mother, she...' Marcus squirmed, not wishing to speak of such things. 'She fell in love with a merchant from Tingor when your father was a boy. He visited Andala every year until his death, waiting until her husband was away, from what I heard. Only dreamers knew the truth. Your grandmother didn't tell a soul.'

A smile played around Jael's mouth. 'So, I *am* Furia's only daughter, then?'

'You are.'

'But Eadmund?'

'Eadmund,' Marcus sighed, sitting down. 'Eadmund is Esk's son.'

'Esk?' Jael was surprised. 'The Tuuran God of War?'

Marcus nodded. 'The gods are powerless against the Book of Darkness. Raemus made it so. Once the prophecy was revealed, once a dreamer had seen what would come, the Tuuran gods sought the Oster gods' help. They came together to plan a way to end any chance of Raemus' return.'

'By doing what?'

'They created three things to stop the woman from bringing Raemus back. The sword, the shield, and the third thing... well, we don't know what that was. That part of the prophecy was never recorded.'

Jael looked puzzled. 'The shield?'

'The sword was passed down, kept safe for you, as was the shield for Eadmund.'

'But why doesn't he have it? Or even know about it?'

'Eadmund was certainly marked as Esk's son, but he was not quite what anyone had hoped for,' Marcus said, trying to be diplomatic. 'The dreamers could see what would become of him. They determined that it was best if he remained in the dark.'

'Oh.'

'He still has some way to go, I think you would agree, before he is ready to play his role.'

Jael couldn't argue with that. 'But does someone know where this shield is? For when it's time? For when he's ready?'

'Yes, I believe there is no reason to worry. When it's time, the shield will be revealed to Eadmund. *If* he is ready.'

***

Edela's daughters had their mother's determination, that was obvious, and Alaric realised that there was nothing he could do but tell them what he knew.

Which was not much. Mostly gossip. But even gossip could be unsettling.

'Well, I have heard a rumour that Marcus...' His voice ran away to nothing as he lost all confidence in what he was saying. He glanced towards the door, certain he could hear footsteps.

'That Marcus?' Branwyn prompted, leaning forward, forgetting all about her cake.

'Well,' Alaric swallowed. 'That Marcus has had dreamers killed.'

'What?' Gisila looked mortified. 'What for? Why?'

'They say he's a member of The Following.'

Gisila and Branwyn stared at each other, confused.

Biddy and Entorp looked at each other, horrified.

CHAPTER SEVENTEEN

Ayla was hit with such a jolt that she lurched off Bram's sea chest, stumbling down the deck as the ship tilted forward before the waves curled the prow back up again, knocking her in the opposite direction.

Bram was quickly at her side, his big arm firm around her shoulder as an enormous wave crashed over the gunwale, drenching them both. 'Where were you going?' he laughed hoarsely, helping her back to the chest.

Ayla didn't know him. She blinked desperately in the darkness as the bitter wind whipped rain across her face. She tried to swallow, panicking because she couldn't. She didn't know him, but he was all she had now.

All Bruno had too.

'Ivaar!' she cried, spinning around, fear tightening every muscle in her shaking body. 'Ivaar is here!'

Her eyes were so wide with terror that Bram shivered. 'You're a dreamer?' he asked, running a hand through his wet beard.

Ayla nodded.

The ship rolled again, and Ayla slid across the chest. Almost off it.

'Here!' Bram called, grabbing a rope from the stern prow. 'Keep hold of this!' He stumbled behind her, losing his balance as the ship rocked, his hands gripping the prow, searching for any sign that they were being followed. It must have only been early evening, but the sky was already dark with storm, and the sea was so wild that he couldn't make out a thing.

He blinked.

Or could he?

***

'Eadmund,' Evaine murmured. 'Leave him. Tanja is there for a reason.' She was naked and not inclined to suddenly lose all of Eadmund's warmth as he shrugged on his tunic and turned around to smile at her before disappearing out of the bedchamber and into the room next door.

Eadmund had wanted to keep Sigmund with them, but Evaine had insisted that it would be less disturbing for the baby to sleep with Tanja. He was so used to her company now that he would not settle without his wet nurse beside him.

And, not knowing babies, and eager to spend his nights between Evaine's moist thighs, Eadmund had relented. But the sound of his son was impossible to resist, no matter how alluring Evaine was proving.

He returned, clutching the baby to his chest, smiling.

Evaine was not. 'He's hungry,' she grumbled, jumping at another rumble of thunder overhead. The storm had been intensifying all afternoon, and the hall had cleared out early; everyone leaving to secure their homes and livestock. 'I cannot feed him.'

'No,' Eadmund supposed, ignoring her grumbles. 'I'll take him back to Tanja. Soon.' He sat on the edge of the bed listening to his grizzling son, who calmed as he wriggled against his father's shoulder. His head turned expectantly towards Eadmund's face, mouth open, looking for milk.

Eadmund smiled, feeling more confident now as he held Sigmund close.

It was a strange situation, he thought, and the looks he had been getting as he walked around the fort told him that everyone agreed. But he felt content having Evaine and Sigmund with him.

He didn't know how long Jael would be away, or what would happen when she returned. But he was not going to give up Evaine and Sigmund.

Not now.

***

Bram couldn't see *Ice Breaker* ahead of them, but he could see a ship following them now. They were not far from Oss, he was sure, but not as close as he'd like to be.

His broad shoulders felt like twisted branches as he stumbled towards the dreamer, who sat on his chest, shivering, drenched, wind-whipped and anxious, much like the rest of them.

'You think it's Ivaar?' he asked, gripping Ayla's arms before his words were picked up and thrown away by the wind. He couldn't make out the ship at all, nor any of its crew. It was just a shadow in the distance, surging closer, then sinking back.

But it was definitely there now. The occasional snap of lightning revealed the truth of that. There was no doubt that the ship was following them.

Ayla barely nodded, her face still with fear. Only her eyes moved about with any speed.

'What else?' Bram asked desperately, pulling her closer, wishing he had a wooden house to shield in like *Ice Breaker*; somewhere to speak without the wind getting in the way;

without the booms of thunder or the rush of waves that tipped the ship up and down. 'Is there anything else you know? Anything you've seen? Anything?' he cried.

Blinking the rain out of her eyes, Ayla tried to recall her dream. It had been brief but so shocking. Fleeting images flashed before her in a jumble. They didn't make sense. 'Brothers,' she said, frowning. 'Three ships. Three brothers. A dreamer. They had a dreamer... in Alekka. More ships.' She stopped and frowned. 'More than three. More men. But not here.' Her wet curls clung to her face, and she brushed them away, trying to see him.

Bram nibbled his hairy lip, considering things.

They had reefed the sail as soon as the storm picked up, trying to keep the ship tightly controlled. He glanced at his helmsman – his best friend, Snorri – crouching over the tiller as it shuddered against him. 'Snorri! Let's shake out the sail!' he called over the noise of the storm.

Snorri's eyes bulged. 'In this shit?' he grumbled crossly, his hands shaking as he tried to control the jerking tiller. 'You've gone mad, Bram Svanter! Madder than usual, anyways!' Snorri was as old as Bram; his helmsman since they had first left Oss as young men. Bram had gotten them all out of more dire situations than he could count. He trusted Bram with his life. But this?

Bram wasn't looking for opinions, though. *He* was the leader of this group of men; their lord, for want of a better word. Every man on *Red Ned* followed him. And he, in turn, kept them all safe.

And one look at the dreamer's terrified face told him that if they didn't pick up their speed, they would not be safe for long.

***

Jael wanted to talk to Fyn. Or Aleksander.

Or Edela.

Marcus had left so much unsaid as he rushed away again, leaving her with a mounting list of troubling questions. But Edela lay in bed with her eyes closed, Aleksander would soon be in Andala with Axl, and Fyn... well, she could only look at him across the table and keep her thoughts to herself.

Whether she trusted Marcus or not, he was making an elaborate show of protecting them both from Tuura's dreamers. He seemed genuinely afraid and had obviously gone to great lengths to hide their conversations.

'Jael?' Kormac asked again. 'Can I pour you another cup of mead?'

They were all staring at her and Jael blinked, realising that she must have drifted away. 'No, thank you,' she mumbled.

'Do you think the elderman will call you to the temple again?' Gisila asked, chopping her omelette into small pieces.

Jael shook her head, glancing at Eydis who appeared to be listening eagerly. 'No, I don't imagine so. He had no interest in helping us at all.'

'Well, I'm not surprised,' Branwyn grumbled. 'We've never had such a reclusive elderman. He seems to have little interest in anyone at all.'

Kormac frowned. 'I'm not sure that's true,' he said patiently. 'But Tuura has certainly become a strange place to be lately.'

'More than strange,' Branwyn insisted. 'I've been telling you for years that we should move to Andala!'

Kormac squirmed, familiar with how that conversation went.

Jael looked at Biddy and Entorp, who both appeared to be avoiding her eyes as they sat around the table that was almost big enough for all of them. 'Well, perhaps with Axl as king it will be the right time?' She shivered suddenly, thinking of Axl. Worried for Axl. It was as though the storm had blown straight through the door. She could almost feel the wind chilling her spine.

Something was wrong.

'Are you alright, Jael?' Eydis asked, sensing her unease.

'Yes, fine,' she said quietly, trying to shake away her unsettling thoughts. 'Just listening to that storm outside. I wouldn't like to be crossing the Nebbar Straights in that wind.'

***

'Thorgils!' Villas screamed over the rushing torrent of rain. 'What are they doing?' He pointed behind him.

Thorgils felt a twinge in his back as he turned, and a sudden tension in his throat. He swallowed, struggling through the wind towards Villas, whose left hand had hurried back to join his right on the tiller that was banging relentlessly against his waist. It was like trying to control a horse in the heat of anger, and his shoulder had gone numb with the effort of keeping the wooden stick where he wanted it.

'*Doing?*' Thorgils wondered, staring at the dark wall of waves rising behind them. 'What do you mean?' He squinted but couldn't see anything. He looked back to Villas, confused.

'Keep looking!' Villas growled impatiently.

And then, Thorgils saw it. A great white flash in the darkness.

Bram's sail. White with a thick, orange stripe, right down the middle.

That was a full sail.

They were getting closer and quickly.

Thorgils clenched his hands into fists, frowning, almost losing his footing as the waves crashed over him. 'Shake out the sail!' he bellowed at Villas, spitting out a mouthful of sea. 'Shake out the sail now!'

***

Meena had remained in Jaeger's chamber all day.

Egil had grown so tired of her tapping that he had left in the afternoon, returning in the early evening to prepare the chamber for his master.

Darkness had fallen some time ago, and Jaeger had not returned.

Egil had brought his own supper up from the kitchen, enjoying a leg of pork with a full goblet of wine, yet he offered nothing to Meena. He wouldn't even look her way.

Eventually, Meena had taken herself to bed.

Jaeger's bed.

That felt strange too.

Everything felt strange, and she wanted to leave, but at the same time, she didn't want him to come back and find that she wasn't there. And, at least, it was a very comfortable bed; warm and soft and spacious, though she felt too shy to do anything but lie with her arms by her sides, feet together, as though she was still in the narrow bed she had always slept in.

Taking a deep breath, Meena tried to remember how it had felt when Jaeger had stared into her eyes, demanding that she leave Berard to be with him.

She wondered if it had all been a dream.

***

'Tie everything down!' Bram roared, swaying up and down the ship, trying to avoid the sea chests that were sliding across the deck. 'Lash these fucking chests to the gunwales before one of us loses our fucking legs!'

Crouching, sodden men, wrapped in furry, rain-drenched cloaks crawled across the deck, waves tipping on top of them, water sloshing up and down as the ship tilted and rocked.

The furious sea was rolling, and the storm was sinking down on top of them, and the ship behind them was not one but three.

The dreamer had been right.

But as much as he felt sorry for her and wanted to help her and her husband, she wasn't important. Nor was he, or, ultimately, even his men. They were mostly alone now, having lost their wives and children to that evil sickness.

Thorgils and Isaura and those children were important. And he had to help them get to Oss. 'Ailo! Irjan! Bothi! Grab the bows and arrows! With me!' Bram screamed, watching as Ailo crouched forward, and with Bothi's help, lifted the wooden panels on the deck that covered their weapon's store, handing out four longbows and four quivers of arrows.

It was going to be almost impossible, but they had to try something.

All three of them struggled over to Bram, who was busy tying himself to the stern. He'd managed to find more lengths of rope which he tied around the small prow as quickly as his slippery, numb fingers would allow, handing the ends to his men; three of his best archers.

Bram wasn't as good as they were, he knew, but once he'd had a fair eye and an arm stronger than anyone on Oss, apart from his brother, Ned. But not many had been able to beat Bram Svanter with a bow.

He shook his wet head. That was a long time ago now.

Bram took the bow from Ailo, and slung a quiver of arrows over his shoulder, spreading his legs apart for balance, pulling back against the rope to see if it would hold. 'The only hope we have is to slow them down!' he cried. 'So let's tear their sails! Snorri! Keep us straight if you can! With a bit of luck, Ver might shoot some lightning their way too!'

Snorri snorted, but no one heard him as he gripped the shuddering tiller, anticipating the next bolt of lightning to hit.

It had to be soon.

The storm was almost overhead.

Ayla swallowed, watching as the four men drew back their bowstrings and released the white-tailed arrows into the night. The arrows were quickly lost in the darkness, but they released another and another. She wondered if they had any chance of slowing down their chasers. The wind was gusting sideways, making it unlikely that they could hit anything other than waves.

Gripping Bruno's hand as she leaned over him, Ayla tried to shield him from the worst of the weather with her shivering body. She had waited so long to be with him again.

She couldn't let Ivaar take them back to Kalfa.

***

'Morana!' Jaeger hissed just as she was about to slither around the corner. He could hear the storm rattling the windows, fluttering the torches that burned along the stone walls of the corridor.

Morana sighed. She was eager to get to her chamber and not looking for any distractions. They needed to be up before dawn for the spell-casting, and she wanted to use all of that time to settle her mind and prepare her body for what would be the greatest spell she had ever cast. 'Yes?' she grouched, her impatience palpable as she yanked her head around.

'You will remember to come to my chamber? When it's time?' Jaeger asked, certain that Morana was rolling her eyes beneath her thick fringe of hair.

'I will,' she said curtly, edging away.

'And you think the weather will allow it to happen?'

Morana's shoulders slumped as she stopped again. 'It will.'

'Good,' Jaeger said gruffly. 'I shall be waiting for you.' And without another word, he left Morana to her impatient grumbling and disappeared in the opposite direction, smiling to himself.

He felt light-headed, excited for what was to come, eager to finally see what the book could do. Yet, there was a part of him that remained on edge. He could feel a new sensation lurking deep inside him. A burning, building rage.

The idea that anyone else would use the book...

It was bad enough that Morana touched it. But he needed her, Jaeger told himself. But she would have to let others see it now. Perhaps they would need to touch it too?

Stopping before his chamber door, he inhaled sharply. It had to happen, he realised. He couldn't use the book or unleash the power he could feel burning to escape its ancient pages.

Not without help.

'Can't decide if you feel like sleeping?'

Jaeger didn't turn around. 'No, I can decide just fine.'

'But surely there's more fun to be had when you're awake?'

Now, Jaeger did turn. Glancing up and down the corridor, he lowered his voice. 'I'm sure your husband would agree, Nicolene.'

Nicolene's eyes glowed with desire. She was still angry, but as she delicately nibbled her lower lip, she knew that she wanted Jaeger more than she wanted to be mad at him any longer. 'He drank so much wine tonight that Haegen almost carried him to bed.'

Jaeger smiled. 'Is that so?' He leaned towards his sister-in-law until his face was almost touching hers.

She didn't move.

'He's a solid sleeper,' Nicolene murmured, her eyes never leaving Jaeger's. 'I don't imagine he'll wake till the sun comes up.'

It was Jaeger's turn to bite his lip as he grabbed Nicolene's hand. 'Well, if that's the case...' And turning the handle, he pushed open the door.

It was dark in his chamber, but the glow of the fire was enough to see by.

Jaeger took Nicolene's face in his hands, kissing her, pushing her against the door. She responded eagerly, pressing her body against his, her lips urgent, her tongue exploring his mouth.

And then they heard a cough.

A tiny, subtle cough.

***

Thorgils held Isaura close, trying to ignore the distant wailing of her children, who were half asleep and distressed that she had left them with their servants and two men they didn't know; distressed that the ship was rolling and the waves were crashing over the sides, and the thunder was booming, and they were at sea, far from home or any certainty they had ever known.

But Thorgils couldn't let them hear. It would only make things worse.

'I think Ivaar's coming!' he called into Isaura's ear over the roar of the storm.

She stilled against him, stumbling as the deck tilted and Thorgils gripped her harder under the arms. 'How do you know?' she almost sobbed.

'Bram's sail is full! It's just a guess, but no one unfurls a sail without reason. Not in this bowl of shit!' It *was* just a guess, Thorgils thought to himself, but the sick feeling in his stomach wasn't just from the sway of the storm, he was certain. 'We're going to have to try and outrun them! We can't be far from Oss now! We just need to fly home before they catch us!' He didn't even wait for Isaura's reply. He probably wouldn't have heard it anyway, and the look on her face was enough to convey the terror she felt at the thought of Ivaar.

If it was Ivaar.

Thorgils shook his head, not wanting to be right.

But what else could it be?

'We need weapons!' he turned and yelled at his nearest man. 'Stygg! Dig out the bows and arrows!'

'In *this* weather?'

Thorgils looked so furious that Stygg scrambled across the deck without another word.

'Keep bailing!' Thorgils urged. 'Keep bailing! And shut those oar holes!' The deck was more than ankle deep in water now as it sloshed back and forth, side to side, up and down. It was not the most pressing problem he had, but it was worth keeping an eye on. Another wave hurled itself on top of Thorgils, and he blinked, shaking the freezing salt water out of his hair as Stygg struggled towards him with the bows and arrows. 'Leave them here! Get some shields, swords too! A few spears! Let's stock the stern full of what we might need!'

Stygg nodded, crawling back across the deck, his urgency now matching the look on Thorgils' face.

Thorgils closed his eyes, thinking of Ran curling under the stormy waves with her three-headed sea monster, Ilvari. He prayed that she would send her monster towards Ivaar and crush his ships.

He didn't want to imagine that the gods were cruel enough to take away everything he had dreamed of for eight years in one stormy night.

***

Jaeger's mind, which was not as alert as his body, stumbled in confusion. 'Meena?'

Meena was too shocked to even tap her head.

She sat up in Jaeger's bed, her mouth open, unable to move.

'*Meena?*' Nicolene was confused, following Jaeger's gaze towards the bed. 'What is *she* doing here?'

'Meena works for me now, remember?' Jaeger said quickly, stepping away from Nicolene.

Nicolene smoothed down her dress, aware of the sudden shift in things. 'I see,' she sneered, not seeing in the slightest. 'And you let her sleep in your bed as payment for her services? *That* thing?' Her nostrils flared in distaste.

Jaeger felt caught.

Frustrated.

'Meena and I are... friends,' he said slowly. 'So, she can sleep where she likes. And I'm sure she'd rather sleep in my bed than Egil's.'

Nicolene glared at Jaeger, not impressed by his attempt at humour. Flicking her hair over her shoulder, she stretched out her neck. 'I didn't realise your bed would be so full this evening. I shall get back to my own.' And spinning around, she reached for the door handle, imagining that Jaeger would stop her.

He didn't.

Thunder rumbled in the distance, and Nicolene turned back to him, scowling.

Jaeger stared at her, not saying a word.

So, clenching her teeth, Nicolene ripped open the door and stormed out of the chamber.

***

The storm was getting worse.

Eadmund lay in bed, unable to sleep. It was still early, he knew, and perhaps that was why he felt so awake. His mind was unsettled, worried about the fort. He had no choice but to worry now. They were his people. He had to make sure they were safe.

The responsibility he felt pressed him down onto the bed, and he didn't even notice Evaine's soft hand as she stroked his chest.

'Can't you sleep?' Evaine murmured, sounding almost asleep herself.

Eadmund put his hand over hers, bringing it to his lips. 'No, I can't sleep in a storm. Not since I stopped drinking so much at least,' he smiled, remembering how Jael had saved him from that.

Forced him to be saved.

Jael.

After all that she had done for him, he felt disloyal lying in the bed that they would have slept in together. If it wasn't for Evaine...

Eadmund sighed, listening as the wind shook the window. He was glad that most of their ships were secured in sheds in Tatti's Bay.

He hoped that Thorgils and Bram weren't out in the storm.

CHAPTER EIGHTEEN

They were gaining.

Bram was sure the ships were gaining on them. The storm was gaining on them too. Buckets of rain washed around the deck, splashing over Ayla's ankles as she waded unsteadily towards the stern, arms outstretched, gripping onto the nearest rope to steady herself.

Bram reached out to her as another wave broke over the ship. The arrows had made no difference that he could see. He had no idea if any had found their mark, but he didn't want to keep sending them out into the watery abyss, wasting them.

He'd wait until the ships came closer.

'We're nearly at Oss!' Ayla screamed in Bram's ear as he gripped her elbow, keeping her upright.

'You've *seen* this?'

Ayla nodded, cringing as a wave crashed next to them; shivering as the water hit her already frozen body. 'Yes!'

Bram edged her towards Snorri. 'Any idea where the fuck we are?' he growled in Snorri's ear.

Snorri shrugged. There was almost no way of telling. They would have expected to arrive in Oss' harbour within a day of leaving Kalfa, which could be around now given the ferocity of the wind tearing into their sail.

He honestly didn't know.

'They'll be on us before long!' Bram yelled at Ayla. 'Unless you can talk to the gods, I don't know what more we can do!'

Ayla wiped the rain out of her eyes, terrified. 'I can try!' she cried, thinking of Bruno; of Isaura and the children. 'Help me! I need my chest!'

***

Meena felt foolish. Humiliated. Worthless and ashamed. Berard had been kind to her. He had offered her a future and showed her respect. And she had chosen his brother, who had immediately stopped noticing her; bored now that he had gotten his way.

'Meena,' Jaeger murmured. 'She's gone now. It's just us.' She had shuffled away to the opposite side of the bed, hiding beneath her hair.

He reached out a hand.

But Meena didn't move.

Tired and impatient, Jaeger lunged for her, snatching her arm, pulling her roughly towards him. 'If you wish to stay with me, then I think we need to discuss some... rules.'

Meena could smell Nicolene on him. Nicolene always smelled strongly of lavender. It turned her stomach. She wrinkled her nose, trying to ignore the pain in her wrist where his fingers were pinching her skin. She pulled against him, confused as to whether she was more afraid or angry.

But Jaeger didn't care about anything she might have felt as he gripped her harder, then pushed her backwards, onto the pillows. He thought of the book, of what Morana would do with it in a few hours. Of Nicolene, who had left.

Of his father and brothers.

Of Berard.

He would destroy all of them. The book would show him the way.

His eyes glazed over as he held Meena down with one hand, tugging his trousers off with the other.

***

Bram wiped a hand across his face, trying to see. The storm was lashing them with rain, thunder, and lightning. Even shouting, his voice was quickly lost amongst the howl of the wind.

Crouching down, he tried to shield the dreamer from the worst of it so she could work her... he wasn't sure what.

Ayla had pulled a bag of stones from her chest, and she now sat wedged into a corner of the stern with Bram protecting her, the stones in her hands, her eyes closed.

Bram didn't know nor care what she was doing. They needed all the help they could get to slip away from their chasers. He shook his dripping hair out of his eyes, not wanting to think about how they were going to get through the entrance to Oss' harbour in this mess. Navigating those ship-wrecking stone spires was a challenge for the sharpest helmsman on the fairest of days. Bram turned around, trying to see Snorri through the driving rain. A shard of lightning struck nearby, highlighting his friend's face; teeth gritted as his body shook with the strain of keeping the tiller tight against him.

Bram swallowed, his mouth dry despite the amount of rain and seawater that had been flooding it.

Ayla could feel him there, trying to keep her safe. The storm was a booming terror, demanding her attention, but she gripped the two stones in her hands as she sat, feeling the rhythm of the ship beneath her, surging on the waves, hoping it would help her slip into a trance.

The ship dipped, and she slid into Bram, but he held her, and she stayed still for a moment, repeating her words over and over; inhaling the wet, salty air; tasting it on her tongue; smelling it in her nostrils; listening to its wild, whistling fury as it burrowed into her head. She tried to imagine Veiga, Goddess of Weather, rising above them, arms outstretched, throwing great balls of dark thunder and spear-tipped shards of golden light down to destroy them all.

Ayla needed to find her. To reach her. She had spoken to the gods before.

She needed to do it again.

And quickly.

***

Eadmund had not been able to get back to sleep, so leaving Evaine dreaming beneath a bundle of furs, he slipped out of the hall. And wrapping his thickest cloak around himself, pulling his hood down over his face, he moved quickly across the rain-lashed square.

He could hear the thunderous growl of the sea in the distance, the eerie scream of the wind as it raced past him. He saw flashes of lightning slice through the dark sky. Ver was in a foul mood, he smiled to himself, hurrying to the gatehouse, determined to get up onto the ramparts.

Eadmund had a bad feeling. Whether it was because of Ivaar or worrying about Thorgils, he didn't know. But something wasn't right.

Of that, he was certain.

***

Thorgils could see them now.

Lightning exploded across the sky like white flames, opening a brief window into the darkness, and standing in the stern, gripping hold of a rope, Thorgils could see Bram being chased down by three ships.

His stomach clenched into a tight knot.

He would not let Ivaar take Isaura.

The waves were higher than Oss' hall, and it felt as though *Ice Breaker* was sinking into them, being sucked down into Ran's desperate embrace. But then they dipped, coming up again, high, high up, and at that moment, as they crested the wave, Thorgils caught a glimpse in another flash of lightning.

He knew where they were.

***

'The spires! The spires!' Snorri shouted, trying to get Bram's attention, his voice quickly lost in a shower of seawater.

But Bram had heard him, and his head was up, spinning around, following the line of Snorri's nodding head. Snorri couldn't take his hands off the tiller, or he'd lose control of the ship altogether.

Another jagged flash of lightning illuminated the sky, and Bram saw them: the towering stones that marked the entrance to Oss' harbour.

And they were full of sail and storm and flying towards them.

He gulped, glancing down at the dreamer. He'd abandoned the gods entirely when they had taken away his family and most of his village, but he found himself begging them to save them all. To save them from the threat behind them and now the even more terrifying one rushing up to meet them.

And below his arms, the dreamer rocked back and forth, mumbling, chanting, gripping her stones. Her eyes closed against the storm.

***

'Fuck!' Villas' eyes were wide with horror as he grabbed the tiller from the man who had given him a break. He could no longer feel the right side of his body and the skin on his calloused hands was ripped raw. Gritting his teeth, he could feel the rough wood dig into his fingers again. 'Fuck!'

Thorgils was next to him. They were approaching the entrance to the harbour fast.

'Reef the sail!' Villas yelled into the squall. 'Reef the sail!'

Thorgils watched as his men raced out of the house, slipping and stumbling towards the sail, rolling it higher, making it smaller.

They needed to slow down.

Villas jerked the tiller back and forth, trying to create some drag.

It didn't matter if they were caught now. Any ship approaching those stones in these waves with this speed had no chance.

***

'Reef the sail!' Snorri screamed to his sodden, terrified men who had all seen fleeting glimpses of the jagged stones, and the high cliffs on either side that were funnelling them straight into Oss' harbour.

Whether onto or around those stones was yet to be determined.

Bram's eyes were up, blinking as one of their chasers crested a wave, then disappeared from view. He kept staring into the darkness, looking for clues in the flashes of light. There were definitely only two sails now, but those two sails were getting closer quickly.

Ayla sucked in a salty breath, coughing as she fell forward, gasping for air.

Bram bent over, grabbing her arm as she started to slide away from him. He sought her eyes, which would not focus on his at all, looking for signs as to what had happened.

Ayla tried to stand, and Bram pulled her to him. 'I must see my husband!' she cried.

'What happened?' Bram wondered urgently, but Ayla said nothing, keeping her head down, her eyes away from his as he helped her towards Bruno.

He appeared unconscious, which Ayla was grateful for. She laid her head on his chest, wrapping her arms around him to stop herself sliding away as the ship reared up again, thunder roaring further in the distance now.

*****

Isaura could hear the panic in the crew's voices as they staggered around on deck, sliding in and out of the house. She'd glanced through some of the holes in the wall and seen why.

Her mind raced ahead, planning what she needed to do if they were to break up on the rocks.

Four children. Three women.

'Ida!' she called to the woman closest to her. 'If anything

happens, you'll take Annet! Selda, you'll take Selene! I'll keep Mads and Leya!' She peered down the end of the house as Thorgils entered, sliding down to her. 'Thorgils!'

He looked ill with worry.

'We're coming in too fast!' he cried, not having any time to be discreet. The children were awake and terrified by the noise of the storm and the violent rolling of the ship. There was no point in pretending that they weren't in serious danger. 'If we hit the rocks...' He shook his head, swallowing, not wanting to imagine what was about to happen. 'Give me one of the children!' he urged, glancing around at the terrified, shaking women who rocked with the ship, banging against one another. 'We'll all keep a child with us! We can get to the rocks! Wait for the storm to pass!'

It wasn't true. Isaura could see it in his eyes.

'Just hold the children tightly!' he pleaded, grabbing Leya who didn't protest as he tucked her into his wet chest. 'Don't let them go now! If we hit, the impact will be hard!'

There was nothing more he could do.

Villas had men in the bow, Thorgils knew. Men on the gunwales, all of them lashed to the ship, just as Villas was tied to the tiller now. He knew those spires better than most. Snorri too. They were old helmsmen, navigating the entrance to the harbour since they had barely any hair on their faces.

If anyone was going to have a chance of getting them in safely, it was Villas and Snorri.

Another crack of lightning and Thorgils shuddered, staring down the length of the house towards the prow as the stone spires loomed like terrifying demons in the darkness. Turning to Isaura, he forced his face into a smile, wanting to reach out and bring her into his arms too, but she needed to keep Mads safe in hers.

His eyes didn't leave her as he fought to keep himself from sliding.

'We'll be on the beach in no time,' he soothed, feeling his

body shake in protest. 'And then we can think about finding a big fire to get you dry. Something hot to eat. Maybe soup. Do you like soup?'

Isaura stared at Thorgils, tears streaming down her cheeks. She was unable to lift a hand to wipe them away. She rocked and swayed, her oddly silent son lying still in her arms, his eyes filled with terror.

What had she done?

***

Bram swayed, tied to the prow, getting a face full of seawater as he tried to make out their distance from the spires. He spat the water back out, turning to Snorri who shook as he struggled with the tiller.

They were edging up to *Ice Breaker*, following Villas in.

It was up to Villas to lead them safely through the jagged stones.

Ayla, lying over Bruno's chilled body, whispered in his ear. 'My love, my love, my love.' She closed her eyes, feeling the sobs rise up in her chest, desperately trying to hold on as the ship rocked, forcing her to loosen her grip on her husband. But whatever was about to happen, she was determined that they were never going to be apart again.

And then a shard of lightning hit the deck, barely a hand from where Ayla and Bruno lay.

Ayla screamed.

Then the ship dropped.

***

Eadmund froze, staring across the harbour to the spires in the distance. Storm crowded for so long and almost disappearing under a thick bank of clouds, they were suddenly visible.

The sky had cleared, and the clouds had vanished, revealing a landscape of stars, and a sliver of moon illuminating the entrance to the harbour.

And two ships.

Eadmund sighed in relief.

Thorgils.

***

Thorgils ducked out of the house, hurrying towards Villas whose mouth was as open as his. 'What happened?' He looked around blankly, confused.

The sea had dropped. The white-capped waves were suddenly timid, barely rolling. The sky was no longer on top of them. It was calm, clear, sprinkled with stars.

The storm had disappeared in the blink of an eye.

Villas shook his head, his eyes never veering from what was in front of them. The storm may have passed, but it was still dark, and there was still the matter of the spires.

***

Bram glanced at Ayla as she stood and looked around, her mouth open, her eyes rounded in surprise.

It was dark, but the light from the stars and the moon showed them all that the storm had gone. It was suddenly so peaceful, so quiet. The wind was there, but it was helpful rather than angry now, and their approach to the spires seemed slightly less daunting.

But then, as Ayla turned to look at the ships following closely in their wake, a shower of arrows shot towards her.

***

'No!' Ivaar reached out, stopping the man who was pulling his bowstring to his ear again. 'No!' He turned around to Borg Arnesson. 'My children might be on that ship! You had better not kill my children if you want that gold!'

Borg looked barely bothered, despite the terror they'd all endured; despite the odd disappearance of the worst storm he'd ever encountered at sea. His luck was in, and he was ready to ride it. 'No more arrows! Just get us through those stones!' Borg yelled to his helmsman before turning to his men. 'Prepare to land fast!' He looked to his left, pleased to see that one of his ships was still with them. The other had disappeared into the waves, which was a loss, but one they could weather, he was sure.

Ivaar frowned, wanting to vomit after the wild ride they had just survived; furious that Thorgils had stolen his wife and children away; ready to destroy both him and Eadmund and take his rightful place as the King of Oss. But above all, he was anxious, remembering the words of the old dreamer, the Arnesson's mother. 'The cautious man will wear the crown. The foolish man will sink and drown.' He turned to Borg Arnesson, whose dark-blue eyes were full of manic energy, fuelled by their brush with death and the reward that waited behind Oss' stones. 'Wait!' he cried. 'Wait!'

CHAPTER NINETEEN

Sevrin and Torstan were at Eadmund's side. The warning bell had rung loudly around the fort, and with the sudden retreat of the storm, they'd all heard it. The ramparts were lined with grim-faced men; on edge, peering into the darkness, watching the faint shapes edging around the spires.

'What do you think?' Sevrin wondered. He couldn't stand still, feeling an urgent need to do something.

Eadmund bit his teeth together.

He knew his brother. Ivaar was too clever to attack Oss with only two ships, surely? Unless he had more coming that they couldn't see yet. 'Light the warning fires!' he called, turning to the nearest man. 'Take five men and get down the island. Bring back anyone who wants to shelter in the fort! Torstan, go to the hall, get the fires burning high. Send Ketil into the square. We need fires, as many as we can! Sevrin, send a group of men down to the drying sheds. Gather all the fish in now!' He glanced around, happy to see another of his friends. 'Erland, organise water! Find any empty buckets and barrels. Bring them into the square. Get the buckets up to the ramparts!'

Eadmund squinted into the distance. Arlo, one of his most experienced archers, was squeezing his way along the narrow ramparts towards his king. 'Get your men ready. And light the braziers up here! If they storm the beach, we burn them!'

Morac staggered up the steep steps from the gatehouse

below. 'My lord?' he panted. 'Is there anything I can do?'

Eadmund's mind went quickly to Evaine and Sigmund. 'Go to the hall. Prepare it as our last defense. If they get through the gates, we'll retreat there.'

Morac nodded, his face reflecting the stark reality of their situation.

If Ivaar got in with enough men, he knew that not one of them would survive.

***

Eydis woke up crying.

Her whimpering was so faint that it didn't wake anyone but Jael. 'Eydis?' Jael whispered, shivering as she leaned over her. The storm had passed, but it was still bitterly cold, which was not unusual for Tuura, she knew, no matter what the season. 'Did you have a bad dream?'

Eydis shook as Jael pulled the furs up to her chin. 'It's Ivaar,' she breathed. 'Ivaar is going to attack Oss.'

Jael blinked, panic flickering in her chest.

Eadmund.

***

Bram crouched over the bleeding body of the dreamer.

Her eyes flickered open. Big, dark pupils jumping out of a pale face; confused, full of fear.

'It's alright,' he assured her gently. 'We'll get that arrow out of your leg. Best you stay down, though, in case they decide to try again.'

Ayla's ears were ringing; the searing pain in her leg was a sudden, unpleasant surprise. She tried to move, worried about Bruno.

'Stay down!' Bram growled, crawling away towards Snorri.

'How is she?' Snorri asked, his eyes never deviating from the spires as he squinted into the darkness, almost missing the bursts of brightness the lightning had afforded him.

'She'll live,' Bram muttered, watching as they passed by another towering stone, holding his breath as they approached the last narrow gap they needed to shoot through. 'If you get us through here in just the one piece that is!'

'Trying,' Snorri said through gritted teeth, pulling the tiller hard to the right, wondering if he'd have any skin left on his hands soon. 'Lucky for me, Villas is up there doing all the hard work.'

Bram turned back to look at their chasers, surprised to see them drifting away.

***

All four children were wailing now; each one being comforted by an adult who felt just as terrified but was trying not to show it. The only true comfort would come when the ship was beached, Thorgils knew. He held his breath, hoping it would happen soon; watching down the end of the house as they edged past the last spire. Breathing out heavily, he turned in the opposite direction, relieved to see *Red Ned* still following in their wake.

Thorgils smiled at Isaura. 'We're through the spires!' he called, trying to cheer the children. 'Now we head for the beach, and soon we'll be in the fort, and you can all have something hot to drink around a blazing fire!'

The children cried even harder.

Isaura wasn't crying, but she looked just as upset. The fear of the spires may have passed, but the fear of Ivaar was looming again. She glanced towards the end of the house. 'Is Eadmund expecting us?' she asked, pointing to the fires burning down the headland.

Thorgils squinted. 'Looks like it.' He frowned, noticing how far along the fires were burning.

Signals.

Signals to the men stationed at Tatti's Bay, guarding their fleet; to the men at Hud's Point, whose farmsteads would be threatened by any invasion, for surely Ivaar would not be foolish enough to only attack through the harbour.

He must have more ships. More men.

***

Aleksander was in Andala, watching Jael walk Tig around the training ring.

She was bursting with pride at how well he was responding to her for a change. She had him under complete control, basking in the rare smile of approval on her father's face as he stood watching with Gant. As always, their heads were together, muttering away to one another, thinking of more ways to help improve both her and him.

The little girl came towards him, straight through the training ring, not noticing Jael or Tig at all. And suddenly the sky darkened. Thunderous clouds hovered low, rushing at him.

She was younger than Eydis, Aleksander was sure, and she was talking, staring at him; her face determined, frowning.

Her eyes urgent and demanding.

He leaned forward, trying to hear her as she strode closer,

and her voice rose. She was small, with dark, curling hair, and a tiny, heart-shaped face, but her voice...

That was not the voice of a girl, but the booming cry of a woman.

When all old kings are murdered,
When ravens claim the sky,
When oceans rage with monsters,
Then all of you will die!

Unless you find the Daughter,
Unless you find the Son,
Unless you find the Sword and Shield,
You will be overrun!

They'll raise her from her tomb,
They'll raise up all her men,
They'll give to her the Book,
And bring the Darkness back again!

'Go!' she yelled, pointing at him. 'Leave this place now! You will all die! Jael will die! Heed my words, Aleksander! You must keep her safe! Go from this place! Now!'

Aleksander jerked awake, panting in the darkness, shivering, wet with sweat.

***

At the first crunch of sand against the keel, Thorgils was jumping down into the dark water with the rest of his men, dragging *Ice Breaker* up onto the beach. Bram's ship, *Red Ned*, wasn't far behind and soon Oss' beach was full of sodden, shell-shocked men, a few shaking women, a handful of crying children and an enormous sense of relief as they all welcomed the feel of stones beneath their wet boots.

All but Ayla and Bruno, who could not walk at all, so they were handed over the side of the ship.

'Ayla!' Isaura rushed to her, leaving the children with her servants.

An arrow was sticking out of Ayla's thigh, and although a ripped piece of tunic had been tied above it, her leg was dripping with blood.

'Quick!' Isaura called to Thorgils. 'We have to get Ayla up to the fort!'

Thorgils nodded, turning back to check the entrance to the harbour once more. But there were no ships coming.

Not yet, at least.

Eadmund was hurrying across the stones towards them, Torstan beside him, a handful of Osslanders rushing past them to help unload the ships. They needed to get everything and everyone inside: sea chests, weapons, sails, oars. They couldn't do much about the ships except beach them, but they could take everything else.

Villas and Snorri looked as though they were ready to fall over. They stumbled across the stones, unsure on their feet, their salt-dry throats already considering whether there'd be a cup of ale on offer, despite the fact that they were too tired to keep their eyes open.

'You made it, then?' Eadmund smiled as he picked up Annet and started walking across the beach towards the hill.

Thorgils was still in shock at how the storm had simply vanished; amazed that they had made it home in one piece. 'I think the gods had a hand in that,' he said quietly. 'What other explanation is there? That storm was about to sink us, I'm sure.' He suddenly realised that he was carrying an open-eared little girl in his arms. 'Although, we would have been fine,' he said quickly. 'We can all swim, can't we?' He tickled Leya under her chin, and she frowned back at him.

'Where have they gone, do you think?'

Thorgils was soaked to his soul; even his eyebrows were wet through, dripping into his eyes, but he raised them anyway. 'Hud's Point?'

'Either there or maybe Tervo or Bara?'

Thorgils shook his head. 'I don't think Tervo. Torborn wouldn't have him there. Bara? Well, Frits Hallstein's always been a stupid shit, so maybe.' He looked around to check on Isaura, who was walking beside Ayla. 'If that's the case though, we're in for it soon.'

Bram ambled past them, lugging his sea chest as though it was a light basket. 'Come on, ladies!' he grinned over his shoulder. 'I need to get these feet of mine in front of some flames before they fall off!'

Now Eadmund did smile. 'Come on!' he called to the men on the beach. 'Let's get inside!'

***

After soothing Eydis back to sleep, Jael had been restless and too distracted to close her eyes for long. She was growing tired of this night, which seemed longer than any she could remember, but dawn would be here soon. So, yawning, she sat up, moving Vella into the warm space she was leaving behind, plonking her next to her brother who lay stretched out against Eydis' back.

Jael frowned, wanting to be back on Oss, helping Eadmund defend the island. How could Ivaar attack Oss, though? He didn't have enough men or ships.

Not enough for what he needed to do.

So he must have help. But whose?

Wrapping her cloak around her shoulders and grabbing her

swordbelt, she put her finger to her lips as Vella popped her head up, and slipped through the door.

***

'Ayla?' Isaura smiled encouragingly as Ayla's eyes fluttered open.

'Bruno?' Ayla asked quickly, turning her head. Disoriented. She must have passed out because she had no idea how she had ended up on a table by a fire inside Oss' hall. She closed her eyes again, aware of an urgent throbbing in her leg, and the swaying of her body, rolling from side to side as though she was still on that ship.

But she wasn't.

Ayla grimaced as Isaura gripped her hand.

'He's here,' Isaura said quietly. 'In a bedchamber, sleeping. He's very weak, but when he wakes, we'll start making him strong again, don't worry.'

Bram stood behind them, looking at the arrow he had just removed from Ayla's leg. Turning to Thorgils, he lowered his voice. 'I have a feeling we owe our lives to that woman.'

'What do you mean?' Thorgils asked, puzzled, watching out of the corner of his eye as everyone rushed about finding dry clothes, filling the tables with food and ale for the wet and weary travellers.

He couldn't believe that they were safe. All of them.

Bram shrugged. 'When she's better, maybe we'll know more, but maybe we won't want to. With dreamers, I've always found, it's better to stay in the dark!' Clapping Thorgils on the back, Bram took himself to the nearest table, collapsing gratefully in front of a cup of freshly poured ale. He watched as Runa entered the hall, her eyes searching the room, meeting his. He saw relief in them, then displeasure as she glimpsed her husband.

'What can I do?' Runa asked, walking towards Morac, trying to avoid staring at Bram. Her eyes rested on the woman lying on the table. She recognised her. 'What happened?'

Morac looked bored. 'She had an arrow in her leg. Perhaps you can help care for her?' He was far more interested in what they were going to do about the ships in Tatti's Bay. If Ivaar was lurking about, they were in danger of having almost their entire fleet wiped out. He sent Runa on her way and turned towards the table where Eadmund sat with Bram, Thorgils, Torstan, and Sevrin. Sighing with tight-lipped irritation, he walked over to join them.

'If we bring back the ships,' Eadmund frowned, 'there's nothing to stop him attacking them at sea. Who knows where he is or what his plans are. And we need all the men we have to defend the fort.'

'Well, Ayla saw three brothers and a dreamer on Alekka. Sounds like the Arnessons to me. And they do have more ships,' Bram said, taking a long drink of ale, grateful to feel moisture in his throat again. 'We had three behind us. One was lost. From memory, the Arnesson brothers have two ships each. So, there's maybe five, plus Ivaar's two ships.'

'But where were the others? If three were behind you?'

'My bet is Bara or Tervo,' Bram mused. 'Mother Arnesson is the dreamer. An old, hairy bitch dreamer from Tingor. The sort of woman who could strip the skin off you with a look.' He shuddered, having had many encounters with the old crone over the years. He'd known her husband who'd been a ferrety, one-armed bastard, killed in a dispute over another man's wife. Unsurprisingly. The Arnessons had a reputation around women, that, as Bram's mother used to say, would curl your hair. 'She must have told them about the gold.'

Morac's head was up. 'Gold?'

Bram's jaw clenched, not welcoming the latest arrival to

their already full table. He didn't move over, and Morac had to perch on the end of the bench as he sat down. 'The Arnesson brothers are gold-hungry bastards. The only thing getting them into their ships, coming here with Ivaar, would have been gold, and plenty of it.'

Eadmund glanced at Thorgils, who, he noticed, was still shaking. 'Go and sit by the fire. Change your clothes. You're not going to be much use to anyone if you end up in Odda's sickbed!'

Thorgils nodded and slunk away, suddenly worried about his mother.

'But Ivaar doesn't want gold, does he?' Sevrin suggested. 'Not really.'

'No,' Eadmund agreed. 'He wants me. He wants the throne.'

'But the Ivaar I remember was no fool,' Bram added. 'He won't come if he thinks he could be humiliated. If he doesn't think he can defeat you.'

'No, he won't,' Eadmund murmured. 'But if he has these brothers on his side, then he likely has more of a chance, wouldn't you say?'

'I would,' Bram agreed, finishing his cup and reaching for the jug. 'So, best we have another talk with that dreamer and see if she had any more dreams while she was asleep!'

***

The knock on the door was sharp, but not unexpected. It was still dark, but Jaeger had been awake for some time, and he stood, dressed and waiting, Meena yawning by his side.

She could barely look at him and had not spoken a word since he'd woken her. She tapped her head anxiously as a sleepy Egil opened the door to reveal Morana.

Morana pulled back her hood, lifting a sharp eyebrow at her hunched over niece, but one look at Jaeger's face told her that there was no point in arguing about it. 'We should go,' she rasped moodily.

Jaeger nodded, pushing Meena forward, both of them wrapped in hooded cloaks. The storm had passed, but it was a fair walk to the Crown of Stones, so it was better to be prepared, or so Egil had insisted. He'd shoved a water bag and a basket of food at Meena, who did not look pleased as she took them.

Morana scowled as Meena passed her, and Jaeger glared at them both, his finger to his lips. 'Let's go. Quietly,' he hissed, leading the way down the corridor, hoping to keep Morana from killing Meena.

At least until they reached the stones.

Jaeger had the book safely tucked beneath his cloak. He could feel it pressing against his chest. There was a sense of comfort in having it so close. He felt calm for the first time in weeks, although it was unsettling to be taking it out of his chamber, to a group of people who would no doubt happily kill him to own it.

But the book was his.

And he would just as happily kill to keep it.

***

Jael rested her head against Tig's. He was sleepy and quiet, and they stayed like that for a while. She ran her hands down his face, wishing they were back on Oss, preparing to ride down the island, across the breathtaking landscape they had both come to love.

Instead, they were back here in the place of nightmares.

Jael had tried not to think about it, preferring to keep her mind occupied with thoughts of Edela and Eadmund.

She yawned, reaching for Tig's bridle. The loss of Eadmund had opened up a hole inside her. She had pushed and pushed against him, and now he wasn't there.

And she missed him.

Jael stilled. Tig's ears flicked.

They could both hear footsteps.

Jael stepped back slowly, her hand resting on *Toothpick*, her skin prickling in anticipation. It had been too long since she had done any training, she grumbled to herself.

Spinning quickly, she came face to face with a sleepy-eyed Fyn.

'Feel like some company?' he grinned.

***

Ayla was sitting up now, a cup of honeyed milk warming her hands. Isaura had gone to try and help her servants soothe the children, who were still confused and in tears, not knowing whether it was day or night.

Bram sat down next to Ayla.

They were alone, by the fire.

'Your leg,' he started. 'It will heal quickly, I'm sure. It wasn't deep.'

She looked up at him. 'Thank you. Isaura said you pulled the arrow out.'

'I did. It's something I'm especially skilled at after all these years.'

Ayla grimaced at a sudden rush of pain.

'It's the least I could do after what you did.' He felt awkward, hiding his eyes from her.

'*I* did?' Ayla looked awkward herself, her attention quickly back on her cup.

Bram glanced around, but they were still alone. 'The storm. The way it just vanished.' He shook his head. 'I've never seen anything like that. It *was* you, wasn't it?'

Ayla blinked at Bram, but her eyes were dark masks, revealing nothing. 'I think it was luck,' she whispered carefully. 'Just luck.'

'Luck?'

Ayla nodded slowly. 'Yes. Luck.'

Bram stared at her. 'Well, if I'm ever in need of some luck again, I think I may pay you a visit,' he said with a smile.

Ayla smiled back before her lips started to wobble as she remembered the words she had heard in her trance. 'Heed my warning, dreamer! My storms are a sign! A message! A cry to arms! For the Darkness is coming and we are all in danger! Man and god alike!'

PART FOUR

The Door

CHAPTER TWENTY

Jael and Fyn walked the horses to the gates, eager to escape the oppressive fort.

'You're sure Aron won't mind you taking his horse?' Jael wondered, ambling along beside Tig.

'He said I could use him while I'm here,' Fyn said sleepily. He was not enjoying Tuura at all, apart from spending time with Jael's two cousins. They were his age, and, like Axl, were proving to be surprisingly good company.

Still, it would be nice to spend some time with Jael.

He was worried about her.

'Well, that's good,' Jael yawned. 'It will be a relief to get out of here for a while.' There was so much to talk about. And nothing she could say. She still had Marcus' stone in her pouch, but his warning about speaking to anyone else rung in her ears.

Jael waved at the soldiers on the gates who squinted in the pre-dawn light, but hopped to action as they got closer, lifting up the thick, wooden bar that secured the gates during the night.

Sticking her foot into a stirrup, Jael hoisted herself onto Tig's back, resettling her cloak. As the gates opened, she took a deep breath, inhaling the smell of last night's storm, and tapped her boots gently into her beloved horse, letting him fly.

***

The Crown of Stones was an ancient landmark, as revered as Skoll's Tree, but not a place that many went. Not anymore. The Following had claimed it centuries before, and their reputation in Hest was terrifying enough to keep everyone else far away.

It was a place of energy and magic, where the Followers believed that Raemus himself had once walked. They came to it each shadow moon, hoping to reach into the Dolma; hoping to feel his dark presence; to connect with him in some small way.

Meena knew it well. It was a place that Varna had brought her many times. Despite her intense dislike of The Following and their intense dislike of her, Varna had been one of their leaders, though she had always disagreed with Yorik Elstad about their one true goal.

Meena remembered Varna and felt sad.

It was not a real feeling, she knew, because Varna had been a cruel grandmother who had mistreated her, not caring for her in any way that she could see or feel. Her shoulders sunk as she thought of Berard. He had wanted to care for her, and she had run away from him, into his brother's arms, only to discover that he did not care for her at all.

They were all eyeing Jaeger. Not wanting to look at him, but eyeing him nonetheless; wondering about the book, Morana knew. She smiled, every one of her fingers and toes tingling in anticipation. She felt light-headed, not having slept at all as she purified both her mind and body in preparation for the spell-casting. 'Give me the book,' she demanded as Yorik approached.

Jaeger frowned at her tone. '*Now*? You don't appear ready to do anything yet,' he grumbled, staring at the huddled Followers in the distance. They gathered inside the stone circle, a murmuring flock of black-cloaked men and women; hiding their faces from him beneath shadowy hoods.

Son of the king.

They did not trust him. Not yet.

'My lord.' Yorik nodded respectfully, trying to get Jaeger's attention. 'We are pleased that you have come. That you have brought us the book.'

'Brought *you* the book?' Jaeger snorted, not noticing the flicker of anger in Yorik's strange eyes. It was still too dark to see much. They had come without torches, eager not to draw attention to themselves as they trekked away from the castle, and some of the Followers were still attempting to light a fire in the middle of the circle.

'Well, of course, the book is yours, as you say. We are grateful for the opportunity to show you what power lies within its pages,' Yorik said, staring intently at Jaeger, almost willing him to hand over the book.

Jaeger reluctantly slipped it out from beneath his cloak. His body twinged as he handed it to Yorik, who tensed in anticipation, gripping his hands around the book's cool leather cover.

Jaeger did not let go as he stared Yorik down. 'This book belongs to me. It revealed itself to me alone, and you will do well to remember that. I am a Dragos. It was meant for me.' His voice was low, edged with menace, and he was pleased to see Yorik take note.

'Of course, my lord,' Yorik said calmly, feeling the weight of the book as Jaeger finally released his grip. He sighed. Oh, the years he had imagined such pure joy. The Book of Darkness! At last –

'We must begin!' Morana snapped, frowning at Yorik's dithering, her attention focused by a clap of thunder in the distance. 'Another storm will be upon us before long.'

Yorik watched as tall flames finally sparked from the fire, snaking into the pre-dawn sky. 'Yes, I fear you're right. It is a sign you know,' he smiled. 'The gods are worried. It is a very promising sign indeed.'

Jaeger glanced at Meena, who was looking through the stones as though planning her escape.

'You will join the circle,' Morana said reluctantly. There was no other way to show him the spell, although she had her doubts as to whether he would see anything at all. He was no dreamer. No elder. No Follower.

He was nothing.

Except a Dragos.

The one who would raise her.

And they all needed him now.

***

Eadmund had not come back to bed, and so Evaine had come to find him, irritated that he had abandoned her. She found him hunched over a table with Thorgils and his equally huge uncle; all three of them drinking.

She scowled disapprovingly as she approached.

Thorgils gulped, recognising the look on her face; still surprised that she was here and not Jael.

Bram appeared just as disturbed by the chill in Evaine's eyes. 'Well, perhaps you and I should go and see how your mother fares?' he suggested quickly, groaning in agony as he stood. The storm had knocked him about so much that he knew he'd look black and blue when he removed his clothes.

Thorgils scrambled to his feet, nodding eagerly.

Eadmund barely noticed that his companions had hurried away. His attention was instantly consumed by Evaine, who softened her expression when she saw the warmth in his eyes.

'Why don't you come back to bed?' she grumbled softly. 'Surely the worst is over? There is no attack. You should get more rest, ready for if it does come.' Reaching out, she grabbed his hand, trying to pull him towards her.

Eadmund had not slept all night, and he was tempted by the idea of Evaine and bed, but his mind was not on sleep. He shook his head, trying to focus. 'An attack may come at any time. And I can't be in bed when it does. We won't survive Ivaar if we're not prepared. And *I* need to be the most prepared of all.' He resisted Evaine's efforts to change his mind, taking another drink of ale.

'But what can you possibly do if you can't even *see* him?' Evaine insisted. 'He is not in the harbour, and you have men on the ramparts. Why not sleep before dawn comes?'

Eadmund smiled, looking towards the doors. 'I think you'll find that dawn is almost here. Besides, if I get anywhere near that bed with you, I won't be able to sleep at all.'

Evaine's face glowed with pleasure, and she relented, coming to sit beside him instead, leaning her head against his arm, not caring who saw. Eadmund was hers now, and soon everyone on Oss would have to accept it.

Jael Furyck would never return.

Morana had promised her that.

***

'Can you see it?' the voice screeched ecstatically. 'Can you see what is coming for her? And here you are, trapped still. Helpless! Dying! Dead already! Supposed to save her, weren't you? Yet, what can you do when you are *my* prisoner? When she will soon be theirs?'

The laughter was unrelenting. Smug and satisfied.

She could feel it crashing against her, claiming victory.

Against her.

Against Jael.

She had to move. She had to do something because she *had* seen it.

She *had* seen what was coming.

And it was terrifying.

***

Jael was breathless as she pulled on Tig's reins, slowing him down, waiting for Fyn to catch up. 'He rides well,' she nodded at Fyn's horse as he skittered to a stop beside her.

'Probably eager to get away from that place too,' he said, just as breathlessly. 'It doesn't feel right in there.' Fyn glanced around, happy to see the sun beginning its slow rise. The constant storms had rattled him, and he felt on edge. Worried about his mother. Ready to go home.

'You're right,' Jael agreed. 'It's as though they're all afraid of something. Or someone.'

'Maybe that elderman?' Fyn wondered as they let the horses walk towards the sun; a building, yellow glow, spreading above the treeline in the distance.

'He is odd,' Jael agreed, wanting to say more. 'Hiding a lot, I think. They all are. But as long as we find out how to get Eadmund back from Evaine, and a way to save Edela, they can keep all the secrets they like. As soon as we get what we need, we'll head for home. We have to. Eydis had a dream. She thinks Ivaar is about to attack Oss.'

'What?' Fyn looked horrified.

'Don't worry, there are plenty on Oss who know how to deal with Ivaar.'

'Do you trust Eadmund to?'

'Of course, don't you?'

Fyn remembered their escape from Hest. Eadmund had

saved Jael. He had thought quickly and acted decisively. 'I do.'

'Good, because I think that Evaine might have bound his heart, but hopefully, Eadmund can still use his head. And as for us?' She leaned over and patted Tig. 'I think it's been too long since we did any training. They must practise somewhere around here. Let's get Aedan and Aron to show us around after breakfast. It's been a long time since I kicked you in the head!'

'Ha!' Fyn laughed. 'And a long time before you will again!'

Jael grinned, enjoying the silence after such a stormy night. She frowned suddenly, peering around. They were in a flat field and in the distance, on three sides of them, were rows of trees. Forest, everywhere they looked. 'Do you hear that?'

'No. Hear what?'

'Nothing,' Jael said, a shiver shooting down her spine. 'Nothing at all. Listen.'

So, he did.

Fyn couldn't hear any noise at all. No birdsong. No insects buzzing. It was so still that he couldn't even feel a breeze. And as he looked around, he couldn't see any birds either.

Jael stared up at the sky. A blue-grey hue was spreading far above them, but when she squinted, she was sure that it was darkening in the distance now. 'Looks like another storm. And if all the birds have gone, it can't be a good sign. Let's head back.'

Fyn nodded, feeling odd. He patted his blowing horse and nudged his boots into his flanks, following Tig. Turning around, he noticed the clouds in the distance.

They were growing bigger and darker by the moment.

***

Jaeger gripped Meena's hand.

He could tell that she wanted to tap her head with it. Her fingers pulsed against his, desperate to escape his hold. But for all that she didn't want to be there with him, he was glad she was.

They stood in a large circle surrounding a fire that spat and crackled in the middle of them all, belching out strange smelling smoke. One of the Followers walked amongst the stones, beating out a hypnotic rhythm on his drum in time to Morana's chanting. Another two Followers were winding their way through the circle, handing out cups of something to drink.

Jaeger wrinkled his nose as they stopped before him. The woman dipped a cup into the foul-smelling liquid and held it out to him. Taking the cup, he drank quickly, wanting to get it over with.

He tried not to retch.

It was warm and thick and tasted bitter. He was certain it was blood.

But whose?

Handing the cup back to the woman, he was surprised to see that she was not finished. Dipping her thumb into the bowl her companion was holding, she raised it to his forehead, drawing on him in a circular motion. Satisfied with her efforts, she turned to Meena and once again, dipped the cup into the bowl and held it out for her to drink.

Jaeger found himself forgetting about Meena's squirming fingers as he drifted away on a tide of unfamiliar sounds and smells. The Followers who had drunk from the cup began to lie down now, keeping the formation of their circle. No one spoke, and the only voice Jaeger could hear as he lay on the wet grass was the grating cry of Morana as she read from his book.

Jaeger's body was throbbing in anticipation. He tried to join in with the Followers as they echoed Morana's words, but he stumbled over them, struggling with a tongue that grew inside his mouth. The words tangled themselves into knots inside his head.

Eventually, he closed his eyes, losing himself in a cold, rushing wind.

It was as though he was flying.

*****

'We have to go!' Aleksander demanded, wrapping his swordbelt around his waist.

Axl, his eyes barely open, was not moving, and because he was gripping Amma's hand, she was not moving either. 'But we have to wait for Gant.'

'We have to go to Tuura now!' Aleksander urged, kicking dirt over the last embers of the fire. 'We have to find horses, leave a message for Gant. We have to go!'

'Aleksander!' Axl called, sitting up, trying to get his attention. 'You can't expect us to follow you without telling us anything! Why would we go to Tuura when I'm going to be the King of Brekka? We need to wait here!'

Amma was worried. Aleksander looked so shaken. His frown was deep, and his eyes were troubled, jumping about with urgency. 'Tell us, Aleksander. What has happened? Why do you want to go to Tuura?'

*****

'Where do you suppose Jael has gotten to?' Branwyn wondered, pacing around the house, picking up the extra bedding, eager to put things into some order. Despite Entorp and Fyn being sequestered with Aedan and Aron, there was still barely enough room to move.

There was a knock at the door, and Kormac, who was just about to go and see to the animals, opened it with a smile, ushering Entorp inside. 'Everyone's up early,' he noted, ducking through the door, glancing up at the sky. 'Looks like another storm soon. Not sure our roof can take many more nights like last night. I'd be surprised if we have any thatch left soon!'

'It *was* a bad night,' Entorp agreed, removing his cloak. 'I don't think any of us slept much at all. Your granddaughter was quite disturbed. And young Fyn headed off while it was still dark.'

Gisila frowned as she combed Eydis' hair. 'Well, hopefully, he's with Jael. This is not the sort of place you'd want to get lost. Not anymore.'

Branwyn sighed 'I agree. Especially after what they tried to do to poor Aleksander. It makes you wonder what is really going on here. There is so much we don't know.'

Entorp sat down on Edela's bed, patting the puppies who were sniffing him for food, eager for their breakfast which nobody was attending to.

He froze.

'What is it?' Branwyn asked.

'Did you see that?' Entorp breathed. 'I think she moved.' His eyes didn't leave Edela's face as he reached for her wrist, feeling for a pulse.

'Did she?' Gisila asked eagerly, rushing to join him at her mother's bedside.

Branwyn frowned. She hadn't seen anything, but she was desperate to believe that something had changed.

That there was some hope.

***

There was a door.

She could see a light; soft, glowing, yellow flames that promised hope.

But so faint. Or perhaps that was just her?

But there was a door.

And she could see a light.

And on the other side of that door was Jael.

And Jael was in danger. Now!

Jael was in danger now!

***

Jael rode fast, frozen by the wind; by the sudden absence of any sun and warmth. It was as though the entire sky was falling on top of them, suffocating them with thick, icy clouds.

She glanced at Fyn. He looked as troubled as she felt. They were both eager to get back to the fort, as strange as that thought sounded to her own ears.

She bent lower over Tig, dropping her head, urging him on.

They could see the gates now.

***

Marcus strode towards the temple doors.

Something was wrong.

The temple was usually filled with a steady stream of hushed murmuring. The elders and dreamers whispered as they walked, talked, and worked. But there was nothing to be heard this morning.

Not a breath. Just silence.

Marcus had lain awake for much of the night, his mind anxious, his body jumping. Storms weren't new, of course, but it was the middle of spring, and he would have expected to see less of them, not more.

Not this many.

Not this violent.

He grimaced as one of his senior elders walked in front of the high doors, a temple guard on either side of him.

Marcus frowned but kept walking.

'My lord,' Gerod Gott said loudly, holding his hand out as Marcus reached past him for the door. 'I would advise you to stay inside this morning. Another storm is coming. And fast.'

Marcus was disturbed by the peculiar look in Gerod's unsettling blue eyes. 'Is that so? Another storm? Well, perhaps I should see how everyone fares in the fort? It's important they're all safe, wouldn't you say?'

Gerod didn't move. He didn't blink. 'Of course, my lord, and I can send someone out to do just that, but first I must ensure that you, as the elderman, are safe from what is coming. It's best that you go with the guards, back to your chamber.'

Marcus turned as another guard came up behind him, and then another.

He stepped away from the doors, dropping his shoulders as the guards grabbed hold of him.

***

'But it was just a bad dream, a nightmare, surely?' Axl insisted.

Aleksander shook his head impatiently. He knew what had happened. He was certain he did. It didn't feel like a dream.

She had come to him.

He shook all over. 'We have to go!'

Axl stepped forward, ready to continue the argument when his mouth fell open. 'What... is... that?' he asked slowly.

Aleksander spun around, his own mouth dropping open in shock.

***

Jael.

Jael.

She had to save Jael.

***

Fyn's eyes widened in horror. 'Jael!' he screamed.

Jael looked around at the sky that was black now; at the storm clouds that were chasing them.

They weren't storm clouds.

Jael jabbed her boots into Tig's flanks as hard as she could, dropping her head even further down his neck. She kicked him again, and he got the message, spurring on with an angry fury, understanding her panic now. He could feel it too. He galloped, his muscles straining, Jael's voice loud in his ear. 'Go, go, go Tig! Go!'

She didn't turn to look at Fyn as she rode past him, feeling Tig thundering powerfully beneath her, his hooves pounding into the soft ground, mud flying everywhere.

Aiming for the gates.

They had to make it to the gates.

***

Eydis stumbled, falling to the floor.

She had stood up as everyone hurried to Edela's bedside, but now she was suddenly overwhelmed by a furious noise; a terrifying screeching that made her put her hands over her ears. It was a desperate cry that no one else seemed to hear.

Kneeling on the floor, Eydis closed her eyes. Her heart was racing, her body shaking. And taking a deep breath to calm herself down, she slipped away.

***

Axl and Aleksander turned back to Amma, throwing her to the ground, Axl's hand over her mouth, muffling her screams.

It was suddenly dark.

So dark.

And that noise?

What was happening?

***

'Edela?' Biddy asked, gripping her hand. She had been up early, milking the goats, trying to be useful. 'Edela?' Entorp had told her that Edela might have moved, and she was disappointed to see that nothing appeared to have changed at all.

Glancing around, she noticed Eydis sitting on the floor, her eyes closed, her hands over her ears. 'Eydis?' Biddy frowned.

'Are you alright?'

'Edela?' Entorp murmured, studying her face closely.

Edela's eyes flickered. 'Jael.'

It was so faint, more of a croak than anything, but they could all hear the urgency in that familiar voice.

'Jael!'

CHAPTER TWENTY ONE

'Open the gates! Open the gates!' Jael screamed, her eyes wide with the fear of what was about to descend upon them.

They could hear it now. Feel it too.

A violent, surging, rushing wave of terror; so close it was almost breathing on them.

'Open the gates!' Fyn screamed with her, his eyes bursting with panic, his voice breaking. 'Open the fucking gates!'

The guards on the ramparts turned at the sound of the panicked voices, their mouths hanging open, their eyes as round as plates. 'Open the gates! Open the gates!' they bellowed down to the men who waited below. 'Hurry!'

The gates opened too slowly for Jael and Fyn's liking. They each had to pull on their reins, skidding their panicked horses as they slipped through the narrow gap that was slowly forming between each gate.

'Close them! Quick!' Jael yelled, riding Tig down the busy main street. 'Get into your houses! Get into your houses now! Shut your doors!' she cried, galloping towards Branwyn and Kormac's house, Fyn close behind her. 'Get into your houses! Hurry!'

***

Kormac looked up.

Gisila frowned, glancing at Biddy, her heart quickening. 'Jael?'

Branwyn was at the door quickly, pulling it open.

'Jael!' Edela opened her eyes, her body shaking with terror. 'Hurry!'

Jael slid off Tig at the door, dragging him into the house past a dumbstruck Branwyn. Fyn pulled Aron's terrified horse in after them.

'Shut the door!' she screamed. Then it hit. 'Get down!' Running to Eydis, Jael knocked her to the floor, pushing her under the bed. 'Kormac! Cover the window!'

The house was quickly filled with the frenzied whinnying of horses, skittering in terror, and then the thunderous battering against the walls; the solitary window shattering before Kormac could get to it as a swarm of ravens flew inside.

Branwyn shrieked, dropping to her knees, covering her head.

'Fyn! Hold the horses! We need to get Edela under the bed!' Jael cried.

Fyn grabbed both sets of reins, pulling them tightly against his chest as the horses panicked.

As he panicked in between them.

Entorp dug his hands under Edela, scooping her into his arms, trying to shield her from the swarming birds. Jael was there quickly with Biddy, helping him to ease Edela under the bed as the birds flapped their wings into their faces, claws out, black beaks stabbing them.

'Aarrghh!' Biddy yelped as the ravens tore at her arms.

'Biddy, get under the bed!' Jael ordered, pushing her down next to Edela.

The puppies raced under the nearest bed as the birds flew around the house, gurgling and croaking, threatening them all.

'Mother! Branwyn! Get under the beds!' Jael shouted over the noise, hurrying to help Kormac lift the table; turning it upright and shoving it against the broken window, blocking any more birds from rushing inside. 'Aarrghh!' A beak snapped at her arm, straight through her tunic, ripping her flesh. Drawing *Toothpick*, Jael spun, slashing the air, trying to kill the fast-moving birds; jumping back as they turned to dive and attack her again. Kormac dropped to the floor, crawling quickly, searching for his swordbelt.

It was so dark now. The birds had covered the smoke hole.

The puppies howled. The horses tried to rear up on their legs at every painful nip as the birds shrilled, smelling blood, eager for more.

Toothpick in hand, Jael kept turning, killing the ravens as they swarmed around her face, biting and scratching at her arms and legs. Kormac found his eating knife and stabbed the last few.

And the house shook.

'What is *happening*?' Branwyn wailed from under the bed where she lay next to Gisila.

'The book, Jael. Get the book.'

It was so faint, but Jael knew that voice. She spun around. 'Grandmother?' Her arms were bleeding. There was a deep scratch across her cheek. Blood was pouring down, into her mouth. Her tunic was in tatters, but for one moment nothing else mattered. *'Grandmother?'*

'Jael. Get the book. Hurry!'

***

Jaeger could see. He could feel. He was there, soaring with the ravens. Watching as they devastated Tuura.

As they tracked Jael Furyck.

He could feel himself smiling; his lips wet with anticipation for her blood.

They would gut her.

But they had to keep going. They could not stop. Not until she was dead. Until they all were. He could feel the rumble of the chant growing inside him like building flames. It was in him, twisting inside his body.

He was in the book.

The book would strike down every one of his enemies.

Soon, he would find where Axl Furyck and his bitch wife were hiding and kill them too.

***

The noise as the birds smashed themselves against the house had them all jumping and shaking. They may have killed the ones inside, but it sounded as though an army of ravens was trying to get in.

'Shields?' Jael asked desperately, glancing around in the near darkness. 'Entorp, hold the horses! Fyn and I have to go!'

'What?' Gisila was horrified.

'Mother, keep Eydis close.' Jael glanced down at Eydis, who she could see shaking under the bed.

Fyn gave the reins to Entorp, while Kormac hurried to find something to use as shields.

Jael looked up. 'They might come down the smoke hole! Biddy, grab some furs. Cover the horses! Cover yourselves! Use anything you can! Buckets! Cauldrons! Cover your heads! And stay under the beds!'

Kormac hurried back from the storage room with two large, wooden lids. 'It's the best I can do,' he said regretfully, looking up as the house became even darker.

Jael took a lid, glancing quickly at her grandmother. 'Keep

Edela safe!' she cried. 'Come on, Fyn!' And with one last look at Kormac, she ran for the door.

'Jael!' Gisila screamed, watching her daughter disappear. 'Where are you going?'

***

The birds surged past the cave in endless waves of shining, black feathers.

Aleksander and Axl lay with their heads pressed against the dirt, watching them, hoping they would keep going, continuing north.

Amma kept her eyes closed, shuddering at the terrifying sound, gripping Axl's hand. She had a mouthful of dust and blood, having bitten her tongue when they'd thrown her to the ground.

She was so scared; she could barely breathe.

But then she sneezed.

Amma's eyes widened in terror as she tried to bury her head.

But even in the furore of the bird's migration, heads turned, bodies changed course, and some of the ravens broke away, swarming towards the cave.

More following.

Axl and Aleksander scrambled to their feet, unsheathing their swords, wishing they had shields.

'Stay behind us, Amma!' Axl yelled.

***

Jael ran out into the street, Fyn right behind her.

It was as dark as night. The ravens covered the sky like storm clouds, their black wings flapping with urgency as they swooped down, attacking the helpless Tuurans who had not made it inside in time.

Jael and Fyn had a wooden lid each, protecting their heads, but the ravens swooped towards them anyway, claws out, ripping their clothing, piercing their skin. Ducking their heads, they batted away the birds, running for the stables as fast as they could.

***

Kormac wished he could reach the smoke hole and block it with a lid but it was too high, and the table was over the window, keeping the ravens out. Although, as he looked towards it, he saw it starting to move; jerking about as the birds hammered on it from the other side.

Entorp stood between the horses, pulling the reins as close to his chest as he could, soothing them as if they were children.

'Eydis,' Edela breathed, worried that she would lose consciousness at any moment. 'Find the page, Eydis. Find the page.'

Biddy had no idea what she was talking about as they sheltered under the beds, listening to the violent battering outside the house.

But Eydis did.

***

'Aarrghh!' Fyn roared as a bird gouged his arm. He shook the flapping creature away, smashing his lid across its back. And then another.

'Beorn! Open the door!' Jael cried, pounding on the stable doors. 'Quick!'

The birds saw them and funnelled into a speeding mass of glistening, black feathers, pointing towards Jael and Fyn. Jael took one look at them and kicked the door open. Fyn ran in behind her, and together they slammed the stable door shut as the birds clattered angrily against it.

'Hold it! Hold that door, Fyn! Help him!' she yelled to Beorn and her men as she ran to the back of the stables, past the terrified horses and the crouching, shaking Tuurans who were sheltering there.

To the room.

Marcus' secret room.

It was locked.

Dropping her sword and lid, Jael dug into her pouch, fumbling, her hands slippery with blood.

She found the key and quickly jiggled it in the lock.

Racing into the pitch-black room, Jael skidded onto her knees in front of the chest, feeling around for the lock. Slotting in the key, she turned it, pushed open the lid, grabbed the book, and ran.

***

Morana was not in Hest anymore.

She was in Tuura, and she could see Jael Furyck, and Jael Furyck was running for her life, that stupid boy beside her.

Morana swooped in, feeling the power of her expansive wings, the iron tang of blood in her mouth. She dove straight towards Jael's neck, but Jael turned just before she reached the door, whipping her wooden lid across the raven's throat with all the strength she had.

The bird screeched in pain, stunned, falling to the ground, blood coursing down its chest; its friends swarming over Jael and Fyn, snapping their beaks as they pulled open the door, quickly slamming it shut behind them.

Morana was back in Hest, cursing and screaming, losing her hold on the raven as it stilled, dying and useless. She lay there on the dewy grass, looking from side to side, smiling again as she watched everyone around her, lost in the trance.

Taking a deep breath, she lay her head back, closed her eyes and started chanting again.

***

The shadows flickered ominously back and forth across the smoke hole.

Gisila closed her eyes, gripping Eydis' hand, holding a shaking Vella in her other arm, reminded of what had happened the last time someone hid under a bed in Tuura.

Eydis could hear Vella whimpering, she could feel Ido shaking as she pulled him to her chest, but it was all so far away. She wasn't really there at all.

The door flung open, then quickly closed, the horses rising up on their hind-legs, whinnying loudly, knocking against the rafters, but Eydis was not there. She was in another place altogether, looking through the book.

She could see each page: the symbols, instructions, lists of ingredients, corrections, notes. It was a thick fog of a daydream, but she found herself lingering on one page, her eyes popping open.

But there was only darkness.

Then the ravens came rushing down the smoke hole.

***

'Shit!' Axl yelled as a raven flew past his sword, snapping at his face. He stepped back and swung around, slashing through the air, but there were so many birds in the cave now, their wings beating loudly, their shrill cries bouncing off the walls like knives.

Black feathers everywhere.

Amma shrieked as a beak pierced her arm.

Axl sliced his sword across its back, glancing at Aleksander. His face was covered in blood, his hands dripping red as he tried to fight them off with a sword and a spear. But it looked hopeless.

More and more birds were streaming into the cave.

They were completely overwhelmed.

***

'Jael!' Eydis screamed as the ravens surged down the smoke hole, filling the house. 'Jael!' Eydis screamed over the terror of the horses and the plaintive wails of Ido. 'Page nine!'

Jael gave Entorp her lid, leaving him and Fyn to protect the horses as she slid under the bed next to Eydis, Marcus' book in her hands. Flicking through the pages, she panted, counting each one until she reached the ninth. 'I can't read it!' It was dark, but she could see well enough to know that she didn't understand the words on the page.

Kormac wriggled out from under the opposite bed and ran to Jael, yelping as he was attacked. 'Here!' he cried, wiping blood out of his eyes. 'Give it to me!' He snatched the book and slid under the bed beside Jael.

The swarming ravens had shut off most of the light, so Kormac had to squint, running his finger under the scrawled words. 'Blood!' he cried at last. 'You have to draw this symbol in blood!' He looked at Jael. 'A dreamer's blood! Your blood! Then you need to say these words!'

Jael reached up to her arm, dipping a finger into one of her many wounds. 'Show me!'

Kormac pushed the book towards her and Jael cleared a spot on the floorboards in front of her, cringing as Tig roared. She knew that sound. He was getting hurt. Both horses were.

She heard the puppies wailing; Entorp screaming out in agony.

Fyn groaning as he tried to protect the horses.

Jael leaned forward, drawing the symbol. 'Tell me the words! What do I say?'

***

'No!' Morana screeched, watching in horror as Jael Furyck started to draw the symbol. 'Stop her! Stop her!'

Meena blinked, trying to pull herself out of the trance but her mind was so hazy. She felt as though she was flying, lost amongst the blur of black wings, following as the ravens dived at the horses, gouging their flesh, hurting them.

Trying to get under the beds.

They wanted to destroy them all. She could feel it.

But most of all, they wanted to kill Jael Furyck.

To stop her.

But Jael Furyck had her own book, and she was going to stop them.

Meena smiled.

***

Jael drew the symbol, repeating the words after Kormac, certain that hers didn't sound anything like his. But slowly growing more confident, she started bellowing them out. And when the symbol was finished, she screamed them out one last time.

The storm of ravens clattered to the floor all around them.

And then silence.

'Tig!' Jael was scrambling out from under the bed, rushing for the horses. Tig was covered with gaping, bleeding holes. Aron's horse looked much the same.

Fyn's arms were a mess, as were Entorp's. Both of them leaned over, panting, their faces contorted in pain.

Kormac squeezed out from under the bed, his frame almost too big to fit into such a narrow space. He pulled Branwyn out after him.

'The boys! The baby!' Branwyn screamed frantically. 'Please! Go!'

Taking one look at his tearful wife, Kormac hunted around for a lid and his sword.

Jael grabbed the other lid and turned to Fyn. 'Let's go!' She glanced at Biddy, who was hurrying to her feet. 'Lock the door. We'll be back as soon as we can. Don't let anyone in!'

'Jael!' Branwyn called. 'Find Alaric too, and Derwa! Bring them here!'

Jael nodded, running after Kormac and Fyn.

***

'What is *happening*?' Jaeger shouted, sitting up in frustration, shocked at how light it was. How long had they been lying there? His back was wet through, his head muddled, his throat so dry that he could barely form the angry words he was so desperate to spit at Morana, who sat up next to him, still gripping his hand.

He yanked it away from her.

'She has a book,' Morana panted, her head swimming with the memory of it.

'*What* book?' Jaeger seethed. 'A more important book than my book? Than *the* book?'

Yorik was up now, stretching his back, his brow furrowed as he held out a hand to Morana, his eyes sharp on Jaeger, not appreciating his vicious tone. Yorik was a measured man. A man who understood that setbacks would happen. But ultimately he knew that they would reach their goal if they were patient enough. 'She has a book that can help her, yes. But we can get that book and besides, it was her brother you wanted more, wasn't it?' He thought quickly, trying to placate Jaeger, to shift his focus away from their failure, towards a new hope.

They needed him. And while it wasn't entirely necessary, it would be easier if he was a willing participant.

Jaeger's head started clearing in the light breeze, his disappointment turning into urgency. He wanted more. He wanted to cause more destruction, more pain, and this time, death. 'Axl Furyck,' he said quietly, watching as the men and women in the circle started pulling each other up, blinking in the morning light. 'Axl Furyck doesn't have a book, does he?'

'I don't imagine so,' Morana growled. 'And even if he does, he is no dreamer. It would do him no good to read a spell.'

Jaeger frowned as he stood, leaving Meena alone on the

sodden ground. 'Good, then you must find him again. And quickly.'

Meena swallowed, wishing that she was back in her little chamber. All alone.

Safe from them all.

***

They were too stunned to move.

Shuddering, breathless, confused; worried that the birds would come back to life somehow and attack them again.

Amma burst into tears as Axl pulled her close.

'I'm sorry,' she sobbed, her face pressed into his torn tunic; blood splattered tatters barely covering his wounds. 'I'm sorry.'

'Sssshhh,' Axl said distractedly, not knowing what to think. He glanced at Aleksander whose eyes did not leave the birds.

'We have to leave,' Aleksander said mutely, crouching down, checking the ravens. They were dead. Definitely dead. 'We have to go to Tuura. They were flying north.' He wiped blood out of his eyes, looking hopefully at Axl and Amma.

And this time, they nodded in agreement.

CHAPTER TWENTY TWO

Kormac pounded on the battered door, his heartbeat loud in his ears. 'Aedan! Aron!' he cried anxiously as Jael and Fyn stood behind him, checking the dead ravens for any sign of movement. 'Kayla?'

The ravens lay motionless all over the street.

Beaks open. Eyes glazed over.

Jael shook her head, turning back to the door as Aedan opened it, throwing his arms around his father, shock all over his bleeding face.

'Are you alright?' Jael asked quickly as they hurried inside, shutting the door behind them, glancing around at the dead birds, the broken furniture, the floor littered with feathers.

Aedan's wife, Kayla, was sobbing as she held their tiny daughter in her arms, tears streaming down both their faces. Aron hurried to his father, sword in hand, his tunic hanging in ribbons from his shoulders.

'Your mother wants you back at the house. It's best if we're all together for now,' Jael said.

Kormac nodded. 'Bring your weapons, boys, and let's get to the smithy. We need some shields.'

'I have to find Alaric and Derwa,' Jael said, cringing as the shock receded and the pain of her wounds started to bite. She stung all over. 'We need to bring them to the house too. Edela has woken up.'

'Has she?' Aron was amazed. 'I'll take you to them.'

Kayla sobbed, not ready to move at all. Kormac put an arm around her shaking shoulders, pushing her gently towards the door. 'Let's get you to Branwyn,' he said kindly. 'We need to look at those cuts. I've a feeling Entorp is going to be very busy with his salves.'

Jael ducked through the door after her cousin and Fyn. 'I'll meet you back at the house. But don't be long. We don't know what else is coming. And we need to block up the smoke hole...' Jael left that hanging in the air, suddenly distracted by the book.

She had to get it back to the secret room quickly.

***

Entorp had dragged the horses out of the house. They were unsure whether they were more unhappy inside or out, but nobody could move with them shuffling about, and the stench of fresh manure was unbearable. He secured them to the rail outside the door, then hurried inside to carry Edela back to her bed.

The puppies shook uncontrollably, not entertaining the thought of coming out from under the bed at all. Branwyn decided that it was the best place for them as she started sweeping the bird carcasses towards the door, eager to get them out of the house.

There were black, shining feathers everywhere.

Dead-eyed birds staring up at her.

Blood already drying on the floorboards.

Branwyn shuddered, leaning the broom against the wall, checking on Eydis again. 'Are you sure you wouldn't like to lie down?' she asked.

Eydis shook her head, happy with her stool next to Edela's

bed.

'Here,' Biddy said as she tried to make Edela more comfortable. 'Let me prop you up a bit.'

Edela hadn't said a thing; not one word since the birds had died and Jael had left, but her eyes fluttered open occasionally, and they all felt encouraged by that.

'We need to get the fire going,' Biddy realised, trying to strengthen her voice. She couldn't stop shaking, worrying about Edela, Jael, Eydis, the horses who were bleeding, covered in holes, the puppies...

And then her mind jumped to Axl, Aleksander, and Amma. What if this had not just happened in Tuura? What if the whole of Osterland had been attacked?

There was a furious rapping on the door, and everyone froze.

***

Alaric's teeth were chattering. He didn't have many left, but he could hear them banging against each other, rattling in time with his creaking bones as he walked. 'But what *was* that?' he asked again, his eyes darting about, searching the street, checking the birds, making sure they weren't moving. 'Who d-d-did this? *How*?'

Jael wasn't listening, though, as she hurried him along, her hand under his arm. Fyn and Aron were helping Derwa on her other side.

The streets were littered with bodies; face up, eyes gouged out.

Animals too.

Both Alaric and Derwa had been in their cottages when it had happened, and they were able to quickly slip under their beds, covering themselves in furs until the terrifying ordeal was over.

Derwa couldn't catch her breath as Fyn helped her through Branwyn's door. 'It's a bad sign,' she said ominously. 'A sign of things to come. Terrifying things. Such things have happened before, but not for a long, long time.'

Jael had her mind on the horses, worried about some of the wounds she'd seen on their hind-legs, and she wasn't paying attention as she pushed Alaric inside.

She froze.

'They want the book,' Branwyn said tightly, her arm around Eydis.

Three temple guards stood there in dark-red tunics. Their faces were stern, their eyes emotionless; surprisingly unaffected by what had just occurred.

'Your aunt is right,' growled the tallest one, stepping forward. 'And you will show us where it is. Now.'

'Book?' Jael shrugged. 'What book is that?' Loosening her shoulders, she readjusted her cloak, exposing *Toothpick's* moonstone pommel. Jael gripped it firmly, her eyes on the guard.

She felt Fyn tense before her, Aron on his right.

'You know exactly what book. Now, give it to me,' the guard ordered, glaring at her.

Jael was unmoved. 'I would think that when addressing a queen, you might try a different tack,' she said coldly. 'But then again, I suppose Tuura is not a place known for its manners. Men here tend to take without asking.'

The guard rose up on the balls of his feet, narrowing his gaze until his eyes almost disappeared. He was a tall man, taller than Jael, and he used every bit of height he had to try and dominate her. 'From thieves, yes.'

'*Thieves?*' Jael's expression didn't alter. 'I have no idea what you're talking about.'

The guards fingered their own swords.

No one moved.

'Perhaps, my lady, it is best if you come along with me. As my guards have said, there is the matter of the book, and what may have happened to it. If you would accompany me to the temple, we can discuss it there.'

Jael spun around, surprised to see Marcus standing in the doorway, ashen-faced but calm, his small, hooded eyes unblinking. He swallowed, and Jael could see the tension in his body reveal itself.

'Of course,' Jael said coolly. 'Since you ask so *nicely*.'

And without looking back, she turned and followed him through the door.

***

A decision had to be made.

Eadmund clenched his jaw, still indecisive, but not wanting to appear so. He could see them all staring at him as he sat on his father's throne.

His throne now.

It hadn't been long since he'd been unable to even wake this early in the day, let alone sit before a hall full of men and women who were looking to him for leadership.

Everyone knew that Ivaar was coming now. But when and where and how?

A decision had to be made.

'Ivaar would not go to Tatti's Bay,' Eadmund decided, at last, sharpening his focus as he watched Thorgils pull Isaura closer. 'Not yet.'

Bram nodded in agreement.

'If he's gone anywhere, he's gone around the headland, past Hud's Point, or to Bara, which means that wherever he is, he's not far away. If he's joined with these Arnessons, maybe they'll have six ships, maybe seven or eight. But they won't go to Tatti's Bay. Sevrin, send someone to the bay. Bring those men back fast. We can rebuild our ships but if we don't hold the fort...' That hadn't reassured anyone, he realised, pushing himself upright. 'We will hold the fort!' he insisted.

'And what of the queen, my lord?' Otto grumbled, his weathered face anxious. 'Can we not send to Tuura for her help?'

Eadmund was surprised to see that he appeared serious, ignoring the rise of Thorgils' furry eyebrows that such a suggestion was coming out of Otto's mouth. He felt an uncomfortable warmth on his cheeks as everyone stared at him, watching as Evaine's pink lips pursed irritably at just the mention of his wife's name. 'No...' He shook his head, arguing with himself. 'No,' he said again. 'We can't afford to lose a crew now. We need all the men we have. Besides,' he continued, trying to embellish his excuse, 'we'd have to send a ship south, around the islands. It would be too risky to head past Bara. There's no time to get Jael or the lords. They need to stay and protect the islands. '

Evaine smiled triumphantly.

She sat next to Eadmund in Eydis' small chair. She had organised a new one to be built for herself, but with all the disruption, and now, the threat of an attack, no one was doing anything except preparing the fort.

The hall fell silent.

The Osslanders were standing and watching Eadmund, desperate for answers; not satisfied with any he had provided so far.

'We'll have more men than Ivaar!' Eadmund rose, strengthening his voice, carrying it to the far reaches of the hall; to those dark, smoky corners where the dissenters and grumblers like to moan and gossip. 'This is not *his* island, not *his* home! We will not let Oss fall! We need more arrows! We must bring everything into the fort to help us survive a siege. To protect all that we have. Do it now! Sharpen your weapons and keep your eyes open. If you find a weak spot, or a problem, bring it to my attention. We must pull together, and all do our part to keep Ivaar and his men at bay!'

There were murmurs of agreement, a few nodding heads, but a lot of worry and fear, Eadmund saw, as everyone gradually dispersed. Frowning, he walked over to Thorgils, Bram, and Isaura. 'Anything from the dreamer?'

Isaura shook her head. 'No. Ayla is still weak from her injury. Her husband is very ill too. Ivaar had him in one of the prison holes for over a year.'

'Well, do what you can to help him,' Eadmund said distractedly. 'And how is Odda?' he asked, turning to Thorgils, whose eyes were on Evaine as she perched regally upon Eydis' chair.

Thorgils blinked. 'Odda is near death, I'd say.' He coughed, glancing at his boots. 'She has not woken for some time apparently.'

Eadmund tried to look sympathetic, though he wondered how anyone could love Odda. She had not said a kind word to Thorgils that he knew of. He thought of his own mother, at the pain of her death, and the emptiness he still felt. 'You should go and be with her.'

Thorgils shook his head dismissively. 'Runa is there, and I can do more than sit and wait for her to die.' It was hard to say, but true. 'Ivaar's coming. And unless Ayla tells us differently, we're going to be in one big shit-heap of trouble soon.'

Eadmund swallowed. He had wanted this. He had wanted Ivaar to come so that he could finish his brother and savour his revenge. But now?

Now, it felt like a petty, childish wish.

Now, he had a kingdom to protect.

***

Jael sat opposite Marcus.

His fireplace contained a heap of ash, and his chamber was so cold that she could see her breath coming in short, white puffs before her.

He didn't appear to notice.

'It has come to my attention that you have stolen a book from me.'

'So your men said.' Jael saw signs of discomfort in his eyes; almost terror. He was trying to mask it so desperately. 'But I do not have the book.'

'There is no point in lying. You will only make it worse. My dreamers will find it.'

'They're welcome to try,' Jael said calmly. 'But I do not have it. I did... find a book, yes... and it proved useful, but I no longer have it. It was lost during the raven attack. I'm afraid I can't help you any further.'

Marcus looked relieved. 'Well, my men will keep looking and if they find out that you have hidden it...'

'What? They will kill a queen?'

'A queen? How are you a queen anymore?' Marcus mocked. 'There is another woman sitting beside your husband now. Sleeping in his bed. How are you the Queen of Oss? You're not even there when they need you the most.'

Jael swallowed, sick to her stomach. Her whole body was punctured and blood-crusted; her worries about Edela, Eydis, and Tig were fighting for her attention and now... 'What are you talking about?'

'Well, now that your grandmother is awake, perhaps she will tell you?' Marcus sneered, standing up, eager to end things, hoping his performance would please the dreamers watching him.

'You mean Ivaar?' Jael asked as she stood. 'Ivaar Skalleson?'

'I couldn't say,' Marcus said, meeting her eyes. 'Best you ask a dreamer. Although, I had heard it rumoured that *you* were one now. But, then again, what use is a dreamer if she can't see what is coming to her own door?' He stared at her with every bit of will he had.

Jael saw what she needed and dropped her head, allowing herself to be ushered outside before the door was banged shut against her bleeding shoulder.

She stood in the cold, dark corridor shivering.

He had warned her.

Oss was in serious trouble.

***

Borg Arnesson looked ready to kill Ivaar as they stood in the rain outside the hall. 'You promised us gold, bastard!' he snorted, pushing Ivaar away from him. 'Gold and blood! Yet, I have no gold, and I've spilled no one's blood! But somehow now, as I stand here in your stinking presence, I'm one ship lighter, having just sacrificed thirty men for Ilvari's supper! So, tell me, Ivaar the Bastard, what are you going to do about that, you feckless cunt?'

Ivaar didn't flinch, ignoring the sour taste of Borg's spittle as it showered over him. Borg Arnesson was smaller than Ivaar but tougher than most men he had met. The sort of man who was wound so tightly that he was ready to kill over the smallest slight. The Arnesson brothers' reputation put the fear of the gods into most clear-thinking men.

But Ivaar had been desperate.

Too desperate to make a better choice.

'And I had been promised fast ships, with the hardest

seamen in Alekka. Yet, here I stand, without my wife and children, far away from my brother and any gold I may have wished to give you!'

Lord Frits of Bara hurried in between the two men, nervously poking his silver-ringed fingers at both of them. 'We are not going to help ourselves or each other if we spend all our breath on arguing!' he grumbled. 'Let's go inside and make our plans. The only way we're all going to get what we want is to find a way forward. In the same direction. And after that storm, I'm sure you could all do with a warm fire?'

Borg and his younger brothers, Toki and Rolan, eyed Ivaar with menace as they turned and followed Frits into his very modest hall.

Ivaar grimaced, watching them go, wondering again at the wisdom of forging an alliance with a trio of turds like the Arnessons. A man's reputation was everything in the islands. But in Alekka and beyond, the Arnessons had no shame in boasting of themselves as weasly thieves, desperate liars, and cold-blooded murderers.

But for Ivaar, they were the only hope he had.

***

'Jael!' Biddy looked relieved as she hurried to the door, helping Jael off with her cloak. It was torn, ripped, bloodstained, and shat on, but Jael couldn't have cared less as she hurried to the bed and her grandmother.

'Are you really back?' Jael smiled, tears in her eyes, clasping Edela's hand. 'It wasn't just a dream?'

Edela was so weak. She couldn't lift her head or even her own hand. But she could almost smile, and she did. 'Jael.' She closed her eyes, the smile still on her face. 'Jael.'

It was just a breath, disappearing into nothing but Jael felt such a lift to hear that voice again. She looked around at everyone, checking their wounds, of which there were many. But none appeared too serious.

Entorp had his jars of salve out and was going from one person to the next, smothering them in foul odours.

Jael wrinkled her nose, gagging. 'You are not coming near me!' she grumbled as he approached. 'Maybe you should take that outside to the poor horses?'

Entorp nodded. 'I've seen to them already, although some of their wounds are deep, but Biddy will help me sew them up soon, don't worry.'

Jael felt anxious for Tig, guilty for bringing him along, but doubting that he would have been any safer with Evaine. She looked around for the puppies who were still cowering under the bed. 'Ido, Vella,' she called gently, but they didn't emerge. 'Come on, now.' Jael crawled under the bed, pulling out one at a time. She placed Vella on the bed next to Edela and plonked Ido on her knee, holding his shuddering, black body close to her own.

'What happened with Marcus?' Branwyn wondered, handing around cups of small ale. 'About the book?'

'What book?' Jael asked, her face blank.

Branwyn blinked, confused, looking at Kormac.

'Yes, my love,' he said to his wife. 'What book do you mean?' Kormac knew as well as Jael that the only way those soldiers and the elderman could have been at their door so quickly, looking for that book, was if they were watching somehow.

And if they were watching then, they were certainly watching now.

'The elderman tells me there is trouble on Oss,' Jael said, gripping Eydis' hand.

Eydis gasped. 'Ivaar.'

'I imagine so.'

Gisila looked impatient and confused, not wanting to talk

about Oss at all; not understanding why they were. 'But what just happened?' She glanced around. Her mother appeared to be asleep again. 'Where did all those ravens come from? And why did they attack us?'

The house was so full. Aron and Aedan were slumped on the floor. Alaric and Derwa had stayed and were perched on stools by the fire. Biddy was helping Entorp administer his salves. Fyn hovered by the door near Kayla who cradled her sleeping daughter in her arms.

They all looked at Jael.

There was not a lot she could say. She had Marcus in her mind.

And the book.

Would the dreamers find where she had put it?

'I don't know,' she muttered, shaking her head. 'I don't know. But they're gone now, and we must focus on what we can do to protect ourselves if it happens again. If it's not more birds, then perhaps it will be something else.'

'Something else?' Alaric panicked, quickly finishing off his small ale. 'What sort of something else?'

Jael wasn't listening, though, as they all started talking over one another, desperate to have their ideas heard, their worries answered. She turned to Edela, thinking back to what had just happened. It flashed in front of her eyes in a wash of black noise.

But one thing jumped out of the blur.

Edela had saved her, as they said she would.

Smiling, Jael leaned over and kissed her grandmother's head. Now, she just had to get them out of here and back to Oss in time to save Eadmund.

***

'They will find the book,' Yorik assured Morana as she stooped before the fire in her chamber, angry and defeated.

She spun around, her eyes flaring. 'And why do you have so much trust that they can do *anything*?'

Yorik was unflustered. 'Because Gerod knows everything that happens in Tuura. He has assumed control now. Marcus?' he smiled. 'There is nothing he can do now. He is merely a figurehead. Gerod runs those soldiers. They are all bound to him. They do his bidding. As are any dreamers who are not already in The Following,' Yorik insisted, attempting to smooth down Morana's hair, hoping to get her to stop fidgeting and spitting. 'They are all there to do Gerod's bidding. You have nothing to worry about. That book will be found.'

Morana's body did not soften in the slightest. Tension made her so rigid that she felt as though her limbs could snap into jagged shards of bone. She gritted her teeth, closing her eyes. 'Jaeger is hungry for more.'

'He is, of course,' Yorik sighed, pushing her gently towards her bed. 'He does not know what we need from the book. What we need from him. That is what you must focus on. Finding the answers to the ritual spell. Making sense of it somehow. These distractions with Jaeger are not helpful, but if you can find Axl Furyck again, that will keep him amused, I'm sure. You must sleep and dream now. We cannot hope to find any answers until you do.'

***

Axl pulled Amma along as she ran her other hand distractedly through the tall, swaying grass they waded through. She tried to smile at him, but her eyes blinked anxiously, and she couldn't stop swallowing.

Once they had been desperate to escape that cave, craving sunshine and warmth, but now they all felt exposed without its thick walls to protect them.

'Do you think Gant will understand the message?' Amma wondered, inhaling the sweet scent of honeyberry flowers that hid amongst the grass; enjoying the rays of sunlight on her face. But as she glanced up, searching the sky, she found herself fearing every bird that flew overhead, every cloud in the distance.

Axl nodded, barely listening. 'I'm sure he will.'

Aleksander watched as they walked ahead of him. Their clothes were in tatters, their wounds exposed and stinging. Everything hurt, but they didn't have time to stop and tend to each other. They had to find horses.

They had to get to Tuura.

CHAPTER TWENTY THREE

They spent the rest of the day clearing up, burning the birds, binding wounds, making pyres for those who had died. The Tuurans shuffled about in shock, jumping at every sound, panicked by every sudden movement, listening for signs that danger was coming again.

There were no more birds, but the stench of blood hung in the air, unnerving them all. More storms threatened. The clouds rolled above them, turning darker shades of grey, clustering into foreboding shapes. Jael worked alongside Beorn and the crew, looking up regularly, eager to make sure that they *were* just storm clouds.

'Some place you've brought us,' Beorn mumbled, picking up a wooden plank and following her inside. They were hurrying to cover any holes in the stable walls before nightfall. 'Think I'd rather be back on Oss, taking on Ivaar. At least that's the sort of fight that makes sense. But this...' Beorn looked around, feeling the pain in his side where a bird had pecked a hole in him.

He didn't have a clue what had happened.

Jael had come to check on Tig who was skittish, reluctant to be left in his stall. 'It doesn't make much sense, I know,' she said quietly, running her hand over Tig's muzzle, trying to calm him.

'But it's magic, isn't it?' Beorn whispered hoarsely, peering at her. 'Some sort of dark magic?'

Jael was desperate to talk to someone; to think of what to do and make a plan. But perhaps the dreamers would hear her? See what she was doing? She had her stone, but no one else did.

And Marcus had made it very clear that they were not safe.

He was in danger, she knew. And if he was in danger, then no one in Tuura was safe.

'Dark magic?' Jael shrugged, trying to smile. 'No, I think all the storms must have worried the ravens, and for some reason, they hunted in a pack. Perhaps they felt threatened?' She stared at Beorn, gripping his arm. 'We just need to secure everything. Make sure nothing can get inside tonight.'

Jael thought about going back to the room, wondering if Marcus was there, waiting for her. But there had been no signal from him, and by the look on his face when she had last seen him, he was not able to go anywhere now.

She sighed, realising that she would have to find answers on her own. Dropping her head, she left the stables, eager to get back to the house to check on Edela.

'Oh, I'm sorry!'

Jael's head jerked up as a woman rushed around the corner, not looking where she was going, banging straight into her. She was about Jael's age, perhaps younger; smaller, rounder, softer looking. Not like Jael at all really. But her eyes were sharp, and Jael blinked at them. 'Watch where you're going next time!' she grumbled moodily before turning away, leaving the woman to look embarrassed as she stood there, watching her go.

***

Haaron's appetite had finally returned after days of self-indulgent moping over the loss of his ships, his men, his pier.

His reputation.

And Varna.

Having Morana in the castle had given him the confidence to see a way forward. He had spoken to the strange dreamer many times now, and her tetchy, reluctant advice had actually helped him craft a way to ease the very real threat his sons now posed to him.

A solution, he thought, that would benefit them all.

Bayla, it seemed, had other ideas as she sat beside him, considering his suggestion with scorn. 'You have food in your beard,' she muttered, pursing her lips.

Haaron, still chewing, wiped one hand through his grey beard and shovelled in another yam, happy that at least his cooks were turning out excellent food without fail. Although, with his harbour in disarray, and being overly reliant upon imported fruit, vegetables, and game, he wondered how long that would continue. 'And what of you, my eldest son?' he mumbled between mouthfuls, turning to Haegen who had frozen, his knife in mid-air.

'Lordships?' Haegen shook his head. 'What do you... I, I don't understand.' He glanced at Irenna, who had stilled beside him.

Karsten, who had little appetite, took a sip of wine and sighed. 'Father means for us to leave the castle. To leave the city.'

'But what for?' Bayla asked. 'And whose idea was that? Your new dreamer's?'

Haaron smiled. 'My wife, still so perceptive, even at such an advanced age.'

Bayla blanched, glaring at her sons, demanding they say something. Their father had obviously gone mad.

'It is the best way forward. We will strengthen every corner of our kingdom. There shall be no lords of Hest that I do not trust,' Haaron insisted. 'It is my sons, and only my sons, who I will put my faith in now. Sending one of you to each corner of the kingdom will help us improve any weaknesses in our defenses. It is the best way to stabilise what we have and build for the future.'

Berard smiled at the slave removing his plate. 'Do you plan to send *all* of us away, Father?'

Haaron considered his least impressive son. He was small, stooping, limp. More like a boy than a man. 'Well, perhaps not you. I don't imagine you want to be a lord, do you, Berard?'

Berard was too interested in the idea to look offended. 'I think that I would not mind such a thing.'

Haegen was surprised by Berard's interest, by Karsten's lack of interest and by his father's sudden desire to get rid of them all. 'But why now, Father?'

'Because it is *time!*' Haaron growled. 'Time for us to consider the future of this mighty kingdom, which is in danger of falling into ruin. And if I do not look forward and plan for what will come after me, then I may as well hand Hest to the Furycks now!' He was irritated. Ready for some wine. Fed up with all of them. 'And where is Jaeger?' he grumbled. 'It would be useful to have all of you here to discuss matters pertaining to our kingdom's future. Does he even *live* in this castle anymore?'

***

Jaeger had been so dazed by the strangely scented smoke that he'd stumbled into bed as soon as he returned from the Crown of Stones, unable to keep his eyes open, pulling Meena under the furs with him.

He had started snoring quickly as he curled up next to her.

And she had lain perfectly still, her eyes wide, desperate for him to stay asleep. She knew that smoke and her head was not affected by it in the same way as Jaeger's. It was Varna's smoke, Varna's herbs, that had helped bring on her trances. And Meena knew how it felt to become lost in it.

But Varna had never cast such a powerful spell.

To control all those birds at once? Turn them into weapons? Force them to kill? *Be* them...

Shuddering, Meena pulled the furs up to her eyes, wanting to disappear, to hide away from what she feared was coming next.

But she knew that it was pointless.

Once, she had been Varna's. Now, she was Jaeger's, and Morana had them both where she wanted them.

***

'Are you sure it's alright for us to stay here?' Isaura asked nervously, looking around in awe at the finest house she had ever seen.

Eadmund and Jael's house.

Thorgils felt sad as he closed the door behind them. He remembered the night he had dumped Eadmund, drunk and unconscious, on the bedchamber floor. How relieved Jael had been that he couldn't even open his eyes.

How eager she had been to leave.

And now she had.

'Eadmund seems quite happy to stay in the hall,' he said mutely, easing Mads down onto the floor.

He had sent Isaura's servants over earlier to warm the place up, and it did indeed feel cosy, with a high fire crackling under a large cauldron that steamed invitingly with fishy smells. He could imagine the look on Biddy's face at the sight of Isaura's servants fussing about in her kitchen.

'Are you alright?' Isaura wondered gently, watching as the girls raced around the house, checking inside the bedchamber, in the storage room at the back of the kitchen, running out to the stables.

Thorgils nodded. 'It's a good house, plenty of room in here for all of you.'

'There's a big tub, Mother!' Annet smiled as she hurried back with wide, blue eyes, grabbing her three-year-old sister, Leya, by the hand and tugging her back to the tub, Mads toddling eagerly after them.

Selene, the eldest at six-years-old, was quiet as she stood by her mother. It had been a terrifying few days, and she had barely spoken since they'd arrived.

Isaura squeezed her daughter's hand. 'Why don't you choose which bed you'd like to sleep in, sweetheart?'

Selene nodded without smiling and walked over to the beds that ran around the walls of the large main room, her shoulders rounded, her head down.

'There's a big bed in here, just for you,' Thorgils said shyly, pointing to the bedchamber. He ducked his head, his eyes on the floor.

'For me?' Isaura asked, walking up to him with a grin. 'Just for me?'

Thorgils turned to her, then glanced back at the children who were suddenly all standing nearby, frowning up at them both. 'For now, I think, don't you?' he whispered, red-faced and uncomfortable.

Isaura didn't think so at all. 'Well, perhaps. We could all do with some sleep, I think. Tomorrow we might feel better.' She looked at her children, who, she could tell, were very out of sorts, then at Thorgils who appeared ready to run for the door.

'I should get back to Odda,' he said quietly. 'It looks as though your supper is ready.'

Isaura smiled. 'Yes, although, after being out in that storm, I don't know if I'll ever have an appetite again!'

The children appeared hungry, though, as they gathered around Selda and Ida, who were standing by the cauldron, bowls in hand.

Isaura followed Thorgils outside, inhaling the smoky air which was much cooler now as dusk settled. She reached for his hand. 'Do you think Ivaar will come soon?'

Thorgils bent down and kissed her so urgently that they both forgot about Ivaar for a moment. 'Ivaar will not take you away from me,' he growled, pulling her close. 'He will never touch you again.'

***

The food tasted like shit.

Bara was a tiny rock full of inbreds, Ivaar decided, and not one of them knew how to cook. And as for the ale...

Frits couldn't stop apologising, staring at Ivaar's increasingly sullen face; gaunter now after weeks of crawling around the hills of Alekka, and now Bara. He had slowly become wistful for his own hall, although the Arnesson's hag mother had happily informed him that it was no longer his. Which was not such a bad thing, Ivaar supposed, imagining how many men Eadmund had given to that cause.

She'd also seen that the queen had left the island, taking men with her as well.

So Oss, it seemed, was light on warriors.

Ivaar smiled, pushing away his plate.

'More ale, my lords?' Frits wondered, rolling out of his fur-lined chair to check on his guests. His hall was so small that there was not enough room for all of Ivaar's and Borg's men, so most were outside in the cold drizzle, drinking around hastily built fires. He could hear them laughing and boasting about how they'd survived the storm. He looked at Ivaar's miserable face, and the surly grimace of Borg Arnesson and felt ready to bolt for the doors.

Borg grunted, holding out his empty cup. Frits flapped his hand at a servant girl and twitched his moustache. He felt uncomfortable with these men here, on his island; constantly doubting his decision to align himself with Ivaar. Although, in truth, his wife had made him do it; almost chewing off his ear at the mere suggestion that he would abandon Ivaar and choose loyalty to Eadmund and Jael instead. Falla was Frits' third wife, and young and ambitious enough to want more than he could ever offer her. And he was old enough to realise that the only way he could keep her in his bed was to tempt her with wealth and status.

And that's where Ivaar had come in.

Frits swallowed, edging towards him. 'The weather appears to be turning again.'

Ivaar barely heard him. He was too busy trying to ignore the sharp-eyed stare that Borg Arnesson was attempting to unsettle him with. 'Another storm?' he muttered distractedly. 'Strange for this time of year.'

That wasn't going to make things any easier.

Frits glanced around as his wife wandered in from the back of the hall. She had changed her dress again. He frowned, sensing her obvious interest in pleasing the men around his table. Men who were younger and slimmer than he had ever been. Men with more hair on their heads and less in their ears. Frits sat up a little taller, sucking in his sagging belly. 'My dear,' he called. 'Will you join us? I think Agda is about to bring out another course.'

Falla Hallstein wrinkled her snub nose at his suggestion. She was almost thirty-years-old and had spent all of those years trapped on Bara, desperate to leave. And now, here was her chance, and if her old husband was not going to make it happen for her, then she was going to make sure that one of these lords would take her with them when they conquered Oss.

There was no way she was being left behind.

'Your old cook needs to throw herself onto the fire and save us all from her food!' she said tartly, turning to Borg, who winked at her. She took a seat next to him, ignoring her husband's fretful looks and the scarred mess that was Borg Arnesson's face. He might have been handsome once, but now it was too hard to tell. But he was young and strong and full of life; Falla could feel that as she smiled at him.

Ivaar rolled his eyes, turning towards the doors. Even a storm would be preferable to this company.

***

'She does not have long,' Runa said solemnly, moving aside to let Thorgils come and take her place by Odda. She glanced up at Bram who waited by the door. 'I'll go and have something to eat.'

'Perhaps you need to sleep in your own bed tonight?' Bram wondered gently. 'You need some rest. It's not easy caring for the sick.'

Runa nodded, reaching for her cloak. 'There's enough food and wood for the night. But I will return in the morning to see how she's faring.' She smiled sympathetically at Thorgils as she headed to the door.

Thorgils stifled a sob. His head was rolling with his body, and he didn't know how he should feel at all. Grief-stricken or elated? Terrified or happy?

Isaura was here, finally. But Ivaar was coming.

And amidst it all, Odda was dying.

He held her hand in his. It felt so cold, as though there was no life in it at all. Her chest was barely moving, and her mouth was stuck open. He wanted to reach over and close it, but perhaps it was the only way she could find a breath now? It seemed to be a struggle for her.

Thorgils looked at his uncle, and his shoulders drooped. 'It's been a long few days.'

Bram murmured his agreement as he pulled over a stool and slipped off his cloak. 'It has. Another one coming tomorrow, I'd chance.'

'How many men do these Arnesson brothers have?'

Bram shrugged. 'About thirty less than they were planning to I'd say after losing that ship. But enough to cause us some sleepless nights.' Pulling his sword from its scabbard, he lay it across his knee. 'They're hard men in Tingor. Their father was a real piece of shit. Set fire to his first wife because he saw her look at another man. Then married her sister... after he'd cut off her husband's head.'

Thorgils cringed. 'Well, they sound like perfect company for Ivaar.'

Bram ferreted about in his pouch for his whetstone. 'I've a feeling Ivaar will live to regret the day he ever tied himself to their ships,' Bram said wryly. 'No one I know ever made a deal with the Arnessons and walked away with his life.'

***

They ate a late supper at Jaeger's table.

Jaeger didn't want to face his father or his brothers. He couldn't even be bothered having to endure his mother. He just wanted to be alone with the book.

Meena sat opposite him, Egil shuffled about in his little corner, but the book was all Jaeger noticed. As soon as their plates were removed, he lifted it onto the table, sighing in relief at the touch of that cool cover; those crackling pages.

He immediately felt right again.

And hungry for more. The power he had experienced being inside the Crown of Stones was exhilarating. He was no dreamer. How could he have seen what the Followers did? What they saw? How was it possible?

But more importantly, how was it possible that they hadn't killed Jael Furyck? That she had somehow managed to stop them? His body shook with a rage that rushed towards his temples. 'I need Morana,' he growled, looking up. 'Why hasn't she come?'

Meena jumped. 'Should I go and get her?' she mumbled, tapping her foot quietly beneath the table, hoping he wouldn't notice.

Jaeger glowered at her. 'Why, when I have Egil? You are not my servant, Meena. Egil is. You are my... assistant, remember?' He attempted to smile at her, but his lips curled unnaturally, and his eyes remained cold.

Meena shivered and remained in her seat as Egil hurried past them and headed for the door.

'And tell her to hurry!' Jaeger grumbled after him. 'She has kept me waiting long enough!'

**

It was dark now, and Jael couldn't wait any longer. She grabbed her cloak.

'You're going out?' Gisila looked surprised as she tucked Eydis into her bed. 'Are you sure that's wise?'

Fyn, who had been thinking that it was time he left for Aedan's, wrapped his own cloak around his shoulders, ready to tag along.

Jael glared impatiently at him, not wanting the company. 'I need to make sure the men are secure for the night. I'm not going to be able to sleep if I don't.'

'I wonder if any of us will be able to sleep,' Branwyn sighed, handing Biddy a cup of passionflower tea. 'Perhaps we need to set a watch to give us some peace of mind?'

'Good idea,' Jael said distractedly. 'I won't be long. I'll take the watch when I get back. Come on, Fyn, I'll walk you to Aedan's.'

Fyn glanced back at Eydis who was yawning, at Edela who had barely said a word since the morning, at Branwyn and Kormac who sat anxiously around the fire with Biddy. 'Should I stay?'

Jael put her arm around his shoulders. 'There's no room for you in here, my long-legged friend,' she said quickly. 'Let's go. Entorp's probably already taken the best bed at Aedan's!'

They left the house quickly, hoping to escape any more protests.

It was dark. Densely so. No stars that they could see. The stink of smoke was in the air, stronger than usual. It was a heady, thick fug of burned bodies; ash and flesh, blood and bone. It curdled Jael's stomach as she walked, trying to piece together what might have happened.

Why the ravens had come.

There weren't many pieces. It didn't take long.

'You take care of yourself tonight,' Jael said quietly. 'Make sure one of you keeps watch. And let's do some training tomorrow. I'll drag the men out there too. We need to be ready for whatever comes next.'

Fyn gulped. 'What do you think will come next?'

'I don't know,' Jael admitted. 'But after what happened this morning, anything's possible.'

***

Morana looked inconvenienced as she dragged herself into Jaeger's chamber. She had been on her way to visit Yorik, but Egil had stopped her, insisting that his master had great need of her.

He did, indeed, Morana could see, peering at Jaeger through her knotted mane as he sat before her, twitching with urgency, desperate to use the book again. She smiled as she shuffled over to the table, enjoying his distress.

'Had a nice sleep?' Jaeger sneered.

'Well, if you wish to know what a dreamer sees, you would be wise to encourage a dreamer to sleep,' Morana sneered back. 'Unless you think I can dream with my eyes open while talking to you?' She turned and glared at Meena, surprised that she was still there.

What did he want with the stupid girl?

Jaeger stared impatiently at Morana. Her tongue was sharper, her voice harsher and her mind quicker than Varna's, but Jaeger didn't care about any of it; he just wanted her to help him use the book again. 'What did you see, then, in your dreams?' he asked, placing his goblet on the table, all of his attention on her.

Meena swallowed, terrified to hear how desperate he sounded.

'I saw the new King of Brekka on his way to Tuura.'

Jaeger froze. 'Tuura? Why is everyone going to Tuura?'

Morana's eyes narrowed, but she didn't say a word.

And nor was she going to, Jaeger could tell. 'And my wife?'

'She is there, beside him,' Morana replied. 'She loves him.'

Jaeger gripped the stem of his silver goblet so hard that he wondered if he could, in fact, snap it. 'Then we must use the book! Kill them both!'

'Of course. We can and we will, but for now, I think you have greater problems to attend to here. With your father. He is sending you away from Hest.'

Meena turned to Jaeger, whose eyes widened in surprise.

***

Berard felt lonely as he stared at his empty fireplace.

He sat in his chair in the dark, remembering how he had watched Meena setting the fire for him. He hadn't been able to sit still, constantly offering to help. She had flapped her hands at him, tapping soot all over her hair.

He smiled.

It was so quiet in his chamber. He had not noticed how quiet until Meena had come and gone. She had only been there briefly, he knew, but he had enjoyed being with someone who didn't sneer at him, or ignore him, or make fun of him.

It reminded him of talking to Jael Furyck. She had listened to him, then warned him about Jaeger, but he hadn't listened to her.

He wished that he'd told her about the book.

Berard was certain that everything had changed when that book had turned up. The brother he knew was long gone now.

And Jaeger had taken Meena with him.

Now she was lost to him too.

Berard's shoulders slumped as he realised that he was fooling himself.

She had never been his to begin with.

***

Jael glanced at Tig as she hurried to the rear of the stables. There were no torches back here, and she merged quickly with the shadows, feeling her way to the door of the secret room, unlocking it with the largest key from her pouch.

But Marcus was not waiting for her.

Jael shut the door quietly, swallowing in anticipation. 'Who are you?' she asked, on edge, preparing for it all to be a trap; planning what she'd do if it were.

'My name,' the woman said, clearing her throat, 'is Hanna.'

CHAPTER TWENTY FOUR

They were morose now. Drinking to the men they had lost.

Ivaar was glad that one of Borg's brothers hadn't gone down in the lost ship, or he imagined they'd be drinking for days. And he needed them to focus on what they had to do next.

Attack Oss.

If only they could agree on how to do it.

Ivaar glared at Frits who was so distracted by what his wife was doing that he could barely hold his attention for a moment. 'Frits!' he grumbled for the third time. 'You need to look at the map!'

It was a shit map, Ivaar decided, to go with the shit hall and the shit food. But there was, at least, a rough outline of Oss on the table; enough for them all to see where they could aim their attack.

Borg's youngest brother, Toki, who barely had a curl of hair on his face, looked confused. 'Why would we creep over rocks when we can just sail straight through there?' Leaning over the map, he pointed to what almost looked like the mouth of Oss' harbour.

Ivaar stared at Toki as though he had spoken Siluran. '*What?*'

Borg pushed Toki out of the way, covering his embarrassment with a blustery growl. 'What my brother is trying to say is that perhaps a direct attack would be our best option.'

'For what?' Ivaar snorted. 'Getting defeated?' He shook his head, looking for some support from Frits who once again had his old, weeping eyes elsewhere. 'The fort overlooks the harbour, and the only way up to it from there is a steep hill. There's nothing to stop you from getting an arrow in the face on that climb. And they'll have enough of those to kill us all.'

'But will they?' Frits wondered, suddenly paying attention. '*Will* they have many arrows? After the attack on Skorro, there might not be many left at all.'

Ivaar was surprised. Someone with an opinion that wasn't stupid and ill-informed. But still... 'We should divide our fleet. If you wish to risk getting shot at, you and your brothers take the fort head on. The rest of us can creep over the rocks to the rear.'

'Are there gates at the rear of the fort?' Borg wondered, glancing at Falla Hallstein as she approached. A fine shape of a woman, he thought to himself, with a face that didn't turn his stomach; obviously imprisoned in an unsatisfying marriage to a limp, old man.

'There's a door,' Ivaar said quickly, trying to keep everyone's attention. 'It's hidden, but I know where it is.'

***

'Why did you give me this?' Jael asked sharply, turning over her palm to reveal the flat river stone. It was the same as the one Marcus had given her.

'That symbol is carved into this room to protect us from the dreamers. I have more of them for you to give to your family,' Hanna said, edging forward, opening her purse and handing Jael three stones. 'My father cannot carry them. It's too dangerous, which is why we made this room.'

'Your father? *Marcus* is your father?'

Hanna nodded sadly.

'But eldermen... they aren't allowed to have children.'

'No. I, I was a mistake, you could say. My father loved my mother, but he had spent his life working towards becoming an elder, so he left her behind in Helsabor. He didn't know about me when he left. He didn't know about me for many years. Not until I came here looking for him after my mother died.'

'Oh.' Jael started to relax. It was too dark to make out much about the woman, but Jael knew that she was the one who had bumped into her earlier that day. She had slipped a note into her hand with the stone, arranging to meet in the room. 'And now? You know everything? He trusts you with everything?'

'He has to. They have slowly killed off everyone else. Every dreamer who was loyal to him has been killed or sent away. They've removed the scribes from the temple too. It's not safe here anymore. My father wants me to leave. He wants me to go back to Helsabor, but we both know that The Following could kill me just as easily there if they had a mind to. They're everywhere, growing stronger each day. Especially now that the Book of Darkness has been found. They are bolder, coming out into the open, revealing themselves without fear.'

Jael frowned. 'I've been thinking about that book today,' she said, taking a seat on the hay bales. 'I was hoping to speak to your father about it, but perhaps you can help me? I think I have a plan.'

***

Aleksander had quickly set a fire, desperate to take the chill out of their weary bones, and they sat around it, defeated, hoping for better luck in the morning. They had walked all day, coming across just the one farm whose two horses had been in the fields when the ravens had flown through. The farmer and his family had sheltered in their home, but the ravens had killed the horses.

Aleksander threw a small branch onto the flames and yawned. His body ached. The arrow wound in his shoulder had been torn open by the birds, and the other cuts they had made nagged at him. His body was not as uncomfortable as his mind, though, which buzzed with anxiety.

He didn't want to imagine what might have happened in Tuura.

'But how do you know it was her?' Amma wondered as they went over his dream again. 'The Widow? Is she even real?'

Aleksander opened his mouth, searching for an escape from the conversation; a way not to have to explain it at all. But he didn't see how he could avoid the truth. Not now. And so he told them about his visit to the Widow, when he had been searching so desperately for some hope that he would be with Jael again.

He told them about what Edela had discovered in Tuura; how his mother and grandmother had both visited the Widow.

He didn't know more than that.

He didn't know who she was or if they could trust her.

But after the raven attack, how could they not?

'I'm no dreamer,' Aleksander sighed. 'But that dream?' He shook his head. 'That was like nothing I've experienced before.'

Amma blinked. 'We have to get to Tuura as quickly as possible. There must be some horses nearby.'

Axl was just as anxious as they were, but the part of him that hoped he was a king now felt slightly more hesitant. 'What if it's a trap?'

'Well, if it's a trap,' Aleksander mused, 'we can hide in the forest. See how things lie. But for now, we should trust in the dream, I think. We'll find out soon enough whether I'm right.'

Axl frowned so deeply that his head ached. He was still not convinced that they should follow the Widow's advice. But he could hear the certainty in Amma's voice and the resolve in Aleksander's. 'Well,' he sighed, 'we'd better get some sleep then if we're going to try and find a way to Tuura in the morning.'

Amma smiled, kissing him on the cheek.

***

'*I'll* do it!' Hanna said eagerly.

Jael was surprised. 'Is there no one else you can think of? No one you trust?' She didn't know what to make of Hanna. She seemed brave, quick-thinking, smart. It would make sense to send her, but she was Marcus' daughter. She doubted he would thank her for sending his only child away on a dangerous mission.

'There's no one else,' Hanna insisted. 'And this is important.'

'It is,' Jael agreed. 'But I'm not sure that it will even work. Who knows what is happening in Hest.'

'I understand, but I can try. I can leave tomorrow. There are merchant ships in the harbour. They come and go most days. You just need to tell me what to do when I get to Hest.'

'You will have to find Berard Dragos,' Jael said slowly. 'He's the king's third son. You'll need to find some way to get him alone. Tell him why you've come. That I sent you.'

'But he won't trust me, will he? Or even believe what I'm saying. He won't just give me the Book of Darkness without any proof that I've come from you.'

'No,' Jael agreed. 'Remind him of the time we ate in the kitchen together, about what he promised me. That he would look after my cousin. Tell him that the book will consume his brother and that if Morana uses it, she will destroy all of Osterland.' Jael's shoulders tightened at just the mention of that evil book. After what had happened with the ravens... she shook her head, wondering if they were already too late.

Hanna nodded, a dark shadow in the dark room. 'I'll try and remember.'

'As long as you remember that it's *Berard* Dragos you need to find,' Jael said, suddenly worried. 'He's our only chance to get that book. But if he still hesitates, tell him that I had a dream about him. He's in danger. He should leave with you. Tell him I've seen him covered in blood.'

Hanna stilled, suddenly aware of the seriousness of her mission.

'Do you know how to use a sword?' Jael asked, sensing her hesitation.

Hanna shook her head. 'No.'

'Do you have a knife?'

'Yes.'

'Well, make sure it's sharp. And if you get into trouble, use it quickly. Slit a throat if you can. Someone with a slit throat is not as likely to scream.'

Hanna shivered. 'I will try.'

'Good. Then you should go and prepare yourself. Find a ship in the morning. Think of a reason for going to Hest. For being there when you arrive. You don't want to arouse any suspicions.'

'I will, thank you,' Hanna said, swallowing. 'My father is locked in the temple now from what I hear. Gerod Gott has taken control. He is a strange, strange man. I hate to think of what he will do to my father, but if somehow you do see him, please tell him that I... love him.' She stood quickly, feeling a sudden burst of emotion about leaving behind the only family she had left.

'I will.' Jael stood, watching her walk towards the rear door. 'Be careful. And good luck.'

Hanna nodded, slipping through the door.

***

Ivaar was sleepy as he stared into the flames. They were mesmerising, and his aching limbs, heavy with ale hung around him, and his grainy eyes started to close.

He thought of Isaura and Ayla.

Had Isaura taken Ayla with her? Were they all gone now?

He sighed. He would miss his children, perhaps, but not his wife. He could get another dreamer, and certainly another wife, and she could have more children, but the thought that Thorgils and Eadmund had taken everything from him now stirred his blood.

His island, his fort, his home, his lordship.

His wife, his dreamer, his children.

And even before that, his throne. *His* throne.

Ivaar's eyes burst open, and he was wide awake again.

He was stuck here with a bunch of bloodthirsty idiots who only appeared motivated by how many people they could kill and how much damage they could inflict while doing so.

It was not a wise man who bargained with an idiot. And although Ivaar considered himself a wise man, he was a man who had run out of options. Frits Hallstein and the Arnessons were all he had now.

He closed his eyes again, determined to get some sleep, for in the morning they would leave to attack Oss and reclaim everything that was owed to him.

***

Eadmund couldn't sleep, despite the comforting warmth of

Evaine as she lay curled into his side. His mind was full of securing defenses, the worrying lack of arrows, approaching storms, how to protect his ships.

Jael.

He was surprised by that. But there she was. Not in the same way that Evaine was in his head. It was different now, but he couldn't stop thinking about what she would do or say. He missed the way she was always chewing over a plan.

He missed her opinions, her advice.

Although, he smiled wryly, it was not really advice when it came from Jael.

It was more of an order.

Eadmund thought of his son in the next room. Ivaar would kill him. He would probably make Eadmund watch before killing him too; before he killed Thorgils and Torstan and Bram, and every man he knew and cared about on the island.

His island.

His and Jael's.

He closed his eyes, at last, remembering Skorro and Hest.

Remembering his wife.

***

Jael crawled into bed beside Edela.

Kormac was on watch now, and she had to get some sleep before she took over from him again. Eydis was curled up with the puppies, and she couldn't see anywhere else to lie.

But she couldn't think of anywhere she'd rather be.

Except beside Eadmund.

Jael sighed, reaching for Edela's hand.

She closed her eyes, the day rushing by in a terrifying blur, but somehow, in the midst of all that terror and destruction, her grandmother had come back.

But for how long?

Jael felt Edela squeeze her hand. She opened her eyes, staring into the darkness, seeing nothing but shapes. It was cold in the house tonight. They had put out the fire early, blocking up the smoke hole.

'Can you hear me?' Jael whispered, staring at the shadow of her grandmother's face. 'Are you in there?'

She felt another squeeze and almost cried with happiness. 'Well, that's good to know, because I need you. You can't leave me. I've lost Eadmund. I can't lose you too. You have to come back. You have to help me get him back.' She tried to blink away the tears rolling down her face.

Tears wouldn't help.

Edela pulled her hand away and reached up slowly, trying to find Jael's face. And finding it, eventually, she gently stroked away her tears.

And Jael cried.

***

Meena felt scared. Terrified.

She reached for the door handle anyway.

'And where do you think *you're* going?'

Meena jumped, biting her tongue as Egil crept up behind her, glaring at her in the dim light of the bedchamber. Glimpses of moonlight shone through the window, and the banked fire emitted a warm glow, but Egil's face was dark and menacing. 'I'm, I'm,' she whispered, trying to find words in the muddle of her mind. 'I'm going back to my chamber.'

Egil frowned. 'Why?'

Meena shook, desperately trying to avoid tapping her head.

She needed to think, and quickly. 'I, I cannot sleep here. I feel strange.'

Egil kept frowning. He was unfailingly loyal to his master, but he simply couldn't understand why he had invited this idiot girl into his bed at all.

But here she was. And if she was here, then she was going to stay here while his master demanded it. And while his master demanded it, he was going to help his master enforce it.

Egil reached out and grabbed Meena's wrist, pulling her away from the door. 'Better get used to it, girl,' he rasped, feeling powerful in his position. 'Because you're not going anywhere unless my lord says so.' And he dragged Meena back towards Jaeger's bed, his rough hands pinching her skin.

Meena gulped, gasping in discomfort, wanting to yank her hand away from him to tap her head. But she was too scared to say or do anything except crawl back into bed next to the still snoring Jaeger.

Satisfied, Egil shuffled back to his end of the chamber, determined to keep one eye on the door all night.

***

Thorgils sat beside his mother's bed on a stool that was too small for him, listening to her chest rattle as her breathing gradually slowed to almost nothing. He wondered if she knew what was happening to her? Whether she could hear him anymore? Feel him next to her?

Whether she'd even care?

It was as though the gods had told him that it was time to say goodbye to one family so that he could start another.

Or were they just teasing him? Taunting him? Because Ivaar was coming and Ivaar was going to try and take back his wife and children.

Thorgils stood, groaning at the stiffness in his legs and back. He felt old. Bram was snoring loudly in one corner of the room, and the fire was burning down to embers, so Thorgils walked over to the wood pile, grabbing another log. Not many left. He would have to go and get some more soon.

But not yet. He didn't want to leave Odda alone.

The flames sparked in protest, disappearing under the heavy log, but Thorgils knew they would emerge soon, so he turned back to his mother, holding her limp hand in his. He blinked in the firelight which was gradually getting brighter now. Odda's mouth still hung open.

But he couldn't see her chest moving anymore.

CHAPTER TWENTY FIVE

Hanna had been up since dawn, packing her few belongings into an old leather satchel. She had her mother's comb, more of the symbol stones, a handful of the gold coins her father had given her, and hopefully, enough food to see her to Hest. She had borrowed an almost-new dress from a friend, and that friend had kindly braided her hair, lending her two brooches and a necklace made of delicate glass beads.

She wanted to present herself as a respectable lady; someone who would fit into Hest, not stand out or be judged as she was in Tuura, where everyone assumed that she was someone she was not. Hanna supposed that she had never given them reason not to think that she was a woman who gave her body to men in return for coins. But the only ones to befriend her had been those sort of women: big-hearted, less inclined to judge. They had taken her in, and her life amongst them had shielded her from any suspicion. When Marcus visited her, no one suspected that his motives weren't simply carnal.

The pretence was uncomfortable, but it had protected them until now, when her father was as unsafe as he had ever been, and she was about to sail into more danger than she could have imagined.

But, she smiled, closing the door to her tiny cottage, she was eager to begin.

***

Ivaar woke with a familiar pain in the side of his head, cringing as he looked around for water. For anything to drink. His throat was so dry.

He blinked repeatedly, trying to pry open his eyes, relieved to hear no rain, no wind whistling around the hall. Yawning, he struggled to his feet, rubbing his face as he peered at the tangle of sleepy, ale-soaked bodies that lay sprawled around the fire. Toe to ear and elbow to nose they had squeezed themselves into Frits' meagre hall.

It was a freezing bitch of an island, and no one had wanted to sleep outside, yet, by the look of how many bodies he could count, most had.

Ivaar yawned again, frowning at the sight of Falla Hallstein as she appeared from behind the bedchamber curtain, Borg Arnesson at her side, his tattooed arm curled over her shoulder, his hand gripping her exposed breast.

Ivaar stilled, cocking his head to one side, feeling as though everything was about to fall apart. 'My lady,' he nodded to Falla. 'And where is your husband this morning?'

Falla laughed, smiling sleepily. 'That old bastard?' She inclined her head towards the floor.

Ivaar looked down, swallowing at the sight of Frits, who lay between two snoring Kalfans, his throat slit, his glazed eyes frozen in shock; dried blood colouring his tunic a deep, dark red. Ivaar licked his salty lips, not wanting to appear as stunned as he was. He glanced up at Borg and Falla. 'I see. Well, it appears that no one has a problem with that,' he said slowly, running his eyes over the men who were busy farting and groaning as they fumbled about, unconcerned that their lord was no more.

'Why should they? They have a new lord, with more ships, more men. More ambition,' Borg snarled. 'Besides, the old man was ready to die. Anyone could see that. And his wife was ready for a new husband. So, we all win, wouldn't you say?'

'Well, as you say, we all win, especially when we get to Oss and dig up the gold.'

'Ahhh, about that,' Borg said carefully, kneading Falla's ample breast with his filthy palm. 'I've sent Toki back to Alekka, to Tingor. It makes no sense to attack your brother without enough men. My cousins will come. They have nine ships between them. At least three hundred men. I'm sure you agree that we need as many men as possible to make a success of our *endeavour*.' His eyes didn't leave Ivaar's. They were sharp, glinting threateningly in the light from the hall doors, open now as men stumbled outside to piss.

Ivaar was sure that he didn't agree, but he appeared to have little choice in the matter, outnumbered now as he was.

***

Gerod was not impressed as he rounded on Marcus. It was early, and he had dragged the elderman from his bed, demanding answers that, so far, were not forthcoming.

Marcus' empty belly growled endlessly, though he had no real appetite.

It only served to irritate Gerod further. 'Jael Furyck has that book!' he hissed through bared teeth. His black hair fringed his face, making his skin appear ghostly white. His clear, blue eyes were bright with anger. 'They saw it! They all saw it! In Tuura! In Hest!'

Marcus did not step back as Gerod challenged him, jutting his pointy chin towards his face. Marcus was taller. Bigger. Stronger. But nowhere near as powerful now. Yet, despite how determined Gerod was to intimidate him, Marcus saw no point in allowing him to have his way.

And he had no intention of saying anything that would lead The Following to the book.

'Then why can't they see where it is now?' Marcus asked calmly. 'If Jael Furyck still has it, why can't they see where it is?'

Gerod glared at the elderman, then snapped his head around, pacing up and down the dark chamber; past the blackened fireplace, around Marcus' chair. 'Perhaps she knows spells? How to hide the book?'

Marcus snorted. 'I'm sure the dreamers will tell you that is not true. As far as I'm aware, she has only just acknowledged that she *is* a dreamer. I hardly think she knows what to do about that yet, especially with her grandmother so ill.'

'Then the girl, the blind girl, she's a dreamer!' Gerod snarled.

Marcus shook his head. 'Perhaps the dreamers are not telling you everything you need to know,' he said carefully. 'Eydis Skalleson? First of all, she is blind. She cannot read a book. And even if she could, she does not know Tuuran. She does not know spells. She does not even know her own dreams yet.' He tried to look disappointed. 'I thought you would have been told that.'

Gerod blinked at the insult. He was sure it was an insult. 'Well, *someone* has that other book. *Someone* knows where it is. And if they don't? Well, perhaps it doesn't even matter. We will kill her anyway!'

Marcus swallowed, trying to keep his face neutral. Gerod had always been so desperate for power, but even though he had now taken it, Marcus could sense his hesitation. 'And you're ready for that, are you? Ready to have the Islanders at the gates? The Brekkans? All of them? You're ready to begin your war? Now?'

Gerod's eyes shone feverishly. 'Her husband would not come to avenge her,' he scoffed. 'Not when he has Evaine Gallas in his bed!'

Marcus shook his head slowly. 'I do wonder who you have

been speaking with to suggest such a thing.'

'He is bound to Evaine. Soul bound now!' Gerod insisted. 'That cannot be undone.'

'So I hear,' Marcus sighed, as if bored. 'But Jael Furyck is still the Queen of Oss, and he is loyal to her, despite any feelings he may think he has for the Gallas girl. As is her brother. And his Brekkan army. And they will come, so you had better be ready to defend this fort if you intend to kill her now.'

**

Hanna swallowed nervously as she approached the merchant ship gently butting the very end of the pier. It looked the least impressive of the four ships in Tuura's small harbour, but she had a feeling that it was the one to try. She had asked around in the tavern and been told that they would be heading south soon. She only hoped that the helmsman could be trusted to get her to Hest. And quickly. She had coins in her purse, and they jingled in time to the nervous beat of her heart.

'Are you Ulf?' Hanna called out hoarsely. Clearing her throat, she tried again. 'Ulf Rutgar? Kirta sent me. She said you were leaving today. That I might possibly find passage to Hest?'

The helmsman turned to squint down at her. He was a roughly hewn man of numerous sea journeys, with a threadbare cloak that gave Hanna hope that he wouldn't mind her coins at all.

'Hest?' he grumbled. 'Looking to find yourself a rich husband?'

'I might be,' she smiled sweetly. 'But I have more than enough coins to get me there if that's what you're worried about. More waiting here if you return me quickly.' Reaching into her purse, she pulled out a gold coin. 'If, of course, gold is what you're after?'

The glint in the helmsman's sharp eyes was encouraging. He looked like a starving dog who'd just been thrown a tasty bone. Hanna stood up straighter, walking towards his ship with more confidence now, eager to be gone.

***

Bayla rapped on Haaron's door until he opened it, grumbling to himself, wondering where his servants had disappeared to.

Why was the King of Hest answering his own door?

He looked at his wife, wanting to feel pleased that she was here, but the scowl on her face was so darkly familiar that he sighed in anticipation of the storm he was about to be battered by.

'What were you *thinking*?' Bayla spat, striding past him.

She had obviously taken the time to work her temper into a frothing, steaming frenzy while she was bathed and dressed. Her hair had been intricately braided, her face highlighted with soft shades of pink. Jewels dripped from her ears, her wrists, her neck.

Bayla had certainly made an effort to come and tell him just how much she hated him.

'I was thinking of the best thing for Hest,' Haaron insisted, hungry and distracted. 'Our sons do nothing. They have learned nothing coddled here like babies. I have failed them all! The best preparation they can have to be king here, whoever it ends up being, is to learn how to lead. How to rule. How to succeed. They cannot, and have not, done that here, hiding behind your skirts and my sword!'

Bayla was surprised by how sensible an argument that was. But still. '*All* of them?' she asked. 'Why *all* of them?' She shook her head, working herself back up into a frenzy. 'I hardly think Berard will end up being king here and Jaeger is your fourth son! Why send them away as well?'

Haaron raised an eyebrow, knowing that Bayla, his sharp-tongued, angry wife, was a smarter person than that. 'Now, now, let's not play games, my dear. We both know that your place in line does not determine where your ambitions lie. And our youngest son is obviously our most ambitious. Or are you choosing to only look at him with one eye now?'

Bayla sucked on her bottom lip, glaring at her husband.

'How does it hurt any of them to become lords? To be in charge of their own domain? To rule their own people? How am I doing anything wrong by suggesting such a thing? They are men! Grown men!'

'You are sending them away from their home! From all they know!'

Haaron laughed. 'They are not little boys, Bayla! They have wives! They have children! They have fought in battles. They are men, Dragos men, but they are not good enough to succeed *me.* They do not know enough. I must leave Hest in experienced hands. Not the soft, weak hands of an entitled brat who thinks that all he has to do is sit on the dragon throne and snap his fingers to keep this kingdom in Dragos hands for all eternity.'

Bayla frowned as he stepped forward, reaching out for her.

'Fine. Send three of them away, then,' she said coolly, shaking him off. 'Surely, three is enough? Send three away, but leave me one son. That is all I ask.'

Haaron rolled his eyes. '*One* son? I don't suppose I need to guess who that would be.'

Bayla looked at him and smiled.

***

Jael laughed at the look on Aedan's and Aron's faces as they glanced at each other. They didn't know what to say, never having fought a woman before. Especially one who was their cousin and a queen.

Fyn knew how they felt, remembering the first time he'd faced up to Jael. He couldn't even hold onto a sword back then. How quickly she had turned him around.

Jael swung her practice sword from side to side, a smile playing at the corners of her mouth. She was desperate for a release from the tension of the past few days. And if it wasn't going to be her hesitant cousins... she looked around the ring. It was a small, pathetic training ring with railings in need of repair. Not big enough to have much fun, but anything was better than waiting inside Branwyn's house for something bad to happen.

'Anyone else?' she called to the men who leaned over the railings, staring at her. The Osslanders made no move to enter the ring. The Tuurans who weren't scowling at her looked on curiously.

But no one volunteered.

Jael didn't move, but her eyes sought out Fyn. 'Well, looks like it's just you and me, Fyn Gallas!'

Fyn gulped as he stepped forward, recognising the glint in her eyes; wishing Thorgils was here to take his place.

'I'll fight you, Queen of Oss,' said a deep voice, rising over the murmuring crowd.

Jael turned to watch one of the temple guards duck through the railings. She recognised him as the man who had threatened her for the book in Branwyn's house. He looked like a commander. Tall, emotionless, broad-chested. Strong. Arrogant.

Flexing one fist, he strode towards her, his other hand wrapped firmly around his practice sword, his eyes on her.

Ready.

Jael smiled.

***

They were all gathered in the hall for breakfast, waiting patiently as the slaves brought around their bowls.

Bayla looked as though she was going to cry, Haaron thought to himself. Was she finally softening in her old age? He shook his head, lifting a spoonful of cloudberries into his mouth. 'And why is it that I've heard everyone's grumbles but yours?' he wondered, turning to Karsten who was ripping off a corner of warm bread to dip into his porridge.

Karsten shrugged. 'Well, I don't see what's wrong with becoming a lord. Leaving here? It's no hardship that I can see, although...' he glanced down the table, to where Nicolene and Irenna had their heads together. 'If you ask my wife, I'm tearing her away from civilisation itself,' he snorted. 'I don't imagine she's going to enjoy Kroll.'

Haaron almost felt sorry for Karsten as he thought of Nicolene stranded in the barren countryside, so far from anything resembling castle life. Haegen was surely going to have a better time with Irenna, who seemed far more inclined to be practical and accommodating. 'Well, there's always Vesta. No doubt your mother is already making plans for your return. She will miss the children, I imagine. Even her own.'

Karsten nodded. 'I expect so, but she'll have Jaeger now, won't she? The biggest child of all.'

Haaron sucked in a sharp breath, almost inhaling a berry. 'Your mother can be very persuasive when she wants to be.'

'That she can. Although, perhaps she has persuaded you to keep the wrong son. It might have been wiser to send Jaeger as far away as possible,' Karsten whispered, his eyes on Nicolene. She seemed oblivious to the fact that he was there, watching as she stared at his brother. 'I'm not sure that Jaeger is such good company anymore.'

Haaron grunted. 'Yes, he has become more unpredictable. Less aware of his place in this family.'

Karsten inclined his head towards Haaron. 'Best watch your back, Father. From what I hear, your new dreamer spends a lot of time in *his* chamber. As does my wife.'

Haaron blinked, surprised on both counts.

***

Aleksander was relieved. They finally had horses. Three of them. Clear-eyed, glossy-coated, well cared for horses. They had even managed to buy some apples, smoked pork, and a wedge of hard cheese from the greedy farmer they had come across, who was eager to part with anything for a handful of their silver coins, much to his wife's annoyance. Greedy, but not particularly savvy, Aleksander thought to himself as he listened to how many more coins still jangled in his pouch.

But now they could ride, although, just as they departed the farm, the rain came down again and they couldn't see anything ahead but threatening storm clouds promising a very miserable journey to Tuura.

But, hopefully, no ravens.

***

Jael felt a sudden lack of confidence as she shuffled her legs apart, balancing herself. It wasn't helped by the way the guard was glaring at her: as though he wanted to break her. Not just beat her, or humiliate her, but actually break her into pieces.

Her limbs felt stiff and heavy, covered in bird holes, stinking of the stomach-churning salve, and she couldn't remember the last time that she'd broken a sweat in a training ring. Shaking her head, Jael walked up to meet her opponent, smiling as she thought of the advice she would have given Thorgils if his mind was as scattered as hers.

'What's your name?' Jael called. 'I'd like to know the name of the man I'm about to defeat.'

Apart from her men, who smiled and nudged each other, the crowd remained mostly serious which unsettled Jael even further. No one in this place seemed alive at all; certainly not the soldiers and temple guards who were there in numbers now, watching on silently.

'Baccus,' he growled, sweeping his sword towards hers, cracking the wooden blades together.

Jael stepped back quickly, lunging to the side, rapping him on the waist. He didn't blink as he charged her, slashing his sword from side to side with speed, trying to get past hers. Jael skidded, digging her feet into the mud, standing and swaying as she parried his blows, feeling the immense power behind them; his determination to defeat her.

Baccus was quickly pushing her back with his sheer strength; the power behind his sword doubling anything she could offer in return.

Gritting her teeth, Jael spun away, out of his reach, kicking him in the hip, changing her angle, smacking her leg across his waist. He turned to smile at her, not troubled in the slightest.

Jael frowned, trying to think, but Baccus was quickly in her face again.

Aedan leaned towards Fyn. 'Baccus is a real prick,' he muttered. 'I hope my cousin knows what she's doing.'

Fyn nodded confidently, not taking his eyes off Jael. 'She does, don't worry.'

Jael jabbed her sword at Baccus' stomach, but he jerked away, feinted left, slipped to the right and punched her straight in the eye.

Jael's head snapped back, shock flooding her body, taking away any pain she should have felt at that moment. She stumbled backwards, shaking her head, cursing herself for being so slow; for taking him too lightly; for not having any ideas at all.

What was wrong with her?

She straightened up quickly as Baccus charged, her ears ringing, black patches flashing in front of her eyes, or at least the one eye that was still open. She shook her head again, trying to clear her vision as she brought her blade up to block his.

Fyn frowned, his shoulders tensing.

Kormac squeezed through the crowd to join his sons. 'What's Jael doing fighting Baccus?' he wondered. 'He's a real prick.'

Aedan laughed.

'You needn't worry about Jael,' Fyn assured him. 'I've seen her defeat men much bigger and stronger than that.' But he felt odd, wanting to take back his words, not wishing to tempt the gods, who were surely always listening to fools like him making such grand predictions.

Baccus wasn't giving Jael any time to come up with better ideas. He hacked his sword towards her face, putting all his weight behind it. Jael jumped back. She couldn't even see out of the one eye that was open. Everything was a muddy haze; the ringing turning to a loud buzzing in her ears now.

Dropping to the ground, she swept her leg towards his ankles.

She always kept knives down her boots, tucked into her socks.

Baccus was surprised by the sharp crack on his ankle bone. He stumbled, grimacing. Jael was up and skipping backwards as he righted himself, both of them shaking their heads now; Jael, blinking quickly, still trying to see, gripped her sword tighter, finally waking up.

Aron elbowed Aedan. 'That was good!'

Kormac didn't smile. 'He doesn't look bothered, though. And I'm not sure Jael can even see.'

Fyn thought that Kormac was right. Jael looked shaken.

Baccus strode towards her. 'Where's the book?' he hissed, baring his teeth. 'I know you've hidden it somewhere.'

'Book?' Jael looked bemused, though with only one eye open that was hard to pull off. 'I don't know anything about a book.' She lunged, slicing her sword towards his throat.

She wasn't fast.

She didn't mean to be.

Baccus easily slapped her blade away, turning his over the top of hers, pushing it down.

Jael slid underneath it, behind him, reversing her sword, slamming the wooden hilt into his lower back. Baccus staggered forward, and Jael spun around quickly, kicking him over. He lost his footing in the mud, falling, his face splashing into a puddle. Jael quickly jumped onto his back, jamming her boot against his shoulder, her sword against his neck.

Fight over.

Jael's cousins turned to smile at Fyn, who sighed in relief.

But Baccus was not done.

And reaching behind himself, he snatched at Jael's ankle, pulling her off her feet, down to the ground, onto her back, rolling over the top of her, wrapping his hands around her throat.

Fyn lurched forward, but the soldier standing next to him stuck out an arm, holding him back.

'You'll not enter the ring!' he growled as more soldiers flocked to him, forming a barricade.

Fyn glanced at Kormac, panic in his eyes. More soldiers and guards surged through the crowd, forcing their way up to the railings, surrounding the training ring.

Keeping everyone out.

Jael could feel Baccus' breath, warm and sour, all over her face. Her one open eye could see clearly now. He was not a man ready to be beaten at all.

His weight took all the air out of her lungs.

His hands took all the breath out of her throat.

She thought of Tarak. Of how close he had come to killing her.

There was no Eadmund to save her now.

CHAPTER TWENTY SIX

'When will Ivaar come?' Evaine wondered irritably. She had grown impatient with everyone's attention being claimed by the impending attack. Nibbling around the outside of a flatbread, she tried to catch Eadmund's eye, but he had turned his head towards the fire as if she wasn't even there. 'What is it?' Evaine wondered. She put down the flatbread, which was stale, and walked around to Eadmund, squeezing herself onto his knee. 'Has something happened?'

Eadmund felt as though he couldn't breathe. The hair on his arms was lifting in warning. Something was wrong. He was no dreamer, but his whole body felt on edge. Even his throat had tightened.

Something was wrong.

***

Fyn panicked, trying to force his way through the soldiers, catching glimpses of Jael's boots banging on the ground, her legs kicking helplessly under Baccus' giant frame.

She couldn't move her arms. Couldn't reach for her sword.

He was strangling her. His eyes were chillingly blank. His

hands squeezed harder and harder around her throat, but his face betrayed no effort at all. He wasn't going to stop, Jael could tell.

He would kill her.

Fyn drew his sword, but the soldiers quickly shoved him back, blocking his path. 'Jael!' he cried desperately. 'Jael! Somebody help!'

Beorn was beside him, sword out, trying to find a way through, his men rushing to his side.

'You would let him kill a queen? In a training match?' Kormac called loudly, desperate to do something; trying to spur the crowd into action. He spun around urgently, imploring the Tuurans, and the soldiers who were blocking Jael's men from getting through. 'For what reason? Are we *murderers* here? Will we do nothing to stop this? She is a queen!'

Jael stopped moving.

Her legs stilled beneath Baccus, her eyes closed.

'Jael!' Fyn cried helplessly. 'Jael!'

Baccus released his hands, slowly pushing himself away from Jael's chest. She quickly brought her leg up to her hand, slid the knife out of her sock, and slammed the blade into the base of his throat, drawing it out again just as quickly. He fell off her in shock, grabbing his neck and Jael was scrambling to her feet, knife in one hand, *Toothpick* swiftly in the other, trying to breathe, crouching, daring him to come for her again.

But Baccus staggered sideways, blood gushing down his tunic as he stumbled to the ground. The soldiers and guards flooded the ring; an angry mass of red and black uniforms. The guards raced to Baccus, the soldiers to Jael.

Jael held *Toothpick* out, keeping them at bay. 'He tried to kill me!' she croaked, her voice a strained whisper as she spun, watching the soldiers edge forward. She coughed, trying not to vomit. 'Everyone saw that! You will take me to your elderman now!'

Fyn, Beorn, and the Osslanders were in the ring, trying to

reach Jael through the swarm of soldiers. Aedan and Aron drew their own swords, preparing to follow them, but Kormac held them back. Jael would have to handle this on her own now.

He pulled his sons away, urging them back to the house.

***

Isaura blanched at the sight of Evaine sitting on Eadmund's lap.

She was an unpleasant, manipulative girl and Isaura wished that she'd stayed in the house. But Thorgils had suggested that Ayla would enjoy some company, so he had dropped Isaura and the children at the hall, then hurried away to take Eadmund's horse for a ride.

Something was wrong, Isaura knew, but Thorgils wasn't telling her anything. Not yet. It would take some time before they grew used to each other again, she knew.

She hoped they would. Hoped there would be time.

That Ivaar wouldn't ruin it all.

'The children look tired,' Ayla said distractedly.

Mads was grizzling, Leya was sulking; Annet and Selene just looked numb as they peered around the hall, not knowing what to do with themselves.

Isaura sighed. 'I'm happy with tired, though,' she decided. 'When we were on that ship...' She felt instantly sick, remembering the enormous waves, the spectre of the stone spires as they lurched out of the darkness. 'I didn't think we'd survive. We were preparing for the worst, but suddenly that storm just vanished.'

Ayla could feel the pain in her thigh, and she adjusted herself on the bench, ignoring Isaura, worrying about Bruno, then smiling at Bram as he entered the hall.

Isaura turned to follow her gaze, relieved to see someone

who could hopefully make sense of everything.

'So, how is he, then?' Bram wondered, sitting down with a thump. 'Or, more to the point, *where* is he? I haven't seen him all day, and there's a lot to discuss.' He reached for the jug that sat in the middle of the table, filling a cup, disappointed to discover that it contained only water.

Isaura looked at Bram, her face blank. 'Thorgils?'

Bram could see that she had no idea what he was talking about. Taking a quick drink, he sighed. 'Odda died in the night.'

Isaura looked shocked. 'Oh.'

'He didn't say a word. Hasn't said a word to me yet, but we need to start thinking about a pyre.' Bram's eyes lifted as a hall door opened and Runa walked in. He smiled. 'Perhaps I can find someone else to help me get things underway while we wait for my nephew. Give him some time.'

Isaura nodded blankly, feeling the sudden urge to take a horse and find Thorgils, but she had no idea where he might have gone.

***

Jael strode across the grand chamber towards the black-robed man who stood waiting before the Fire of Light, flanked by a cluster of red-breasted guards.

There was no sign of Marcus.

Perhaps they had simply removed the pretence now, Jael thought as she tried to blink her right eye open. Gotten rid of Marcus entirely? But would they be able to find the book?

'Your guard tried to kill me,' she rasped loudly, coming to a stop. 'Why is that? Is Tuura an enemy to the Slave Islands now? An enemy to Brekka? To try and kill a queen?' She shook her ringing head. 'That would be a declaration of war! My brother and my husband would come for you with all their ships, all their men. Is that what your dreamers are advising you to do? Start a *war*?' She was furious, her anger boiling like water.

Gerod was quickly on the front foot, incensed by her arrogance. 'Tried to kill *you*? In a fight you willingly participated in?' He laughed, and it echoed high up to the rafters. 'But surely you are not that naive? With all the experience you have? To think that there are no risks involved in fighting a skilled warrior? A man who is bigger, stronger, *better* than you? It seems to me that you simply failed in your judgement. What else was Baccus supposed to do but try to win the fight? Was that not the point?'

Jael was unnerved by how quickly he had turned the truth upside down. She smiled coldly. There was no joy to be found here, she realised. No answers at all. And, if The Following controlled the elders, the dreamers, the temple, and the soldiers... well, they were in about as much trouble as they could possibly be. 'As you say, perhaps it was just a misunderstanding. But I would think it always advisable *not* to try and kill a queen if you don't want to turn your neighbours into enemies. Not until you're ready to go to war, at least.' Jael didn't take her one eye off Gerod's pale, shining face.

Gerod's eyes widened as he glared at her. It was a look so intense that Jael could tell that he was imagining killing her. Slowly. He was dangerous, she knew, and he had done something with Marcus. And now, without Hanna, there was no one who could help him.

No one but her.

'I shall heed your advice, my lady,' Gerod said smoothly, walking up to Jael, pointing her back towards the doors. 'But for now, I think it best if you return to your family and have that eye seen to.'

'And what of the elderman?' Jael asked, walking back to the doors. 'When will I see him again? He promised to meet with me. There is more I need to know.'

'*Know?*' Gerod shook his head, bemused. 'As far as I'm aware, and from what the elderman told me, you know everything you need to know. There is nothing more to be found here. As soon as your grandmother has recovered, you should return to your husband. I'm sure he is spending every waking moment thinking about you.' And smiling, Gerod guided Jael through the open door.

Jael stopped, turning around, determined to say something more, but Gerod quickly slammed the door in her battered face.

***

It felt good to be back on Oss, Isaura decided as she walked to the house, the children running ahead of her in the lightly falling rain, and yet she did not want to get comfortable, to make assumptions. For, if Ivaar took the fort it would not feel good to be back at all.

He would kill Thorgils. Perhaps her too.

At least, she thought to herself, he would never hurt the children.

The children stopped just before they reached the house. They saw Thorgils waiting for them by the door, and none of them wanted him to be there at all. They missed their island and their home, but most of all, they missed their father.

Mads burst into violent tears, throwing himself to the ground before scrambling back to his mother, who lifted him into her arms, wincing at the ear piercing sound she knew so well.

'You have a way with children,' she laughed, trying to make Thorgils smile.

Thorgils didn't smile.

'Selene, Annet, take your sister into the house,' Isaura said firmly. 'Get your cloaks off and ask Selda to dry them by the fire.' The girls hesitated, eyeing Thorgils with scowls, but one look at their mother and they grabbed Leya's hands, pulling her towards the door.

Thorgils felt even worse. Any thoughts he might have had of a new, happy family had only been a dream, he realised.

This was Ivaar's family.

Not his.

He shrugged, walking towards Isaura who was pulling Mads' hood up to keep the rain off his little, blonde head. 'You think it's the beard?' Thorgils asked seriously. 'Perhaps it's too big and scary?' He opened his eyes wide at Mads who howled even louder.

Isaura wasn't sure what to do. She cooed in Mads' ear, trying to calm him, but every time he looked at Thorgils, he cried even louder.

Thorgils held out a filthy thumb, pushing it towards Mads, who ignored it, and turned his head away, resting it on his mother's shoulder. 'Well, perhaps it's a sign from the gods that I should stop avoiding things and get back to Odda's.' His voice caught then, tears in his eyes.

Dropping his head, he tried to move past Isaura.

'I'll come with you,' she said gently. 'You're not alone now. I'm here.'

Somehow, Thorgils heard her over her son's grizzling, and he stopped, thinking that those were the nicest words he'd ever heard. He turned, reaching for her hand. It was wet but soft and comforting, and he squeezed it, smiling at her wailing son who had turned his head around again to see what was happening.

Accidentally catching Thorgils' eye, Mads quickly twisted his head as far away from him as possible.

And this time, Thorgils laughed.

***

'Jael!'

Biddy hurried to the door as Jael stepped inside. It was only just after midday, she was sure, but with the window blocked over it was dark and oppressive in the house.

Kormac was there with Aedan and Aron, who weren't going back to the smithy until they knew how Jael was. And she didn't look good.

Biddy fussed around Jael, trying to remove her cloak, shaking her head at the bruises around her neck, grimacing as she peered at her swollen eye. The puppies rushed around her feet, climbing her legs, almost themselves again.

'What did they say at the temple?' Kormac wondered, standing up to offer Jael his stool as she approached the fire. 'Did you speak to the elderman?'

Biddy glanced at Entorp, who had uncorked a jar of salve as he approached, making everyone cringe.

'You are *not* going to put that on me!' Jael grumbled moodily. She quickly changed course, walking over to check on Edela, who appeared to be sleeping. Leaving her in peace, Jael stepped back to the fire, keeping well away from Entorp. 'I saw someone else. A thin, pale man. Dark hair. Strange eyes. I don't know his name. But he was unhelpful. Threatening, even. He appears to be in charge now.'

She watched them all watching her, questions poised on the tips of their tongues, desperate to know more. There was no Gisila or Branwyn – they had left earlier to take Eydis for a walk – but everyone else knew what had happened in the training ring and they were not inclined to be satisfied with nothing.

'Sounds like Gerod Gott,' Kormac murmured. 'He's a senior elderman. Always wanted to be *the* elderman from what I hear.'

'Mmmm, well maybe he is,' Jael rasped, holding her hands

to the flames. 'There was no sign of Marcus anywhere.'

'But, but that soldier...' Fyn spluttered as he sat down and removed his muddy boot, looking for the stone that had been rolling around under his foot all morning. 'He tried to kill you! He wasn't interested in anything but killing you!'

He wasn't wrong, Jael thought to herself. She had felt that too; seen it in his eyes. But why?

'Here,' Biddy said, handing her the cup of warm chamomile tea she had been drinking. 'This might help.'

'Yes, thank you.' And sitting down, at last, Jael took a sip, appreciating the warm liquid as it eased her raw throat. 'No!' she grumbled as Entorp approached her eye again. 'If you bring that salve near me, I will hit you, Entorp Bray!'

Biddy smiled, watching Entorp creep away. 'But you really should let him if you want to see out of that eye again quickly. The way things are going around here, you might need to.'

'Jael.'

Jael turned to the bed where Edela lay, her eyes fluttering open. She handed Biddy her cup and hurried to her grandmother's side, pleased to see a hint of life in Edela's face. They had started feeding her. Not much, just little spoonfuls every now and then. Liquids too. Healing herbs. There was almost colour in her cheeks, but she was still so weak.

Edela frowned, blinking rapidly at the sight of Jael's face. 'What were you doing?'

'It was just a fight, Grandmother. Nothing more than I've done countless times.' She shook her head. 'I just wasn't myself. Wasn't thinking clearly enough. It's my own fault.'

'But what about the...' Edela whispered faintly, trying to catch her breath.

Jael leaned forward, placing her ear close to Edela's lips. 'The what?'

Edela sighed heavily, closing her eyes again. Exhausted. 'Baby.'

***

'Eadmund, what is wrong with you today?' Evaine glanced towards her father, raising her eyebrows in irritation. Eadmund was so distracted, not listening to anything they were saying to him. 'Didn't you hear my father?'

Eadmund rubbed his eyes, turning to Morac who waited before him. 'I'm sorry, no, I didn't. What were you saying, Morac?'

'The pyre is ready, my lord,' Morac muttered. He had despised Odda Svanter, as had most, and he felt no desire to provide her with anything for her departure to the Otherworld. But, he knew that his king would think otherwise, so he had made every effort to ensure that her pyre was of a fairly high standard.

'Good,' Eadmund sighed, not looking forward to it at all. 'I'll go and find Thorgils. See if he's ready to begin. We don't want the next storm to come halfway through the burn.' He turned his head, listening to the sudden, raucous crying from behind the curtain.

Evaine didn't even blink.

'Should you go and check on Sigmund?' Eadmund wondered.

Evaine fiddled with her amber brooch, thinking how plain her jewellery looked; how ordinary her dresses appeared. If she was going to be queen here, she needed to start looking like one. 'Why?' she asked blankly. 'Tanja is back there with Runa. They don't need me as well.' She laughed, smiling at her father, who did not smile back.

Thorgils opened the door for Isaura, who walked into the hall with her son in her arms. Eadmund was happy to see them together again, for, although Thorgils had just lost his mother, he had gained a new family.

Eadmund could sympathise with the pain of losing a parent. He kept hearing Eirik's voice, barking at him. He could almost see his father rolling his eyes as he tugged impatiently on his beard, displeased with every decision he made.

But most of all, he kept imagining his father's fury at the absence of Jael. Eirik had chosen Jael to be the Queen of Oss, not because she had married Eadmund, but because she had earned it. He had believed in her; believed that she would look after his kingdom and his son.

And now she was gone, and Eadmund knew that it was all his fault.

***

Jael glanced around, but no one was looking her way.

She turned back to Edela who appeared to be sleeping again, checking under her pillow. She had placed one of Hanna's stones beneath it, not wanting anyone to invade Edela's dreams.

It was still there.

'Jael?' Entorp murmured as he approached with another jar. 'I have something else that might help your eye. It smells good, I think.'

'How many of these jars do you *have*, Entorp?' Jael wondered, frowning apprehensively as he uncorked it, but the smell was subtle, floral even, and her stomach did not protest. 'Well, alright then,' she said, sitting forward, her body throbbing where Baccus had choked her throat, crushed her chest, punched her in the eye.

She felt uncomfortable all over, but none of the wounds bothered her as much as the one she felt to her pride.

'What were you thinking, getting into a fight with a soldier?' Biddy grumbled.

'He offered to fight Jael,' Fyn said, rushing to her defense; feeling guilty that he hadn't been able to help her earlier. 'It was only supposed to be a training match. He tried to strangle her to death!'

Branwyn gasped as she stood in the doorway. 'Jael! Are you alright?' She rushed inside, Gisila and Eydis right behind her.

Gisila took one look at her daughter's face and put her hands over her mouth.

'Jael?' Eydis was frantic, not knowing what was happening. She had been upset while they were gone; on edge, desperate to get back to the house.

She had a growing sense of unease and was desperate to speak to Jael alone.

Jael reached for Eydis' hand, shooing away Entorp who had surely slathered her in enough of his salve for now. 'I'm fine, Eydis. Just a black eye, which is my own fault for being too slow-witted to see what was coming.' She smiled and squeezed Eydis' hand, guiding her down to the bed. 'I've looked a lot worse, just ask Biddy!'

Biddy nodded, glancing at Gisila who was sucking in her cheeks.

'Why don't you go and have some of Biddy's tea, Mother?' Jael suggested. 'It might calm you down.'

'Yes, that sounds like a good idea,' Branwyn agreed, peering at Jael's eye. 'That looks painful.'

'It doesn't hurt,' Jael lied, distracted by the overwhelming sense of unease coursing through her body. She needed some help.

She needed to speak to Eydis and Fyn.

***

'What were you *thinking*?' Gerod seethed, rounding on the dreamer. She was a young woman, new to the Chamber of Dreams. It was a great honour to be accepted into the chamber. Not all dreamers rose to such high status within the temple. But those who did were required to dream for the elderman. They were given orders to focus their dreams on whichever subject the elderman requested.

The dreamers who resided in the chamber now were those who had been taught dark magic, passed down through generations of The Following. They knew how to manipulate events and people, as though they were pulling on invisible strings; strands so delicate that only the dreamer could see them.

They had marked out their enemies, binding those who caused trouble or chose to go against The Following. And once bound, they could always find ways to control those people for their own ends.

'You cannot just kill her!' Gerod yelled. 'Without my authority? Without my explicit order? What were you thinking?' They needed that book. And he was beginning to realise that Jael Furyck might be the only one who knew where it was.

The dreamer blinked slowly, her eyes glazed, still lost in the trance she had gone into when she was controlling Baccus. She dropped her head to her chest, avoiding his wild eyes, certain she should feel embarrassed.

'Find me that book!' Gerod growled, looking around the chamber. It was a wide, almost-round room on the very top floor of the temple; an addition built many years ago, exclusively for dreamers. A bare, cold chamber, it had enormous smoke holes in the roof to expel the smoke from their dream walking fires.

Of which there were many.

'Find me that book and then we will kill her! Then we will kill them all!'

CHAPTER TWENTY SEVEN

It was not much, Thorgils thought, embarrassed on behalf of his mother for the meagre offerings he had scattered around her wrapped body. He wasn't sure why he felt that way. Odda certainly wouldn't have cared what anyone thought.

Stepping back, he smiled sadly, wiping his nose on the back of his hand.

'It looks fine,' Isaura assured him softly, slipping her arm through his.

Thorgils shrugged, unconvinced. 'Well, I'm sure they'll be able to hear her grumbling in the Otherworld soon.'

Isaura didn't think he was wrong.

The pyre did look fine. Perfectly fine for a woman like Odda Svanter, who had left her life with as much as she had come into it; whose one achievement had been the tall, red-headed man who stood sadly before her shrouded body, torch in hand, having just set fire to the tower of wood carefully stacked beneath her.

Thorgils' chest heaved as he sobbed, ducking his head, his tears dripping onto the muddy ground.

Torstan came forward and took the flaming torch from his hand, patting Thorgils on the back before turning to Eadmund, who was far away, remembering his father's pyre; smelling the smoke already snaking up to the clouds, blown about on a steady wind.

His father's pyre and now Odda's.

And then whose?

How many more would they need to build when Ivaar came?

***

Jael felt a sense of peace as she sat down in the wooden house. If only *Sea Bear* were full and they were about to depart for Oss.

'What do you mean *trapped*?' Fyn asked anxiously.

They were each holding one of Hanna's stones.

No one else was on board.

Jael kept looking through the holes in the wall, wanting to ensure it remained that way.

'The elderman told me that The Following has taken over Tuura.'

Fyn looked confused.

'They are dangerous,' Eydis shivered. 'So dangerous.'

Jael was surprised. 'You know this? How?'

'I have seen them in my dreams, in hooded black robes. They want to kill you. I feel it so strongly.'

'Yes, I think you're right, Eydis. But not just me. Everyone. Everyone in Osterland. All of us. And now that the Book of Darkness is in Hest with Morana, they have a chance of doing it. Look at those ravens,' she breathed. 'How else did that happen if not for Morana and that evil book? And that guard today? He looked as though he wasn't even there. There was something wrong with him.'

'What do you mean?' Fyn wondered.

'Hanna said that the soldiers were bound by the dreamers. Just like Eadmund, I suppose.'

'But Evaine was not controlling Eadmund, was she?' Eydis

suggested. 'Just forcing him to love her?'

Jael saw a vision of Evaine sitting on Eadmund's knee. Sparks of anger and pain burst inside her heart. 'Yes, but maybe being bound opens you up to more than we realised. Perhaps once you're bound, they can control you?'

'At least we have our tattoos,' Fyn said, relieved that his mother had taken him to Entorp before they'd left.

'But not everyone does. And tattoos won't save us from ravens or whatever it is that Morana is planning next.'

'What should we do?' Fyn asked, rubbing his fingers across the smooth stone. 'What can we do?'

It was a good question.

'I can't get that book again. It's too much of a risk, but perhaps you can dream about it, Eydis? Look for answers. If that book counters dark magic, there must be a way to unbind the soldiers or anyone who isn't in The Following willingly.'

'We have to set them free,' Eydis whispered, shivering. 'They will not let us leave here until we do.'

***

Berard had his head down as he walked towards the castle doors, struggling to decide how he felt about everything. The thought of starting a new life away from his family appealed. He could imagine himself as a lord, not cowed by his father or his brothers, but master of his own domain.

He smiled, thinking that perhaps it was just what he needed. To be far away from judgement and scorn. Respected, admired, noticed even, by men and women who would follow him.

But...

His family had always thought him entirely useless. And perhaps there was a reason for that? Why did he think that he stood a chance of being able to achieve anything on his own, away from them? Berard shook his head, his shoulders sinking as he approached the doors.

'Berard!' Haegen grumbled, turning back to his brother. 'Come on! It will be supper before we even *get* to the training ground!'

'Ahhh, don't worry, Brother,' Karsten laughed, limping beside him. 'It won't take us long once we get there. We'll only need to look at Berard for him to drop his sword and surrender!'

Berard muttered to himself, not wanting to train with his brothers at all. But now that he was going to be out in the kingdom on his own, he would not have them to protect or defend him anymore. He would be the Lord of Solt, responsible for all the men, women, and children in his fort and beyond.

And he wouldn't be much of a lord if he couldn't even protect himself.

Lifting his head, Berard scurried after Haegen and Karsten.

***

'How is she?' Jael wondered as she sat by the fire, defrosting her toes. Her head was ringing with the sound of angry ravens, with Marcus' warning, and with her father's voice, loudest of all.

You have to *do* something, he kept urging furiously.

Biddy looked up from spooning thin broth into Edela's mouth. 'Eating, which is good,' she smiled. 'Better than good. Much better than I ever thought possible.'

Jael felt her shoulders relax as she stroked Vella, who lay curled up on her knee. The puppies had barely left the house since the raven attack.

She didn't blame them.

Eydis sat on a rug by her feet, Ido over her lap. Fyn had left with Kormac and his sons to collect more iron ore to make weapons. Branwyn and Gisila had gone to buy extra food from Tuura's small market. With so many mouths to feed and the fear of what might happen next, they were all eager to be as prepared as possible.

Biddy saw that Edela's eyes had closed, so she wiped her mouth with a cloth and stood up, leaving her to sleep. 'How about a hot drink, Eydis?' she asked. 'It's not very warm today with that wind out there and all these holes in the walls now! I wouldn't mind something warm myself.'

Eydis nodded, and Biddy left the bowl in the kitchen as she hunted around for three cups. 'How is that eye feeling?' she wondered, ripping up handfuls of peppermint leaves and adding them to the bottom of the cups. She used her apron to lift the cauldron of hot water off its hook and took it to the kitchen to pour over the leaves.

'It's going to make sleeping interesting tonight,' Jael grinned, ferreting in her pouch.

'I'm not sure that any of us are going to be sleeping anyway,' Biddy shuddered, thinking about those evil birds. She walked back to Jael and Eydis, handing them a cup each. 'Careful, it's hot.'

'Thank you,' Jael said, taking her cup and slipping a stone into Biddy's hand.

'What's this?' Biddy asked, frowning.

'That stone will stop the dreamers watching or hearing you,' Jael said quickly. 'Eydis has one. I've put one under Edela's pillow. I have one too. You'll have to give it back to me when we've finished talking. Until we make more, those are all I have.'

'You think the dreamers are *watching* us? All the time?' Biddy was suddenly fearful as she perched on the very edge of a stool, forgetting all about her own cup of tea as she looked the stone over.

'Yes, so we can only talk if we have a stone and the people we're talking to have one as well. We're trapped here, I'm certain now. The Following has taken over. I think they're holding Marcus prisoner in the temple. They've bound the soldiers and anyone who is a threat to their rule. They must be working with Morana. Why else would those birds have come here? Eydis is going to try and dream about the book Marcus gave me. It's the only way I can think of to get us out of here. It must have something in it that can break the binding spell.'

Biddy stared at Jael, too stunned to speak.

'It does,' came a faint whisper from the bed.

***

Karsten's lips curled back in anger as he lunged for Haegen.

He wasn't angry at him. It was just Haegen's unfortunate luck that he looked the most like their youngest brother; almost as large, with the same golden hair, the same almond-shaped eyes.

But he was not Jaeger, and Berard was desperately trying to remind Karsten of that. 'We should go back to the castle!' Berard called as Haegen ducked another vicious blow. 'Think of your wounds!'

Berard was right, and his plea was perfectly timed as Karsten's knee gave out and he staggered to a stop.

Haegen knocked Karsten over, dropping on top of him, his sword at his brother's throat. 'You *are* in a foul mood today,' he panted, rolling away, wiping blood from his mouth. Karsten had been vicious, more intent on attacking him than training. 'You shouldn't be so impatient to get your strength back. It will come in time.'

Karsten was too angry to speak as he struggled back to his

feet, whacking away Berard's attempt to help him up.

'Leave him be, Berard!' Haegen warned. 'Unless you want a black eye too?' He felt his face, certain that his left eye was already closing up. 'Maybe we should just leave Karsten to train with Jaeger? The two of them could try to kill each other while we watch?' He grinned, but neither Karsten nor Berard looked amused. 'What?' Haegen wondered as he walked over to a stone bench and sat; sweat-drenched, sore, bleeding, but happy. He was feeling strong again.

Unlike his brothers.

Berard came to join him, scowling.

'Why are *you* so angry?' Haegen wondered. 'That's not like you. Aren't you happy to be leaving? Becoming a lord?'

'Are you?' Karsten snorted, pacing back and forth in front of them. He had no intention of sitting. He wanted to stretch out his knee. He wanted to get stronger. Tougher. Back to himself again. 'You're going to keep smiling, are you? As though what Father is doing is perfectly normal?'

Haegen did smile. 'I think he's making an interesting choice,' he admitted. 'But it will be good for us. That we can become lords? Get experience ruling? I like the idea. And Vastera's no shithole, so even Irenna's looking forward to it.'

Karsten stared at Haegen as though he'd gone mad. 'And you?' he growled at Berard, hoping to find someone who still possessed some sense.

Berard blinked. 'I... I can see Father's reasoning,' he said diplomatically. He was starting to become nervous, realising that he would have no wife to take with him. No wife, no children, and now, not even a servant.

He would be going to Solt alone, leaving Meena behind with Jaeger, which, he supposed, was what she wanted. But still, it didn't feel right.

'His *reasoning*?' Karsten laughed bitterly, adjusting his eye patch as he finally sat down. He glanced around the empty, muddy ring. There were other training grounds dotted around the city but this one, tucked down a road next to the castle, was reserved for the royal family. Slaves stood around the edges of the ring, cloths draped over one arm, holding jugs of ale and cups, waiting to attend to whatever needs the royal princes might have. 'His *reasoning* makes no sense. He's keeping Jaeger here when it's Jaeger who's responsible for everything that's gone wrong! It's Jaeger who's the biggest threat to him!'

Haegen looked surprised. 'Calm down, you idiot!' he grumbled. 'It wasn't all Jaeger's fault. Why would you say that? What could *you* have done in his place against that sea-fire?'

'Always so reasonable, Brother!' Karsten spat. 'But you'll see. You'll see how he destroys everything. How he destroys every one of us, piece by piece. I heard Varna tell Father that once. That if he wasn't careful, the Bear would destroy us all!'

***

Edela didn't appear to have the energy to say anything else. She blinked at Biddy, then closed her eyes again.

'It's how we broke Eadmund from Evaine's binding spell,' Biddy explained as they stood around Edela's bed. 'Your grandmother remembered a symbol from that book. Entorp carved it into Evaine's floor, under a rug. She must have found it, though, and destroyed it as poor Eadmund is trapped again.'

Jael remembered how it had been in Hest. How Eadmund had come back to her so briefly, before he was gone again. She sighed, watching Edela try to nod her head. 'But there must be another way to break Evaine's spell? A different symbol? She says that she's bound Eadmund to her soul now. That if she dies, he will still be bound to her.'

Edela's eyes popped open. She had never heard of such a thing. 'Eydis,' she said hoarsely. 'Eydis can see the book.' And she closed her eyes, her head sinking heavily into the pillow, exhausted.

She would try and find that book too.

It was time for her to have a dream that wasn't about that evil cave.

***

'Oh!' Meena exclaimed, smacking into Berard, who was hurrying around the corner towards his chamber.

Berard leaned forward, reaching out to set Meena right. 'I'm so sorry! I wasn't looking where I was going,' he muttered, his tongue tangling as he glanced at his boots; mud-covered, much like the rest of him after Karsten and Haegen had cheered themselves up at his expense.

Meena looked just as awkward as they stood before each other. 'You are... going back to your chamber?' she asked, looking up and down the empty corridor. Not being able to find Egil, Jaeger had sent her to search for Morana. He was irate, desperate for her to come and look at the book again.

Meena was reluctant to even go back. She had thought of escaping, but with her aunt's ability to dream even without the Book of Darkness, she realised that there was no point.

'Yes, I have no appetite tonight.'

'Oh?'

'There is much to do, I suppose, and not many days left to do it,' Berard said thoughtfully, realising the truth in that statement. 'I have a lot on my mind.'

Meena felt an urge to offer her help, but she didn't dare open her mouth. She tapped her head instead.

'Meena!'

Meena jumped, dropping her eyes to the floor.

Jaeger strode down the torchlit corridor towards them. 'Meena!' he growled. 'Where have you been?' Gripping her arm, he yanked her hand away from her head, turning her towards him. 'And where is Morana?' He didn't even acknowledge Berard.

Meena grimaced in discomfort.

'You shouldn't grab her like that,' Berard mumbled, trying to meet his brother's eyes, hidden in the shadows as they were.

'What? What did you say?' Jaeger's head snapped towards Berard. 'She is not your servant anymore. Go find yourself another, and leave mine alone.' And gripping Meena even harder, he pulled her down the corridor.

Meena's head shook as she hurried after him on her tiptoes.

Berard watched them go, digging his feet into his boots. He felt incensed, worried for Meena, and completely helpless all at the same time.

***

Haaron edged his chair closer to Morana, wanting to see her eyes. 'Perhaps I am being too generous to my wife?' he mused. 'Letting Jaeger stay? Perhaps it is better that he goes? I can keep one of the others instead. Berard is useless, no threat to me, I'm sure. But Jaeger...' He shook his head. 'I was half asleep when Bayla pounced on me.'

Morana narrowed her eyes. 'You want *my* approval?' Her lips twisted into a sneer. 'Do what you want with your sons. I do not know them.'

Haaron peered at her, confused. 'But you suggested that they were a threat to my throne.'

'And they are. Every king's sons are a threat to their throne, especially ambitious ones.' Morana cracked her neck, sliding forward on the stool. 'But you must ask yourself what you care about more? Your throne or your wife?' She turned her head, fixing one eye on him. 'I see your wife. She loves you still. But if you change your mind and send away her favourite child?' Morana shrugged. 'It is your choice to make, and you know her better than I...' She hunched back and sighed, certain that Jaeger would be stalking the corridors, looking for her again.

Haaron studied the dreamer closely. 'He is no threat to me, then? Not yet, at least?'

'He is a threat to everyone, that one,' Morana said slowly. 'But when I see him, I see a broken, little boy. He hides in his chamber, shunning his brothers, plotting ways to kill the Furycks. If you are *that* worried about what he might do, why not just kill him?'

Haaron was shocked that she would be so bold. Her haggard face didn't even move as she spoke. Her eyes were lifeless.

'But of course, if you *do* kill him, your wife will hate you until her very last breath.'

Her words were no more than Haaron already knew, but it left him cold to hear them delivered so starkly. It was a choice that only he could make.

Bayla or the Bear?

***

Ayla couldn't walk easily, so Bram had helped her to a table by the fire, and Isaura had brought her a cup of wine and a plate of food. She smiled gratefully at them both, wishing that Bruno was sitting with them. He was still very weak, and it was too early to tell if his body would ever recover from the torturous conditions he had endured as Ivaar's prisoner.

Bram grinned at her. 'I'd eat up if I were you. I imagine

that'll be the last you see of food like that for a while, what with Ivaar coming for us soon!'

Isaura shivered as she scanned the hall, looking for her children. They had already eaten and were trying to befriend two cats, or rather, they were chasing the poor cats under the tables, snatching at their tails. She turned to Ayla. 'But why isn't he here yet? They were right behind us. Where did they go?'

Ayla ignored her plate of food, which did look appetising, but she was too troubled to eat. 'He *will* come,' she said with certainty.

'You saw this?' Bram leaned forward, ale dripping from his enormous beard. 'In a dream?'

Ayla nodded. 'But it was different than before. I see more ships coming now.'

Bram frowned, motioning Eadmund and Thorgils over. 'You still see those brothers with Ivaar? The Arnessons?'

'I don't know their names,' Ayla said quietly. 'But I see more than brothers. I see a whole family. Ships in a great line.'

'When, Ayla, when?' Isaura reached out, gripping Ayla's hand.

'They are... preparing,' Ayla said dreamily. 'I see them making plans.' She closed her eyes, searching back into her dream. 'They killed a lord. Slit his throat.'

Eadmund's eyes widened. 'What? *Who*?'

Ayla shrugged. 'He was old, but his wife was not. She was happy when he died.'

'Frits,' Eadmund and Thorgils said together.

'There must be something we can do?' Isaura pleaded. 'We can't just sit here and wait for them to come for us!'

Thorgils put an arm around Isaura's shoulder. 'We're prepared, don't worry. They can come, but we're prepared. This old fort has withstood greater forces than Ivaar can muster, isn't that right?' He looked at Eadmund who did not appear as confident as he was trying to sound.

Eadmund swallowed, clearing his throat. 'Thorgils is right.

It's much easier to hold a fort than break into one. They're going to have to work very hard to come even close. Don't worry. We can hold them out.'

But one look at Ayla's terrified face told him what trouble they were in.

***

'You have to give me the stone,' Jael said, sensing that everyone would soon return to the house for supper.

Biddy turned the stone over, running her fingers around the twirling symbol. It was similar to the one Entorp had carved into Evaine's floor. 'Why don't we ask Entorp to make more? He has brought all number of things in his sea chest. Not just salves! We could collect more stones, and he could paint the symbols onto them?'

Jael shook her head, feeling foolish. 'Well, of course. That's the obvious thing to do! Give me the stone, and I'll go and find him.'

Biddy smiled as she stood. 'I have no idea where he is. He's been all over the fort today, helping the injured, checking on the horses. I don't imagine he'll have anything left in his little jars soon!'

'Well, perhaps we should put him to work making some more. It would be good to start preparing ourselves for what might lie ahead.'

Biddy held out her stone to Jael, then gripped it tightly, her eyes darting about anxiously. 'What about Aleksander? He could come, couldn't he? Help us get out of here?'

Jael opened her mouth to answer but stopped herself, suddenly certain that Aleksander was already coming.

***

Another chorus of squawking chickens in the catacombs.

Morana could barely contain her annoyance as she shook her wild hair. If Yorik was the leader of The Following, why was there always so much debate about everything? How could anyone rule when they cared about other people's opinions?

Morana glowered at the cloaked figures as they stood in a circle around her and Yorik, calling out to him, demanding to be heard. Occasionally, they would look at her, both irritated and curious. She was a stranger to most of them, and not one of them liked her, she knew.

But *she* was the only one able to get near the book, so what *they* thought didn't matter in the slightest. 'We must not lose sight of our one true goal!' Morana bellowed, out of patience at last. 'To bring Raemus back! We are closer than we have ever been, but I still need some time to translate the ritual. The spell... its texts are... complex.'

'Varna could have translated it!'

Morana spun, her eyes twitching, peering at the woman who spoke. '*Varna*? Varna did not want to bring Raemus back. She wanted the book for herself! She would have given it to Haaron Dragos! Used it to help him conquer Osterland!' she yelled. 'Varna was not your friend!'

Her voice careened around the walls, echoing sharply, and the Followers shrunk back beneath their hoods, looking for Yorik to step in.

He did.

'Morana is right,' Yorik said calmly. 'We need Jaeger to bring Raemus back. He is captivated by the book. Lost to it. Desperate to feel its power again. We must cast another spell to keep him happy, especially after what happened with the ravens. He needs to trust us.'

'But this other book,' a man spoke up. 'If Gerod has not located it, then they can simply stop us again.'

Morana smiled, turning to Yorik. 'Not if we cast our spell on someone who doesn't have the book.'

***

Eadmund and Thorgils had left the hall to check how things stood from the ramparts.

Thorgils squinted at the harbour entrance, wondering who was lurking out past the stone spires. He wanted to drink until he couldn't feel the pain in his heart, but he had stopped himself because the pain in his heart would be even greater if Ivaar came for Isaura and her children. As strange as it all felt, as difficult as the road ahead appeared, he didn't want to lose the hope that was here on Oss.

Not after so many years alone.

'We need Jael,' Eadmund murmured, rubbing his forehead. 'And Axl. Bringing Brekka's fleet with them. I should have sent for her.'

It was too dark for Thorgils to see Eadmund's face. He didn't know whether he missed his wife, or felt love for her anymore. But he could hear very plainly that Eadmund wanted Jael to come.

But could she?

Would she?

'Jael would come if she could,' Thorgils decided, at last, listening to the moody howl of another approaching storm. 'Nothing would stop her.' He turned to Eadmund. 'But I'm not sure there's time to send for her help. Not anymore. Ivaar must come soon.'

Eadmund ran a hand through his beard, knowing that his

friend was right; imagining his father's disappointment in him. King for barely a moment and he had already put his people in jeopardy by making the wrong decision.

***

Kormac and Branwyn were loud snorers.

Jael wondered how anyone had managed to fall asleep at all. She supposed that Entorp and Fyn weren't having much more fun with Kayla and Aedan's daughter, whose first teeth were coming through.

Apparently, that was not a good thing.

Jael frowned, trying to make out the rafters in the darkness; listening to the wind wailing around the house; certain there was a flea in the bed. It wasn't Oss. And it wasn't her house. And she wasn't sleeping next to her husband. And he was no doubt sleeping with another woman.

But Evaine Gallas was not the Queen of Oss.

Not yet.

She kept seeing the ravens. Those birds had been turned into weapons. And they were all but helpless against them.

What would Morana try next?

Jael yawned, closing her eyes, reaching down to place a tentative hand on her belly, before quickly moving it away.

CHAPTER TWENTY EIGHT

Irenna stood in the entranceway, dressed and ready to head to the markets before breakfast. She had been unable to sleep. The thought of moving her family to Vastera was both exciting and unsettling.

Mainly unsettling, though.

Haegen had taken it in his stride. He was the opposite of Karsten and Jaeger, and she was grateful for it. Her head was a jumble of things to remember, and his steady support was a welcome bolster.

Nicolene looked surprised as she came down the stairs. 'Where are *you* going so early? Off to meet your lover?'

Irenna frowned, glancing around, but Haegen and Karsten were already in the hall, eating with their parents. 'What are you talking about, Nicolene? I'm just going to the markets.' As much as Irenna had tried to forge a friendship with her sister-in-law, none had eventuated, and she would not miss her when she left.

Nicolene laughed at the shock on Irenna's face. 'Who goes to the markets before breakfast?'

Irenna was already feeling flustered and she had no inclination to stand around enduring Nicolene's insinuations. She pulled her basket to her chest, turning towards the doors. 'There is a lot to do before we leave. I can't imagine I'll find much linen or silk in Vastera. And you'll have even less on offer in Kroll, it being so far from the coast. Then there are furs for winter. And I want some candles, honey, wine...'

Nicolene sighed, not wanting the reminder of how Karsten had been given the worst of the lordships. Lord of Kroll; a landlocked dungheap, by all reports. 'Well, perhaps I'll join you, then. Wait here while I get my things.'

Irenna's mouth was open, readying a stream of protests but Nicolene was already running back up the stairs, heading to her chamber.

***

'How's the eye this morning?' Kormac wondered, joining Jael at the training ring.

'What eye?' Jael asked, winking the one eye that was open. The other was swollen, closed up, covered in a purplish yellow hue, but Biddy had assured her that it already appeared to be improving.

Kormac nodded towards the ring as the Osslanders trained, battering each other enthusiastically with wooden swords and shields. He shook his head. 'I still can't understand what happened yesterday. Why Baccus would do that?' Glancing around, Kormac lowered his voice. 'I've had a lot of dealings with him over the years. He was always a bastard, but not a murderer. That wasn't the man I remember at all. But I suppose I could say that about many people around here now.'

Jael had set Entorp to work, making more stones. Hopefully, he would have enough to give to everyone soon but until then... 'People change. Places change. I barely recognise Tuura now, which, for me, is a good thing, I suppose.'

Kormac looked awkward, eager to change the subject. Evva had not been his daughter, but her death still haunted him. No one enjoyed being reminded of that night. 'Edela is healing well, so hopefully, you won't have to stay here too much longer,' he suggested.

Fyn approached the railings with a wide smile. 'What did you think?' he asked breathlessly, looking back to where his opponent was picking himself out of the mud.

'About what?' Jael wondered blankly.

Fyn looked crestfallen. 'Nothing,' he said slowly, slouching his way back into the ring.

'Fyn!' Jael called, smiling now. 'It was good! I think you would've knocked Thorgils over with that kick!' Oh, how she missed Thorgils.

Thorgils who had saved her grandmother.

Thorgils who was looking after her husband.

She hoped he was alright.

***

'Hello,' Isaura smiled, opening the door to find a bashful looking Thorgils standing there. His eyes were puffy, and he smelled as though he'd spent most of the night in the hall and needed a good bath. She reached out and touched his hand.

Thorgils looked down at her, his weary eyes sparkling. 'Hello.'

'How are you?' Isaura wondered. 'Did you sleep?'

Thorgils grinned, listening to the squealing children as they raced around inside the house. 'I don't think so. But I can sleep when I'm dead. There's too much to do for sleeping!'

Isaura's smile faltered as she felt the cold grip of fear around her heart. 'Will you come in? We have porridge and berries. Honey and warm bread too.'

'Well, that sounds pleasant,' Thorgils said shyly. 'Although,

I eat a lot more than when you last lived on Oss. I'm not sure your servants will welcome my arrival.'

Isaura laughed, pulling him inside. 'I'll have to tell them to prepare more in future,' she said, closing the door behind them, listening to his stomach growl. 'A lot more!'

***

Irenna was pleased that Nicolene had brought her servant along as that servant was now weighed down with cords of linen, wool, and silk as she waddled behind them both. Nicolene had commandeered two male slaves as well, and they trailed at the rear carrying baskets full of beeswax candles, rounds of hard cheese, jugs of wine, and tiny jars of preserved fruit.

'I'm just going to take a look down here!' Irenna called, squeezing past a merchant who immediately lunged at her, trying to tempt her with an amber necklace she had absolutely no need for.

Nicolene rolled her eyes. She was bored now, satisfied with what she had purchased, and ready to head back to the castle for breakfast. She couldn't imagine the dire shed of a hall that she would soon be moving into. Her shoulders sunk at the thought of being stuck so far away from everyone with just Karsten and their two squawking sons for company.

'You *do* like to get up early,' Jaeger murmured, stopping behind her.

Very close behind her.

Nicolene was caught between wanting to still be annoyed with Jaeger and feeling excited to see him again. 'We're leaving in a few days. There's much to prepare,' she said sharply, shooing away the servant and slaves.

'And how will you enjoy your new life in Kroll, I wonder?'

Jaeger teased. 'Lady of the Arse-crack of Hest!'

Nicolene decided then that she was far more annoyed than excited, and she pushed past him. 'Why don't you go back to your servant?' she sneered. 'No doubt she's waiting in your bed!'

'At *this* time of day?' Jaeger laughed, nonplussed. 'I doubt that. And besides, there are plenty of other places she never goes.' He didn't move, watching as she stalked away.

But not very far.

Nicolene stopped, turning towards her brother-in-law, more excited than annoyed now. She put a finger to her lips. 'What places?'

***

'What do you think your sister is doing on Oss?' Jael wondered, trying not to sound as bitter as she felt as she walked Fyn back to Aedan's. 'Having her own throne built?'

'I imagine so, and having dresses made and ordering servants to do her hair and bathe her every day.' Fyn frowned, certain that Evaine would be flouncing around, acting like the queen she wished she was. Although, part of him hoped that that was the case as she would be far too occupied to do anything to hurt his mother.

His mother. He was happy about that. News that Evaine was Morana's child, not Runa's, had come as a relief.

It would be so much easier to kill her.

If Jael didn't get to her first.

'Well, hopefully, Eadmund will be too busy to notice,' Jael said. 'It appears that Oss is about to be attacked by Ivaar. Or has been. Which, I suppose, comes as no surprise. It was only a matter of time before he came back.'

Fyn turned to her, his eyes wide with worry.

'Ivaar only wants Eadmund,' Jael reassured him, patting his arm. 'You've no need to worry about Runa. He won't hurt her.' She blinked, surprising herself, but it was true, she realised. Ivaar was jealous of Eadmund. He wanted revenge. He wanted to assume what he saw as his rightful place on the throne of Oss.

He wasn't about to kill everyone.

She hoped.

***

The ritual spell Morana needed to translate was a winding maze of words that were both familiar and yet not familiar at all. And because Jaeger would only let her look at the book in his chamber, she found herself constantly back at the beginning each time she arrived, stumbling over the same confusing passage that never became any clearer.

She could feel Jaeger's breath as he loomed behind her, sensing his displeasure at having to share the book with her.

'*And*?' he muttered impatiently.

Turning around, Morana cocked her head. 'When did you last eat?' she wondered, noticing how his desperate eyes sunk into his face; how prominent his cheekbones appeared as he glared at her.

Jaeger ignored her. 'The ritual? Have you translated it?'

Morana turned back to the book. 'No, not yet,' she grumbled.

'But what about Axl Furyck? You do know exactly where he is now?'

'Yes.'

'When, then?' Jaeger asked impatiently. 'When are we going to the Crown of Stones again?'

Morana snorted. 'You should eat something. Rest. I will

come for you at midnight, so be ready. But for now, I must concentrate. We will never be able to unleash the true power of the book if I cannot unravel this spell!'

Jaeger grunted, prowling around behind her, his eyes rarely leaving the book; flinching every time she turned a page.

Meena, sitting on the bed, shivered, tapping her boots on the flagstones. They were going to hurt Axl Furyck, she knew.

Try to kill him.

More than just him.

But what could she do to stop them?

***

Entorp had worked quickly, and by late afternoon, they all had stones, and everyone knew that they were in danger.

But no one knew what they could do about it. Not without that book.

'I can't take it out of the secret room,' Jael insisted, sipping from her cup of small ale. 'It's safer where it is for now. And Edela thinks that Eydis can see the book without us needing to actually have it.'

Eydis felt nervous, hoping that Jael was right. 'I can feel the dreamers,' she said quietly. 'I can feel their eyes searching for us.'

'So can I,' Jael agreed. 'But where do you think they all are?'

Alaric was there, sitting on Edela's bed. 'There is a special chamber in the temple,' he said cautiously, worried that the symbol stones were just a flimsy theory, not guaranteed to work at all. He was expecting the door to be smashed in at any moment by angry soldiers with swords out, ready to take them away to the temple. Everyone was staring at him, though, and Alaric was quickly flustered. 'The Chamber of Dreams is a place where they send the most talented dreamers in Tuura. The elderman gives them... tasks. Sets them to dreaming for the answers he seeks. When I worked at the temple, it was my job to record the dreams they had there.'

'Well, Gerod must have them dreaming about you,' Branwyn murmured to Jael.

'And the book,' Biddy added, darning one of Eydis' socks by the fire. 'Without that book, who knows what the ravens would have done to us.'

Kormac was still shaking his head in disbelief. 'So, there is no one we can trust in Tuura? Not a single person?'

'I don't think everyone is bound or a member of The Following,' Jael said. 'You're certainly not. But how do we find out who is without alerting the dreamers? The only people we know we can trust are the ones in here, as well as Aedan and Aron, and Beorn and the crew. And Marcus.'

Branwyn looked doubtful. 'Do you think you can trust him?' She glanced at Edela, who was asleep. 'Mother didn't. And look at what he tried to do to Aleksander.'

Alaric nodded. 'He may well be a member of The Following too.'

Jael frowned, thinking. She shared many of the same fears. 'I trust him,' she said at last. 'His daughter is risking her life to try and get the Book of Darkness. And he gave Edela that book. Gave it to me, too. He knows where it is. He could have easily turned it over to this Gerod. But he didn't.'

'Jael's right,' Kormac agreed. 'We have this book *because* of Marcus. It doesn't mean that we have to trust him entirely, but right now, it makes no sense not to.'

Branwyn nodded reluctantly. 'I agree. But if the elderman's a prisoner in the temple, and there's no one to trust anymore, what are we going to do?'

***

Eadmund tried to resist the pull of Evaine as he sat talking to Ayla. Evaine's eyes followed him everywhere he went, but they were especially sharp with displeasure whenever he was near the dreamer.

'Isaura told me about your dream walk to try and save my father,' he said, feeling the ache of grief, still so raw. 'I wanted to thank you. For trying.' He kept his voice low, which was unnecessary. The hall was humming with activity as everyone rushed about, preparing for the attack they assumed would come soon.

Ayla looked away, embarrassed that she had not done enough. 'I'm sorry I couldn't warn Eydis in time. He was a good man.'

Eadmund swallowed. 'He was. He didn't deserve to die that sort of death.'

'No,' Ayla agreed.

'Was it Ivaar?' Eadmund asked quickly. 'Did Ivaar do it?'

Ayla hesitated. His eyes were so desperate. 'No, he didn't,' she said, shaking her head. 'It wasn't Ivaar.'

Eadmund felt as though he'd been punched in the stomach. 'But who was it, then?'

Ayla clasped her hands together in her lap, feeling a twinge in her thigh. 'I don't know.'

'Then how can you know that it *wasn't* Ivaar? Perhaps you're wrong?'

Ayla sat quietly for a moment, considering that. 'I was kept prisoner by Ivaar for over a year. In his bed. At his side. I could not escape.' She felt sick, not wanting to relive the memories. 'I know Ivaar better than I would wish to. He wanted your father's throne, but I don't believe that he ever had the stomach to kill him. He loved him too much.'

Eadmund looked horrified. '*Loved* him?'

'He was a boy who was abandoned by his father. Abandoned in favour of another son. His mother killed herself because he chose your mother. In his eyes, he lost both of his parents because of you. He wanted to destroy you, not Eirik. He only wanted his father's love.'

Eadmund sat back, sighing. 'So, now he is coming to destroy me at last?'

'Yes, and to take back those things he believes are his. His island, his throne, his wife and children. His dreamer.' She shivered.

'And will he?'

'For a long time I had such a strong vision of him sitting on that throne,' Ayla said, her eyes moving to the fur-lined chair that Evaine was fussing over. 'That vision is not as strong anymore, but he will come with many men. It's hard not to see him being victorious.'

'This fort is solid. It can withstand a lot,' Eadmund insisted.

'Yes, I can see that,' Ayla said. 'But eventually, your people will run out of food and water. They will die from starvation. Those who aren't injured or suffering from disease by then.'

It was a grim reminder of what might come. A siege was about more than the strength of your walls, Eadmund knew. It was as much about the strength of your people to withstand deprivation and hardship. He looked into Ayla's eyes. 'Perhaps it doesn't have to come to that. There may be something you can do to help us.'

CHAPTER TWENTY NINE

It was early in the evening, but Jaeger had already fallen asleep, and Egil was nowhere to be seen, so Meena had made the most of the opportunity to escape the castle.

She had begun to feel like a prisoner, although she wondered if that was just in her head. Jaeger barely spoke to her now. Like a new toy abandoned quickly, he appeared to have tired of her. And Meena didn't know whether she wanted him to notice her again, or to forget about her so that she could leave and return to her chamber.

But what would she do there without Berard to care for?

Soon, he would be gone.

'Meena!' Berard smiled, leading his horse into the stables, surprised to find her waiting for him. 'Not trying to move in here again, are you?'

Meena swallowed, suddenly nervous, shuffling her boots in the straw, avoiding his eyes. She had come hoping to find Berard, thinking that if she told him what Jaeger and Morana were doing with the book, that perhaps he could stop them somehow. But now that she was here, she realised that doing so would only put him in danger. 'I, I should be getting back to the castle. It will be supper soon.' Meena could almost feel Morana's hands on her, dragging her away.

She turned, hurrying through the doors before he could stop her.

'Meena, wait!' Berard handed the reins to the stable boy and ran after her. 'Why are you leaving?' he called.

Meena slowed down, letting him catch up with her, not wanting to make it worse. 'I, I just... came to look at the horses,' she mumbled, her shoulders up around her ears.

Berard looked confused. 'You did?'

'I like horses,' Meena whispered truthfully. 'I always wanted to have one.'

'Well, you didn't need to leave. Come back. Stay as long as you like. I have to get to the hall for supper, but you take as long as you want to.'

His voice was full of kindness, and Meena felt her shoulders relax. She lifted her head, meeting his eyes; wishing she could tell him what Morana was planning. But she couldn't. She didn't want to put him in danger.

Dropping her eyes to the ground, she sighed. 'Alright.'

***

Ayla leaned forward. 'Me?'

'Can you dream walk again? To Jael?' Eadmund whispered, not wanting Evaine to hear. 'I need her help. I need her to go to Andala, to get the Brekkan ships and their sea-fire.'

Ayla's eyes widened. 'I...' She saw Evaine stalking towards them and paused, watching how Eadmund's attention was immediately consumed by the girl.

'Sevrin and Otto are over there, waiting on you,' Evaine said sharply, glaring at Ayla. 'There is much they need to discuss. Important things, they said.'

Eadmund nodded. 'I'll be there in a moment, I just have to finish this meeting.'

Evaine looked furious. '*Meeting*? About what?'

Eadmund didn't want to mention Jael's name, but he struggled to think of an excuse.

'The king needs information about Ivaar,' Ayla said hurriedly.

'I see,' Evaine muttered. 'Well, hopefully, that won't take much longer.' And eyeing Eadmund, she walked slowly away, turning around every few steps to scowl at Ayla again.

'Thank you,' Eadmund smiled. 'So, can you? Will you? Dream walk to Jael?'

Ayla took a deep breath. 'I can try.'

***

Karsten watched Nicolene as she ate.

She usually picked at her food, but tonight she appeared ravenous; finishing off her bowl of soup and quickly starting the next course of crab claws. She was not looking forward to going to Kroll, he knew, and yet, there she was, smiling as she chatted to Irenna and Bayla as though nothing was bothering her at all.

Haaron watched Karsten watching his wife. If what Karsten suspected about Jaeger and Nicolene was, in fact, true, it was a good thing they were leaving so quickly. Although, he considered, it would be the perfect way to get rid of Jaeger without being blamed for his death. He smiled as he pushed his plate away, frowning suddenly at the thought of Morana.

He had trusted Varna implicitly. But he didn't know her daughter and Morana had made it plain that she had no interest in getting to know him. It was difficult to listen to advice from someone who didn't appear to care one way or the other.

And if she was working with Jaeger against him...

'I shall miss this hall,' Haegen murmured, watching the

servants shepherd the children away from their table.

Haaron blinked at his son, noting the sentiment in his eyes. He turned to follow his gaze towards his grandchildren, remembering when his own children were that small. That innocent.

They had all looked up to him once. Wanted to be like him. And now?

According to Morana, each one of them wanted his throne. Each one of them was, therefore, a threat to his life, and yet, when he looked at Haegen, his eldest boy, he saw genuine sadness in his eyes.

'I'm sure your mother will visit regularly,' Haaron muttered, feeling uncomfortable.

'And you?'

'Me? Well, I have the kingdom to care for. Much rebuilding to do. I have plans for a wall, you know.'

'A wall?'

'From the Tower, all the way across the pass.'

'A good idea,' Haegen agreed. 'You could build further towers along it?'

Haaron nodded. 'Yes, I was thinking that.'

'Well, it does sound as though you'll be busy. Too busy for visiting.'

Haaron glanced at his son, who looked down, continuing with his meal. 'Yes, too busy for visiting,' Haaron almost whispered to himself.

***

Ayla sat by the fire. It was a lovely house, she thought, although Isaura seemed a little on edge and uncomfortable being in it.

'Selene! Don't touch that!' Isaura snapped, her usually calm face pinched with displeasure as her eldest daughter backed away from the bone-handled knife she was about to pick up.

'Are you enjoying being back?' Ayla wondered gently.

Isaura sighed. 'I'm not sure how I feel.' She lowered her voice, her eyes darting around the room. 'The children are unhappy. Asking questions, not sleeping. And I just don't know what will happen next. I don't fear for them, but I worry about Thorgils and Eadmund and everyone else.' She looked at Ayla, reaching for her hand. 'I worry about what Ivaar will do to us.'

'Well, perhaps there is something we can do about Ivaar,' Ayla said quietly. 'I've come for your help.'

***

Dusk had fallen before Axl, Amma, and Aleksander were near a cave or shelter of any kind, so they stopped for the night in a small clearing, some way off the road. It reminded Aleksander of the first place he had camped with Edela on their trip to Tuura.

Thankfully, it wasn't snowing.

They were tired and wet through. It had rained steadily for most of the day and Axl had struggled to get a fire going, but, at last, the flames appeared to have settled into a promising rhythm. He suspended the rabbit Amma had prepared over their makeshift spit, his stomach gurgling.

Amma, who had not enjoyed preparing the rabbit at all, felt sick and she couldn't stop shivering. Axl reached out for her, wishing he could offer her some warmth, but everything they had was wet, including the horses, who didn't appear bothered in the slightest as they quietly pulled on long shoots of grass nearby.

Aleksander yawned, rolling his shoulder. It was healing but

slowly. Resting his head against the wide trunk of an oak tree, he tried to imagine how far they were from Tuura. He had been this way so recently that it wasn't hard to get his bearings. His best guess was that they had two more days on the road.

'Perhaps you'll have another dream tonight?' Amma suggested.

'I don't think it works like that,' Aleksander smiled wearily, not wanting another dream at all. 'I think we're doing what she wanted, so hopefully, there's nothing more to say.'

'Well, maybe that's for the best? I can't imagine it's very comforting to have a dreamer inside your head.'

'No. No, it's not. But if it helps us save everyone, then it's worth all the bad dreams in the world.'

***

Morana sat in a chair by the fire, staring at the wall.

Coming to Hest had been unpleasant.

Too many people.

Needy, demanding, stupid people.

She sighed, closing her eyes, feeling closer than ever to the supreme bliss of limitless death and ultimate power. To exist as a god, but better. The gods and goddesses were pathetic tools of Dala, of Vidar, of whichever weak master they served. So protective of life. So afraid of death. But Raemus? Raemus *was* the Darkness. All things would be possible once he returned.

If Jael Furyck didn't get in the way.

Eadmund Skalleson was no longer a factor, she was certain, but Jael Furyck was roaming Tuura with a book that no one in The Following could find. And that book was useful enough to battle the Book of Darkness, she knew.

But if she could work fast enough, distract them all, keep

them thinking about Tuura, about the book, about Jael Furyck, then she could finally translate the rest of the ritual spell.

And then, before long, they would raise Raemus from his death-prison.

Morana smiled, desperate for the night to hurry along.

***

Karsten couldn't sleep.

He felt sick. Angry. Humiliated. His wife lay next to him, not sleeping. But she was pretending to. He knew Nicolene. He knew her sounds and the ones she was making were not the ones she made when she slept.

Was she planning to leave in the night? Waiting for him to fall asleep?

Karsten's fists pulsed in angry balls by his sides as he lay there, thinking about his brother. His wife. Wondering who he would kill first.

How he would do it.

His own brother?

It was too painful to feel real. The night of Lothar Furyck's murder, he had raced back to try and stop Jaeger's own wife from being stolen away. Jaeger's thanks had been to take Nicolene from him.

Karsten clenched his jaw, desperate to keep his tongue inside his mouth.

The right time would come to expose their deceit.

And he would wait for it.

***

Isaura glanced at Ayla, wondering if she was ready to begin the dream walk. Ayla didn't look comfortable as she sat on the floor before the fire, her legs crossed, her brow furrowed in discomfort. Or perhaps she was just concentrating, Isaura wondered.

They were alone in Eadmund's small, rundown cottage. Despite a healthy fire before them, the wind was whistling through holes in the crumbling walls and Isaura was convinced that they would have been warmer outside.

She gripped the drum, waiting, her mind wandering to Ivaar. He would be so desperate to come and claim them both. There had to be something they could do to stop him.

Perhaps this was it?

Ayla exhaled, trying to ignore the pain in her leg as she turned to Isaura, slowing her breathing, feeling her body unwind, limb by limb, her mind with it. 'Start drumming.'

***

Axl smiled at Amma as they lay on the grass; close, but not as close as he would have liked. Not with Aleksander there. Not after what Amma had been through.

Not when she was still Jaeger Dragos' wife.

Yet here he was, heading for Tuura, when he wanted to be in Andala with Gant, preparing their forces to attack Hest.

Hest had plenty of men, but no ships. And if he was the King of Brekka now, then he was a king with an impressive fleet. And, if his grandmother lived and she could help him make sea-fire, they could sail to Hest and destroy the Dragos'.

Take Hest. Claim it for Brekka.

And he would become a powerful king.

He could see his sister's frown and hear his father's

disapproval, but he closed his eyes and ears against them both. Revenge would be his to claim, for Amma.

***

'Meena,' Jaeger purred, crawling across the bed towards her. 'Meena, Meena, Meena.'

Meena sat up, shuffling away from him, her eyes wide with terror.

'What do you *do*, Meena?' he asked.

He sounded odd, she thought, feeling more uncomfortable by the moment. Her skin itched. She wanted to scratch her arms and legs. 'D-d-do?' she stuttered. 'Anything you w-w-want.'

Jaeger stopped, his face almost touching hers. 'Anything I want? Hmmm...' He cocked his head to one side, watching as she tried so hard not to scramble away from him. He could almost taste her fear as he reached out a hand, running it over her tangled web of hair. 'Have you ever thought of a comb, Meena?' he wondered suddenly. 'You really should use a comb. It would help with this...' He waved his hands around, frowning. 'Mess.'

Meena gulped. Jaeger was acting so strangely.

'Morana is hiding things from me,' Jaeger murmured. 'So many things. She said she could read the book. Promised me that she could read it. I killed her mother because she could read it! And now? Now, all I do is wait,' he growled, his eyes darting around the candlelit chamber as he rocked back on his heels. 'I wait on her because she has all the power over me.' He snapped his head to Meena. 'You see that, don't you?'

Meena nodded quickly.

Jaeger crept towards her again, his mind whirring so fast that he couldn't keep up with it. 'So, you will finally *do* something Meena. My Meena. My little Meena.' He rubbed his finger over the bump in the middle of her nose. 'You will go to Morana's chamber. You will bring me Varna's books, and we will look at them together. They must still be there, mustn't they?'

Meena looked horrified. She opened her mouth in protest, but Jaeger reached out and pinched her lips closed.

'Good!' he smiled, then turned away from her, exhausted, yawning. 'When Morana is here next, you will go. I will keep her away from you, don't worry. I will protect you.'

Meena sat there as he muttered sleepily to himself, her body taut with fear.

Morana would know.

She would know.

She saw everything in her dreams.

***

Evaine fell into a satisfied heap beside Eadmund, who didn't appear to notice as he lay there, barely moving, staring into the darkness. As much as she knew that he was hers, he seemed so distracted. His mind was occupied with thoughts of his brother and the island, she knew, but there was something else, and she didn't know what it was. 'Eadmund,' Evaine murmured, laying her head on his chest. 'What is wrong?'

He blinked, noticing her at last. Laying a hand on top of her head, he stroked her silky hair, feeling it slither over his chest as she wriggled into a comfortable position. Eadmund sighed, content for a moment, knowing that in the next room, their son lay sleeping.

And he couldn't let Ivaar take either of them away from him.

He hoped that Ayla could get through to Jael.

He needed her help.

***

Ayla fell forward, gagging, struggling for air. Spent.

'Are you alright?' Isaura asked dreamily, straining to see through the smoky haze. 'Did you find Jael?' Dropping the drum, she felt around for the water bag, taking a quick drink before handing it to Ayla.

'Yes. No,' Ayla said breathlessly, coughing. 'She is shutting me out.'

Isaura frowned, feeling as though Ayla's voice was echoing all around her. 'Why? How? How can she do that?' And reaching for the water bag again, she took another drink.

Ayla opened her eyes wide, trying to clear her mind. She didn't know. 'I've never experienced it. It's as though she's invisible. I cannot see her at all.'

Isaura was confused. 'You don't think she's... dead, do you?' She hurried to her feet, desperate to escape the thick fug of smoke choking her throat.

'Dead?' Ayla frowned. 'No, death is something else. Death is emptiness. Peace. No, this was as if she was hidden behind a wall. Locked away from me.'

Isaura stood in the doorway, inhaling the cold air. 'From *you*?'

'From me. From dreamers.' Ayla struggled to her feet, limping to the door, eager for a breath of the night air herself. 'But why? What doesn't she want us to see?'

***

'The walls are closing in, Edela,' the voice crowed. 'While you lie there, lifeless. Useless. No help to anyone. The walls are closing in, and soon they will crush you all.'

Edela squirmed, impatient to leave these nightmares behind now. She was growing stronger. She didn't need to dwell in this stinking, black cave any longer, listening to that cackling voice as it tried to intimidate her.

She was ready to walk all the way through the door and slam it shut behind her now.

Everyone was in danger.

Everyone she loved.

And they weren't getting out of Tuura without her help.

PART FIVE

The River

CHAPTER THIRTY

Morana came for them at midnight.

Jaeger felt as though he'd only just fallen asleep. His eyes were grainy, still half closed. He was unsteady on his feet as he stumbled down the corridor after her, dragging Meena behind him.

Thunder growled in the distance, and he frowned at the idea of trekking out to the Crown of Stones in another storm, but The Following would not abandon their sacred place.

So they walked to the stones and lit their fire in the rain, preparing to cast another spell.

For him.

Jaeger scowled impatiently as he stood with Meena, watching Morana mark where each person would lie with a small stone; watching The Followers fan out, murmuring amongst themselves as they took their places in the circle. Flames spluttered, fighting against the drizzle and the piles of herbs being thrown on top of them. Eventually, they burst into life, belching out thick puffs of fragrant smoke.

'Perhaps you should join the circle now?' Yorik murmured, ushering them towards Morana.

Meena pulled against Jaeger, wanting to leave, smelling the familiar scent of herbs that would take them into another trance.

She wanted to go back to the castle.

Jaeger yanked her towards him. 'You're sure it will work

this time?' he snarled. 'That we will *actually* kill a Furyck?'

'They won't even know what is happening,' Yorik insisted. 'But will we?'

'Of course,' Yorik smiled. 'We will be there.'

***

'Wake up! Wake up! Ride to the river! You know where it is! You have been there before! I will help you! Ride! Ride! Ride!'

Aleksander's head jerked forward.

Blinking rapidly, he tried to open his eyes. It was too dark to even see his hands, but he could hear that urgent voice, booming in his head.

The Widow.

Aleksander scrambled to his feet, reaching for Axl, his mouth so dry that he could barely speak. 'We have to move!' he croaked, tying his swordbelt around his waist, grabbing his cloak.

Axl shook himself awake. 'Move?'

But Aleksander had already gone, feeling his way towards the horses who were whinnying, pulling against their ropes. Did they sense his panic, or something else, he wondered? He could feel rain, getting heavier. Clouds were covering the moon and stars. It was not going to be an easy ride. 'Amma! Wake up! We must leave! Now!'

Amma lurched forward. Their fire had gone out. She was shivering. Damp. Confused.

Aleksander didn't know what he was doing or saying. There was nothing to see except the darkness, which, in itself, was unsettling. But he was sure that what was coming would not be good. 'Amma, come!' he called as Axl hurried her towards the horses. 'Axl, grab your cloaks! Quick!'

Axl was alert now. 'What's happening?'

'I don't know, but we have to leave!' Aleksander boosted Amma up onto her horse who was panicking with her, skittering across the wet ground.

Axl finished wrapping his belt around his waist, then hoisted himself up onto his own horse. 'Where are we going?'

Aleksander tried to get his bearings. The wind was picking up around his ears, clearing his sleepy head. 'The river.' Instinctively he turned his horse's head to the right. 'Come on! Let's go! Ha!' he cried, nudging her flanks, pointing her towards the trees.

And the voice kept echoing in his ears. 'Ride! Ride! Ride!'

***

Eirik Skalleson sat on his chair in Oss' hall, frowning at her.

He was not happy. 'You have left.'

Jael didn't know where to look. Finally, she braved his eyes. 'Not forever.'

'You're sure about that?' Eirik sharpened his bushy, white brows, displeased. 'Sure you haven't just escaped because the challenge was too hard? She took Eadmund, so you gave up?'

Jael shook her head, straightening her back. 'I'll return as soon as I can.'

'And what if you're too late?' Eirik stood, walking towards her with ease. There were no aches or pains for him now. 'What if Ivaar sits on my throne when you come?'

'But I can't leave Tuura. We're trapped here.'

'Eydis can help you.'

Jael blinked as he reached her.

'When all is lost, when you are blind, Eydis can see. That is what her mother told me before she died. When the darkness comes, that is when Eydis will see.'

Jael looked at Eirik, confused. Sad. She had missed that crumpled face.

She reached for his hands, but he drifted away, and she stood in Tuura's main street. It was dark and cold and stunk of smoke and dying things.

She shivered, hating this place; hearing her mother's screams, remembering herself shaking under that bed, trying so desperately to keep Axl quiet as he wriggled beside her, tears running down his cheeks.

Closing her eyes, Jael tried to find a different dream.

'Jael!'

It was Axl, and he was screaming.

'Jael!'

***

He was running.

Powerful, long strides. Thick claws digging into the earth. Frenzied breath coming in bursts. Tongue flapping.

Inhaling the familiar scent.

Of Amma Furyck.

He could feel his teeth grinding, sharp-edged, desperate; his lips curling.

Thundering through the forest.

After that scent.

***

His horse's ears flattened back.

Aleksander saw that in a burst of moonlight before he heard the noise.

He thought it was thunder; the storm approaching from behind.

They were winding their way through the dense forest in the darkness; moonlight shining in intermittent patches. His horse had a sense of space that he didn't possess, so he gave her room to find her way, trying to ignore the terror of tree trunks leaping out from the shadows, stopping his heart.

Aleksander wanted to swallow, but his mouth was dry with fear.

'Go right! Right!' urged the voice in his head, and he yanked on the reins.

His horse was terrified, he could tell.

So was he. Something felt frighteningly familiar.

Aleksander glanced behind himself.

And then he found out why.

Amma screamed.

Teeth glowed in the darkness.

Hundreds of pairs of teeth.

Wolves.

***

'Jael!' Edela called out loudly.

But Jael was already out of bed. She stumbled around, trying to avoid tripping over the fire pit, jumping at a booming clap of thunder that shook the house.

Everyone was awake then.

'Jael!' Eydis was creeping towards her, hands out, feeling her way across the room.

The puppies had quickly retreated under the bed again.

Jael searched for her swordbelt, disoriented, cursing herself for not keeping it close by. Finding it, at last, slung over her cloak, she hurried to tie it around her waist. 'I have to go and get the book! Axl's in danger!' she cried, running to the door.

'What is happening?' came Branwyn's frantic cry as she rose up on her elbows.

'I have to go!' Jael called. 'Barricade the door after me! And light a fire!'

More thunder crashed overhead as Jael reached the door. 'Biddy! Get Eydis. Take her to Edela! Keep them safe!' She threw away the barricades they had put in place after the raven attack, pulled open the door and froze.

The house was surrounded by soldiers.

***

'Wolves!' Axl screamed. 'Wolves!'

The river, Aleksander panicked. Where is the river?

He was as terrified as his horse, whose nostrils were flaring, smelling what was coming for them all. He tried not to remember Ren, his horse who had been killed by wolves.

He couldn't let it happen again.

But there wasn't one wolf or even a pack.

There were hundreds of pairs of eyes; panting, rumbling bodies surging towards them.

'Go! Go!' Aleksander bent lower, urging his horse on. He couldn't smell the river, just rain and fear. 'Go!'

'Left!' He heard her, at last. There was a calm certainty in that voice. 'Left! Now!'

Aleksander tugged on the reins, listening to Axl and Amma, still close behind him. At least he hoped that was the sound he heard. He couldn't turn around now.

It was too dark. He couldn't see.

He was lost.

Where now?

'It's coming! It's coming! You'll need to jump! Faster!'

***

Jael slammed the door.

Kormac was scrambling around in the darkness, trying to find his tinderbox.

Aleksander. She could feel Aleksander's terror.

Jael stared at the door. There was nothing she could do. There were too many soldiers. Only Kormac could offer her any help to fight her way through them.

There had to be something she could do!

'Grandmother?' she cried desperately.

'It's the same,' Edela murmured, panicking. Trying not to. 'Do you remember the symbol?'

'No!' Eydis called from beside her, where Biddy was keeping her close. 'It won't work! They are too far away. We need a different symbol!'

Jael hurried to her side, gripping Eydis' hand, remembering Eirik's words. 'Eydis, think. See the book. How can we save them? Which page?'

Eydis shook all over, her head tumbling with symbols; none of which felt right. She shut out all the noise until the only sound she could hear was the rhythmic thudding of her heart.

She knew this book. It was a book of light, white magic.

Her grandmother's book.

Eydis gasped, surprised by that.

But there was no time; she had to find the page.

'The wolves are coming,' Edela said faintly. 'They smell blood.'

Then Eydis knew.

'I see it!'

***

Axl could hear the rushing of the river, over the rushing of the wolves, over the screaming of Amma, and the pounding of his heart.

He could hear the rushing river.

But it was too late.

Up snapped a jaw, clamping down on his horse's hind-leg and he tumbled over in a crashing roll of horse and ground and legs and teeth. 'Aarrghh!' he screamed, drawing his sword and slashing into the night.

Wailing and whimpering.

'Axl!'

He heard Amma's terror.

'Amma!'

He heard Aleksander's scream and then more horses tumbling, and the low growl from bellies, and the tearing of flesh, and the desperate need to feed.

And then the pain.

***

'Cut me!' Eydis cried. 'Make me bleed, Jael! I will draw it! I can see it!'

Eydis pulled away from Biddy, dropping to the ground, feeling around, pushing the rug away until she felt bare floorboards.

Jael grabbed Eydis' hand, unsheathed her knife and sliced it across Eydis' left palm. She rolled her fingers into a fist, squeezing them together. Dropping the knife, she dipped Eydis' finger into the bloody wound. 'Draw!' she urged, pushing Eydis' finger to the floorboards. 'Draw!'

Eydis knelt there, closing her eyes, seeing the symbol glowing in the darkness, burning like white flames. She began drawing, listening as the words echoed around her head like a howling wind. And she repeated them loudly.

'Wait! You need more blood!' Jael dipped Eydis' finger into her bleeding hand again, then placed it quickly back on the floor.

And Eydis kept drawing the symbol as she chanted, while everyone around her held their breath.

***

Aleksander staggered, panting, his sword out.

The river was there.

The river was there!

He'd pushed his injured horse into the water, and she was trying to swim, but Axl and Amma were underneath a pile of furious wolves, trapped with their own horses.

Aleksander stepped forward, bellowing, trying to draw the wolves away.

***

Jaeger fought his way towards Axl Furyck.

He could see him. He could feel his body shuddering with the need to dig his teeth into his flesh.

To tear him to pieces. To end him.

And then his bitch wife.

He could smell her terror as he leapt over her, surging towards Axl Furyck, jaw extended, ready to sink his teeth into him.

And then a searing stab of pain.

And he was whimpering, awake, panting, back at the stones, sitting up, confused.

Jaeger looked around at the bodies collapsed in a circle. No one was moving. The storm was still raging, and they were still in their trance. He screamed in frustration, hoping The Following could finish what he could not.

***

Aleksander dragged Axl away from the dead wolf, searching for Amma. He followed her terrified sobbing in the darkness, his bloody sword extended, his head swivelling with speed.

The wolves crept closer and closer, enclosing them as they backed up slowly towards the river. Low growls rolled through their bodies to the backs of their teeth. Salivating. Ready to launch.

Blood dripping from fangs.

'We have to run,' Aleksander said calmly, pulling Amma to her feet. She stumbled against him, shaking all over.

Axl could barely stand. His ears were buzzing as he swayed next to Aleksander, panting.

Two against how many?

They kept backing up, hearing the river; sensing how close

it was.

'On me, Axl,' Aleksander said. 'I'll take Amma.' And then, before another heartbeat. 'Now!'

And the three of them turned, running, stumbling as fast as their bleeding limbs would take them towards the water; listening to the thunderous pounding of paws and claws and blood-thirsty fury behind them.

'Jump!' Aleksander cried, throwing Amma into the water, plunging in after her.

Axl, staggering, limping, had one foot in the air, ready to follow them. Then he felt the fangs pierce straight through his leg.

He screamed.

***

Morana was victorious.

She had the King of Brekka in her teeth. She could smell his fear, taste his blood, and her body vibrated with victory as she tore at him, shaking her head from side to side.

She would devour him whole.

And then he was gone.

And she was gasping, falling back to earth.

***

Eydis slumped forward, exhausted.

'Eydis?' Jael swallowed. 'Eydis?'

No one knew what had just happened.

The flames were glowing now, and Kormac was creeping around lighting lamps as Jael pulled Eydis into her arms. 'Eydis?'

'The wolves have gone,' Edela said breathlessly from her bed. 'The symbol worked, Eydis. They are gone. I feel that. Do you?'

Eydis nodded against Jael's chest.

Gisila was beside herself. 'What has happened? Mother? Jael? *Somebody* tell me!'

***

'Axl!' Aleksander screamed, reaching for his arm again.

The sky was bright with stars now, glimmering reflections on the dark water, but Axl had drifted away from them as they weaved down the cold river on a steady current. Aleksander had a firm grip on Amma; one arm around her chest, pulling her close to him.

But he couldn't reach Axl.

And Axl didn't appear strong enough to reach him.

***

'That book! That book!' Morana seethed, crawling around in the darkness, heaving air into her burning lungs. 'Gerod has to get that fucking book!'

Jaeger didn't care what she was saying.

He didn't care that she was irate.

He was irate!

Launching himself at Morana as she struggled to her feet, he knocked her to the ground. 'You bitch!' he screamed. 'You useless bitch!' His teeth were bared, glowing white before her eyes, his spittle flying in the wind. 'You had me kill your mother! For what? What have you done? With the most powerful book ever written? You've done *nothing*! Nothing but failed me! And they still live, don't they? They all still live because of *you*!' He was roaring, his eyes bulging, shaking off the hands he could feel pulling on his arms.

He wrapped his fingers around Varna's throat.

Jaeger shook his head.

Morana's throat.

He squeezed and squeezed and then stopped, dropping her back to the earth.

'Stop it!' Yorik bellowed furiously. Anger burned in his mismatched eyes as he clung to Jaeger's arm.

'You need *me*!' Jaeger yelled, throwing them all off as he stood. 'You need *me*, and you will remember that! Without me, this book means *nothing*, and you know it! Without me, you cannot bring her back!'

Jaeger blinked as he stared at Morana.

Morana blinked as she turned to Yorik.

How did he know that?

***

Amma was clinging to Aleksander's chest, so he had his arms free as he stretched for Axl with everything he had.

Axl, who had been his annoying little brother since he could remember.

Axl, who was hopefully now his king.

And on his eighth try, Aleksander finally caught him, just

by his fingertips, but he wasn't letting go.

He gritted his teeth, holding on as the river ran and the sky lightened, and they were nowhere near shore, and all of their horses were lost, and Amma was sobbing, her head buried in his chest.

But the wolves had gone.

CHAPTER THIRTY ONE

Morana could barely control the fire burning inside her mouth. She stomped along with her staff, ready to shove it down Jaeger's throat as they all walked back to the castle.

That he would dare *touch* her? *Threaten* her? She shuddered, and her hair shook like a tree in a storm, vibrating with intensifying rage.

Yorik grabbed her arm, his face once again a mask of calm. Jaeger was right, he knew, and there was little they could do except continue to keep him on side. 'Perhaps it is time that *I* had a look at the book,' he announced.

Jaeger came to a halt.

Morana's mouth fell open as she stumbled to a stop beside him.

'You?' Jaeger said slowly. 'Why you?'

'I do not doubt Morana's skill,' Yorik said diplomatically. 'But I understand your desire to advance things more... quickly.' He avoided Morana's eyes, which he was sure were popping out of her head. 'I have my own knowledge of these things. I may be able to help.'

'Help to do *what*?' Jaeger wondered.

'As you said yourself, we need you to raise her. And we cannot do that until we translate the ritual spell. Morana understands much of it now, but one passage remains a problem. With my help, perhaps she can finish the translation, and we can make a start? A shadow moon is coming. It's an opportune time. We must be ready.'

Yorik spoke so commandingly that both Jaeger and Morana held their tongues.

'And what can she do, this woman? Why do we need her?' Jaeger asked.

'The book was hers once,' Yorik explained. 'She, and only she, can bring Raemus back from the Dolma.'

But Jaeger had stopped listening. He was suddenly ravenous, noticing Meena for the first time as she twitched beside him, tapping her head. 'Come to my chamber, then, tonight. Both of you. We shall see what use you are then, Yorik Elstad.' He turned to walk away. 'But don't be seen coming into the castle. Take the back entrance. I don't want to draw any attention to what we're doing.'

Yorik tried not to smile, which was easy when he looked at Morana's scowling face. 'Of course. Perhaps it is best if you go on ahead, then? We will wait and find our own way.'

Jaeger didn't even acknowledge him as he dragged Meena away.

Most of The Following had already passed them, but Yorik waited for the last stragglers to disappear, wanting to speak to Morana alone. He held his finger to her lips, sensing her need to burst into flames. 'Patience, now,' he urged. 'Think of how long we have waited. Think of those who came before us who never had the opportunity we have now. It is not about *who* translates the ritual. It is about being able to use it at all!'

Morana sighed, her temper receding slowly.

Yorik had always been calm in the face of her fury. He would watch her spark and explode and barely blink. 'Fine!' she spat, at last, banging her staff onto the ground before shuffling away into the darkness.

***

The hammering was insistent.

Jael frowned, striding to the door, *Toothpick's* hilt exposed, her hand hovering near his pommel, considering what was possible.

Kormac had a sword, but there was no one else. Fyn, Aron, and Aedan were far away. Beorn and the Osslanders were in the stables.

It was possible, but...

Jael reluctantly pulled open the door.

Gerod was there, black-robed, striding into the house. 'Take the girl!' he ordered to the temple guards behind him.

Jael was surprised. 'No!' She quickly moved to block his path. 'You will not take her!'

'Take the girl!' Gerod repeated sharply as the guards rushed towards Eydis, who clung even tighter to Biddy.

'Wait!' Jael yelled. 'Why?' She drew *Toothpick* from his scabbard, holding them all back, though she knew she wouldn't be able to for long.

'You won't give me the book, so I am taking the girl. Perhaps it will encourage you to change your mind?' Gerod growled, nodding to his guards to get on with it.

'Wait!' Jael tried to think. 'What will you do to her?'

'Whatever we like until you give us the book,' Gerod snarled. 'You think you can come here? Use that book against us?' He shook his head, clicking his tongue. 'You are not welcome here, Queen of Nothing. And that book is not yours. Give it to me, and we will allow you all to leave. Don't and...' He stared at Eydis, his eyes glinting angrily in the flames.

'I will go!' Eydis insisted boldly. 'Let me go, Jael! You cannot give them the book!'

Eighteen years ago, when Jael had been younger than

Eydis, men with swords – angry, seething men – had burst into a cottage and attacked her and her mother, raping them both. Repeatedly.

She glanced at Gisila, who looked terrified.

Everything Jael had done in those eighteen years was meant to take her as far away from that moment in her life as possible. And she would never consign another person to that torturous fate.

Not someone she loved.

Not Eydis.

'I'll give you the book.'

***

They had floated down the river as it frothed and rolled, and then, thankfully, calmed to gentle ripples, and eventually, they had crawled onto the bank, half drowned and so cold that they could neither feel, nor think.

But they appeared to be safe for now.

Aleksander dragged Axl to a small huddle of bushes surrounding a solitary tree and leaving Amma with him, he disappeared to find twigs and branches to make a fire. His hands were shaking, and his body was wet and weak, but somehow, he managed to collect an armful of most of the things they would need. His tinderbox was still in his pouch, which had remained attached to his belt, but everything was sodden, and it had taken some time to get his flint to work with the sodden tinder and the sodden twigs to make flames.

Amma's teeth were chattering as she tore off another strip of her dress and tried to tie it above Axl's gaping leg wounds. He hadn't stopped shivering. He looked so pale and exhausted. They all were, she supposed, but the teeth marks in his legs were particularly deep, gushing a never-ending flood of bright blood down his mottled skin. She needed to stop it, but her hands weren't working, and she couldn't tie a very tight knot.

'Here,' Aleksander said, his own teeth chattering just as loudly as Amma's as he took the cloth and pulled tightly. 'That's good. Now we just need some more to cover it.' And reaching down, he tore off a strip of his own tunic. His legs were bleeding, but his wounds were not that deep. They would heal.

So would Amma's.

Axl's were a worry, though.

Axl groaned. 'Where are the horses?' he asked, trying to keep his eyes open; worried by how light-headed he felt. 'Where are we?'

The sun had risen now, but it was a cold morning. Grey clouds rolled above their heads, and it looked like more rain would come soon. 'The horses are gone. I don't know where we are. When Edela and I went to Tuura, everything was frozen. Nothing looks familiar here. Not yet. But all you have to worry about now is lying there while we get you warm.'

'My legs,' Axl grimaced, trying to reach down to see what had happened.

'The wolves had a nibble on you,' Aleksander grinned, wrapping the strip of tunic around Axl's deepest wound. 'You need to stay still until we can stop that bleeding.'

Axl shuddered. His ears were buzzing so loudly that he was sure he was about to pass out. And then Amma smiled at him, and he gripped her hand, laying his head back against the tree they had propped him against, trying to breathe. 'Are you alright?' he whispered faintly.

'Yes,' Amma said, kissing his forehead. 'I am.' She turned to glance at Aleksander as Axl's eyes closed, his head drooping to one side.

How were they going to get to Tuura now?

***

'Jael, no!' Eydis panicked. 'Don't let them have the book!'

But Jael had no choice. 'I will bring it to you.'

'You will *give* it to me,' Gerod insisted. 'Now!'

Jael blinked slowly. 'I will *bring* it to you and then you will have it. I give you my word.'

Gerod glared impatiently at everyone gathered in the house; a large house full of people he had no time for. Inhaling sharply, he narrowed his eyes at Jael. 'Within the hour, or my men will return. And they will kill your family, one by one.'

Jael frowned. 'Why?'

'*Why?*' Gerod looked surprised that she would dare ask such a thing. 'You do not belong here, and it is up to me and me alone how you will leave. On a pyre or on a ship.' And with one last seething look at Jael, he spun around and headed back through the door, the guards turning to follow him.

No one said a word.

'Jael?' It was Edela who finally broke the silence, reaching out a withered hand to her granddaughter.

Jael blinked, hurrying to her grandmother's side.

'Your stone,' Edela whispered. 'Leave it behind, in the stables. They cannot find it on you.'

'I will,' Jael nodded. 'There has to be a way out of here. Back to Oss. We just need to find it.'

Edela smiled weakly. 'We will. Now hurry.'

Everyone looked anxious as Jael grabbed her cloak. 'Kormac.' She motioned her uncle over to the door, lowering her voice. 'I'll go to Aedan's before I get the book, and tell them what's happening. Don't worry, I'll be back soon.'

Jael opened the door, hoping she meant it.

***

'You need to stay alert,' Jael said to Beorn, her one open eye on the Osslanders, who were mostly still asleep, curled up on the straw. 'I don't know what will happen now. Talk to Fyn if you can't find me.'

'And why might I not be able to find you?' Beorn wondered, rubbing a hand over his grey-and-white beard. 'You planning on disappearing? Leaving us all here?'

Jael frowned. 'I'm going to the temple.'

'Now? Why?'

'Either I do, or they take Eydis.'

'What? Why?'

'To threaten me into giving them the book. So, I'm giving them the book, but I don't know what that will mean for me. You'll need to work with Fyn and Entorp to get everyone out of here if I don't come back.'

She swallowed.

Beorn swallowed.

'I have to leave my stone here, so we can't talk again. Not until I say. Just promise me something, Beorn. Don't leave Tig or the puppies behind. If there's a rush to escape, take them with you.'

Beorn nodded. 'Of course. But don't get caught in that temple.'

'That's my plan. Now go back to the men. I have to get the book and get to the temple quickly.' Jael squeezed his arm. 'Stay safe.' And she turned away, ignoring Tig, who she could hear blowing and snorting in annoyance behind her as she headed for the secret room.

***

'The bleeding has stopped,' Amma sighed in relief, but one of Axl's legs looked particularly bad, and she couldn't help glancing at Aleksander, who appeared as concerned as she was.

The wolves had bitten through to the bone in two places, and Axl had lost a lot of blood; his face was the colour of snow.

'Where are we, do you think?' Axl wondered again, trying to take his mind off the pain. He could see that they were still near the river. It was wide, winding through a low-lying field. In the distance stood a thick row of trees. It looked nothing like where they were before.

Aleksander had been wondering the same thing himself. The fire had helped warm them, but they needed shelter. And they needed horses.

Axl couldn't walk anywhere.

'I'll head off, see where we are. See if I can find a village or even just a farm. Food, shelter, maybe more horses.'

Axl didn't look hopeful that any of that sounded possible. 'We have to get to Tuura,' he said faintly. 'Before something else happens.'

'If we can get back to the main road, then we still have a chance of Gant stumbling across us in a few days,' Aleksander insisted.

'If he gets the message,' Amma said miserably.

'Of course he will,' Aleksander smiled. 'Now, why don't you get comfortable next to Axl. I'll go and find some more wood for the fire and then take a look around.'

'Thank you,' Axl mumbled, closing his eyes. 'You saved our lives.'

Aleksander shrugged. 'Well, it's not going to do us any good if I can't get us to Tuura, is it? Get some sleep, Axl. It will help your leg heal. I'll be back soon.' And winking at Amma, he disappeared around the tree, wishing that at least one of their horses had survived.

***

The giant door was dragged open, creaking and groaning as Jael waited to be ushered inside the temple.

She wondered where Marcus was.

If he was still alive.

Two elders, hooded in black robes, stood on either side of the door, motioning her inside. Jael didn't want to even step over the threshold, not without her sword drawn. But what could she do with it anyway? The temple guards were lining the walls of the cavernous grand chamber, their dead eyes fixed on her, swords at their sides.

'You have the book?' Gerod hissed impatiently, striding forward, flanked on either side by more guards.

'I do,' Jael said slowly, drawing it from beneath her cloak, wishing she didn't have to hand it over; not when there were symbols in there that she was certain would help Eadmund escape Evaine. But she would come back for it when they found a way out of Tuura.

Gerod snatched the book from her, glancing at it dismissively as he flicked through the pages before tossing it into the nearest fire.

Jael couldn't help the gasp that rushed out of her mouth, nor the look of horror on her face.

Gerod laughed. 'What a lot of time and work someone put into that,' he sneered. 'And for what? To help *you*? Why? Why do you need anyone's help? You, Furia's daughter, so powerful that you need a little book to defeat us!'

Jael tried to forget the book. There was nothing she could

do about it now. She had to get out of the temple and back to her family, but by the look on Gerod's face, it didn't seem as though he was inclined to let that happen easily. 'I don't know anything about this prophecy, or what you want with me. I have no idea why I'm important to you at all,' she tried.

Gerod shrugged indifferently. 'You're not. Not anymore. Not to us, nor your husband, who has another woman in his bed. Soon *she* will be his new queen.'

Jael's expression didn't alter, but she felt a twinge in her stomach. 'I'm well aware of that. Why do you think I left?'

'You don't wish to return to Oss?'

'My place has always been in Brekka.'

'Hmmm, Brekka,' Gerod mused, pacing back and forth in front of her, his long, black robe swirling around him. 'There won't be a Brekka soon. Or an Oss. It will all be gone. *You* will all be gone. Soon.' He lunged at her suddenly, the whites of his eyes glowing maniacally. He was not as tall as Jael, though he seemed to rise on his toes, trying to be. 'You may return to your family, but first... I shall take your sword.'

Jael stiffened, rolling her tongue over her teeth. 'What need do you have for a sword when you have the Book of Darkness?'

'Me?' Gerod smiled. 'None at all. But it would be remiss of me to leave that sword with you. We all know the damage that sword could do in your hands.' He reached for it. 'You choose. Your sword or your life.'

Jael felt sick.

Gerod didn't blink as he glared at her.

She saw the guards creeping in from the walls. More elders had flocked to the grand chamber. Perhaps as many as thirty were clustered around the fires now, watching her. And even if she somehow got through all of them, there were more inside the temple chambers, she knew.

Many more.

Jael slid *Toothpick* from his scabbard, handing him to Gerod without a word.

He took the sword in both hands, curling his wet lips in distaste, holding it as though it were diseased. 'Leave. Go back to your family. Say your goodbyes. You do not have long now.'

Gritting her teeth, Jael turned away from him, towards the doors, trying to forget the image of Gerod's smiling face as he held her sword.

***

'Locked out?' Eadmund frowned at Ayla as they sat at a table in the corner of the hall. 'What does that mean?' He had waited for Evaine to leave for the tailor's, not wanting her to see him with Ayla, who she had made a point of disliking; not wanting her to know that he was trying to contact Jael at all.

Ayla looked up. 'It means that she doesn't want anyone to see what she is doing or dreaming or saying. She doesn't want us to see her at all. She has locked a door.'

'On purpose?' Eadmund wondered.

'Yes, I think so. Dreamers can spy on anyone they choose if they are skilled enough. If you are to keep a dreamer out, you must actively close your mind.'

'How?'

'Symbols, perhaps. You can use symbols to bring anything to you, to keep anything away. But dreamers?' Ayla shook her head. 'I don't know of a symbol that does that.'

Eadmund glanced around, nodding at Bram and Thorgils as they entered the hall, but not inviting them over. He looked back to Ayla. 'Why would Jael want to keep out dreamers? Why now?' He was troubled. 'I need to get through to her. Urgently.'

It was something that had kept Ayla awake for much of the night. She had never come across such a thing, and she was as desperate as Eadmund to get Jael and the Brekkan fleet to help them. 'Perhaps I can try Eydis?' she suggested. 'Tonight?'

Eadmund swallowed, suddenly anxious for his little sister. 'If it is not too much for you?'

'No, I couldn't even begin last night. I can try again. If it will help?'

'Do *you* think it will?'

Ayla nodded. 'I see a wave of ships. Angry men. Desperate for gold.'

'*Gold*? And Ivaar? Do you still see Ivaar?'

Ayla frowned. 'Yes. Ivaar wants you. He wants to be king here. But the men beside him? Their eyes gleam with dreams of gold and maybe something else...'

'What?'

'Power. They want to be king here too.'

***

When Borg Arnesson and Falla Hallstein weren't rutting like dogs in their bedchamber, they were rutting like dogs in the hall.

Ivaar refused to sit inside and listen to it any longer. Rain and high winds had battered the tiny island of Bara for days, and his mood was as grey and morose as the clouds hanging above him.

'You prefer the rain to the company of my brother and his new wife?' Rolan Arnesson wondered with a grin, sitting down beside Ivaar on the rocks, staring out at the crashing waves as they pounded the shore.

'I prefer the arms of Ran and the teeth of Ilvari to the sound of those two fucking,' Ivaar spat moodily, fed up with how badly everything had gone. 'It's not why I came here. Not what I thought we would be doing.'

'True, but what else is there to do on this shithole? You're just jealous that Borg's taken the best looking woman here!' Rolan elbowed Ivaar, who looked ready to kill him.

'We had enough men to attack Oss without your cousins.'

Rolan shrugged, resigning himself to not being able to improve Ivaar's foul mood. 'We did, but Borg wants more now that he's married Falla. He wants to be a king.'

Ivaar felt a chill that had nothing to do with the icy rain running down his neck. 'King of what?' he scowled.

'Of the Slave Islands, of course.'

Ivaar frowned, realising that he had misjudged this brother as being the smartest of the three inbred fools. '*King*? But...' His face made a series of strange expressions as he fought the urge to throw Rolan to the ground and rip out his eyes. 'King of the Islands?' He shook his head in disbelief.

Rolan started to look uncomfortable as he ran his fingers through his freshly combed beard. 'Well, now that Borg has a wife, he wants to settle down. And the King of Alekka is going nowhere, not with that fleet of his. But the King of Oss?' Rolan smiled. 'With your help, we will kill your brother and take the islands for ourselves. I'm sure Borg will reward you. Make you a lord.'

Ivaar blinked. 'Make me a lord?' He scrambled to his feet, losing his temper at last. 'I *am* a fucking lord!' he cried, striding away, back to the hall.

Back to Borg Arnesson, who was no doubt fucking his new wife.

CHAPTER THIRTY TWO

Jael took the sword, looking it over with an attempt at interest.

It was well made; similar in length and weight to *Toothpick*. Double-edged with a silver and copper inlay of wave-like patterns, a leather grip and a shell-like pommel.

A beautiful, expertly crafted weapon.

But it was not *Toothpick*.

It was not the sword she was meant to have.

'Thank you,' Jael said mutely, unable to raise a smile.

Kormac didn't blame her. He knew the story of her sword; how vital it was to the prophecy.

Edela glanced at her granddaughter, concerned by both the destruction of the book and the loss of the sword. It certainly made their situation even more precarious.

'How about a cup of chamomile tea?' Biddy suggested as she bustled about, trying to be useful. Branwyn's servant, Berta, had left to look after her father, who had been seriously wounded in the raven attack, so Biddy had assumed control of the kitchen.

It helped to give her something to focus on.

'And something to eat, perhaps?' Edela said. 'I think I'm almost hungry.'

Biddy would have smiled if she didn't feel so petrified. 'Well, I'm making flatbreads, and there's some smoked cheese. How does that sound?'

Edela nodded, resting her eyes for a moment, listening to her stomach growl in anticipation.

'Those soldiers have gone,' Gisila sighed, closing the door. 'Finally.'

That was something, Jael supposed. She glanced around the house. Biddy had rushed to the fire to flip her flatbreads. Eydis sat by Edela, the puppies curled up beside her. Kormac had taken a seat next to Branwyn, preparing to sharpen his own sword, but Gisila couldn't sit still.

She was in a complete panic.

'Can we dream walk? Maybe Axl and Aleksander could help us?' Gisila wondered.

'They cannot,' Edela sighed. 'Not now. The wolves have hurt them.'

'What we need is to find a way to break the binding spell,' Kormac said calmly, running a whetstone down his blade. 'To free the soldiers. There are some good men among them. If we can free them from this spell, they would help us, I'm sure.'

'But would that be enough to defeat The Following? With all those elders and dreamers in the temple? No one is safe here while they live. While the Book of Darkness is in that woman's hands,' Gisila panicked.

'Don't forget Marcus' daughter,' Branwyn said, trying to soothe her sister. 'If she can steal the book they won't be such a threat, will they?'

Jael frowned, running her eyes over the sword that wasn't *Toothpick*. She wanted to reassure them all, but as much as she hoped that Berard would help Hanna take the book from his brother, she had felt his fear growing in her dreams. He was becoming more and more afraid of Jaeger.

And if Berard refused to help her, then Hanna didn't stand a chance.

***

Berard hunched over sadly, watching Meena scurry away from the castle, heading towards the markets.

She looked as nervous as ever.

'Berard!' Haaron grumbled. 'Your head is facing the wrong way!'

Berard turned back to his father who had been talking with all four of his sons about the defenses he was planning to construct. Around the harbour. The castle. Across the mountains.

Only Haegen seemed interested.

Jaeger was eager to get back to his chamber for his meeting with Yorik and Morana.

Karsten was eager to launch himself at Jaeger and take off his head.

And Berard... well, Berard was suddenly unable to think of anything but the fact that they were leaving in five days and Meena would be all alone with Jaeger. Jaeger, who was so unlike the brother he used to have that he barely recognised him anymore. Jaeger, who seemed more and more like the man who had punched his first wife in the stomach, killing both her and their unborn son.

He remembered how Jael had begged him to look after her cousin. She was worried enough about what Jaeger would do then. But now? Now, he seemed even worse. How could he go and leave Meena alone with him?

'What do you think?' Haaron asked, nudging his smallest son.

Berard blinked himself awake. 'I think it makes sense, Father,' he said mutely. 'When word spreads of what happened here, it will embolden our allies and enemies alike. Those who thought they never had a hope of defeating us might chance their luck. We need more protection.'

'Good!' Haaron was surprised that he had been listening. 'And that's something I want you three to remember. Build walls! Bolster your defenses! If our enemies come here, they will come everywhere. They will seek to attack Hest from every angle. Try to conquer us piece by piece. That's why I'm sending you away from here. Part of the reason, at least. To strengthen our borders.' He thought of Lothar Furyck and sighed. 'It was not so long ago that we were thinking of claiming Helsabor. Now we must push back against the very real possibility that our neighbours will unite to do the same to us.'

Haegen was pleased to see that Haaron was back to himself. He felt relieved. As much as he would have preferred to defeat the Brekkans now, he realised that what his father was pursuing made more sense.

Strengthen your defenses, then attack.

'Let's go back inside before your mother starts screaming from the doors!' Haaron smiled, enjoying the image of his furious wife, who had already sent a slave out to hurry them up.

No matter how bitter she became or how ornery and old he felt, he could not help but love Bayla.

If only she felt the same way.

***

Aleksander had not found a soul. Not a house, nor a horse. But he did have a rabbit, a fish, and an idea of where they were now.

Unfortunately, it was not where they needed to be.

Amma left Aleksander to take the news to Axl while she busied herself gutting the fish. She was so anxious about Axl's wounds and worried about how they would find Gant, that she barely noticed how unpleasant a task it was this time.

'I can't walk.'

'I know,' Aleksander sighed. 'But I can carry you.'

Axl laughed. It hurt. 'You can't carry me. Not that far.'

'I'm going to make a rack and tie you to it,' Aleksander grinned. 'So, I was wrong. I'm not going to carry you. I'm going to drag you!'

Axl raised his eyebrows, looking at the state of Aleksander who was covered in cuts and bruises, his arms hanging at his sides in exhaustion. He appeared ready to fall over. 'And you think you can *do* that?'

'I can try. It will give me something to do instead of sitting here moaning with you. If we don't get back to the road in the next few days, Gant will pass us by. He's not going to take the army off the road. He's not going to lead all those men through the forest. So, we just have to be by the road, waiting.'

'You could go on your own.'

'I could,' Aleksander agreed, having thought the same thing himself. 'But you're in no shape to protect Amma if something happens. And I don't think she could protect you. I'm sure you'd both rather we stuck together?'

Axl felt embarrassed. 'Makes sense.'

'Good, well you stay there,' Aleksander smiled, 'and I'll go and find some branches.' His stomach rumbled, and he remembered the raspberries he'd found. Jael's favourite. Tipping them out of his pouch, he handed them to Axl. 'Here. Something to keep you going.'

Axl took them gratefully, starving himself. 'Amma?' he called. 'Would you like some berries?'

Amma shook her head, certain that she was hungry but too ill with nerves to think of eating. The fish guts had quickly turned her stomach, and she almost retched as she threaded a sharpened stick through the cleaned carcass, jumping at every pop and crackle from the fire.

Waiting for another attack to come.

***

Fyn and Entorp had been relieved to see the soldiers abandon the house and they hurried inside, eager to see how everyone was.

'You look much brighter,' Entorp smiled, pulling a stool towards Edela and uncorking his jar of salve. The colour of her cheeks was encouraging. Her eyes seemed alert, and her nose immediately turned up at the smell emanating from his jar.

Jael hurried to the door, taking Fyn and Eydis with her, eager for some fresh air. 'So,' she said, glancing around as they walked away from the house, relieved to see that they were not being followed by anything other than two waddling ducks. 'Tell me what you know about this book, Eydis. Why do you think you can see it?'

'I think it was my grandmother's,' Eydis said quietly. 'That it was her voice I could hear, showing me the right pages, telling me what to say.'

'Is your grandmother still alive?' Fyn wondered, loping along beside her, one eye on the road ahead, checking for any obstacles in Eydis' path.

Eydis shook her head. 'No, she died before my mother left Tuura.'

'But she was from here, wasn't she? And a dreamer?' Jael wondered, bringing Eydis towards her as a huddle of soldiers approached. They paid them no mind, though, as they hurried on down the street.

It started to rain. Just a light drizzle, but no one was keen to turn back yet. They were all tired of being confined in such a small space; not ready to feel like prisoners again.

'She was a dreamer, yes,' Eydis said, pulling up her hood. 'Her name was Samara.'

'Well, we can't ask Marcus about the book now,' Jael

frowned. 'But perhaps you could ask your grandmother? Is that possible, do you think? Can dreamers talk to spirits?'

Eydis looked terrified by the idea.

'Perhaps Edela would know?' Fyn suggested, sensing Eydis' panic.

'Good idea,' Jael smiled. 'We have to find some way to break this binding spell. The quicker we can get back to Oss, the better.'

***

The waiting was eating away at them all, and the need to keep as many stores reserved as possible meant that meal times had quickly become something that no one looked forward to.

Evaine pouted as she sat beside Eadmund. 'Leek soup?' And lifting her spoon, she dribbled the very thin liquid back into her bowl. 'Why are we eating so much leek soup?' she grumbled. 'I told the cook to prepare a suckling pig tonight!'

Eadmund smiled tightly. 'I heard. Yetta came and told me, but Evaine, we can't eat as though every night is a feast. We have to ration. That pig needs to stay fat for when things get hard. If we can't defeat Ivaar easily, our only hope is to hold him out, and we won't last long if there's no food left before he even gets here!'

Evaine harrumphed loudly, pouting some more.

Morac looked embarrassed by her childishness. Runa, sitting next to him, was not surprised. There was nobody as self-centred as Evaine and for some reason, despite having Eadmund all to herself, living in the hall with him, and having Jael gone, she had been in a foul mood for days.

Eadmund had too much on his mind to give any further attention to Evaine's sulk. He glanced at Ayla, who sat at the opposite table, helping her husband to eat. Bruno Adea had finally been carried from his sick bed, and although he looked frail, he seemed pleased to be with her.

Evaine glared at Ayla, watching as Eadmund's attention kept drifting towards the dreamer. She was convinced that Ayla was doing something to Eadmund to take him away from her. But how was that even possible when he was bound to her soul?

Evaine was so overcome with jealousy that she could barely see straight. Eventually, she pushed her bowl away, slopping soup everywhere, and hurried up from the table, disappearing behind the green curtain without another word.

Morac glanced at Runa in surprise, but Runa kept her eyes down, not wanting any part of it. He swallowed, trying to smile at Eadmund, who looked confused. 'Evaine has never been especially fond of leek soup,' Morac said weakly.

Bruno barely noticed the ruckus as Ayla offered him a piece of bread. It was left over from breakfast and hard to chew on, so she dipped it into his soup to soften it first. He sighed, relieved to be out of that hole, to be away from that island.

To have his beautiful wife next to him again.

He took the bread, too full to eat any more but not wanting to disappoint her. She needed him to get strong quickly, he knew, because of what was coming. He had barely eaten in a year, though, and his appetite was so small that he was full almost immediately.

But he bit into the slice of soupy bread for her.

'I have to go and see Isaura again tonight,' Ayla said quietly.

Bruno frowned. 'You'll try again?'

'Yes, I'll try Eydis this time. There has to be a way to get through to Jael. Ivaar cannot come. I won't lose you again.'

Bruno felt his body tense at the sound of that name. He wanted to vomit. He had eaten too much. He needed to lie down. He'd been out of bed for too long, and his body felt weak, but more than anything, he wanted to kill Ivaar Skalleson for what he had done to his wife. He reached for the plate of bread.

'I think I'll have some more,' he said firmly.

***

'Hmmm,' Edela murmured, smiling at Eydis who suddenly looked much taller, but so worried as she sat beside her.

They all looked worried.

'I do remember Samara Lund. But not well. What about you, Derwa?'

Derwa had come to check on her patient, and she was pleased with her progress. She had set Biddy to work on a tonic and another broth, and now she sat hunched over on Edela's bed, shooing away Vella, who was trying to lick her ankle. 'Samara?' Derwa nodded. 'Yes, a very skilled dreamer, I remember. Younger than us. She was friends with my sister.'

Derwa had her own stone now, so they felt free to talk around her.

'She was Rhea Thorsen's cousin,' Derwa added. 'You remember Rhea? Strange girl, that one.'

Edela blinked.

'What is it?' Biddy wondered, trying to shift her into a more comfortable position. After so long in bed, Edela's skin and joints were suffering, and Biddy was conscious of moving her regularly.

'Rhea Thorsen,' Edela whispered, 'was Aleksander's grandmother. The one who was thrown out of the temple for seeking out the Widow.'

'Oh.' Biddy looked surprised, turning to Eydis who looked confused, and Derwa whose mouth was hanging open.

'Well, things are getting very interesting, aren't they?' Edela smiled. 'And you, Eydis, have just found yourself a new cousin.' She closed her eyes, exhausted, thinking of Aleksander, who she knew was in trouble.

Just as they were in trouble.

And there had to be something she could do about all of it.

***

Aleksander was happy with what he'd managed to construct from six sturdy branches and two cloaks. Thankfully, between all of their pouches, they'd found two fishing hooks and just enough line for Aleksander to tie the cloaks to the branches. And within a few hours, his makeshift stretcher was born.

After easing Axl onto it, Aleksander had picked up the arms, tested that it would hold, and they'd headed off towards the forest.

It was slow-going, though.

Aleksander lugged the weighty stretcher behind him, feeling as though his wounded shoulder was about to drop off. He gritted his teeth, brushing away Amma's offers of help, and eventually, they made their way across the wide expanse of field and bog, into the forest, which is where everything suddenly got much harder.

'I could walk, you know,' Axl kept muttering from the stretcher, listening to Aleksander's grunts of discomfort as he stumbled over rocks and tree roots, slipping on pine needles, falling into leaf-covered holes, getting stuck between trees.

Aleksander lowered the stretcher to the ground at last.

They had not made much progress, but dusk was already upon them, and they needed a fire. Aleksander looked around. It was the clearest spot he had found all day, and it would at least enable them to lie down in some sort of comfort. 'No! You can't!' he groaned, bending over, hands on hips, his chest heaving as he tried to catch his breath. 'Axl, you can't walk!

But you will when your legs get a chance to heal. So, just rest! I'll go and find some wood and something to eat.' He looked at Amma. 'Find what you can. Moss, twigs. Gather anything small. Dry is good. And stones. Make a circle. I'll be back soon.'

Aleksander didn't wait for the well-meaning protests that he knew would come. He disappeared quickly into the tall, densely packed trees, conscious that sounds of the approaching night were already upon them.

He had to hurry.

Axl sighed, dropping his head back onto the stretcher. 'I'm sorry,' he said faintly. 'Sorry for this mess I've landed you in. And it looks as though it's about to get even worse too.'

'I'd much rather be in a mess with you than stuck in Hest with him,' Amma smiled, turning away, remembering Aleksander's instructions. 'But don't worry, soon we'll find Gant, and he will have horses, and we will get to Tuura!'

Axl tried to cheer up, seeing how brave she was being. His legs were throbbing, though, and he was starting to shiver. 'We w-w-will.' He wanted to see Gant, to have an army behind him, to destroy whatever was doing this to them.

And then he would turn that army towards Hest and Jaeger Dragos.

***

Egil ushered Morana and Yorik into the chamber.

Jaeger had been looking forward to this all day; playing over in his mind how it would go; what he would say. Toying with the idea of killing them both, then blinking that thought away.

How would he read the book without them?

'Wine?' Jaeger asked impatiently.

'No, thank you, my lord.' Yorik shook his head, eager to get to the book.

Jaeger grabbed his own goblet, following them to the table where the book lay, open and waiting.

Yorik could barely breathe as he approached the ancient book; his body tingling, almost tearful to think that their dreams were finally within reach. He closed his eyes, inhaling its intoxicating scent.

'I don't imagine you'll be able to read much with your eyes closed,' Jaeger muttered.

Yorik blinked, composing himself. 'No, of course not, but for what we need to do, we must have a clear mind. You understand?'

Jaeger didn't, but he followed them to the book, watching closely as Yorik sat down in front of it, Morana hovering over his left shoulder. Yorik reached out slowly to touch the book and Jaeger wanted to scream. But he drank his wine and flexed his fist and glared at him instead.

Morana guided Yorik to the part of the book she had been working so hard to translate. It was written as though an afterthought, on the inside of the back cover, next to where that page had been torn out.

Yorik ran his hand over the jagged edge, wondering if Raemus' own hand had been there, then frowned. 'Well, I see. That doesn't make sense, does it?' His eyes met Jaeger's as he leaned forward. 'Morana is right, there are some words... some phrases in here that are strange. Confusing.' He motioned for Morana to sit beside him. 'But I'm sure we can figure this out together,' he smiled at her.

Morana didn't smile back.

She felt much the same as Jaeger, not wanting Yorik's hands anywhere near the book; grimacing as he caressed the pages, touching each delicately drawn symbol, running his finger under every line of text.

She swallowed, irritated, biting her tongue; too distracted

by a loud buzzing in her ears to think of anything at all.

***

Eadmund kissed Evaine quickly, then edged towards the bedchamber door.

'Where are you going?' she asked sharply. 'You only just came in!'

'I have to go and speak to Thorgils,' Eadmund lied. 'I have some things to organise.'

Evaine huffed and puffed her way over to him. 'Surely you've organised everything you could possibly organise by now?'

Eadmund felt weary, and his smile was forced. 'Evaine, we're about to be attacked. Ayla has seen that and –'

'Ayla!' Evaine spat. 'Why do you care so much about what *she* thinks? She worked for Ivaar! How can you even think to trust her?' Reaching out, she turned Eadmund's face towards hers, running her hands down his hairy cheeks. 'Why would you take notice of *anything* she says?'

Eadmund felt a sudden need to throw Evaine onto the bed and lift up her nightdress. She was wild, and her eyes were frenzied with jealousy, and it heated his body quickly. She wanted to possess all of him, and he was filled with the desire to lose himself in her until nothing else existed. But he shook his head, knowing that there would be no Evaine, no Oss, nothing at all if he didn't find a way to keep Ivaar out.

'Ayla was Ivaar's prisoner. The last thing she wants is Ivaar to come. He will take her back, kill her husband.'

'So she says.'

'Well, Isaura says so too. And besides, Ivaar wants to kill me, and that has nothing to do with Ayla at all,' Eadmund insisted, pushing Evaine away, sensing that he had to leave before he could no longer control himself. 'Now, go and see Sigmund. I'll be back soon, I promise.'

Ayla was doing the dream walk at the cottage again and this time, Eadmund and Thorgils were going to watch.

He didn't want to be late.

***

Jael kissed Eydis' cheek as she tucked her into bed, placing a hand on Ido, who lay with his head on her chest. His sister was still happily sniffing about for crumbs.

Eydis had been excited to find out that she was Aleksander's cousin. Thinking that she had a family she didn't know about had distracted her for the afternoon. Now, though, Jael needed to get her thinking about the book.

'You must try to find your grandmother in your dreams,' Jael reminded her. 'She guided you to the answers when you needed them, and now we need the biggest answer of all. A way to set everyone free from the binding spell, so we can go home to Eadmund.'

'I'll try,' Eydis nodded sleepily. 'I'll try. Goodnight, Jael,' she yawned.

'Goodnight, Eydis.'

***

Meena could barely breathe as she shuffled outside Morana's door.

She knew that Morana was with Jaeger, but...

Morana would know. She would know.

Know that she had been in her chamber. Know that she had stolen a book.

Meena rubbed her fingers together, biting her lip, her eyes constantly fleeing down the darkened corridor, certain she'd heard footsteps.

Tapping her head with one hand, she reached for the door handle with the other before changing her mind entirely and running away down the corridor as fast as her shaking legs would carry her.

CHAPTER THIRTY THREE

Eadmund and Thorgils sat far enough away not to be a distraction, although the bed groaned every time Eadmund moved, and eventually, he left to sit on the floor.

Ayla knelt in front of the fire, ignoring everyone.

She focused on her breathing; on the rhythm of the drum; on the feel of the floorboards against her knees. She felt every sense heighten, becoming aware of her body, and then, bit by bit as she started chanting, slowly leaving every part of herself behind, drifting into the twisting, hypnotic flames.

Drifting towards Eydis.

Eydis.

She needed to see Eydis...

***

Axl had fallen asleep early, and Aleksander couldn't stop yawning. He was ready for sleep himself, but he could see that Amma was wide awake.

It was so loud in the forest, and her senses were overwhelmed. She couldn't stop thinking about the wolves, imagining that every rustle, every wail and howl was going to lead to another attack.

'It's alright,' Aleksander murmured, watching her eyes jump about in terror. 'That's what a forest sounds like.' He hoped that he was right, but he couldn't hear anything out of the ordinary. Just crickets and owls, bats and foxes.

The odd hedgehog.

Hopefully, no wolves.

Amma swallowed, wanting to feel reassured, but it was impossible after what they had been through. 'Do you think the Widow is trying to protect us?' she whispered.

Aleksander had been thinking about little else all night. 'Yes,' he said. 'It doesn't make sense, but yes. She woke me up in time to get us to that river. If she hadn't...'

'And you really think it's her?' Amma yawned, reaching over to pull Axl's cloak up to his chin. Neither she nor Aleksander had cloaks, and it was freezing, but they had no more fishing line and their cloaks needed to remain on the stretcher.

Aleksander nodded. 'I do. I remember her voice. It's her, I'm sure.'

'But I thought that she was evil?' Amma mumbled, finally lying on the ground, resting her head on the pile of damp leaves she had been making into a pillow. 'Why is she helping us, I wonder?'

'I don't know, but we can only hope she keeps trying to. It feels as though we're going to need it.'

Amma closed her eyes, not wanting to sleep at all; not comforted by Aleksander's words, nor the sounds of the forest, but desperate, just for a moment, not to feel scared.

***

Gerod stood before Skoll's Tree.

It was his favourite dream to have, Morana knew. She rolled her eyes, bored as she hiked towards him, wanting to get it over with. It had not been a good day, and she just wanted to sleep and find her own dreams, hoping that the answers to the ritual were waiting for her.

'Morana,' Gerod sighed in relief. 'You've come!'

'It appears so,' she grumbled, waiting while he walked to her, his eyes shining in the moonlight. 'And you have news, I hope. About the book?'

'Oh, yes,' Gerod purred. 'It is no more. I threw it into the fire myself, before taking Jael Furyck's sword from her.' He smiled, enjoying the shock on Morana's face.

Morana almost jumped in the air. 'You *burned* it?' She shook her head with glee. 'That book? Ha! Well, that is some news. You have done well, Gerod. Yorik will be pleased, I'm sure.'

Gerod puffed out his chest, appreciating the compliment. 'And the Book of Darkness?' he wondered. 'When will you be performing the ritual?'

Morana's smile vanished. 'Soon,' she glowered, not wanting to reveal her own failure to him; not wanting to talk to him about it at all. Yorik had been no help, in the end, and she was still no closer to translating that troublesome phrase. But that was not something she wished to share with Gerod Gott. 'The shadow moon will be upon us in four nights. We will be ready by then.'

Gerod looked pleased, wanting to ask more but Morana had already turned from him, and he was left watching her slink away, merging silently into the shadows as though she had never been there at all.

He turned around, walking slowly back to the tree, remembering how his mother had brought him here as a child; how he had found her body hanging from a branch, swinging in an angry breeze.

***

There was another wall.

Ayla couldn't get through.

Eydis had shut her out as well.

What was going on?

'There is no way through there,' said a melodious voice.

Ayla spun around, surprised to see an old woman. Not that old, she supposed. More middle-aged than old. But very familiar. Her hair was as dark as storm clouds, but her eyes were a cheerful, cornflower blue, and she was standing by a tree, smiling.

'I am Samara,' she said. 'Eydis wanted me to come, so I came. But she didn't realise that she had locked us all out.'

'But why?' Ayla wondered. 'It was the same when I tried to reach Jael Furyck.'

'Ahhh,' Samara murmured, moving closer. 'They are hiding from dreamers because dreamers are trying to hurt them.'

Ayla looked shocked. 'What dreamers would try to hurt them?'

'The ones in Tuura. They are under orders to dig into their dreams and find answers, so Jael and Eydis have wisely shut them out. They have all shut them out. They are trying to stay alive. And now, without the book...' Samara looked worried, not knowing what she could do to help.

Ayla frowned. 'Do I know you?'

Samara smiled sadly. 'No, but you knew my sister. She was your mother.'

Ayla gasped.

'We were separated as children. No one knew that we were sisters. We were kept apart so that if one of us was discovered or killed, the other's line would continue.'

Ayla looked confused.

'We were the keepers of the book,' Samara explained. 'Not the Book of Darkness, but the Book of Aurea. Your mother had one copy, and so did I. Before I died, I left mine in the temple, with the elderman. Naively so, for I did not realise how deep the roots of The Following had entwined themselves around that sacred place. And nor did he. And now he is a prisoner in the temple, and my book is destroyed. And Eydis is trapped there. They all are.'

'But my mother's copy? She did not pass it on to me,' Ayla said.

Samara's eyes lit up. 'No. You were gone, and she worried about you. You loved your husband, but she saw a dark cloud hanging over your future. You were far away from being able to help Tuura.'

'Then where is it?'

'I don't know, which is as it should be. But she would have made sure that you could find it when you needed to. You will know where to look and when.'

'But...' Ayla glanced down at her hands, and when she looked up, Samara had gone, and she was alone in front of the wall that stretched far up to the dark, threatening clouds above her.

Reaching out, Ayla placed her hands on the roughened stone. 'Eydis,' she breathed. 'Eydis, it's Ayla. I need your help. Please, let me in...'

***

Jaeger ran his fingers around Meena's belly button, distracted.

Yorik and Morana had left, and he felt a sense of relief that the book was his again. Meena had no interest in it, nor it in her, he knew. Egil was no threat, but those Followers? He frowned.

They wanted to take the book away from him. He could feel it.

Or kill him.

His eyes flared in the darkness. He knew that they needed him, but did they need him alive?

'You're sure you looked everywhere?' he grumbled.

Meena nodded, shivering beneath him. 'There were no books. Morana must have hidden them. She must have s-s-seen what you wanted to do.'

Jaeger looked away, sighing. He felt powerless, caught in a web. Bound to the will and whim of Morana and Yorik.

Not how he expected to feel at all.

Meena wanted to roll away from him and hide under the furs. She envied Berard and his brothers who were leaving, taking their families and going far away from the castle. She wished she could go along. But to do so would cause more problems for Berard.

Jaeger would certainly hunt her down.

Or would he?

Perhaps he wouldn't notice if she just slipped away? Perhaps he would be too busy with Morana and the book to even know she had gone?

***

Eydis could hear the anticipation that hung, heavy in the silence as she sat eating breakfast.

'Did you see anything?' Jael asked at last. 'Did you have any dreams about the book or your grandmother?'

Eydis squirmed. Fyn was sitting next to her, she knew. Jael was on her other side. Edela was still in bed. She didn't want to let anyone down, but... 'No. I didn't have any dreams at all.'

The disappointment was loud. The escalating fear, even

louder. Eydis' cheeks warmed with discomfort. She didn't know what to say.

Jael filled a cup with milk. 'Here, have a drink,' she said kindly, placing the cup in Eydis' hands. 'It doesn't matter. You're not alone in trying to find the answers we need. Edela looks ready to get to work. And I may be of some use too.' Turning around, she glanced at her grandmother, who was being spoon-fed porridge by Gisila. She did not look happy.

That was a good sign.

'Jael's right, Eydis,' Edela said between mouthfuls. 'You're not alone. We will find answers soon. There's a way out of this place, don't you worry.'

Branwyn spooned another boiled egg onto Fyn's plate, glaring at Kormac, inclining her head towards Jael.

'What is it?' Jael wondered.

'It's nothing,' Kormac mumbled, frowning at his wife. 'Probably nothing. Just a thought I had.'

'About?'

'Well,' he started, his fair skin turning pink as everyone stared at him. 'I wondered about the idea of the binding spell, as though it were a rope. And I thought of the fort. The fort is like a rope around us all.'

Entorp, who was sitting next to Kormac, almost dropped his cup of milk. 'Yes!' he exclaimed. 'You're right!'

Biddy looked confused as she handed around a bowl of berries. 'Do you mean they have put a spell on the fort itself? Because, if that were so, then *all* Tuurans would be bound, wouldn't they?'

That had everyone frowning.

'Not necessarily,' Edela said, waving away Gisila's spoon. She tried to sit up, but Gisila pushed her back down.

'Mother, you're not strong enough yet.'

Edela sighed, exhausted, realising that her daughter was right. Her head sunk heavily into the pillow. 'They could have used candle magic to bind the soldiers. And then used symbols to reinforce it,' she added.

'Perhaps there are symbols around the fort. In the walls?' Entorp suggested.

Edela nodded. 'Yes, that would work!'

'Well, we can't all go peering at the walls of the fort,' Jael said. 'Perhaps we can leave you to do that on your own, Entorp? Maybe Fyn can help you?'

Fyn sat up straighter, eager to be useful.

Branwyn smiled proudly at Kormac, who blushed further. 'You don't need to be a dreamer to have a good idea, it seems!' she said, kissing his hairy cheek.

***

Morana hopped around the fire, pulling on her socks.

Yorik sat on the bed, watching her. He had never seen her so happy. 'You're pleased, then?'

'I am!' she exclaimed, sitting down to pull on her boots. 'Now that Gerod has destroyed that book and taken the sword from Jael Furyck, there's nothing to stop us!'

'Nothing but the puzzle of that final phrase,' Yorik reminded her. 'It makes no sense at all.'

Morana was suddenly serious. 'No, it doesn't. And we are running out of time. I had thought it would unravel itself more quickly than this. But the shadow moon is approaching. We cannot miss it!'

Yorik frowned, knowing that she was right. He reached for his black robe, though it was already a humid morning and he was not inclined to dress in such heavy wool. 'And if we do bring her back, what if she takes the book? It was hers for so long. What guarantee do we have that she will even *want* to help us bring Raemus back?'

Morana dismissed his fears. 'We have no option,' she insisted. 'And whatever she will be when she returns, we are not without power. I have studied the Book of Darkness. We are not without power. And now that Jael Furyck is impotent, without her sword, her husband, or that pathetic book, we have a clear path to Raemus. No one can stop us now!' Her eyes widened, and they were mad with ecstasy. 'We cannot give up! He is within reach!'

***

Aleksander had dreamed of Andala and the tiny bed he used to share with Jael, wondering how he had ever complained about it being too small and uncomfortable. He was becoming so used to sleeping on lumpy dirt that the idea of that bed felt like a luxurious fantasy.

That and Biddy's cooking.

He thought about that too.

When he wasn't thinking about Jael.

'Aarrghh!' Axl groaned as he was knocked against the side of a tree, whose low branches then scraped across his legs.

'Sorry!' Aleksander called over his shoulder, glancing around at his uncomfortable patient. The forest was growing denser, and he was doing his best to manoeuvre the stretcher through the tightly packed trees with shoulders that felt full of knives. 'It's getting a bit tight up here!'

He was right, Amma thought, squeezing between two trees. If things continued like this, they would soon be boxed in. And that idea terrified her.

Aleksander looked up at the sky, whose low clouds appeared to be touching the high canopy of the forest.

He hoped that he was leading them in the right direction.

***

Ayla's news about Eydis had kept Isaura awake for much of the night. And when she wasn't worrying about the fact that no help was coming, she was having nightmares about what Ivaar would do when he arrived.

She yawned as she trudged along the beach with Thorgils, watching the children chase Bram around on the stones. He was slipping and sliding, fooling them into thinking that he was about to fall over, but just as they lunged for him, he'd suddenly right himself and charge after them.

There was much squealing, and laughter and Isaura smiled to see it.

Thorgils did not.

'They seem to like Bram,' he mumbled moodily.

'Well, he has a way with children, I suppose,' she said tactfully, 'having had children himself. It must be so hard for him to have lost them all. His whole family? All at once?' Isaura looked at Bram, not imagining how anyone could cope with such loss.

Thorgils felt embarrassed. 'True. Perhaps they can help each other feel better?'

Isaura sighed, listening to the gleeful giggling of her children, mixed with the plaintive cries of the seabirds who swooped down, searching for dried bits of seaweed and twigs to add to their nesting holes in the cliffs. 'Are you sure you have to go?'

'To Hud's Point?' Thorgils asked. 'Best that I do. Eadmund needs someone out there he can trust. I'm taking Torstan with me, but I've asked Bram to stay behind and look after you.'

Isaura was grateful for that. 'But what if Ivaar doesn't sail around the headland? What if he comes over land? Towards you? There's nothing down there but a tiny hall and a few old farmers!'

Thorgils smiled broadly, trying to reassure her. 'Then I'll be the first one to Ivaar's throat. Don't worry. There's nothing I wouldn't do to keep him from you. From all of us. Ivaar is not going to take Oss!' He pulled Isaura to him as the wind picked up her long, golden hair, blowing it behind her like a sail.

He was never going to let Ivaar take her away from him again.

***

Ivaar sipped morosely from his cup, wondering if he was about to meet the same fate as his father.

He had barely slept, and his mind was drifting like a drunk man at sea. He rubbed his eyes, trying to ignore the almost-toothless grin of the woman whose bed he'd ended up in. She was no beauty. And even that was kind to say, but it was better to be humping than just listening to Borg and Falla doing it.

But still, he wished she'd just fuck off.

'My cousins should arrive today, or perhaps tomorrow,' Borg grunted, flopping down onto the bench beside him, nudging his tattooed shoulder into Ivaar's. 'Best we start knocking these cunts into shape. Time to stop the ale, I'd say.'

Ivaar didn't even look his way. He'd thought about simply taking his two ships and disappearing in the night. But he didn't know where he'd go.

Not anymore.

A man with two ships and a lot of enemies had few options.

Borg nudged him again. 'Lost your tongue, Ivaar the Bastard?'

'I think you're right,' Ivaar said, at last, through grinding teeth. 'They have my dreamer with them, so it may be that she knows our plans.' He felt oddly wistful for Ayla. He'd always felt a sense of comfort in having a dreamer around.

Knowing what was coming.

He wondered if she saw what was coming for him now.

***

Entorp and Fyn had tried not to draw any attention to themselves as they wandered around the fort in the pouring rain for much of the morning, acting as though they were deep in conversation.

Every now and then one of them would drop to the ground as if to pick something up, or to check their boots for stones, taking the opportunity to look at the great wall that circled Tuura, but they found nothing. The wall was mostly constructed of stone; its foundations older than anything in Osterland.

But they could find no symbols carved into it at all.

It was disheartening and neither wanted to go back to the house and disappoint everyone.

Entorp frowned. 'I was sure we'd find something.'

'So was I,' Fyn sighed wearily, wet through and miserable. He looked up at the sky. 'Will it ever stop raining?' he grumbled as they finally trekked back to the house.

Entorp smiled, following his gaze. 'It does rain a lot in Tuura. But this weather feels even worse than anything I remember.' He stumbled to a stop.

'What is it?' Fyn wondered, peering at the street, assuming that Entorp had tripped over something.

'The towers,' Entorp whispered hoarsely. 'Look at the towers.' He knelt in the mud, pretending to adjust his boot while Fyn scanned the fort. There were four towers positioned along the wall, equal distance apart. They were large towers with two floors; wooden ramparts connecting each one to the next.

The soldiers spent much of their time in those towers.

Entorp stood up, enjoying the look on Fyn's face.

'But how can we get in and find out if there are any symbols inside them?' Fyn wondered.

'Well, I think Kormac and his sons might come in handy for that,' Entorp grinned as they hurried back to the house.

***

The thought of seeing Axl's face when he told him the news about Osbert had spurred Gant on through six long days in the saddle. He was numb and stiff and yet, still grateful that he had a horse, and could at least feel his feet, unlike most of the poor souls who had traipsed behind him in the never-ending rain. So, it came as a bit of a disappointment when Gant finally arrived at the cave to find that no one was there.

No one was there, but a message had been left for him in stones and twigs:

GO TO TUURA

Gant stood and stared at those words for a time. Some of the sticks and smaller pebbles had been moved – displaced by animals, he supposed – but the message remained clear enough. And so he stared at it, and then at the piles of dead ravens littered around the cave floor.

There was dried blood everywhere.

Somehow, Gant knew those two things were related. Why else go to Tuura?

Why ever go back to Tuura?

Dropping his shoulders, he turned to leave. Tuura was another three or four days away. Not the news he wanted to deliver to his men who thought they were nearly home.

But if their new king had gone to Tuura.

Well, he sighed, then they were going to Tuura too.

CHAPTER THIRTY FOUR

Aedan and Aron swallowed at the same time, looking as apprehensive as their father as they stood around the three loaded carts.

'It's simple,' Kormac said in a hushed voice. 'We've repaired their swords, sharpened their axes, fixed their tools, and now we're just going to deliver them, as we would on any other day.' He pointed to the cart on his right. 'Aedan, you'll go to the eastern tower. Aron, you'll take this pile to the northern tower. And I'll take the rest.'

His sons nodded nervously.

'Make sure you help them carry the weapons inside. See if you can find a way to have a look around,' Kormac reminded them.

'But where do we look?' Aedan wondered, pulling on the three braids of his short, coppery beard. 'Surely they haven't carved these symbols in plain sight?'

That thought worried Kormac too. 'Well, try your best to check the walls and floors that are exposed, that's easy enough I'd say. It may be that they're hidden, and we won't see them at all, but if you have a chance alone in the tower, look behind things and try not to get caught!'

***

'I'm not sure why you have to keep rubbing this evil stink all over me, Entorp Bray!' Edela spluttered. 'I don't blame Jael for wanting to vomit every time she smells it. I feel the same!'

Entorp's eyes widened in surprise. Edela almost sounded like herself again. It cheered him to see it. 'Well, perhaps you don't need it anymore? You seem almost recovered.'

'Not quite,' she said, exhaling heavily, resting her head back on the pillow. 'But I am feeling stronger. I just need to have some useful dreams. It's been too long since I was much help to anyone. We're all in this mess because of me.'

'Yes, but you nearly dying has led us here to something important. Something we need to stop. Saving Tuura, destroying The Following.' Entorp could feel his heart pounding at the memory of what they had done to his family. After hiding from the pain for so long, he felt a sudden thirst for revenge.

He was not a violent man, but The Following had taken everything from him. Nothing they did now would bring back his wife and children, but if he could rip out their heart, it would go some way towards healing his own.

'I know that book,' Edela murmured. 'I saw every page of it when I was here in the winter. I ran my hands over every scrawl, every symbol. And, old though I may be, I know that every one of those pages is in here somewhere.' She tapped her head. 'So, I think I had better get some sleep and try to tease out some answers for what we need to do.'

'And a way to save Eadmund,' Eydis reminded her.

Edela frowned. 'Yes, that too. Your poor brother has not had much luck lately, has he? Twisted around the finger of that evil, little bitch.' Edela ignored Entorp's surprised blinking that she would speak with such force in front of Eydis. But Edela still remembered the look in that girl's eye, so vicious and victorious as she plunged the knife into her stomach. She shivered, reliving the strange sensation.

There had been no pain, only shock.

'Edela?' Entorp was worried.

'I'm still here,' she assured him. 'But I'm tired now. I shall close my eyes for a while. One of those puppies would help me sleep. They are quite soothing, I find, when they lie still.'

Entorp smiled, reaching down for Vella who already had her paws on the bed, ready to accept Edela's invitation. He placed her on the furs and turned to Eydis, who had been yawning uncontrollably next to him. 'Why don't you get some sleep as well, Eydis? I'll just sit at the table with my ink pot and some vellum. Perhaps something will come to mind for me also?'

***

Aron stopped outside the tall, stone tower, his shoulders up around his ears, worried that everyone would hear his knees knocking together.

He knew the soldier, Horsa, who raised a hand to him as he approached. 'Surprised to see you here, Byrn, what with all the trouble your cousin's been cooking up lately.'

Aron shrugged, pulling back the sacking he had laid over the weapons and tools to keep off the rain. 'My cousin? In the training ring, you mean?' He laughed, shaking his curly, brown hair, trying to sound casual. 'Not sure what Baccus thought he was doing, but it didn't look like he had training on his mind to me.' Aron lifted out an armload of swords and walked towards the guard tower. There were two levels. He didn't know how he could possibly get up to look inside the top one.

'Well, I guess she's not as tough as they say if she's going to moan about being in a real fight.' Horsa picked up a pair of fetters and a long axe and followed him into the tower.

Aron realised that he needed to get Horsa on side quickly. 'True. But then, she's from Brekka, and they're all a bit soft down there!'

Horsa sniggered. 'Especially the women, from what I hear. In all the right places!'

Aron wasn't listening as he adjusted his eyes to the dingy room. There was only a tiny smoke hole leading up to the next floor, and with the fire burning high, it was murky and airless. A couple of torches flickered from sconces along the walls. Narrow beds lined one side of the room. Barrels and shelves ran down the other. A long table surrounded by stools sat to the right of the fire pit.

Aron's eyes were everywhere as he carried the swords to the table and carefully laid them down.

'So, when do you think she's leaving, then, your cousin?' Horsa wondered, rubbing a dirty hand across his meaty lips as he added the fetters and axe to Aron's pile.

Aron turned to leave, tripping over his feet, landing on his elbows with a thump.

Horsa laughed. 'Ha! Runs in the family, I see.'

Aron scrambled to his feet. 'I seem to remember Baccus being the one with a knife in his throat,' he grinned, brushing himself off. 'What's going on up there?' he wondered, looking up at the rafters, listening to the thumping of boots across floorboards.

Horsa grunted, uninterested. 'Training. Same old thing, day after day.' He narrowed his beady eyes. 'Not looking to become a soldier are you, Byrn? I doubt your father would like that! Who would do all his odd jobs?' he laughed, walking Aron back to the door.

'Well, I've never really wanted to be a blacksmith,' Aron said quite truthfully. 'Maybe if I could... look around? See what you do?' He tried to sound casual, but his voice was quivering.

Horsa didn't appear to notice. 'Spose you can,' he shrugged, motioning towards the stairs. 'Maybe it's better than smithing, I don't know. You can tell me.' And turning, he wandered up the stairs.

'I'll just make sure my cart is secure!' Aron called, hurrying through the door. 'I'll meet you up there!' He waited until Horsa had disappeared up the stairs, then quickly raced back inside, dropping to the floor, peering under the bed.

'Left your cart under there, did you?' Horsa wondered as he stepped back down the stairs, frowning.

Aron hit his head on the bed frame as he shuffled out. 'No, but I must have dropped my knife when I fell over. Thought it might be under there. My father will kill me if I come back without it. He's only just given it to me!'

Horsa smiled. 'I know how that goes. I'd better get upstairs before there's a grumble on. Come up when you're ready.' And he waddled back up the stairs, leaving Aron dizzy with panic, scrambling about on the floor, checking behind and under every bed and stool.

And then, just as he was about to give up, he found it: a symbol, carved into the stone wall behind the great barrels of ale. Swallowing and glancing back at the stairs, Aron rocked and pushed the barrel further away from the wall. He pulled a scrap of vellum and a stone from his pouch, and with shaking hands, held the vellum over the symbol and rubbed the stone furiously over it. Folding everything up and stuffing it into his pouch, he hurried up the stairs, worried he was about to faint.

***

'Not dead yet, I see,' the voice sneered. 'What a shame. I was quite enjoying your company. Having you here with me, in this prison? It was so nice to have someone to talk to after all these years.'

Edela was not on the raft this time. She was not bound.

She was standing in the cave, feeling the certainty of her boots on rock. The dark air felt familiar and heavy, crushing her with its force.

But she was standing. 'You will not win!' Edela cried, but her voice was as faint as a whisper.

The laughter was a shriek of anger. 'You think *living* is winning? That you defeat me by *living*?'

Edela frowned, wanting to turn and leave now. This wasn't the dream she needed to have. There were no answers here.

She closed her eyes, trying to catch her breath; to fill her lungs with air.

She needed to go.

'We will be together soon, Edela,' the voice promised. 'This? This is just where I wait to return. And soon, I will. Can you feel that? How close I am? How close I am to your precious Jael now... the one who is supposed to stop me. But will they stop her first? I think so.'

Edela swallowed, blinking, gasping.

Disappearing into the darkness.

***

There was a lot to talk about that night.

And a lot of people all wanting to talk at once. But ten people around a table made for six would not do, so they spread out, eating from stools, from the floor, barely noticing the taste of Biddy's long slaved over stew as they fought to be heard.

Except for Entorp. 'This tastes good,' he smiled shyly at Biddy.

She beamed at him, pleased that someone was enjoying it.

She had no appetite herself, so she was busy spooning some into Edela's mouth instead.

'I'm not a baby bird, Brynna Halvor!' Edela grumbled. 'No need to feed me like one. Give me the spoon!'

Jael looked around at her grandmother. 'Well, anyone who insists on lying about in bed for so long must be spoon-fed, don't you think, Biddy?'

Biddy nodded. 'Indeed. We can't have our patients thinking they can feed themselves.'

Edela wriggled, worried that her bones were too fragile to even lift her body. But there was no time for fragile. She pushed herself up, determined to get to the edge of the bed.

'Mother!' Gisila and Branwyn exclaimed, scrambling off their stools, hurrying to her side.

'You're not ready,' Branwyn insisted.

'Not yet,' Gisila added.

Edela frowned at them both. 'Ahhh, two daughters now. Twice the fussing.' She rolled her eyes. 'Stop mumbling and help me. I'm tired of this bed, and there is too much to do for me to lie around in it any longer. I am back!'

Jael smiled, happy to hear it. She turned to her cousins. 'So, both of you saw a symbol?'

Aedan nodded. 'And they're the same.' He took Aron's scrap of vellum and placed it next to his own. 'Both in the same place on the wall, near the floor, behind the barrels of ale.'

'And how many men are in each tower?' Jael wondered.

'Well, during the day, maybe ten,' Kormac said uncertainly, looking at his sons for support.

Aron nodded. 'They take shifts at night, so five sleep below while the others are up on the top floor, then they swap.'

'So, they would only come down to swap over?' Jael ran a hand over her mouth, looking at Entorp. 'If we can get in before that happens, we might be undisturbed.'

'Except by those five men!' Biddy exclaimed, helping Edela to stand. 'Slowly now, slowly,' she muttered. 'And what will you do about them?'

Jael shrugged. 'We'll think of something, I'm sure.'

Biddy frowned, not liking the sound of that. 'But it's all pointless, surely? Won't the dreamers know that their spell has been broken? Won't they see or feel it?'

Jael looked at Edela, who was being shuffled slowly towards the table.

'Possibly, yes.' Edela sighed heavily, exhausted already. 'You will need to put the symbol from our stones next to it first, I think. The symbol that keeps the dreamers out. Once that is there, cut through their symbol. What do you think, Entorp?'

'Yes, that makes sense. It would hide the fact that the symbol was broken. The dreamers wouldn't know.'

Jael smiled, feeling around her right eye. She could almost see out of it again, which would come in handy now that they had the beginnings of a plan.

The beginnings of a way out of Tuura.

***

Evaine crawled towards Eadmund, her skin glowing brightly in the candles she had lit around the chamber.

Eadmund could barely breathe. She looked exquisite. Her eyes were so full of desire for him. And yet... 'I don't think we should use the candles, Evaine,' he said as she stopped, her lips about to touch his. 'We may need them soon.'

Evaine sat back on her heels, looking as though Eadmund had just spat in her face. 'What? What are you talking about? *Candles?*' She shook her head, and her blonde hair swept across her tiny breasts. 'You're thinking about candles? *Now?*'

Eadmund froze, caught between his irritation over the candles and his throbbing, almost uncontrollable need for

Evaine. 'We shouldn't waste them.' He glanced around the bedchamber. 'And you have...' There were at least twenty candles that he could count, and beeswax candles were considered a luxury long before they had started planning for a siege. More of a luxury than the plain soapstone lamps most Osslanders used to light their homes. Oss' best candles were imported from the Fire Lands. They needed to save them. 'Better to use lamps,' he smiled in the face of her frown.

Evaine looked at him blankly. 'Eadmund, what are you talking about?'

Eadmund blinked, wondering himself. She was so beautiful. Mesmerising. He couldn't take his eyes off her. His body was urging him on, but something was holding him back. Something he couldn't put his finger on.

Eventually, he sighed, reaching out his hand. 'Come back,' he murmured. It was impossible to resist her. He couldn't stop himself.

He had to have her.

'No more talk about candles?' Evaine purred, crawling back to him, her frown easing, her tongue teasing his lips. 'You're ready to forget everything but *me* now?' She put her hands on either side of his face.

Eadmund closed his eyes. 'I'm ready.'

***

Marcus' bowl remained untouched.

Gerod wasn't sure that he should care. He was convinced that they didn't need him anymore.

The elderman, Jael Furyck, her family, her men...

Surely they were all dispensable now?

But, despite his rise to power in Tuura, the true leaders of

The Following remained in Hest. And Yorik and Morana were keeping him on a tight leash.

'Your book is burned to ash,' Gerod smiled, watching Marcus twitch. He wanted more than a twitch, though. 'And the sword is mine, so Jael Furyck is powerless now. Although, soon it won't matter. Soon, they will raise her, and she will destroy you all.' Gerod strode back and forth in front of Marcus, who lay on his bed in the darkened corner of his chamber, facing the wall.

A lamp burned softly on a table near the fireplace, but here, in the back of the long room, Marcus could escape into the shadows and hide away.

Gerod licked his lips, sliding his knife from its scabbard. Bending down to Marcus, he brought the blade to his throat. 'But they haven't said that they need you. Not that I remember hearing.' He smelled fear now. It made him happy. He pressed the tip of his blade against Marcus' neck, feeling it break his skin.

Marcus had no desire to die, yet at the same time, he had started to wonder what point there was to being alive any longer. What hope that he could escape? That Jael Furyck could do anything without her sword?

Then he thought of Hanna.

And the Book of Aurea.

There were two copies. Not many people knew that.

'You can kill me,' Marcus breathed, blinking away the sharp pain in his neck. 'You have no reason not to. But there are dreamers everywhere in Osterland. In every kingdom. They will see this. They will see if you kill Jael Furyck. Armies will rise against you. They will find a dead elderman, discover all the dead dreamers and elders you have buried here. Find a dead queen and her men. Before you're ready?' He tried to sound calm, but his ears were ringing. 'Perhaps it will not matter? Perhaps you are close to what you wish to achieve? But do you want to be remembered as the one who ruined everything?'

Gerod was not inclined to listen to anyone's advice. Especially not someone he had wanted to kill for so long. The sanctimonious, pointless man who lay before him had been asking for his death for years, but... Gerod pulled his blade away. 'You will do well to realise that I have shown you mercy. As you say, we are not quite ready. But the time is nearing when we will be.' And standing, he slipped his knife back into its scabbard. 'And when that moment comes, I shall be here, by your side, ending you.' He stepped away, towards the light. 'You have nothing left now, Marcus Volsen. No one will mourn you when you're gone.'

***

Hanna stood in the bow of the merchant ship.

She had barely slept since they left Tuura. The crew worried her. She was the only woman on board, and she'd spent most of the journey squirming away from leery looks and groping hands. Many of the men looked embarrassed when she caught them; others were bolder and held her stare, their eyes roaming her body freely.

Thankfully, Ulf seemed focused on getting his gold, and he made a point of barking at anyone he found getting too close to her. But Hanna wondered if even he could stop a man who decided to make good on his stares.

And Ulf was not always awake.

Hanna knew that she had to sleep, though, for they would be in Hest in a few days, and she would need to think and act with clarity and speed as soon as she arrived.

They had pulled in to shore every night so far. The weather had been foul, and Ulf had wanted to protect his ship. But to make up time, he had left them out at sea, sailing through the night and Hanna was grateful. She was impatient to get to Hest, wondering how she was going to convince Berard Dragos to help her steal the Book of Darkness.

Whether that was even possible, she didn't know.

Opening her purse, Hanna felt inside for her symbol stones. Wrapping her chilled fingers around one, she thought of her father, desperately hoping that Jael Furyck had found a way to save them all.

***

It was a different kind of dream. Not a dream walk. Not a memory.

Was it a vision of the future?

Jael didn't know, but Oss seemed different. Darker. There was no Ketil, no Una beside him. No smell of charred meat. The tables were empty. The familiar, mud-caked square was free of people and animals altogether.

It was eerily quiet.

She looked around, but the only thing she could see moving was a thick cloud of low-lying mist creeping towards her.

Jael shivered, placing her hands on the table. She snapped her head to the right. Eadmund, Sevrin, and a man she didn't know were suddenly there, sitting at the next table as though they had been there the whole time.

They didn't acknowledge her at all.

'They must be coming soon,' Sevrin grumbled. 'If Ivaar has sought help, it should have arrived by now. What's the delay? Or are they holding back simply to torture us?'

'I don't know,' Eadmund sighed, as irritable with the waiting as Sevrin. 'Ayla sees a large fleet. She sees ambitious men. More than one.'

'Well, it would be a bad case of the fates if Ivaar went and fucked his own chance of overthrowing you by getting too greedy!' the large, bearded man laughed.

'Eadmund!'

Jael clenched her jaw.

'Eadmund! Supper is on the table. What are you still doing out here?' Evaine snapped as she grabbed Eadmund's arm, attempting to pull him away from his conversation.

Eadmund turned to her and Jael was pleased to see annoyance in his eyes. 'Evaine,' he said firmly, 'we're discussing things here. I will come to the hall when we're done. You start without me.' He stared at her and waited, watching as her face twisted and her lips pouted, and she finally relented, releasing his arm.

'Fine. But do not be long. The food will get cold!' And with a moody growl, she swung around, heading in the direction of the hall.

Jael watched as Eadmund turned back to his conversation without even blinking.

'If only Ayla had been able to get through to your wife,' the large man muttered. 'Or your sister.'

'Ayla said that they'd locked her out. She couldn't get through. They were doing something to stop the dreamers watching them.'

'That doesn't sound good. Perhaps they're in danger?' Sevrin wondered.

'I hope not. I just wish that I'd sent someone to Tuura. We need her help.'

Jael felt a tightness in her stomach.

Oss.

She thought of Eirik and all that she had promised him.

Oss...

CHAPTER THIRTY FIVE

'What are you doing here?' Meena was too surprised to feel shy as Berard crept up behind her. She glanced around, but he was alone.

They were alone.

Meena was on her knees by the stream where the slaves and servants would come to bathe and wash their clothes. She was relieved that it was the latter she was doing, not the former.

'I followed you,' Berard mumbled. 'I have been... worried. About how you are.'

'Oh.' Meena picked up her cloak, which she had been scrubbing in the cool water. As desperate as she was for his help, telling Berard what Jaeger and Morana were doing would only get him in trouble.

She wanted to cry, but instead, she ducked her head, hiding her eyes.

Berard bent down beside her, trailing his hand in the water. It was a fine morning, and he had no cloak himself, but he didn't need one. Summer was fast approaching, and he could feel a trickle of sweat running down his spine, or perhaps that was simply brought on by discomfort? 'You're alright, then?' he wondered, trying to see Meena's eyes underneath her wild hair. 'My brother, he is treating you well?'

Meena didn't want to look at him. She was a terrible liar.

'Meena,' Berard sighed, dropping to his knees, lifting her

chin. 'I want to help you. If, if Jaeger is mistreating you, I could help.'

Meena turned her face away, imagining Morana watching her. 'He is... not,' she said firmly. 'He is treating me well. You should go. He would not want to see you here, talking to me.' She scrambled to her feet, hurrying away, dripping her cloak behind her.

Berard blinked in surprise, convinced that she was about to say something else. And he wasn't sure he believed anything she had said.

But what could he do?

'I'm leaving!' he called after her. 'In three days...' His voice trailed off, disappearing beneath a chorus of quacking ducks as they came in to land on the stream.

Meena didn't turn around, so Berard took a slow, deep breath, curled his shoulders forward, and walked away.

***

'It sounds bad,' Beorn agreed. The soldiers were now keeping them away from *Sea Bear*, and he was starting to go stir crazy. Stuck in the stables. Wandering around the bleak fort. Unable to leave.

Jael didn't want to think about how bad it sounded because she was not on Oss, preparing to defend it with Eadmund. 'But they can hold out. That fort is old, but it's strong. The walls are thick.'

'And Ivaar doesn't have any sea-fire,' Fyn added as he stood, jiggling anxiously before them. 'The gates might hold?'

'Well, now that Edela is better, perhaps she can remember how to make it?' Jael said, an idea forming quickly. 'It would come in handy if we can get in behind the ships attacking Oss.'

'If only we still had the catapult,' Beorn grumbled, frowning at Tig who knocked his muzzle into him, trying to get Jael's attention.

'I've seen how quickly you can make a catapult, Beorn,' Jael smiled, feeding Tig another carrot.

'True.'

'It's one day's sailing from here to Andala. Maybe another day to make the sea-fire, and build the catapult, then we head for Oss.'

'But...' Fyn said, looking less hopeful. 'We don't even know if Edela can remember how to make the sea-fire.'

***

'I wrote it down!' Edela announced cheerfully. 'And tucked it into a little box under the floorboards in my cottage.' Her eyes twinkled. 'I couldn't trust myself to ever remember it again! And I had Aleksander hide a few extra jars too. Just in case.' She was sitting at the table, her cheeks pink, her eyes alert.

'But what if they can't hold out?' Eydis panicked.

Jael put her arm around Eydis' tense shoulders. 'Your brother can hold them out,' she said firmly. 'If he knows that we're coming, he'll hold them out.'

'But how will he know?' Eydis wondered.

Jael smiled at Edela. 'Because I'm going to go to Oss and tell him. Tonight.'

***

Axl had turned feverish, so Aleksander left him with Amma, and hunted through the forest, desperately trying to remember anything Edela had taught him as he'd followed her about over the years. She had always been trying to teach him and Jael about whatever plant she was handling, but they had both been far too busy rolling their eyes to listen carefully.

Aleksander could imagine Edela rolling her eyes at him now.

If she was still alive.

He needed to find herbs to stop Axl's fever and heal his wounds, but in the dull light of the forest, he was struggling to find anything that would be of use. Dropping to his knees, Aleksander dug around the forest floor and finally, happily, found a small yarrow bush struggling out from behind a tree trunk. The delicate, green leaves were just what he needed for Axl's leg wounds. Pulling the entire bush out of the ground, he stood, shaking leaves from his knees before turning back around and cocking his head.

The tree was a white willow.

White willow...

And dropping the yarrow bush, he dug out his knife and chipped off some of the bark. Chewing on a bit of that would help Axl's fever.

Satisfied with that as a beginning, Aleksander slipped the bark into his pouch, picked up the bush, and headed back to his patient.

**

Jaeger scratched his head. He needed a haircut, though he wondered if it mattered anymore.

His mind kept wandering to Axl Furyck and his wife,

imagining her in his arms. His bed. Next to him as he sat on his throne. King of Brekka.

'Do you agree?' Haaron asked shortly, glaring at his son, annoyed that he wasn't listening.

Jaeger yawned. 'Agree?'

'That we need to bring in more shipbuilders. At this rate, we'll have no more than half a fleet by winter. Eldon was saying that his brothers are skilled shipbuilders. They live in Solt. I shall have Berard send them back here when he arrives. We need to double this speed, don't you agree?'

Jaeger nodded, not caring.

'Good,' Haaron said, irritated both by the slowness of his shipbuilders and the disinterest of his son. He walked Jaeger out of the shed, back towards the castle. 'I thought you might have shown more interest,' he snapped. 'You're hardly going to be able to take back your wife and exact your revenge upon the Furycks without ships.'

Jaeger spun towards his father. 'Is that so?' he growled. 'You'd be surprised what I can do without ships, Father!' And he stalked off ahead of Haaron, desperate to get back to the book.

Haaron swallowed, surprised by his son's tone, which was odd, he thought, having been on the receiving end of Jaeger's angry outbursts for over twenty years.

Something was different, though, but what?

***

Jael vomited behind the shed.

'Are you alright?' Fyn asked, not knowing what to do.

'Fine,' she said dismissively, clearing her throat, wiping a hand over her mouth, wishing she had some water. 'Let's get going. I want to check on Kormac's progress with the weapons. We're going to need a lot more than we have, especially if Gerod has a mind to take the rest of ours away.'

Fyn didn't stop frowning as he followed her.

'Speaking of that slimy shit,' Jael grumbled, surprised to see Gerod walking towards them, flanked by two columns of temple guards.

'Still here, I see,' Gerod smiled serenely, his cheeks shining like newly polished apples. His eyes, though, remained frozen with menace. 'I am surprised. What exactly is keeping you here now?'

'You.'

He laughed. 'That's right, me! Well, not much longer now, I promise.' He glanced at Fyn, who was glowering at him. 'From what I hear, your brother is in a bad way. Your husband, if you can still call him that, is about to be in a bad way. And you...' he sighed happily, 'you are right where we want you.' Gerod nodded to the guards to carry on ahead of him. 'Now, if you'll excuse me, we need to go and remove your men's weapons. Just in case you were planning something... foolish.' And, sweeping his black cloak around himself, he knocked into her shoulder as he passed.

Jael watched him go, too surprised to be annoyed.

Fyn spluttered beside her. 'But, but... what are we going to do now?'

***

Morana studied Haaron, wondering why she was bothering with the pretence. She needed to be upstairs in Jaeger's chamber, studying the book instead.

'You have no explanation?' Haaron wondered as he walked

to the window, peering down to the harbour. 'You see nothing unusual about him?'

Morana yawned. 'Your son is angry. I see a lot of anger in him. But it is buried deep. He is angry at you. It is hard-worn, built up over many years.'

Haaron sighed. That made sense, of course, but there was more, he knew. He remembered what Karsten had warned, about Morana spending her time in Jaeger's chamber. Turning, he studied the dreamer as she wriggled on the stool, ignoring the cup of wine he had given her, shaking her bird's nest of hair. 'Do you see much of Jaeger?' he asked lightly. 'Do you dream about him?'

Morana stopped wriggling and looked up, her eyes sharp. 'Why are you asking?'

'I don't know you, Morana. Not yet, at least,' Haaron muttered, walking back to the fire, dragging a stool towards her. 'And you seem reluctant to tell me much about anything. Your mother... she was very helpful to me. She cared about my future. About my kingdom.'

Morana tightened her jaw, her irritation with that statement palpable. 'Perhaps my mother told you what you wanted to hear, instead of what you *needed* to hear,' she sneered. 'You disliked your son from birth. Jealous of how much love your wife gave to him. More than the others. He was sickly, small, not expected to live. In fact, he almost died, didn't he? But he was brought back from the shadows of death. So your wife loved him and ignored you. And you hated him with every breath you took because of it. My mother helped that feeling to fester into a stinking wound that you've carried around and picked at all through his life.' Morana sat up straighter, narrowing her gaze. 'How did that help you or your son? Now he hates you, and so does your wife!'

Haaron didn't move.

Her words jabbed at him, and he felt the truth in them. 'Then how can you sit there and say he is no threat to me? That there is nothing wrong, nothing I should worry about?' he snorted. 'Your words make no sense. They are just a jumble of sounds intended to distract me from what is right in front of my face! Something is wrong with my son, and you will not tell me the truth!'

Morana was unmoved. 'You are a king, with a son you have maligned since birth. How should you expect him to be?' she asked coldly. 'All I can do is tell you what I see. Not make up tales to help you sleep at night! I see no new threat in him at all. He has always hated you, and always will.'

Haaron stared at Morana, feeling a sharp pain in his head.

He barely knew the woman, but he was sure that she was lying.

***

'You're not as happy as I thought you'd be,' Morac noted as they watched Eadmund up on the ramparts, issuing orders, his arms flailing about with urgency. His men were bringing up wood, attaching sharpened poles to deflect any attempts to use ladders against the walls.

'Who would be happy living like *this*?' Evaine grumbled, jiggling Sigmund against her shoulder, certain that he'd just vomited down the back of her newest dress. 'About to be attacked by some ever-increasing, invisible army? All of Eadmund's attention is on the fort when it's not on that dreamer!' she spat, glancing around, but there was only Runa nearby, talking with Isaura.

Morac frowned. 'Would you rather he *wasn't* paying attention to protecting us from an attack?' he wondered incredulously. 'You do realise that Ivaar wants to kill Eadmund, and if he sees that boy,' he said, pointing to Sigmund, 'he will kill him too! Ivaar will not let Eadmund live if he gets into the fort.' He glared at Evaine, wishing that she would heed his warning.

She didn't.

'But what does *that* have to do with the dreamer? Why is he always with *her*?' Evaine frowned, watching Ayla approach Runa and Isaura, all three of them looking her way.

Morac would have shaken her if she wasn't gripping a baby to her chest. 'Evaine,' he hissed. 'That dreamer is the only way Eadmund has to see what is coming. To see what he can do to keep us safe. Save your jealousy for when Ivaar and his allies are defeated, and we are free. It will not help Eadmund, and ultimately, it will not help you to be obsessing over her!' And feeling himself losing any sense of control over his temper, he stepped away from his daughter and hurried past Runa towards the ramparts, determined to see if he could do anything to help.

Runa avoided Morac's eyes as he marched past. She had been helping to care for Bruno in an attempt to stay away from him. 'And how is your husband today?' she asked, smiling at Ayla.

'Much better,' Ayla said with a happy sigh. 'He walked around the hall this morning. His legs are becoming stronger.'

'I'm glad,' Runa said. 'It must have been so hard being without him all that time.'

'It was, yes,' Ayla admitted. 'I sometimes wondered if I would ever be with him again. I did not see a future with him in my dreams.'

'But you saw Ivaar?' Isaura asked anxiously, watching out of the corner of her eye as Mads waddled through the mud after a chicken.

'I did,' Ayla said quietly. 'I saw Ivaar as king here for a long time.'

Runa's eyes widened. 'And now?'

'Now, I see fire,' Ayla breathed. 'Always fire.'

CHAPTER THIRTY SIX

'No!' Jaeger was incensed. 'Why would I let it out of my sight?'

He rounded on Morana who stood by the window, wishing she could run her knife through him and take the book. She sighed impatiently. 'I need more time with it. Keeping it with me would help.'

Jaeger eyed her suspiciously, shaking his head. 'First, you tell me you can read the book, then you can't. Then Yorik tells me he can, but he can't. And now? Now, I'm supposed to trust you to take the book away, as though somehow taking it out of my chamber will help you understand it better?' He sucked in a breath, scanning the room. 'No, you can't! And where's Meena?' he grumbled.

Morana tried not to roll her eyes. 'Perhaps she's run away?'

Jaeger looked surprised. 'Run away to where? She has nowhere to go. She has no one but me.' He looked at the door.

Now, Morana did roll her eyes. Why was he so obsessed with her hideous niece? 'Perhaps she prefers the company of your brother?'

Jaeger froze, then turned his head ever so slowly back to Morana. 'My *brother*? Berard? You've seen them together?'

'I have,' Morana smiled. 'Often. Whenever she is not here, I imagine she goes to find him. They are very close.'

Jaeger looked incredulous. And then, quickly furious.

Morana dropped her smirking face to the floor, hiding

behind her hair.
  Gleeful.

***

Aedan, Aron, and Kormac sat around the table, practising the symbol with Entorp. All four of them would be going to the towers to carve it into the walls, before cutting through the ones that were binding the soldiers. And somehow, Jael would have to ensure that every tower was safe for them to work in.

But how? She didn't want to kill those soldiers without reason. They were bound, innocent, and they needed their help.

'What about a diversion?' she suggested, glancing at Beorn who she had brought to the house for a good meal and a long talk to plan their escape. 'If they think there's an attack, they'd all head up top, wouldn't they?'

'But how would we get outside the gates?' Beorn mumbled, his mouth full of warm apple cake. 'We can't do it inside the fort. We'd just get ourselves in more trouble.'

Jael frowned, sneaking Vella a piece of cake. She turned to Entorp. 'Can we put them into a deep sleep?'

Edela, back in bed again, smiled. 'Oh yes, we can do that!'

***

Jaeger stormed through the castle, checking in every chamber, but he couldn't find Meena. He did, however, find Berard who was with Karsten and Haegen in the training ring.

'Where is she?' Jaeger snarled, bursting through his

brothers, ignoring their grumbles, striding towards Berard who was sitting on the stone bench, red-faced, catching his breath.

Berard yelped as Jaeger dragged him to his feet, pushing him against the castle wall. 'Wh-wh-what?' he stuttered, dropping his sword to the dirt in fright. Jaeger's eyes were not registering anything other than the violent desire to kill him. 'Wh-wh-who?'

Haegen and Karsten were quickly at Jaeger's side.

'Whoa, little brother,' Haegen said with a tight smile. 'What's going on?' He stepped in front of Berard, pushing his chest towards Jaeger who ignored him as he continued to lunge at his cowering brother.

'This is nothing to do with you, Haegen!' Jaeger spat, slamming his hands against his chest. 'Get out of my way!'

Karsten clenched his fists, ready to intervene.

'I don't know where Meena is!' Berard cried. 'I haven't seen her since this morning!' He bit his lip, wanting to stuff the words back into his mouth.

'*This morning*?' Jaeger growled, poking his head around Haegen as he fought to push him out of the way. They were grappling now, arms everywhere. 'And where were you this morning?'

'Aarrghh!' Berard cried as Jaeger escaped Haegen's hold, grabbing his neck, digging his nails deep into his skin.

Karsten jumped in to pull Berard away. 'Why not pick up a sword, Brother?' he challenged, pushing Berard behind him.

'Not helping!' Haegen grunted as he finally shunted Jaeger away. 'I think it's best if you leave, don't you?' He held out his arms, trying to shepherd Jaeger out of the ring, but Jaeger dropped his shoulder and punched Haegen in the chest. Haegen staggered backwards, trying to suck in a breath.

'What is going on?' Bayla called from the edge of the training ring, where she stood with Nicolene and Irenna. 'What are you all *doing*?'

Karsten threw himself onto Jaeger's back before he could

catch Berard.

'What were you doing with Meena?' Jaeger screamed, trying to shake off his brother. 'Where is she?'

Irenna hurried towards Haegen, who ignored her, charging after Jaeger. 'Haegen!' she implored. 'No!'

Jaeger threw Karsten to the ground, then turned and grabbed Berard by the throat again. Haegen hooked Jaeger around the neck with his forearm and dragged him backwards. Jaeger ducked out of his hold, turning to punch him again. Karsten took out Jaeger's legs, smiling as his brother tumbled to the ground, jumping on top of him, trying to keep him down. Catching sight of Nicolene, Karsten punched Jaeger in the mouth, pulling his fist back, ready for more.

But Berard grabbed it. 'No!' he shouted. 'No!'

Nicolene looked unconcerned as she watched the scrambling Dragos brothers rolling around in the red dirt. Three of them fighting for control.

One desperately trying to scramble away.

Bayla strode towards them. 'You will stop this now!' she bellowed in her loudest voice. '*Now!*'

Her sons froze, glancing up at their mother as she bent down, pulling at Karsten's tunic, forcing away Jaeger's hand. Furious. Upset. Determined to stop them. 'You will get up!' she ordered. 'You are princes here! Princes, embarrassing yourselves! Embarrassing your wives! Embarrassing *me!*' And seeing that they had all stopped, at last, she inhaled sharply, spinning around, sweeping her dress behind her as she stalked away.

Her four sons lay sprawled in a red-faced, bloody heap, watching her go.

***

Deciding that it was best to have fewer distractions for Jael's dream walk, Kormac took everyone to visit Aedan after supper, leaving Jael, Edela, Biddy, and Entorp behind.

'What do we do about The Following?' Biddy wondered, poking at the fire, trying to resurrect the dying flames. 'If we manage to destroy the symbols in the towers without getting caught, without the dreamers seeing, how do we stop The Following?'

'We have to kill them,' Jael said as she leaned towards the fire, gripping a cup of cold fennel tea. She felt odd. As eager as she was to dream walk to Eadmund, she was starting to wonder what she would find when she did.

Entorp nodded in agreement. 'Yes, we must kill them. They are too blind to see what is right anymore. Their hearts are black, filled with evil. And they know dark magic. They will not be swayed from their path now. If we do not kill them, they will kill all of us. Everyone that lives. That is what they desire above all things.'

'Well, then,' Jael said. 'We have to get into the temple. But those doors...' She looked at her grandmother, who appeared ready to fall asleep.

'Those doors have stood for centuries,' Edela murmured. 'And they are not going to be opened willingly. We know that.'

'Unless we can get someone on the inside to open them for us?' Biddy suggested.

'But who?' Entorp wondered, stretching out his legs until his cold toes almost touched the flames. 'There is no one in there who could help. They're all our enemies now.'

'Maybe not,' Edela said quietly, closing her eyes which felt far too heavy to keep open any longer. 'Alaric may know of someone who could help us?'

It was a thought. Not an especially promising one, but still...

'I'll go and get him tomorrow,' Jael said. 'I'm sure he'd like to come and see you again.'

'Mmmm,' Edela yawned. 'I think I may just have a little

sleep, but do wake me up when you're ready to begin. I don't want to miss the fun of watching you dream walk!'

Jael cringed. 'Yes, well no doubt you can point out what I'm doing wrong.'

'No doubt I can...' Edela smiled, her voice trailing off to a whisper as her head dropped to one side.

***

Jaeger rose out of his seat, pushing away Egil who had been trying to press a cold cloth to his mouth. 'Where have you been?' he snarled, his bleeding lips curling with anger.

Meena blinked. She had been gone for most of the day, and she knew that Jaeger would be wild. But she had not expected this level of fury. 'I, I, I...' She dropped her sack to the floor and with it her head, her eyes chasing the lines around the flagstones, frantically trying to focus on something that wasn't the fear of what was to come.

'Go!' Jaeger growled at Egil. 'Leave us!'

Egil scuttled towards the door, glaring at Meena as he passed, furious to have been sent away like a slave.

'Where have you *been*?' Jaeger demanded again, striding towards the shaking mass of hair. 'All day?'

'I was washing,' Meena tried, her voice barely a whisper.

Jaeger shook his head, unsure if he had heard her correctly. '*Washing*? Washing what?'

'My cloak,' Meena mumbled. 'My dress. I only have one of each. I, I had to wait for them to dry.'

Jaeger frowned, looking down at her sack. 'And what's in there?'

'Herbs,' she said. 'I'm having trouble sleeping. I remembered something my grandmother used to make to help her sleep. I, I went to the winding gardens after my clothes dried. I am sorry.'

Jaeger narrowed his gaze, finding it hard to see anything sinister in what she was saying, but still... 'And what of Berard? Why were you with him?'

Meena swallowed, feeling her legs start to tremble. 'He, I, he, he came to the stream when I was washing my cloak. I...' She felt so hot. Uncomfortable. Desperate to tap her head. 'I don't know why.' She looked up, letting him see her eyes. Wondering if that would help or only make it worse.

Jaeger was quiet, feeling his racing heart calm as he peered at her fearful face. Berard was pursuing her. Trying to take her back from him. But Meena was his. It wasn't her fault that Berard seemed intent on starting a war.

It wasn't her fault.

Jaeger put his hand under her chin, tilting it towards him. 'Berard will be gone in a few days, so until then you will stay in here. I will have Egil bring everything you need.' He leaned forward, pulling her into him. 'There's no need to go anywhere now, Meena. You'll be safe in here with me.' Jaeger kissed her, feeling an urgency to claim her as his.

His.

Not Berard's. Just like the book wasn't Morana's.

He needed to feel powerful.

They needed him. Meena needed him.

He was powerful.

Powerful.

***

After two solid days of arm-breaking stretcher pulling through the forest, they finally made it to the road; to the place where Aleksander hoped that Gant would find them.

Axl was shivering less now. His wounds looked cleaner too, and Amma, who was checking on him regularly, could only hope they remained that way.

Night was falling, and Aleksander was ready to drop to the ground, but he managed to make a fire, and with Amma's help, he hastily prepared a rudimentary shelter of branches; quickly covering it with their cloaks as the rain came down again.

'What if they've missed us? How long should we wait here? What if Gant's not even coming? What if Osbert still lives?' Axl grumbled, not ready for sleep even though he'd been yawning since the sun had set. He shifted his hips, trying to get more comfortable in his dirt and leaf bed, disturbed by the increasing wail of the wind as it wound its way through the tall trees they were sheltering behind. Their fire was flickering in protest, and the rain had brought a bitter chill with it, so they were watching the flames closely.

Aleksander knew that he needed to keep watch, but he was so tired and sore. His hands were blistered, shredded from gripping the stretcher; from dragging it over roots and rocks and pulling it through trees. The strain of carrying Axl had left his shoulders numb, and the worry over whether the wolves or ravens would return remained ever-present. 'Axl,' he murmured. 'It's too late for that many questions. Get some sleep. We can talk...' he yawned. 'We can talk in the morning. Get some sleep.' Aleksander glanced over at Amma who had been asleep for some time. She had barely spoken since he'd dragged her out of the river, but her eyes revealed her unspoken terror that they would be caught.

That somehow, Jaeger Dragos would capture her and take her back to Hest again.

Aleksander wondered the same thing himself.

With the Book of Darkness in Jaeger's hands, he didn't need ships or an army to reach them it seemed.

Not anymore.

***

Evaine was unsatisfied.

Eadmund had rolled over, apparently uninterested in anything else, but she was not done. Not done at all, and yet he was almost snoring, she could tell as he mumbled and sighed and barely answered her.

Evaine frowned, sniffing loudly, folding her arms across her breasts.

Cold.

Lonely.

It was not how she imagined it would be. Eadmund's wife had gone, he was bound to her, and they had a son together. But why wasn't it enough? Why didn't she feel secure? Safe? Blissfully happy, as she had always imagined she would.

Pursing her lips, Evaine pulled the furs up to her shoulders, grumbling loudly. She looked over at Eadmund, then quickly away.

But he didn't move.

And as she listened, his snores grew even louder.

Banging her fists uselessly by her sides, she stared up at the rafters and sighed.

***

Jael swallowed. She was actually nervous. If she had been holding a sword in her hand, facing an axe-wielding Hestian, she would have felt prepared. Confident.

But pretending to be a dreamer?

Perhaps last time had happened by chance? Merely luck?

'Go on,' Edela urged, watching from her bed. 'You're ready. You have always been ready for this, Jael. Just close your eyes and grip that ring and think of Eadmund. Don't let go. Throw the herbs onto the flames. Think of Eadmund. We will be here when you return.'

Jael was on her knees before the fire, holding Eadmund's wedding band in her hand; the one he had so readily given to Eydis in Saala. She could hear the rain thundering onto the roof. She watched it dripping onto the flames; heard the wind, shaking the door.

And she thought of Eadmund, who she had chosen, then lost.

And she missed him so much that she ached.

'Do you remember the words?' Entorp murmured, pounding on his drum.

Jael nodded and picked up the bundle of herbs, throwing them onto the spitting flames. She closed her eyes, listening to the rolling rhythm of the drum as it kept time with her heartbeat. Rolling like thunder, like waves, like the waterfall in Oss she loved so much.

And she started chanting.

***

'Bayla?'

'You're alone?'

Haaron had fallen asleep in his chair and he was momentarily confused as he opened the door wider, ushering her inside. 'Yes, come in.'

Bayla looked uncomfortable as she stalked past him, wishing to be anywhere else. 'It is about our sons,' she said as Haaron closed the door and followed her to the fireplace.

'About our kingdom.' She glared at him. 'It is falling apart.' Her face remained hard, but her voice wavered.

'What do you mean?'

Bayla sat down in the chair Haaron had only just left. It felt warm. 'I found all four of them trying to kill each other today.'

'Why?' Haaron sat opposite her, picking up a log and throwing it onto the flames.

'I don't know. Everything feels different. Ever since the Furycks were here. Ever since they humiliated us and destroyed our fleet. Ever since...' She looked towards the fireplace, watching as the wood caught.

'Ever since what?'

'Ever since Varna died.'

'You hated Varna,' Haaron said wryly.

'Yes, but,' Bayla swallowed, not wanting to form her fears into words. 'Perhaps she helped... keep everything safe. Keep us safe.'

Haaron had thought the same thing. Without Varna, it felt as though the scales had tipped; as though she had taken his luck with her when she died. There was no proof, nothing to latch onto that was real, but he had not felt right without her.

Morana was not Varna, and he did not trust her.

'Perhaps,' he sighed. 'But it may all have happened anyway. With four sons, it was inevitable that they would turn on each other eventually. Another reason I thought to send them away. If only...'

'If only what?' Bayla edged towards him.

'Well, I think, perhaps we are keeping the most ambitious of them all, which may, of course, be your intention. I hardly think you'll mourn my passing. And you've always seen him as king here, I know.' Haaron rolled his hands over the arms of his chair, clenching his jaw, not wanting her confirmation of his long-held assumption. 'But, if Jaeger does claim power here, I don't imagine that he'll be content to let his brothers live. He may have to go through them to fulfill his ambition. Two of them, at least.'

Bayla looked indignant on many counts, but more than that, she felt confused. She could not deny that Jaeger had changed. She had always supported him and his claim to the throne, but after what she had witnessed in the training ring, she suddenly feared what his rise would mean for them all.

***

So much fire.

Eadmund couldn't catch his breath. The smoke was thick; the screaming and panic so loud that he couldn't think.

He couldn't think!

There was nowhere to go. They were in a stone prison.

A prison that was on fire.

He turned to Bram. 'Get Evaine!' he cried. 'Get my son! Please!' He pointed to Sevrin. 'More buckets! More water! Hurry!' But Eadmund could feel the fingers closing around his heart. They were cold and hard.

They were squeezing.

He needed to move, but he didn't know what he could do.

He couldn't think!

The banging was getting louder. Like a drum. Thunderous hammering. Urgent, demanding.

'Eadmund!'

They kept calling for him. Everyone wanted his attention. He was their king. He needed to save them.

'Eadmund!'

Eadmund turned slowly, confused, searching through the thick plumes of smoke. He knew that voice. 'Jael?'

Jael's body tensed as he turned, then relaxed.

Eadmund.

'You've come!' He looked relieved, rushing towards her, his arms outstretched. 'There's no time! We have to go! Quick. I need to get my son, make sure he's safe! Where's Axl? Where are your men?' He looked around, searching through the flames, the smoke.

'Eadmund.' Jael reached for his hands, trying to calm his panic. 'Eadmund, it's a dream. I came to speak to you in your dream.'

'But...' Eadmund spun around, his heart skipping, the smoke choking his throat.

And then nothing.

It was all gone, and they were standing in the cool darkness, and there was snow on the ground, and they were beside Eirik's pool.

Jael blinked, wistful for the time they had spent there together, but she could already feel the strain of holding the trance. She did not have time to lose focus. 'Eadmund, I'll be here as soon as I can. I'll bring the Brekkan fleet. Look at me, Eadmund. I know you're in trouble. I know about Ivaar, but you have to hold him out. And wait. I will come.'

Those eyes.

The moonlight reflected off the dark water, and he could see those eyes so clearly. He stepped forward. 'Is Edela alive?'

Jael opened her mouth, conscious of the loud humming in her ears. Her hold on the dream was fading. There was little time left, she knew. 'Take this.' She reached out, placing a stone in his hand. 'Remember this symbol. Promise me. Promise me. Don't tell Evaine. Go to Ayla when you wake up. Tell her that this symbol will keep out the dreamers. It will keep out Morana. Have her make one for you. For her. For Thorgils too. Keep the stones with you.'

Eadmund closed his hand into a fist. 'I will.'

'I have to go,' Jael said quickly. She wanted to touch him, but he wasn't hers. She could feel it still. 'Don't forget the symbol. And don't forget that I will come. Soon.'

'Jael.' He touched her hair. No braids for a change. Long and flowing, dark waves of hair, shining in the moonlight, hanging over her well-worn, blue tunic. 'Stay safe.'

She nodded, not wanting to go. 'You too. And whatever you do, don't tell Evaine about this dream. Trust me. Don't tell Evaine, please.' And closing her eyes, Jael felt herself falling backwards. 'Please,' she murmured, her words lost amongst the hum as Eadmund faded into the night and Oss slipped from her grasp.

PART SIX

The Plan

CHAPTER THIRTY SEVEN

'Eadmund?' Evaine reached out, sleepy-eyed and confused. 'What are you doing?'

Eadmund had lurched out of bed, panting as though he'd been running. He could feel sweat trickling down his temples. Pressing his feet onto the floorboards, he looked down at his hand, still curled into a fist, remembering the dream.

He glanced around for his tunic and trousers, trying to keep his eyes open. He had to go. He needed to find Ayla.

'Eadmund?' Evaine crawled towards him, shivering. 'Where are you going? It's still dark. Come back to bed. I'm cold.'

Eadmund wasn't listening. He opened his fingers, but there was no stone. 'I have to go,' he mumbled, sitting down to pull on his trousers. 'There's a lot to do.'

'In the dark?' Evaine grumbled. 'Eadmund...' She crept up behind him, pressing her body against his, seeking his warmth. 'It's not even dawn. Surely you don't have to go just yet?'

Eadmund was caught, listening to Jael's voice urging him to hurry to Ayla before he forgot the symbol. And then, just as quickly, not caught at all as he felt Evaine's breasts on his back, and her lips on his neck.

He turned to her and smiled.

***

It was too early to do much, but Jael couldn't sleep. The smoke had wound itself around her thoughts all night, and her dreams had been multi-coloured and strange, filled with confusing visions.

Seeing Eadmund had left her sad, and she was eager to ride away from the fort, despite the foul weather. But she didn't dare go near Tig now. And she knew that she would not have been let through the gates if she'd tried. So, she walked down the main street instead, hoping that Eadmund had remembered the dream.

Hoping he'd remembered the symbol.

But most of all, she hoped that she was right. If she couldn't get everyone out of Tuura alive, then Oss was in danger of being overthrown. And that would mean death for Eadmund and Thorgils, she knew.

Jael stopped, frowning. The sun was struggling to rise, but the dull, grey light was enough for her to recognise where she was, and squinting into the distance she spied Alaric's door.

Smiling to herself, she changed course and headed down the alley.

***

'Where were you going before?' Evaine yawned contentedly, twisting her fingers in Eadmund's chest hair. She liked sleeping. A lot. And with Tanja looking after Sigmund now, she was able to catch up on all the sleep she'd lost when he was born.

'I wanted to get up on the ramparts. Take a look around.'

'In the dark?' Evaine murmured. 'But what would you have seen?'

Eadmund stroked her hair. She had just washed it, he could tell. It smelled faintly of peppermint. 'You'd be surprised what you can see with a bit of starlight,' he whispered, watching as her eyes closed, feeling her chest moving steadily against his.

Evaine didn't reply and Eadmund slowly eased away from her, leaning her gently against the pillow. She mumbled but didn't attempt to open her eyes again, so he slipped out of bed, pulling on his trousers.

He needed to see Ayla.

***

It had taken Jael a while to rouse Alaric, and when he creaked open his door, he looked half dead.

'Has something happened?' he panicked, glancing behind Jael.

'No,' she said, pushing past him. 'I just need to talk to you.'

Alaric locked the door behind her and yawned, wanting to splash his face with some water. He was not used to being awake so early, and he could barely see straight.

Jael studied his cottage. It wasn't the best place to be talking, but it was early. Hopefully, they would have time before anyone with a mind to eavesdrop was out on the street, eavesdropping. 'You know the temple,' she whispered. 'And I need to know how to break into it.'

Alaric's sleepy eyes were quickly as wide as plates. 'Break into it?' he breathed, his mouth opening and closing like a panicked fish. 'Break into it? Oh.' He stumbled down onto his bed. 'But there are not enough of you. To fight against all of them?' He shook his head, shuddering.

'Alaric,' Jael said calmly, watching her breath smoke out before her as she took the stool opposite him. 'If you want Tuura to be free, if we are going to escape, then we have no choice. The Followers are in the temple. We have to get in there and stop them, or they will kill all of us. And soon.'

Alaric thought of Edela. He couldn't let anything happen to her. 'There is a door you could try,' he sighed. 'The door to the kitchen. From there you can get into the temple. But they will surely see you coming!'

'Perhaps,' Jael mused. 'I just needed to know what was possible before I came up with a plan. A door to the kitchen will help,' she said. 'Thank you.' And standing up, she headed for the door. Turning around, Jael looked at the cold fire pit and the meagre supplies on Alaric's solitary shelf. 'Why not grab your cloak and come with me? I'm sure you could do with a hot breakfast?'

Alaric brightened at the thought of it. 'Well, perhaps I shall just check on Edela,' he said eagerly. 'See how she's faring?'

Jael smiled. 'Come on, then, before the rain comes down again.'

Alaric scrambled to find his cloak, listening to the happy rumble in his empty belly.

***

Ayla and Eadmund hurried away from the hall, turning down the alley towards his old cottage. Eadmund had not wanted to talk inside, where he knew that a sleeping Evaine was only just through the wall. He wondered how he could be so disloyal. But he knew that he could trust Jael.

Jael was trying to protect Oss.

They had arrived at his cottage without Eadmund uttering

a word. Ayla was puzzled, but she did not question what was happening. Eadmund didn't want to light a fire, but they needed to see, so he pulled out his tinderbox and sparked the lamp alight.

Ayla sat on the bed, waiting patiently, and finally, he brought the flaming lamp towards her, placing it in her hands. He took the leather satchel from his shoulder and laid it on the floorboards, pulling out a folded piece of vellum, a quill, and a jar of ink. Bending down, Eadmund uncorked the jar, dipped his quill into the ink and began to draw. He could see the symbol in his mind. It reminded him of a symbol he had once seen on a shield.

It was easy to remember, and it did not take him long to finish.

'I've had a dream,' Eadmund said softly, handing the vellum to her, keeping hold of one end. 'Jael came to me last night, with this. She said that the dreamers can't see past it. That we need one each. On a stone. To carry with us. Thorgils too.'

Ayla frowned. She didn't recognise the symbol, but it looked Tuuran. 'I can do that,' she said slowly. 'That must be how they are locking me out. But it makes you wonder why, don't you think? Why do we need to be afraid of dreamers?'

Eadmund did not want to stay long. 'I don't know. She did mention Morana.'

Ayla shook her head. 'Who's that?'

'An evil woman. A dreamer. A witch. She hated my father. I think she killed my mother. She is...' He ducked his head, feeling a tightness in his chest. 'She is Evaine's real mother.'

'Oh.'

Eadmund didn't look up. He felt uncomfortable, disloyal for being in the cottage with Ayla. 'But Evaine never knew her,' he insisted. 'Not while she was growing up. She didn't know Morana was her mother.'

His desperation to defend Evaine worried Ayla. Isaura had told her that Evaine had bound Eadmund to her soul. It was a strange thing that she had never heard of before. But it was apparent that he was hopelessly tethered to the girl.

Ayla had seen him over the winter, and his love for Jael Furyck had been obvious. She had felt it. But this? With Evaine? She smiled kindly. 'I'll make the symbol stones for us. We cannot speak about it again, though. Not until we have them,' she warned. 'Jael is telling you this for a reason. Something is wrong in Tuura.'

Eadmund nodded.

'And, I think, if I may say,' Ayla said gently. 'It's best if you keep the stone a secret from Evaine. Morana will have a strong connection to her, whether Evaine knows it or not. For Evaine's own good, and your son's, it's best if this remains between us.'

'Agreed.' Eadmund stood, glancing at the light filtering from under the door. The sun was definitely up now. 'We should go.'

Ayla blew out the lamp and put it to one side, then folded up the vellum and slipped it into her purse. 'Is that the only reason Jael came to you? The only thing she said?' she wondered, suddenly desperate.

'No.' Eadmund helped Ayla to her feet. 'No, she told me that she was coming,' he smiled, feeling a ray of hope. 'Jael is coming.'

***

Morana creaked out of bed with speed, grimacing and grinning at the same time. She padded across the chamber to Meena's old bed where she had laid out her mother's books the night before.

She'd had a dream.

An idea about what that troublesome phrase meant.

Impatiently sweeping her hair away from her eyes, she

hunched over, fingering through the crackling pages of the smallest of Varna's books, squinting in the faint morning light that seeped through the window above her.

And then, finally, there it was.

The answer she had been waiting for.

Screeching in pleasure, Morana skipped around the fire, head back, mouth open; the relief a welcome balm for her tattered confidence.

She couldn't wait to tell Yorik.

***

No one was speaking at breakfast.

Jaeger's lips were fat, cut where Karsten had punched him. Haegen's jaw was bruised and swollen where Jaeger had hit him. Berard sat hunched over his porridge, upset about it all; wanting to make things right, but at the same time, doubting that it was even possible anymore.

'And how is your packing going?' Bayla asked Nicolene, eager to break the uncomfortable silence.

Nicolene didn't look up. She had spent most of the night arguing with Karsten, insisting that he had no reason to be jealous. It was an argument she had fought hard to win, but she wondered why she had bothered. She much preferred the company of the youngest Dragos to his bitter older brother. 'Fine. It's going fine,' she snapped, inviting no further questions.

Bayla felt mournful, thinking of her grandchildren, who, she was surprised to discover, she would miss. Although, having her sons so far away meant that she could spend much of her time travelling, and little time at all with Haaron. She eyed him with a scowl as he sat there noisily slurping his porridge, looking like a tiny, old man.

Not a king. Not the man she had married.

Not the man who could put their family back together.

Or their kingdom.

'Well, that is good to hear. It will be nice for us to enjoy the feast tomorrow night and not have to worry about getting up too early.'

Berard squirmed, wishing that his mother wasn't determined to throw a lavish farewell feast for them. He doubted that anyone would have anything to say to each other by then. He glanced at Jaeger, worried about what he might have done to Meena.

Had he hurt her?

Killed her?

'Berard,' his father said, interrupting his morbid thoughts. 'I want you to come with me after breakfast. We must choose some weapons for you to take. You're going to have to manage yourself on the road. You'll be responsible for the men you're taking. You'll need to know how to lead them. How to protect them.'

Berard gulped, not convinced that there was any point to him having weapons at all. He nodded mutely, smiling at the slave who reached for his bowl, his mind running quickly back to Meena.

He needed to know that she was alright.

***

Gerod was growing impatient.

He paced the grand chamber, striding across its wide flagstones, past the stone columns that reached high up to the cavernous ceiling, walking around the three long fires blazing down the centre of the temple, towards the towering doors.

And back again.

The shadow moon was almost upon them now, and yet the dreamers had reported nothing from Hest. Nothing to tell him what to do with Jael Furyck and her men. Nothing to confirm that the ritual was going ahead as Morana had suggested.

Nothing about their plans for Marcus.

Gerod stopped before the Fire of Light, losing himself in its mesmerising flames; imagining that day, centuries before, when Raemus' dragon, Thrula, had brought it to life with one powerful breath.

And it had burned ever since.

That is what The Following believed, just as they believed that Raemus had never truly died. That he waited in the Dolma for them to bring him back.

But when?

And in the meantime, he had the woman who could stop it all, here, within reach. Although, she was without her sword now. And the book. Gerod smiled, imagining how much that would be irritating the smug bitch. But even without the sword and the book, he sensed that she was going to cause trouble. Clenching his jaw, he turned away from the flames.

He would go to the Chamber of Dreams. Seek out the dreamers. They were working hard, day and night, he knew, but their visions had so far been mostly irrelevant. They had nothing to tell him about Jael Furyck.

It was as though she was invisible.

CHAPTER THIRTY EIGHT

'If we slip in through the kitchen door while they're asleep...' Jael mused.

'It will be locked!' Alaric exclaimed, shaking at the mere thought. He couldn't imagine attempting such a reckless thing. With the elders so close? The dreamers? All controlled by The Following? Reaching for another flatbread, he smothered it with honey, his eyes darting about, studying the eager faces sitting around the table. 'It is locked every night before the kitchen staff take to their beds.'

'Locked how?' Kormac asked, wondering what tools he could use to break through the door.

'With a bolt and a key,' Alaric muttered, thinking hard. 'Two bolts, if I remember rightly. One top, one bottom.'

'For a *kitchen*?' Biddy looked surprised, filling Alaric's cup with fresh milk. 'The elders are not a trusting bunch, are they?'

Edela was at the table, sitting between Jael and Alaric. 'And what about you, dear Alaric?' she smiled. 'Is there anyone you know in the kitchen, perhaps? Someone who would be inclined to leave the door unlocked?'

Alaric shook his head quickly. 'No, no, no. I should not think so. No.'

Edela fluttered her eyelashes as she sipped her milk. 'Oh, that's a shame. Are you sure now? No one at all?'

Alaric suddenly took great interest in his plate, avoiding her eyes. 'Well, there might be someone I know, someone I could ask. But... even if I could trust her once, how would I know that she was not bound to The Following now?'

'It's a fair point,' Branwyn called from her chair by the fire. She was cradling her red-cheeked granddaughter, who was busy sucking on a cloth. 'We must assume that everyone in the temple is bound now.'

'What about Berta?' Kormac wondered. 'Her sister works in the temple kitchen, doesn't she?'

'Does she?' Jael looked hopeful. 'Well, perhaps you could go and visit her, Branwyn? See how she is? Maybe she would let you talk to her sister?'

Branwyn sat up immediately. 'Well, yes, I can do that. Here, Kayla, take the baby. I need to get myself ready. Gisila, why don't you come with me?'

Gisila, who was sitting on her bed, braiding Eydis' hair, looked up. 'Yes, alright, I'll just finish here.'

'It's too dangerous,' Alaric fretted.

'We have to get into the temple,' Jael insisted. 'We must rescue Marcus. Kill Gerod. Free Tuura. Take back my sword. We can't do any of that if we can't even get inside!'

***

Aleksander had left Amma and Axl early that morning, determined to see if he could find Gant; worried that perhaps Axl was right and they had simply missed him.

Or worse.

He had started walking down the road, trying to guess how many stones were rolling around in his boots. Wishing he had a horse.

And then the rain had come down.

Great sheets of icy water soaked him through until his boots squeaked and his trousers rubbed together, and the back and front of his tunic stuck to his skin like a wet dog's fur.

He thought of Andala and Jael and a fire.

And then he heard a low, groaning sound. Thunder? Aleksander squinted, wiping the rain from his eyes. The road was muddy and narrow, surrounded on both sides by tall fir trees. Not the best place to be standing in a storm. He glanced up at the dark sky, considering his options: he could disappear into the trees, or run further ahead to find a clearing to wait out the storm.

Then he frowned.

That wasn't thunder.

And running now, slipping in the mud, he felt his spirits lift as he raced down the road towards the Brekkan army. 'Gant! Gant!' Aleksander's voice was lost amongst the heavy rain, and he was out of breath and ready to drop to the ground, but he could see Gant now at the head of a long line of soldiers.

Warriors.

Brekkans.

They had come for their new king.

Aleksander threw his head back into the rain and howled with happiness.

***

'You have done well!' Yorik's calm demeanour was replaced with childlike glee as he took Morana in his arms, overcome with relief. 'I always knew you would find the answer!'

Morana stepped back, eyeing him moodily. 'Is that so?' She walked around the only room of his very modest cottage. It was no better than the stone chamber her mother had spent her life in; sparsely furnished with a bed, a table, a chair, a small fire pit, and a chest.

It was a solitary, meagre life for the most powerful man in Hest.

Was he *really* the most powerful man in Hest?

'What do you mean?' Yorik was quickly calm again.

'I had a dream. You were planning to have the Followers take over, find the answer without me,' she snarled, rounding on him, her tongue sharpening. 'You did not appear to believe that I would find the answer at all.'

'Morana,' Yorik smiled patiently. 'Translating the ritual was all that mattered. Not *who* translated it.' He reached for her hands, trying to soothe her ragged mood. 'I am pleased that *you* managed it, of course, but it hardly matters in the end. We are all working towards the same outcome.' He didn't blink as his eyes claimed hers. They were forceful and demanding of her. Wanting her submission. Needing to see her bend to his will.

There could only ever be one true leader of The Following.

And it would never be Morana Gallas.

***

Gant quickly found Aleksander a horse, and together they rode back to Axl and Amma.

The rain had eased to a steady drizzle, and Aleksander was able to make himself heard. But what he was saying made no sense to Gant.

'Ravens? Wolves? You think they were sent to *kill* you?' He shook his damp hair, his weary, grey eyes filled with disbelief.

'Jaeger Dragos has the Book of Darkness,' Aleksander said with a sigh. 'And that's a problem for all of us. Who knows what it can do. All I can tell you is that we're lucky to be alive.'

'But why Tuura?' Gant wondered, eager to get out of the saddle, despite the fact that it was barely midday.

'Jael's in danger,' Aleksander said, suddenly overcome with fear. He'd spent all of his energy on trying to save Axl and Amma, and now that he finally had, the worry about Jael came rushing towards him like a wave.

'How do you know?'

Aleksander dropped his head. 'I had a dream.'

Gant laughed. 'Why is everyone turning into dreamers all of a sudden?'

'No, not that sort of dream. A dreamer came to me, told me to leave, to get to Tuura. Said we're all in danger.'

'What dreamer?' Gant asked suspiciously.

'The Widow,' Aleksander mumbled, glancing around, but Oleg had slipped back to check on the men, and they were alone.

Gant's eyes widened. 'The Widow?' He rolled his tongue over his teeth. 'The Widow? The same woman who kills people for gold? Who hides away in case someone finds her because she's responsible for so much evil? *That* Widow? I thought she was just a myth? A story to scare children?'

Aleksander didn't know where to begin. 'Trust me,' he said in the end. 'I know it makes no sense. You just have to trust me. She warned me about the ravens. Warned me about the wolves coming too. She guided me to the river so that we could escape.'

Gant felt too tired to argue, so he frowned instead.

'What about Osbert?' Aleksander wondered. 'How did that go?'

'Go?' Gant sighed. 'That was easy enough. The men were relieved, ready to follow Axl. Happy to be rid of the little worm.'

'And you?'

'Me?'

'Killing him like that?'

Gant inhaled sharply. 'I could have challenged him to a fight. He could have died with a sword in his hand. But he was no brave warrior or noble leader. He was a shit-stain on the arse-crack of the Furycks. He wasn't worth Vidar's time.' He looked away, into the trees. 'How far away are we now, do you think?' he wondered, quickly leaving that subject behind.

Aleksander was surprised to see Gant so affected by killing Osbert. He wasn't sure how he would have felt himself. Murdering a king would have attracted the attention of the gods, especially a Furyck king. And he knew that Gant was superstitious enough to be unsettled by that.

But hopefully, the gods would be grateful for what he did, rather than choosing to punish him for what was truly a merciful act for all of Osterland. 'Up here,' Aleksander said, pointing to the left, recognising the strange, leaning tree that marked their shelter. 'Best dismount here.'

And clambering down from their wet horses, and feeling their wet clothes sticking to them, they disappeared into the trees.

***

Berard knocked on the door, his heart racing.

He had seen Jaeger with his father, inspecting the building of the new piers. He knew that he didn't have long.

'My lord?' Egil answered the door to Berard's disappointed face. 'I have not seen you here for some time. Your brother is not here, however. Perhaps you can come back later?' His rotund frame filled the entire doorway, and he made no move to step aside.

'Oh,' Berard swallowed. 'Well, in fact, Egil, I wondered if I had left something here. Perhaps I could come in and quickly see?'

Egil frowned, certain that he had not seen anything out of place, but he could hardly refuse a son of the king, no matter how keenly his master guarded his chamber. 'Of course,' he muttered reluctantly, ushering Berard inside. 'Although, I have cleaned this place from top to bottom many times since you were last here and I've not found anything belonging to you. What is it that you're missing?'

Berard had thought of his excuse ahead of time but promptly forgot it as he stepped into the chamber and came face to face with Meena.

Her eyes widened in surprise at his unexpected arrival.

'My lord?' Egil prompted. 'What have you lost?'

'Oh, oh...' Berard clutched at the strands of memory that were evading him. 'My, ahhh, my tweezers.'

'Your *tweezers*?' Egil frowned. 'Well, I shall take a look around.'

'Thank you, Egil,' Berard said quickly. 'They were my grandfather's, you know, very special to me. And I feel quite lost without them. I've looked everywhere I can think of. I just don't want to leave them behind when I go. I've never had a pair like them.'

Egil wandered up and down the chamber, taking his task seriously as Berard stepped nervously towards the table where Meena sat.

She was shaking.

'Are you alright?' he whispered, watching as Egil checked under Jaeger's bed. 'He hasn't hurt you?'

Meena gulped, her eyes snapping to Egil as he emerged, shaking his head.

'Nothing there, my lord,' Egil groaned, staggering back to his feet. 'I'll keep looking.'

Berard's eyes rested on the book that lay on the table. He was surprised to see that Jaeger was keeping it out in the open now. But then again, he was surprised by everything Jaeger was becoming.

'I'm alright,' Meena murmured as Egil walked to the other end of the chamber. 'You shouldn't be here.' She was tapping her head frantically now. 'Go. Quickly.'

She looked terrified. Berard wanted to take her with him.

'I'm sorry to say, my lord, but I cannot see your tweezers,' Egil said as he returned, red-faced, glaring at Meena.

'Well, I do appreciate you looking, Egil,' Berard smiled, trying to sound cheerful. 'Please keep an eye out for them, though. They might turn up. No doubt just after I've departed for Solt!' He walked to the door. 'Goodbye, Meena,' he nodded. 'Egil.' And dropping his head, Berard slipped out of the room.

Egil shut the door firmly, and Berard was left in the corridor, fighting the urge to go back inside and rescue Meena.

'What *are* you up to, Little Brother?' Karsten mused from across the corridor. He had a toothpick between his teeth, which he removed as he considered Berard. 'I would think, after yesterday, *that* would be the last place you'd want to go?'

Berard looked up and down the torchlit corridor. 'I've lost something,' he muttered. 'I thought it might be in there.'

'What? You mean your servant? That bug-eyed girl?'

Berard bristled, hurrying forward. 'She is not a *bug-eyed* girl, Karsten! She is an innocent woman being kept prisoner by Jaeger, and I wanted to see if she was alright. After what he did to Elissa?' he hissed, shaking his head, realising that his tongue had run away with him. 'I must go. As you say, it's better if I'm not here.' And turning away, he made to leave, but Karsten grabbed his arm.

'Why does Jaeger have her in there?' he wondered quietly. 'He has his own servant. Why does he want her?'

Berard shook his head. 'I don't know,' he admitted. 'But I don't think she's safe there with him.'

Karsten let go of his brother's arm. 'Come on,' he said. 'Let's go for a walk. You can tell me all about it.'

Berard didn't think that sounded like a good idea, but Karsten was already striding off ahead without him, so with one last look at Jaeger's door, Berard scrambled after him.

***

Morana was in a frantic state as she shuffled through Varna's prized gardens, foraging for what she would need for the ritual. Many of the herbs required were those she used regularly: mugwort, fennel, rosemary. But others were more obscure: snakeweed, crab apple, plantain. She hoped that her mother had thought to plant those.

It was not just herbs that would make this ritual work, though. There were mushrooms, seeds, stones, and bones to find. Mead and food to prepare. Gold coins to collect. Yorik had offered to help her with the preparations, but she was surprised to realise that she did not want his company. And besides, he was going to have the more unpleasant task of talking to Jaeger.

It was time the Bear found out what role he needed to play.

***

Amma was overcome with relief at the sight of Gant. She threw herself into his wet arms, sobbing. 'Thank you!' she cried. 'Thank you!'

Gant was quickly uncomfortable with her affection, having been the one who had just murdered her brother. He eased Amma out of his arms, turning to Axl. 'You've had a nice little adventure, then, my lord?'

Axl stared up at him. 'My lord? Is that what I am now?' He couldn't even stand, was wet through and stinking, covered in bird holes and blood-crusted wolf wounds, aching all over and absolutely starving.

But the happiest he had felt in a long time.

'It is.' Gant couldn't help but smile as he looked down at the pale-faced, shaking mess that was his new king. 'I'm just sorry that it took so long. Three years too long.'

'True,' Axl laughed. 'But I don't plan on being a king who holds grudges. Except, perhaps, against one man.'

Amma looked at her muddy boots, not wanting to think of Jaeger again.

'Well, now that you have an army of men and a fleet of ships behind you, King Axl of Brekka, I imagine there's something you can do about that. And soon.' Gant glanced around at their lopsided shelter which had suffered under the onslaught of rain. 'But perhaps we need to get out of here first and see what all this fuss is about in Tuura? Your men should be here soon. And then we can find you an amenable horse for the rest of the way.' He looked around at the three of them: filthy and wet, their clothes ripped to pieces, wounds everywhere. 'For all of you, I think.'

Axl smiled, liking the sound of that very much indeed.

CHAPTER THIRTY NINE

Ivaar stood next to Borg Arnesson, watching as the ships were pulled ashore.

He tried to keep the shock from his face; the sheer surprise he felt at how many there were. He made some quick calculations as Borg clapped him on the back, whooping with joy.

'My cousins!' Borg cried, smiling at Falla. 'We breed like rabbits in my family!' He patted her belly, anticipating the many sons she would give him.

The new King of the Slave Islands would need a hall full of sons.

Falla did not look so enamoured with the hairy, tattooed men who were clambering down into the water, calling to her husband. They would all need feeding and housing, and the ale was almost gone.

She hoped Borg had plans to leave straight away.

'Well, that should give us... sixteen ships!' Rolan Arnesson exclaimed, tipping the last of his ale down his black-bearded mouth. He lifted his empty cup towards Falla who glared at him and turned away, heading back to the hall. 'Enough to defeat your brother?' he asked, nudging Ivaar.

Ivaar felt sick.

He had two ships. The Arnessons now had fourteen. 'I would think more than enough,' Ivaar said distractedly. 'Where did your family get so many ships from?'

'We've had a good few years since our fathers died,' Borg said, picking his nose. 'They never had much ambition. Too easily led by their cocks. Not enough up here.' He tapped his black hair, grinning. 'We decided to do things differently. Going up the Frozen Road, raiding. We took a lot of ships. Built a few more. And now?' he sighed happily. 'Now, we're ready to rule.'

***

Eadmund sunk into his chair. He could do no more to secure the fort. Everyone had come in from the outlying farms. Their weapons stores were healthy. They had a surplus of food. The fort itself was solid. They had done what they could to reinforce the gates, digging out ditches around the walls, hammering poles into the trenches, sharpening their tips into spears.

No assault their enemy made would come easy.

If they got through the stone spires in the harbour.

Warning fires were waiting, ready to burn all the way from the fort to the headland when it was time.

They would know.

Now, they just had to wait.

Eadmund reached out for his son as Tanja approached, cradling him in her arms. 'Here, give him to me,' he smiled. 'I'll take him for a while.'

Tanja looked surprised but grateful. She handed Sigmund to his father and hurried to the kitchen, eager for something to eat. Evaine had barely looked at the baby since they'd moved into the hall, and it was only Runa who Tanja could turn to for a break.

Eadmund's confidence was growing around his son. He sat back further, letting Sigmund sink into the crook of his arm. He didn't look especially happy but Eadmund made a few faces and soon Sigmund was making faces back.

They sat like that for a time, oblivious to everyone else in the hall.

Bram watched them from a table in the corner, where he sat with Ayla and Bruno. 'It's a hard man whose heart can't be tamed by a wee babe,' he said wistfully, feeling the great hole in his own heart, big enough to sail a ship through.

Ayla saw the pain in his eyes. She could feel the grief floating all around him like a hazy cloud. 'Perhaps there is another chance for you one day?' she suggested quietly. 'Another chance for you to have a family?' She glanced at Bruno, remembering the plans they had made just before Ivaar had taken them both.

Bram shook his head. 'At my age? Ha! I think the only women who'd want to share my bed now would be toothless grandmothers!'

Bruno chuckled softly. He had insisted on being helped out of his sick bed, desperate not to spend any more time away from his wife. 'Well, some women do like what an older man can offer,' he said, winking at Ayla. He was some twenty years older than his wife, and as far as he knew, that had never been a problem for her.

'It's true, Bram,' Ayla smiled shyly. 'Older men have more experience. They are kinder. Wiser.'

'Well, I don't deny that,' Bram grinned. 'But they're also fatter and hairier, creakier, smellier, and far less inclined to do much at all. Set in their ways. Miserable. Deaf!' He scratched at his bushy, grey beard, smiling as Isaura held the door open for her children who raced inside out of the rain. 'Which, I suppose, does make it easier to put up with screaming babies!'

Isaura saw Ayla, and the children spotted Bram, and they all came hurrying over.

'Still raining, I see.' Bram nodded as Isaura shook her cloak by the fire. 'Maybe another storm's rolling in? This place does like to keep you on your toes!'

'Yes, which might keep Ivaar away a little longer, don't you think?' Isaura wondered, taking a seat next to Ayla, smiling as Mads toddled straight over to Bram, eager to be lifted onto his knee.

Ayla glanced at Bruno, who looked as doubtful as she did. 'We can only hope so. A little bit longer would be helpful, I think,' she said quietly.

Nobody heard her, though, as Selene chose that moment to chase Leya too close to the table, knocking the ale jug onto the floor.

***

Branwyn and Gisila returned from their visit to Berta with bad news. Her sister had been removed from her employment in the temple kitchen.

'But...' Branwyn smiled, lifting the flap of her purse. 'She was so unhappy at being let go that she stole some things from the kitchen, including this key to the door!' She plonked the large, iron key on the table, staring at the beaming faces sitting around it. 'They made her leave in such a hurry that she was planning to sneak back in and take her things.'

'What about the bolts?' Entorp reminded her, frowning.

No one was beaming then.

'What if we snuck in during the day?' Jael wondered. 'Just one of us. If we could hide in the kitchen somewhere, we could undo the bolts after the kitchen staff had gone to bed. Let everyone else in?'

Fyn avoided Jael's eyes, hoping she wouldn't ask him.

'*If* there's somewhere to hide. *If* you wouldn't be seen sneaking in. It sounds far too risky to me,' Biddy said anxiously.

'I agree,' Gisila muttered. 'In the daylight as well. You'd be seen!'

'What is Berta's sister's name?' Jael wondered. 'And can we trust her?'

Branwyn looked at Gisila, then nodded. 'Her name is Briga. She seemed angry enough about Gerod and the elders not to be bound in any way. So, likely we could get her to help us. If she snuck in, it wouldn't be such a surprise to see her there, I suppose. She could say that she was returning the key or looking for something she'd left behind?'

Jael smiled at Branwyn. 'That sounds like a plan to me.'

***

There wasn't much to Hud's Point, and Thorgils and Torstan had quickly gone stir crazy.

There was a small hall – a *very* small hall – with one long table running down the middle of the low-roofed, ramshackle building. Four beds. One fire. A handful of stools and nothing to do but sit and wait and listen as the weather battered the hall's wooden planks, that were old and rattling and needed new nails, and the lady of the hall battered her long-suffering husband with a constant stream of rasping insults.

To escape the sound of both, Thorgils and Torstan had spent most of their time outside with the men they had brought to help them keep watch over the headland. There weren't many – only six in all – but it was enough to ensure that a pair of eyes was continually scanning the horizon. Although, in this weather, Thorgils was beginning to wonder if anyone would be stupid enough to cross the Akuliina Sea, which was a wild bitch at the best of times.

'They won't come at night,' Torstan insisted as they stood near the edge of the cliff, straining their eyes to see through the low-lying clouds.

'Maybe, but Bram says those Arnessons are arrogant shits, so it's possible they'll do something stupid. But still, having just sailed through those spires in the dark, I say good luck to them! Hopefully, they'll pack a spare pair of trousers!'

The crease between Torstan's eyebrows did not ease. He clenched his jaw. 'In this weather, we're going to have a hard time getting our signal fires going.'

'True,' Thorgils grinned. 'Which is why we brought the fastest horses on Oss with us. Don't worry.' He patted his friend on the shoulder. 'We'll give them enough warning, and we'll get back to the fort in time.' He was trying to appear confident, but his insides were churning at the thought of how many ships were coming.

How many men?

Too many, was the answer they all feared.

***

'My lord,' the dreamer murmured.

Gerod had just screamed at them until his shiny cheeks had turned a deep purple, and his ice-blue eyes were popping out of his face.

She was hesitant to speak at all.

Gerod rounded on the young woman, who was new to the chamber. He didn't know her name, nor remember her bringing one dream of relevance to him at all. He sighed impatiently, running his hands over his slippery, black hair, smoothing it down on either side of his cheeks, calming himself as he did so. 'Yes?'

'I had a dream,' she said nervously, looking at her clasped hands. 'The Brekkan army is marching to Tuura with their new king, Axl Furyck.'

Gerod glared at her. That put him in a bind. 'Why?'

'He is worried, my lord, about his grandmother. His family. He fears they are in danger.'

'And he is bringing his entire army with him?' Gerod's eyes widened. 'Well, that is interesting news. Finally, finally, someone has something worthy of my attention! And what is your name?' he asked, looking the girl over, wanting to remember her.

'Thea,' she said with a small smile now.

'Good girl, Thea,' Gerod purred. 'You will reach out to Morana tonight. I shall be interested to see what she thinks about this development. It will surely be time to kill Jael Furyck and her men now.'

***

They had decided to break into the temple on the night of the shadow moon, hoping that its cloak of darkness would aid their plans. But there were less than two days to prepare and a lot of decisions to be made. Everyone needed to know what to do and when.

And they desperately needed more weapons.

After a morning spent in the smithy with Kormac, Jael had come back to the house, eager to check on Edela, who was annoyed that she was still, for the most part, bed bound.

'You think I should just lie here and wait to be carried onto the ship?' Edela grumbled. 'Like an old invalid? While you're all out there, risking your lives? You only came here because of me, and now I can't do anything to help you!' Her shoulders dropped in frustration.

Jael tried not to smile. 'You were almost dead! How can you forget that? We'd like to take you back home alive!'

'Home?' Edela wondered, peering at Jael. 'And where is that to be, I wonder?'

Jael peered back. 'Well, you tell me, Grandmother. Wouldn't you like to go back to Oss and see to Evaine?'

'Oh.' Edela's eyes rounded at the thought of that. 'Yes, I would. But without that book, we are going to have to find another way to save Eadmund. Especially with the –'

'We need to focus on what to do once we're inside the temple,' Jael said sharply, standing up and walking over to the fire to add another log. It was not an especially cold day, but Edela had lost so much weight that she felt the cold more than ever, Jael knew. 'We have to find Marcus, but if he's still alive, I imagine he'll be heavily guarded.'

Edela's mouth was still hanging open in surprise at having been interrupted so abruptly, although, she wondered why she was surprised at all; Jael had been interrupting her since she was old enough to talk. 'Yes, I imagine so,' Edela said with a frown. She did not like the man, and she'd been disturbed to find that he was now their ally. 'But unless you kill everyone in the temple, we will have no chance of escaping anyway.'

'And what about Axl and Aleksander? Have you seen any sign of them in your dreams? Are they alright?'

'Oh yes,' Edela smiled. 'They are coming. Axl is the King of Brekka, at last, and he is coming for us.'

***

The pleasure of sitting on a horse again was rapidly outweighed by the discomfort of keeping his feet in the stirrups, so Axl just clung onto the reins instead, leaving Gant to tie his horse onto his and pull him along.

It was not the finest start to his reign, Axl grumbled to

himself, but his men seemed pleased to see him. Perhaps even relieved. And as strange as it felt, he realised that he had to lead them now.

But into who knew what?

'I wish we had a dreamer,' he sighed to Amma, who rode alongside him. 'A little grey-haired one.'

Amma smiled sadly, thinking of Edela. 'Well, perhaps we'll find one just like that very soon.'

Aleksander turned around in his saddle. 'We're not too far away now. Another day, I'd say.' He felt the familiar clench around his heart when he thought of Tuura. It was even worse now that he was forced to see his mother in a disturbing, new light. He didn't want to believe that she had done anything to try and hurt Jael.

'And what do you think we're going to find when we get there?' Gant wondered from Aleksander's left.

'No idea at all. The dream warned of everyone being in danger. But from who or what, I don't know.'

'Perhaps we're too late?' Axl worried.

'I hope not,' Aleksander frowned. 'But we'll know soon enough. Best we put our minds to thinking of a way to get in. They've built some tall walls since the last time you were there.'

Neither Axl nor Gant wanted to think about the last time they were in Tuura. And nor did Aleksander, so they stopped talking altogether, fumbling quickly with their hoods as the rain came down again.

***

Meena was growing bored with her confinement.

Egil had gone in and out of the chamber throughout the day, and he had locked the door each time. Apart from Berard's unexpected visit, she hadn't seen a soul.

It was warm, and Meena wanted to feel a breeze on her skin; water, air, anything but this stuffy chamber with only Egil for company. She sat on the bed, her chapped hands twitching in her lap, wondering how she was ever going to escape while she remained locked in.

There was a sharp knock on the door and Egil creaked to his feet, shuffling over to it with a moody frown. His eyes widened as he unlocked the door, slowly pulling it open.

'Why are you locking yourself in?' Morana scowled, creeping past him, her shoulders hunched tightly around her ears. 'I can assure you that any danger coming your way is not going to be stopped by a lock!'

'My master is not here.' Egil swallowed, hurrying behind Morana, who had edged her way towards Meena.

'Your *master?*' Morana sneered, twisting her head around. 'What would I want with him?' she laughed. 'No, I have come looking for an assistant. Someone who knows exactly how to help me.'

Meena looked horrified, staring quickly away from the dark pits of her aunt's searching eyes.

'Do you know of anyone like that, Meena?' Morana asked sweetly. 'Anyone who could *assist* me?'

Meena gulped, resisting the urge to shake her head. What was the point? Morana had come for her, and she had no choice but to go.

'I'm not sure that my master –' Egil spluttered.

'Your *master?*' Morana rounded on him. 'Your master is welcome to come to my chamber and tell me all the problems he might have with me taking an assistant. For what I need to do, in such a short space of time, I require help. Tell him that!' And snatching Meena's sleeve, she yanked her niece to her feet. 'Now, come along, little mouse. We don't have any time to waste!'

Meena yelped, stumbling after her aunt as she dragged her

past Egil, too terrified to take any pleasure in the disturbed look on his face.

***

Biddy had spent a busy afternoon with Entorp and Derwa, picking herbs for the assault on the towers. They planned to put the soldiers to sleep, and Derwa knew where all the right herbs were located for that. But how they were going to get the mixture inside each tower was a problem that nobody could find an answer to.

'Do they make their own food?' Jael wondered.

'I think it comes from the hall kitchen,' Kormac said, taking a bite out of his chicken leg. 'They had to build a hall recently to fit in all the soldiers. From what I know, most sleep there. Meals are served there. Perhaps food is taken around to the towers too?'

'Can we find out?' Jael wondered. 'Is there anyone you know who works there?'

Branwyn smiled, passing Entorp the bowl of baby turnips. 'Funnily enough, that's where Briga has just started working!'

'I'm starting to like the sound of this Briga,' Jael grinned, not having an appetite for anything but trying to force herself to nibble her way through a piece of rye bread; anything to stop Edela from glaring at her. 'Perhaps you can visit her again tomorrow? It's best if I'm not seen near her.'

Branwyn nodded eagerly. 'Of course.'

'Good. If we can break that symbol in the towers without being discovered, then we can focus on getting into the temple and rescuing Marcus. We'll need every pair of hands for that.'

'What about Axl and Aleksander?' Gisila asked anxiously. 'Shouldn't we wait for them? If they have the army, doesn't it make sense to wait?'

'They may be bringing the army to Tuura,' Edela yawned from her bed. 'But no one will be letting them in if The Following has its way!'

***

The Following did not gather in daylight.

Ever.

For many, their allegiance to Raemus had always been carefully masked from those around them. Most Followers lived in the kingdom as lords and ladies, farmers, merchants, armourers, even servants. Only a handful were bold enough to wear their distinctive, hooded robes in public.

When it was time to convene a meeting, Yorik would send word through a small network of slaves who were loyal to him, and when night fell, the Followers would creep around the cobblestoned streets, winding their way through the cramped buildings towards the entrance of the catacombs. It was concealed in the weaver's house, beneath his workshop. A trapdoor in the floor revealed a stone staircase that led to the hidden passageway. And there they would begin their journey through the skull-lined catacombs, towards the round meeting chamber, deep under the castle.

But on this humid afternoon, there was only one unsettled, impatient man waiting for Yorik to speak.

'Is this where we will perform the ritual?' Jaeger asked, glancing around at the unfamiliar symbols carved into the stone walls, illuminated by the torches that Yorik was patiently lighting. He was amazed to think that such a place existed beneath the castle he had spent his whole life in.

That he had known nothing about it.

He wondered if his father knew?

'Here?' Yorik's expression did not waver. 'No, we will go to the Crown of Stones again, but this time we will take something with us.' He motioned with one hand towards the shadows, lifting a torch out of its sconce with the other. '*Someone.*'

Jaeger felt a surge of excitement. This is what he'd been waiting for. He followed Yorik through an archway.

Into a round tomb.

It stunk of rat shit, and what else, Jaeger didn't know, but he couldn't feel any air coming in. He could barely breathe at all.

Yorik didn't seem to notice, though, as he carried on. 'Her name was Draguta,' he murmured. 'She gave birth to Valder Dragos, first of your line.'

Now Yorik had Jaeger's attention. 'The one we are bringing back was Valder Dragos' *mother*?' He looked down at the stone coffin. It was high-status, he could tell, covered in detailed reliefs of big-eyed dragons and long-tongued creatures he didn't recognise. And on the very top, near where you would expect a head to be lurking beneath the thick stone lid, the masked face of what appeared to be a woman rose up, wild hair flaring out from her head like stone branches.

'Yes, she is your ancestor, and the book has chosen you to help us bring her back.' Yorik tensed, wondering how Jaeger would react.

'How?'

'With blood,' Yorik smiled. 'We will need your blood.'

CHAPTER FORTY

Meena didn't know which was worse. She had been freed from Jaeger's chamber, but now she was locked in Morana's.

'You are here to be of use to me, girl! Not to stand there, shaking all night,' Morana snarled, picking up her pestle and grinding the henbane seeds she would add to the ritual mead. 'And all night it will be, I promise! I must stay awake now, preparing myself, so you will stay awake with me, watching if I start to tire. Keeping me alert. No food or drink shall pass my lips. My body must be deprived of everything now to enhance my dream state.'

Meena didn't like the sound of that. 'Jaeger will be mad,' she mumbled, her chin on her chest. 'He'll come looking for me.'

'I doubt that,' Morana snorted, glancing at her. 'What does he want with you anyway? Do you have some magical skill with cocks?'

Meena looked so horrified that Morana burst out laughing. 'So it's your conversation he enjoys, then? Or perhaps your pretty face?'

Meena didn't say another word as she ripped plantain leaves into the copper bowl Morana had given her.

'Smaller pieces!' her aunt grumbled. She turned back to her pestle and mortar, closing her eyes, wanting to infuse her own power into the seeds. It all needed to be perfect. Every tiny component had to work together in harmony.

Her stomach growled, and she frowned, suppressing a yawn.

It was going to be a long night.

***

Bayla watched her children leave the hall, wondering why she was even bothering to hold a feast tomorrow night. Her sons were not talking to each other, Karsten and Nicolene didn't appear to be on speaking terms either, and Haaron was, as always, entirely useless.

Power and wealth were all that Bayla had sought since she was a girl. Her status as the queen of the greatest kingdom in Osterland mattered to her. Once, she'd had a strong husband and fiercesome sons by her side, all working together as a family to ensure that the Dragos legacy continued.

But now?

Sighing, she got up from the table. Now, her family had splintered, her kingdom was broken, and she didn't know what to do about any of it. She had gone from feeling powerful to vulnerable in a heartbeat.

'You look tired, my dear,' Haaron murmured, stopping beside her.

She snapped her head around. 'Well, you look half dead. And there's food in your beard again!' And with that, she strode off towards the stairs, not wanting another reminder of how far they had come from the people they had once been.

Haaron brushed a hand through his beard. He had been spending his days rushing from one corner of the city to the other, desperately trying to resurrect his piers; to hurry along his shipbuilders; to grumble at the stonemasons as they started construction on his new walls; to speak with the merchants who were complaining about having to beach their ships up the coast.

But his wife never noticed any of that, he knew.

She just saw a hopeless, old man.

And right then, with his body aching and his spirit defeated, he thought that she was probably right.

*****

Jael sat on Eydis' bed stroking Vella, who was getting comfortable on one side of her. Ido was already asleep on the other.

The lamps glowed warmly around the house as everyone prepared for bed.

'Are you alright?' Jael wondered. 'You've barely spoken today.'

Eydis could feel tears coming. She had been holding them in for days. 'I miss my father,' she whispered. 'So much.' And her eyes filled with tears that quickly spilled down her cheeks. 'I want to go home.'

Jael squeezed her hand. 'Oh, Eydis,' she said softly. 'I'm so sorry for you. I had a dream about your father the other night. Did I tell you?'

Eydis wiped her eyes. 'No,' she sniffed.

'He told me that in the dark you could see. He said that your mother told him that before she died.'

Eydis felt strange all over. And so very alone. She had Jael. Fyn was always somewhere nearby. There was Biddy, Gisila, Entorp, and Edela. But her parents... she felt such overwhelming pain that she would never be with them again. She wanted to feel her father's arms as he pulled her close; to hear her mother sing her to sleep. She squeezed Jael's hand back. 'If something happens to you...'

'*Nothing* will happen to me,' Jael promised. 'Nothing, Eydis. I'm taking you home and when we get there, Eadmund will be waiting. And we'll get rid of Evaine and Morac and Ivaar. And we'll start our new lives together, you and me and Eadmund.'

Eydis closed her eyes, wanting to believe it could be as simple as Jael said, but the voice in her head boomed loudly, promising dark things to come.

***

Karsten stopped outside Berard's chamber.

Nicolene had gone on ahead. He wasn't looking forward to another night in her frigid company. She had not uttered a single word to him since their last fight, and although he thought that it was better than listening to her screeching at him, there was nothing worse than sharing a bed with a woman who wasn't talking to you.

'You should do something,' Karsten said quietly. '*We* can do something.'

Berard looked confused. He had not drunk much wine, but his head felt scattered, with worry for Meena, and with all the things he still needed to organise for his departure. With Jaeger and the book too. 'Do something about what?' he muttered with a frown.

'Meena,' Karsten whispered, leaning closer. 'You can take her with you.'

Berard looked horrified. 'How? I can't do that. She's in Jaeger's chamber. He would know!'

'Depends how we do it,' Karsten smiled, eager to irritate his youngest brother, and taking away his bug-eyed toy was surely going to do that. 'He doesn't need to know until you've gone.'

Berard peered into Karsten's conniving eye, trying to see

if he was just teasing him, but he appeared serious enough. 'But how would we?' he breathed, glancing up and down the corridor.

'Well, let's go inside and come up with a plan.'

'What about Nicolene?'

Karsten snorted. 'I don't imagine she'll miss me tonight.' And he followed Berard inside his chamber, wondering exactly how they could get Meena away from Jaeger without him noticing a thing.

***

Jael couldn't sleep.

Her mind kept wandering to Eadmund; feeling his hand touching her hair as they stood by Eirik's pool; remembering the look in his eye that, for a moment, had made it feel as though he was hers again. And then everything faded, and she was back in Tuura, her mind skipping quickly to the temple.

To Gerod tossing the book into the fire.

Jael yawned. She could only hope that Eydis or Edela could help her get Eadmund back somehow.

Gerod.

What a bastard.

Rolling over, trying not to wake Eydis, Jael closed her eyes, wanting to see Eadmund again. To hear his voice. But instead, she started thinking about Fianna. She was at the training ring in Andala, listening to the cheers go up as Harald defeated Gant, watching Fianna hand the note to her man.

Gerod, she had ordered. Give the note to Gerod.

Jael shivered in the darkness.

***

It was well past any time that Meena might have expected to be asleep, and Morana was showing no indication that she was about to let her stop and rest. There had been no food on offer either. The fire was too busy heating Morana's cauldron of ritual mead. It smelled awful and as well as longing for sleep, and food, and her freedom, Meena was desperate for a breath of fresh air.

Mercifully, there was silence while Morana carried out her preparations. Occasionally, she would call on Meena to assist her, to hand her things or stir her cauldron. But mostly she left her alone.

Meena glanced at her aunt. She seemed wide awake. She wondered why Morana had wanted her help at all. Her mind kept wandering to how angry Jaeger must be that she wasn't in his chamber. She listened for the bang on the door that she was certain would come at any moment.

Morana coughed loudly, struggling to her feet, eager to stretch out her legs. She had spent much of the night on her knees and was suffering because of it. She was almost surprised to see that Meena was still there. 'Why do you like the hunchback so much?' she wondered sharply, shuffling over to check on the cauldron. 'When the Bear likes you? Why do you prefer the hopeless hunchback? What use is he?'

Meena jumped. 'I, I, I... don't,' she spluttered.

Morana's laugh was a coarse cackle, delighting in Meena's discomfort. If the lamps in the chamber had been brighter, she knew she would have seen her cheeks burning red. 'Not that it matters,' she sneered. 'Your hunchback will be dead soon.' And leaning forward, she picked up a log, placing it under the cauldron.

***

'Make it look as though you're raiders. Thieves. Searching for treasure, women, whatever raiders do when they... raid.' Gerod turned around as he spoke. He was younger, much younger. His hair shone like polished ebony; his pale-blue eyes were feverish.

The men before him were...

Jael shuddered as she watched.

The men before him were...

She could smell them. Knew what their beards felt like rubbing against her face, her mouth. Knew the strength of their hands as they grabbed her body and pinned her down, ripping her dress, hitting her, pushing her, forcing her, bending her over.

Hurting her.

She couldn't breathe.

'So, raid, pillage, rape, cause a great big mess and in the middle of it all, make sure you kill the girl.' Gerod strode to the fire in the centre of the cottage, holding his hands out to the high flames.

The huddle of large, fur-cloaked men stood behind him, blinking at each other, wondering if they'd been dismissed.

'How will we know where to find her?' a blonde-haired man asked.

Gerod sighed as if bored, walking towards him. 'She will be in her aunt's cottage. Her aunt is to be married, so banners will fly outside to mark it. But I will ensure that someone is on hand to guide you in the right direction.' He narrowed his gaze. 'Do not hesitate. After you have killed her, cause some more mayhem and then disappear. Do not let anyone catch you, for if you do...' He studied them carefully. 'It will not go well for you. Our dreamers see everything. They will know if you have failed to cover your tracks. No gold will exchange hands if you do not do as I have instructed.'

The five men nodded, shuffling out of the small cottage. Jael swallowed, desperate to look away, but just as desperate to lunge for Gerod and throw him into the fire. But she was stuck to the floor, her body gripped by terror.

Ten years old.

She was only ten years old.

***

Although Jaeger had been annoyed to discover that Meena had left with Morana, he had been too preoccupied by his conversation with Yorik to give it much thought. But as he lay in bed, unable to sleep, the absence of her niggled at him.

It was a warm night, and Jaeger kicked away the furs. His ankle was aching, and he tried to turn his mind away from the pain and the absence of Meena, towards the ritual.

He was excited by the thought of raising the woman, Draguta; a woman he had never heard of before. His family had always proudly proclaimed that their line began at Valder Dragos. So, why was this woman both important, and yet, completely hidden from their history?

He was going to help raise her with his blood, Yorik had said. And then he had added: a lot of blood. He would have to put his life in Yorik's hands. But what need would they have for him once they had his blood? After that, why would they require him at all?

They wanted to raise Draguta. And she, in turn, would bring back Raemus.

But what of him?

He turned over, angrily bashing his pillow into a more

comfortable shape. If Yorik and his Followers thought that he had no part to play in the future of Hest, in the future of Osterland...

They were wrong.

They would need him.

He would make sure of it.

***

Bruno was moaning.

Ayla leaned over him, stroking his shoulder, soothing him back to sleep. She smiled sleepily, happy that he was there, next to her again. He was growing stronger. And when he was ready? Ayla knew that he would try to kill Ivaar.

Sighing, she lay back down, wishing she could fall asleep. She wanted more dreams. There was so much that she needed to know.

Over and over again, she saw a great line of ships sailing towards them. It sent a shiver through every part of her. But she wanted to see where they were, to know how long it would be until they were here.

And as for Jael Furyck coming to rescue them?

When Ayla thought of her, she saw fire. She was trapped by flames. Imprisoned by evil. Ayla could feel that. Jael had told Eadmund that she was coming to help them. But as much as Ayla wanted to believe her, she didn't see that.

She saw Tuura burning. And soon.

CHAPTER FORTY ONE

Hanna's mouth was so dry that she was struggling to swallow.

Six days on the ship as they had blown down the Osterland coastline had eroded her confidence. She wondered how she had ever thought herself brave enough to find Berard Dragos and convince him to steal the Book of Darkness for her.

But now she had no choice. Now she was here.

'We will wait here until tomorrow morning. One day only,' Ulf growled between hacking coughs as one of his men helped her over the side. 'Right here. Remember that. Remember your path back here. If you get lost, tell someone to point you to Balder's Cove. And do not be late. I already have one gold coin from you. Perhaps I don't need another?'

Hanna nodded quickly, too nervous to speak. Her blue eyes were big and blinking as she stood on the white sand beach, swaying in a blustering wind.

'Head up through those rocks, over the hill. That path will carry on to the left. It will take you all the way to the city.' He pointed to a well-worn dirt track leading up to the rise.

Dawn had barely broken, but Hanna could see well enough where she needed to go. Nodding again, she forced her legs to move. 'Thank you,' she croaked, adjusting her cloak as she turned towards the path. Looking over her shoulder, she called out. 'I'll be back by tomorrow morning!'

She hoped that they would wait for her.

***

Meena's eyelids felt like heavy curtains as she traipsed beside her aunt, her head pounding in time to the tapping of Morana's enormous wooden staff as she walked.

'I doubt anyone has ever walked slower than you!' Morana screeched, turning to slap Meena on the side of the head. 'We'll be all day if you do not shake yourself awake!'

Meena did shake then, with fear, as she picked up her feet and quickened her pace, gripping the handle of the basket she carried in her sweaty palm. She didn't know how long her aunt would keep her, but she was sure that the longer she stayed with her, the more furious Jaeger would become.

They were walking along the gravel road that led away from the castle, over the hill, towards who knew where. Morana certainly wasn't saying. The sky was a deep, dull grey, and although it was just past dawn, it was hard to tell. The wind was blowing angrily around them as they walked, and Meena could smell rain coming.

There was no one on the path, except...

Morana frowned at the young woman who was walking quickly towards them. She appeared to have come from out of nowhere. Stabbing her staff into the gravel, Morana threw back her hood.

Hanna stopped at the sight of the wild looking woman, who was most certainly a dreamer, and the wild looking girl cowering next to her with bulging eyes.

'Who are you?' Morana asked suspiciously.

Hanna gulped, trying to form words but those dark eyes were interrogating her, and she worried what they might find. Then she remembered her stone. 'I am Hanna,' she said, almost boldly. 'Who are you?'

Morana ignored her question. 'Where have you come from?'

'A ship,' Hanna said. 'I have come to visit my cousin. Why do you ask?'

Morana studied her. She was pretty and well spoken, unlike the shaking mess standing next to her. She couldn't see anything else, though, which surprised her, but she didn't have time to stand about engaging in pointless chatter. 'Well, move out of our way then... *Hanna*,' she growled, poking her staff at Hanna, who stumbled as she hurried around them.

Morana glared at Meena who was watching the woman walk away, then spun around. 'And what is your cousin's name?' she snapped.

Hanna stopped, glancing over her shoulder. 'Alika Salvar,' she said as calmly as possible, feeling her knees knock together beneath her dress. 'Do you know her?'

Morana turned away, stomping up the hill.

Hanna shook her head and continued on her way. It was early, and she doubted that anyone from the castle was up and about yet. She would have to find some way of getting a message to Berard Dragos.

She needed to speak to him as quickly as possible.

***

Jael woke in a cold sweat, her heart pounding.

Her dreams came rushing back to her in horrifying waves, and she tried to shake them away. Biddy was spooning her hotcake mixture onto the griddle, murmuring to the puppies who were waiting by the door, ready to go outside. Jael sat up, knowing that she needed to get out of bed, but her nightmare had a firm grip on her and would not let her go. She was overcome with the strangest sensations. It was as though there was no past or present, just a shifting focus between then and now.

She was still in that cottage, watching those men.

'Jael?' Biddy was at her side. 'Are you alright?'

It was a dim light that filtered down the smoke hole, but Jael could see the concern in her eyes. She nodded, unable to speak. Biddy laid a hand on her shoulder, and she flinched.

'Jael?' Biddy asked again.

Jael heard her father's booming voice telling her to come back from that dark place. She had been so quiet and lost when she'd returned home from Tuura all those years ago. Ranuf had barked at her and pushed her and never once let her sink back into that place again.

Not when she was with him, at least.

It was all that he could do.

'I'm here,' Jael said, at last, clearing her throat. She glanced around the house, avoiding Biddy's eyes. 'We have a lot to organise today.' Standing up, she reached for her trousers, feeling her amulet swinging between her breasts. Her father had given it to her when she'd come home, promising her that Furia would always protect her.

That nothing bad would ever happen to her again.

Biddy didn't look any less worried. 'I'm making apple hotcakes,' she smiled. 'I thought Eydis might like them. And you.'

Jael grimaced, shaking her head. 'Not for me. I have to go and see Beorn. We need to finalise our plans for tonight.'

Gisila muttered to herself as she helped Eydis dress. 'Are you sure it's going to work?' she asked anxiously. 'That they won't know we've broken their spell?'

Jael shrugged as she sat on the bed, pulling on her boots. 'I've no idea,' she admitted. 'But we'll know tonight. I'm sure if the dreamers see what we're doing, they'll make a fuss. So, we'll need to be prepared either way.'

'Did you have any dreams?' Gisila wondered. 'Anything that would help?'

Jael froze, one hand on her cloak, her shoulders tightening themselves into knots. 'No. None that would help,' she said stiffly, wrapping her cloak around her shoulders and reaching for her swordbelt. 'How about you, Eydis?'

Eydis, who was still half asleep, shook her head. 'None that would help. Or that made sense.'

'Never mind,' Jael yawned, bending down to pat the puppies who were desperately trying to get someone to let them outside. 'What about you, Grandmother?'

'Me?' Edela croaked, stretching her arms above her head as she considered getting out of bed. 'Oh, yes, I had a very useful dream indeed!'

***

Gerod never had an appetite in the morning. He preferred to take his meals at midday and dusk, so he was up early, stalking the many chambers of the temple, checking on the elders and dreamers as they went about their morning tasks, his sharp eyes impatiently scrutinizing their every move.

'Thea, isn't it?' he asked the mousey girl who looked petrified to be called upon as he entered the Chamber of Dreams. 'Tell me, what did Morana say when you told her about the Brekkan army's approach?'

Thea had barely roused herself out of bed and quickly draped her cloak around her shoulders as she stood, shivering before him. 'I did not find her, my lord,' she mumbled.

Gerod twitched with displeasure. 'What? What was that you said?' he hissed through clamped teeth. 'You did not... *find* her?' He shook his head slowly. 'But how is that possible? Only the elite dreamers are admitted into this chamber. How is it possible that you cannot accomplish the simple task of dream walking?'

Thea felt her body warm with embarrassment. The other dreamers, all seven of them, remained quiet behind her. They were much older women; more experienced, but not better dreamers, she was certain. 'Perhaps she was not asleep, my lord?' Thea suggested quietly.

Gerod bit his tongue. 'Not asleep?' he growled. 'Your excuse is that the fault is not your own, but Morana's? That she was *not asleep*?' He looked incredulous, his anger spiking.

'If Morana is preparing to perform the ritual tonight, then she would be purifying herself,' one of the other dreamers spoke up. 'She would not eat, nor drink, nor take any rest, my lord.'

Gerod rounded on the snowy-haired woman, his eyes bright with rage. 'You think I don't know what a dreamer must do before a ritual?' he snorted, annoyed that he hadn't thought of that himself. He glared at them all. All those useless, pathetic women who had done nothing; who had told him nothing in days. He rounded on Thea. 'You will leave this chamber! Get your things. I have no need for someone who does not even understand the basics of what is required here. Go back and join the rest. I shall promote another,' he snarled. 'Someone with more... experience.'

Thea's eyes filled with tears of shame as she turned back to her bed.

Gerod ran his eyes over the rest of the dreamers. 'You will all try and make contact with Morana, Yorik, any of them. I need to know what I'm to do with the Brekkan army when it arrives, if, of course, this idiot girl was even right in what she saw in the first place! But if you fail to get through to them, well then, I shall simply have to take matters into my own hands.'

***

They all gathered around Edela, waiting to hear about her dream, but she was more interested in breakfast. Her stomach was gurgling expectantly, and she hoped that Biddy would not burn her hotcakes.

'I dreamed of the elderman,' Edela said, at last, realising that no one would move until she revealed what she had seen. 'He is locked in his chamber.'

'He's alive, then?' Jael asked.

Edela nodded. 'He is. But he does not believe that he will live much longer. That strange man, Gerod? He comes to him every day to threaten his life. And he means to take it. Along with ours.'

Branwyn swallowed. 'The elderman may be alive, Mother, but how does that help us?'

'Because I saw something, my dear,' Edela said patiently. 'Something I had completely overlooked when I was in his chamber. There is another door.'

'Two doors?' Jael had been so focused on speaking to Marcus that she had not noticed another door either.

'Yes, there is a room through a little alcove. He keeps his books in there. His chest. And hidden behind a curtain is another door. And that door leads to a corridor which goes directly to the kitchen.'

'Oh,' Jael smiled. 'That *was* a good dream to have, Grandmother.'

***

Aleksander felt almost refreshed when he woke up. It was the first time he had slept through the night in longer than he could remember. A night where he had not had to keep watch; where the pain in his shoulder had not kept him awake; where he had not been disturbed by strange dreams.

And yet, despite a lack of exhaustion, he felt a growing sense of discomfort. The Widow had come to him and warned him of the danger that Jael was in, but it felt as though he had been wading through mud to try and reach her ever since.

He feared they were going to be too late.

The ravens. The wolves.

The sick feeling in the pit of his stomach kept growing.

'Ready?' Gant wondered, cracking his neck as he stopped before the fire. They had been up before dawn, eager to get back on the road. 'Looks as though we might actually have a fine day ahead. That should help us get to Tuura by dusk I'd say.'

Aleksander looked hopeful, then frowned. 'But what will we do when we get there?'

Gant laughed, motioning to the men who were preparing themselves for another march: dousing fires, packing saddlebags, wrapping belts around their waists. 'I say we knock on the gates and ask to come in. Politely, of course,' he grinned. 'We Brekkans are known for our exceptionally good manners.'

'Well, I suppose we do have one or two men. It might make them more inclined to let us in. Or less.'

Gant kicked dirt across the nearby fire. 'I keep imagining what Ranuf would do. And it would not be subtle. If Gisila or Jael were in danger, he would burn the whole place down.' Gant dropped his head. Memories of Tuura were stirring, and they were never pleasant. 'So, we get there as fast as we can, find out how the land lies, and then we act. Maybe, just maybe, this dreamer of yours was wrong.'

Aleksander rolled his shoulder, reaching for the reins, hoping more than anything that she was wrong.

'Let's get moving!' Gant bellowed, nodding at Axl, who was being helped onto his horse. 'We can be at Tuura before nightfall if we make a start now!'

***

Hest's sprawling markets quickly overwhelmed her senses, and Hanna's nervousness was swept away on building waves of colour and noise as the merchants rushed past her, setting up their stalls for the day.

She bought a sausage and a couple of wild plums because although she was too uptight to feel hungry, she needed to stay alert, and food would surely help.

It was going to be a long day.

As Hanna wandered around the markets, squeezing between the aggressive merchants, resisting their offers, she noticed children darting in and around the stalls, stealing fruit, chasing one other, getting into trouble. Most were filthy, dressed in torn clothing. None wore shoes.

All of them looked hungry.

She followed one boy who had slipped an apple up his tunic and run off quickly, keeping one eye on her.

'Wait!' Hanna called. 'Wait! I just want to talk to you!'

The light-haired boy slowed down. He looked about eight-years-old, maybe older. He was small and wary of her, with big, brown eyes that never stopped moving, checking if she was alone.

Hanna had one hand out as she approached. 'Please, I just want to talk to you.'

'About what?' he asked quickly, ready to run if she got close enough to snatch him.

'I'm looking to pay someone to help me deliver a message.'

He frowned. 'Pay with what?'

Reaching into her purse, Hanna pulled out a large, gold coin, gripping it tightly.

The boy raised his eyebrows, unable to mask the glint in his eye at such a treasure. A gold coin? He could feed his family for a year or more on that. More, much more, he was sure. He edged towards Hanna, wondering if it was a trap, but too eager not to want to try and see if, perhaps, it wasn't. 'Who do you want to get a message to?' he asked.

Hanna glanced around, feeling exposed. 'Come with me,' she said quietly, nodding towards an archway up ahead. 'We can go somewhere more private.'

The boy flinched, digging his toes into his hole-ridden boots. 'No! You tell me here. I'm not going anywhere with you!'

Hanna sighed. She didn't blame him. Why should he trust her? 'Alright,' she said softly. 'But let me whisper it in your ear. I don't want anyone to hear me.' Slipping the gold coin back into her purse, she took out two symbol stones and reached out a hand, hoping he would stay.

He shrugged, standing his ground, resisting the urge to run. He wanted that coin, and she didn't have a mean looking face.

Hanna crept closer, until she was standing near him. She bent down, placing the stones in his hand, whispering in his ear. 'I want you to find Berard Dragos and give him one of these stones, then tell him that Jael Furyck has sent him a message. He needs to meet me to hear it. It's urgent. Make him understand that. He must tell no one. And make sure you tell him to keep the stone. It stops dreamers from hearing or seeing what he does.' Hanna peered at the boy, whose eyes were wide, his head nodding. She worried that she had told him too much to remember. 'Do you understand?'

He kept nodding.

'Tell him to meet me here. In there.' Hanna pointed to the archway. She had walked around the marketplace a few times now, and it was the most private area she had found. She would have to spend the day there, waiting, hoping that he would come.

'I'll tell him. I'll find you for my coin,' the boy said impatiently, jiggling on the spot, eager to leave.

'Only if he comes,' Hanna warned. 'Make sure he comes.

And bring back my other stone. Then you will get your coin.'

But the boy had already run off, winding his way through the merchants like a tiny snake. She looked after him with a frown, not knowing if he'd ever come back.

***

Morana had brought her to the Crown of Stones.

Meena hated this place, where the black-robed Followers hid their faces and danced in time to mysterious, languid rhythms that only they could hear. They brought fresh blood and herbs, old bones and stones. They painted symbols, killed animals, caused mayhem, cast spells.

And Morana was preparing to do it all again.

Tonight.

Meena stumbled around the circle, wanting to crawl away from her aunt. Morana was busy running through how the ritual would go, making sure that she had thought of everything they would need. She hadn't noticed Meena in some time. If she were to just slip through the stones...

'You!' Morana growled as Meena staggered to a halt. 'You have my basket?'

Meena tapped her head, shuffling towards her aunt.

Morana dug into the basket. 'We are going to cleanse the circle,' she said firmly. 'I want everything ready. Everything must be perfect for tonight.' And pulling out a hazel switch, she handed it to Meena. 'You will get on your hands and knees and sweep the circle clean. Carefully. I will lay out the stones.'

Meena took the switch and placed the basket on the ground, looking up at the sky as the rain came bucketing down. Dropping to her knees in the dirt, she started sweeping.

***

Berard walked down the castle steps, his head pounding, eager for a swim, despite the rain. It was a humid morning, and he was determined to escape before Karsten pounced on him again. He was leaving tomorrow, but he wanted to run away from all that saying goodbye would mean.

From having to face Jaeger entirely.

Karsten had suggested a number of ways that he could steal Meena away from Jaeger, but for every idea he considered, Berard quickly found a reason why it would fail.

Jaeger was not the brother he knew, and at every turn, he felt the terror of being crushed by him. He worried about what that would mean for Meena, if she tried to leave and he failed her.

His shoulders were curled, and the crease between his soft grey-blue eyes was deepening with every step. He heard the familiar, frantic hum of the markets and turned his head. In his hurry to leave the castle, he had not thought of breakfast. Breakfast would mean his mother and father, Karsten, possibly Jaeger.

He had just wanted to avoid them all.

Sighing, Berard ignored the growling protest of his empty belly and headed across the square, deciding that he would eat after his swim.

'My lord!'

Berard looked around in surprise as a small boy ran towards him. He did not turn away, but nor did he look eager to linger. There were always beggars hanging around the markets, often children, who pleaded for food or wine or coins. It was hard to say no. Mostly, he didn't. 'Yes?' he asked impatiently. The boy was very thin. Berard felt bad for him.

The boy's big eyes ferreted around expertly. He motioned

for Berard to bend towards him, then placed a stone in his palm. 'For you. From a lady. She wants you to come. To meet her.'

Berard stepped back, staring at his hand, confused. 'A lady?' Wrapping his fingers around the stone, he looked around. 'Who?'

'I don't know, my lord,' the boy admitted. 'She said...' he lowered his voice, 'that Jael Furyck sent her with a message. That it was important. For you to have the stone to keep away the dreamers.'

Berard's own eyes were wide now. 'Jael?' He slipped the stone into his pouch and scratched at his beard. 'Where?'

The boy took off, motioning for him to follow, and with one quick look back at the castle, Berard scuttled off after him, heading towards the markets.

CHAPTER FORTY TWO

Jaeger had had enough now.

He strode up to Morana's chamber and hammered on the door, but no one came. In the end, he forced it open, further annoyed to find that Meena wasn't there.

He thought of Yorik.

Perhaps he would know what Morana had done with her?

***

The boy ran fast, and Berard panted as he tried to keep up with him, desperate not to lose him in the maze of merchants and stalls.

Eventually, he came to a halt as the boy stopped, pointed to an archway and disappeared back amongst the crowd.

Berard paused, suddenly wary. That archway led to nowhere, he knew, just a dark, dead end. Taking a deep breath, he walked under it anyway, his eyes widening as a young woman stepped into the light.

'Hello,' she said quietly. 'Are you Berard? Do you have the stone?'

He glanced behind himself, then nodded. 'Who are you?'

'My name is Hanna. Jael Furyck sent me.'

Berard hurried forwards, gripping her elbow, leading her further into the darkness, towards a stone bench; eager to be as far away from prying eyes as possible. He indicated for her to sit, the whites of his eyes bright in the shadows. 'Why? Why has she sent you here?'

There were many ways Hanna had thought about beginning, but she was so nervous that she simply blurted out, 'Jael wants you to take the Book of Darkness from your brother!'

'What?' Berard sat down, dazed. 'What are you talking about? How could she...' He trailed off, his mouth hanging open in confusion.

'We know he has it,' Hanna went on. 'Jael is a dreamer. Her grandmother has seen it too. The book is more dangerous than you know. Your brother and Morana... they have been trying to hurt people. In Tuura, they have already caused a lot of harm. People have died.'

Berard didn't know what to think. 'How do I even know Jael sent you? And why should I listen to anything she says anyway? She murdered her uncle! Destroyed our ships!'

'Jael didn't kill her uncle, her brother did. He found Lothar beating his mother. They just wanted to leave before the body was found. And she has had a dream about you.'

Berard sat up straight. 'She has?'

'She says that you're in grave danger. You should come with me, Berard. Get the book and come with me. I have a ship.'

'But I'm leaving. Tomorrow.'

'Leaving for where?'

Berard dropped his eyes to his lap, trying to think. 'I... the book... it is changing my brother. *Has* changed him,' he admitted, looking up. 'He is not the same.'

Hanna felt impatient, but even in the shadows, she could see Berard's pain. 'The book steals souls. The souls give the spells more power. A person without a soul is no longer a person. If your brother spends his time near the book, it would make sense that you're losing him.'

'But can I get him back?' Berard asked weakly, already knowing the answer.

Hanna shook her head. 'I don't know. But if you do not take the book, your brother and Morana and The Following will destroy everything in Osterland. They seek the return of the Darkness, and that means the end of all life.'

Berard swallowed, thinking of Meena. 'But even if what you say is true,' he whispered. 'Even if I were to believe you, I cannot *get* the book. Jaeger keeps it in his chamber. And no one is getting in there.' He gulped, staring at the archway, conscious of how long he'd been; wondering who else that boy was talking to.

'There must be some way you could get it. He must leave sometime?'

'I have to go!' Berard stood up, overwhelmed by discomfort and terror. 'I cannot be here, talking to you. I have to go!'

'Berard!' Hanna hurried to her feet. 'The stone I gave you. It stops dreamers hearing what you say, seeing what you do. Please, whatever you do, keep it on you. Morana is dangerous, and the dreamers in Tuura will warn her if they see a threat to the book or your brother.'

Berard nodded quickly, turning to leave. 'I cannot get the book,' he mumbled. 'You should go back to wherever you came from. I cannot get the book.' And he hurried through the archway without looking back.

Hanna frowned, watching him go, wondering what she was going to do now.

***

Ivaar had left the hall just after dawn, desperate to think.

Borg's cousins had been smart enough to bring barrels of ale with them, and that had kept them all entertained since their arrival. But despite all the drunkenness, they were actively preparing to depart for Oss the next day.

They had talked and argued and somehow planned a strategy. And now... now they would eat, drink, sacrifice to the weather gods and dream of the destruction they would cause and the kingdom they would claim.

Ivaar felt sick.

His men had looked at him with discomfort, seeking his leadership, and he had avoided their eyes, hiding his away, trying to find an answer that he could bring to them.

But it had been days now, and he still had no ideas.

He walked along the beach, reluctantly heading back to the stinking little hall, his shoulders heavy and his spirit bleak. The Arnessons would take Oss. Kill everyone. Likely him and his men too.

And he would help them.

'You do not like our company, Ivaar the Bastard?' Falla spat as she sauntered towards him in a thin, white dress.

Falla Arnesson now, Ivaar reminded himself. Not a woman to be seen talking to. Not alone. Not in *that* dress. Borg had already fought two men who'd dared to admire her plump figure.

'You prefer to talk to the birds?' she laughed, but there was no amusement in her eyes, only cold ambition and utter dislike of him.

'Well, lady, I am a man who misses his wife and children. It's not easy to live in another man's hall when you have your own.'

'*Had*, from what I hear,' she sneered, apparently not bothered that her dress was flapping around, exposing her legs.

The weather was rolling in towards them again, and Ivaar could smell rain. He wasn't sure whether that was a good thing or not. As impatient as he was to leave the island, he was less eager to start the journey that would end everything he had so desperately wanted to achieve.

'Now, you're just a man. Not a lord! Not a husband or a father. Just a nothing!' Falla laughed.

Ivaar bit his teeth together, unsure if he had ever met a more disagreeable woman. Perhaps Jael Furyck? No, he thought to himself. No, she was fierce and brave and beautiful, but this woman? She was coarse and vile and conniving. And he knew that she was trying to get him in trouble with her thin dress.

And Ivaar did not need any more trouble. 'Well, as you say, I'm nothing. But I'm also cold, so I think I'll return to your hall, now that I've had some time to think.'

'*Think*?' she snorted, following him. 'Think about what? Betraying my husband, perhaps?'

Ivaar kept walking.

'That's what Mother Arnesson warned!' she shouted over the cawing seabirds. 'She warned Borg that one of his men would betray him! Will it be you, Ivaar the Bastard? If it is, I promise it will be the last thing you ever do!'

Ivaar frowned, striding away, impatient to escape her screeching which was as grating as the song of the angry birds that chased each other above his head.

***

'Brother!' Jaeger called as Berard emerged from the markets. 'What are you doing here?'

Berard froze, hoping the woman had not followed him. He glanced around guiltily.

'Are you hiding from someone?' Jaeger wondered, peering behind his brother.

Berard shook his head, his damp, brown curls shuddering

around his face. The rain was turning heavy, and he was keen to get inside the castle and away from Jaeger. 'No, no, I was just seeing if there was anything I might want to take with me tomorrow.'

Jaeger stared down at Berard's empty hands. 'But you found nothing?' he asked suspiciously, not noticing the rain at all. He wasn't sure why he was suspicious, but he had stopped trusting his brother some time ago and now saw everything he did as a potential threat.

Berard moved past Jaeger, brushing against his shoulder. 'I must go,' he mumbled. 'I have a lot to organise. I need to see Father and –'

'Wait!' Jaeger gripped his arm tightly. 'Have you seen Meena anywhere? Or Morana?'

Berard felt a tightness in his chest. 'Meena? Why? Has something happened?' He turned, searching his brother's scowling face for clues.

'*Happened*?' Jaeger laughed. 'To Meena? No.' He shook his head. 'Morana has commandeered her for the ritual.' He swallowed, realising that he had said too much.

'Ritual?' Berard's chest tightened further.

Jaeger let go of his brother's arm, laughing even more, attempting to cover his slip. 'Well, she's always doing some strange thing, I suppose,' he said casually. 'Being a dreamer.'

Berard didn't move. 'Oh, yes, of course. Well, I'll tell Meena that you're looking for her if I see her. But I doubt I will.' And he turned away from his brother, hurrying towards the castle before Jaeger could say another word.

***

Jael had second thoughts about meeting Beorn at the stables, not wanting to bring any attention to their plans. She went to Aedan's house instead, picking up Alaric on the way.

Kayla sat in a chair by the fire, nursing her daughter as Jael, Fyn, Entorp, and Alaric stood around the table with a sheet of vellum, a quill, and a pot of ink.

'It doesn't have to be perfect,' Jael said encouragingly, noticing Alaric's hesitation. 'We just need an idea of what the inside of the temple looks like. How to get from the kitchen to the other chambers. Where we might expect to find the dreamers and elders. And the guards. The fewer surprises, the better.'

Alaric took a deep breath and picked up the quill, dipping it into the pot of indigo ink. He scratched it against the vellum, making hesitant, shaky lines that he eventually started joining up, creating chambers. He could see the temple with his eyes closed after working there as a scribe for nearly fifty years, and his hand became steadier as his confidence grew.

He stepped back and looked at the basic outline he had made. 'This is how it was when I was last there,' Alaric explained. 'They didn't have temple guards then, so I can only guess where they might be sleeping.' He frowned, pointing to a large chamber, leading off the kitchen. 'Probably here. Where the scribes lived. Where I lived, once. But they will not all be sleeping, will they?'

'No, some will be guarding the temple. Walking around. Watching the doors,' Jael muttered, staring at the map. 'And where do you think Gerod might have put my sword? If he kept it at all.'

'Oh, I think he would have kept it,' Alaric said. 'A sword that important? Perhaps they will even try to use it themselves?' He pointed to a very small room near Marcus' chamber. 'This is where the scrolls were kept. There are locked chests in there. Lots of shelves. A room of secrets. Only the elderman ever had the keys. Perhaps the sword is in there?'

'Well, it sounds as though we'll need to find those keys,' Jael murmured. 'And one guess who has them now.'

***

Gerod was growing anxious as he paced in front of Marcus.

The elderman was not a dreamer, he knew. There was nothing he could tell him, and yet, Gerod felt as though he had no one else to turn to for answers.

Marcus sat before the empty fireplace, cold and hungry. He could feel the angry heat lifting off Gerod, and it disturbed him. He had never liked the man, predicting his bold-faced ambition on the very first day they had met, many years ago. They had both put their names forward to become the elderman, and Gerod had been furious when the Elder Council had elected Marcus. But that had been long before The Following had corrupted the temple, bending those who chose to be compliant to their will.

Murdering those who did not.

'The Brekkan army is coming,' Gerod said, leaning towards Marcus, searching his eyes for signs that he had any information about that.

Marcus' eyes revealed his surprise but disguised his relief. 'Why is that?' he asked casually.

Gerod lunged at him, blinking in Marcus' face. 'You tell me! Why are they coming here? What do they know? What do they seek to do?'

'Why don't your dreamers tell you?' Marcus wondered sharply. 'I'm not a dreamer. I have no knowledge of what they are doing or why.' He sat back in the chair, uncomfortable with Gerod's proximity. He was a disturbing man, with eyes so frantic they unsettled him. 'Why are you not asking your leaders in Hest or your dreamers? I cannot help you.'

Gerod stepped away, his nostrils flaring, his mind flitting all over Osterland. 'How could Axl Furyck know what we are doing?'

'Axl Furyck? What makes you think that he's coming here because of you? His grandmother is here. He doesn't know if she's dead or alive. He would want to find that out, surely?'

'With an army?'

'You will start a war if you attack them,' Marcus said plainly. 'A war you must be prepared to finish.'

Gerod rounded on him. 'With the Book of Darkness, we can destroy anyone! You know that. We will destroy *every* kingdom!'

'Of course.' Marcus didn't flinch. 'As you say.'

The elderman's calmness disturbed Gerod even more. He strode towards the door, gripping his bony, white fingers around the handle as though he would break it. 'My dreamers can see into your thoughts,' he warned. 'They will find any secrets you're keeping.'

Marcus held his breath as Gerod left the chamber, slamming the door behind him. He glanced towards the alcove.

Through that alcove was his chest, his books, his clothes.

And another door that led to the corridor.

And his spare set of keys.

***

Berard was beside himself.

He had abandoned all thoughts of breakfast and scuttled straight upstairs to his chamber instead. Jaeger, he knew, was not in the castle now. He could go to his brother's room, take the book, give it to Hanna. Leave with her, even.

If she had not left already.

He shook all over as he sat on his bed, wet through but not caring.

Egil would be in the chamber. And Jaeger would return before he was across the square and he would surely kill him.

Berard didn't know why Jael had sent Hanna. Why she had dreamed of him at all. She sensed danger. That unsettled him too. What Jaeger was doing with Morana and the book...

He closed his eyes, wanting to shut it all out.

But he could leave. Tomorrow he *was* leaving. He would be away from it all. He would be safe in Solt. Although Hanna had said that they were hurting people.

That they wanted to kill everyone.

How could he run away like a coward and leave Meena in such danger? Berard opened his eyes and sighed, feeling as pathetic and pointless as his father had always insisted he was.

Not brave in the slightest.

Admitting defeat, he lay back on the bed, closed his eyes and saw Meena's terrified face.

***

They had finally decided upon a route around the temple, but Jael didn't feel overly confident with so little time to plan; with not quite enough weapons; with no real knowledge of how many people they would have to face once they got inside.

They would simply have to react in the moment.

'Do you think we can do it?' Fyn wondered, kicking a stone down the street. 'It feels as though we'll be blind in that temple.'

Jael tried to look confident as she wandered beside him, but she felt ready to fall down. Her stomach was rolling, and she wondered if she would, in fact, vomit again. 'We can,' she said. 'It's the only way we'll get out of here alive, and we need to get home as quickly as possible to help Eadmund.'

Fyn nodded but still looked troubled.

'When a fight seems impossible, you have to find a reason to keep going. You have to claw your way to victory because giving up would mean losing everything you ever cared about.' Jael stopped and turned to Fyn. 'Think of your mother. She's stuck there on Oss with Morac and Evaine. And getting out of here means that we can go back and make all of that right. We can get rid of both of them!'

As pleasant as that thought sounded, Fyn did not look convinced in the slightest.

Jael sighed. 'Come on. Perhaps you just need something to eat!' She grabbed his arm, pulling him along, past a column of soldiers who eyed her as though they would happily tear the skin from her bones.

Jael ignored them and thought of her advice to Fyn. She had her own motivating reason to keep going now.

Gerod.

***

Jaeger became more enraged as he stomped back through the castle, searching for Meena. Yorik had been of no use. He had no idea where Morana was, and he was far too busy preparing for the ritual to give it much thought.

Jaeger's mind taunted him as he checked in every chamber, twisting his thoughts into dark conspiracies. He worried that she might have escaped. That someone had helped her.

Berard?

Morana?

They both wanted to hurt him, he was sure. Or his father?

'You look tired,' his mother smiled, walking out of the hall, her youngest grandchild, Kai, in her arms.

Jaeger scowled at her with such ferocity that Kai burst into tears. He blinked, finally breathing, quickly irritated by the noise.

'What is it, Jaeger?' Bayla implored. 'You are not yourself these days. What is wrong? Please, tell me.' She patted Kai on the back, uncomfortable with his tears, quickly looking around for a servant or Nicolene.

Jaeger ignored her, his attention suddenly claimed by the two bedraggled women walking through the castle doors: Morana, followed by an exhausted-looking Meena.

Jaeger left his mother to deal with the wailing toddler and hurried to them. 'Where have you been?' he growled, snatching Meena's hand, dragging her towards the stairs with a violent glare at Morana. 'Where have you *been*?'

Meena could feel Jaeger's fury as it pulsed through his arm, down to the hand that was squeezing hers so tightly. She was too terrified to speak as he pulled her up the stairs behind him.

Jaeger squeezed harder, unable to stop himself. 'You belong to *me*, Meena, not Morana! You should not have left like that!'

Meena almost lost her footing as she stumbled after him, lurching again from one horrible situation to another; watching in misery as he yanked her past Berard's door. She was so distracted that she tripped over, crashing onto the flagstones with a crack.

Jaeger glowered at her, even more incensed. 'Get up!' he seethed, tugging on her arm.

Berard, roused from his bed by the commotion, opened his chamber door, his eyes rounding in horror at the sight of Meena on the ground, his brother, red-faced and mad-eyed, towering threateningly over her. 'What's going on? What are you doing?' he cried, bending down to help Meena up.

Jaeger pushed him out of the way, shunting his brother against the wall. 'Leave her alone, Berard!' he yelled, and as Meena scrambled to her feet, he quickly pulled her down the corridor towards his chamber.

Berard could hear Meena sobbing as she stumbled away.

Taking a deep breath, he hurried down the corridor in the opposite direction, determined to find Karsten.

CHAPTER FORTY THREE

They stood around the cauldron, watching as Entorp lifted it up, tipping its boiling contents into a cloth-covered, stone bowl. Once the liquid had cooled, it would be poured into water bags and those bags would be taken to Briga.

Biddy looked nervously at Derwa. 'You're sure this will work?'

'Well,' Derwa muttered, moving her long, white braid away from the flames. 'I do hope so. It has worked before.' She glanced over at the table where Edela sat, sipping her tea. 'Hasn't it?'

'Oh yes,' Edela smiled. 'It has. It should keep them asleep for a few hours. We don't want to knock them out for days!'

'No,' Entorp agreed, easing the cauldron back onto its hook. 'But nor do we want them to wake up before we're done!' He swallowed, staring at Biddy whose face was a ghostly mirror of his own. He could feel his heart quickening as he thought of having to go into the tower; worrying what he would do if the soldiers were wide awake.

'You needn't worry about that,' Derwa tried to reassure him as she shuffled back to the table. 'There's enough belladonna in there for a good nap.'

Entorp took a deep breath to steady his nerves, deciding that he needed to check the contents of his satchel again. The afternoon was already moving quickly, and he wanted to be prepared before night fell.

Biddy brought him a cup of chamomile tea. 'Here. It's cold, but it might help.'

Entorp turned and saw the concern in her eyes as he took the cup and sat down on the bed. 'Thank you. It might.'

Biddy walked over to let the puppies out, wondering when Jael would return. They'd barely seen her all day. 'And you think that Briga will be able to get the mixture into their food? Without being noticed?'

'She seems like the sort of woman who won't have a problem, if you ask me,' Branwyn smiled, trying to lift everyone's mood as she crawled around on her hands and knees, picking up all the things her granddaughter had dropped on the floor. 'I doubt anyone would want to question Briga if she got caught!' Looking around her house, she felt a pang of sadness that she would be leaving. After living here with Kormac for eighteen years, she'd never really imagined being anywhere else.

Until she knew what The Following had done to Tuura.

Now she couldn't wait to escape.

***

Jael and Fyn had spent most of the day ferrying weapons into the stables with Kormac, Aedan, and Aron, trying not to draw any attention to themselves. It had taken many trips, but finally, everything was in place.

Every sword, shield, and axe that Kormac had been able to make, find or borrow.

Hidden amongst the hay.

Jael smiled at Beorn, who did not smile back.

'You really think this will work?' he grumbled.

'It has to work. We need to get out of here quickly. We have to get to Oss,' Jael insisted, holding out an apple for Tig.

'There's a lot that could go wrong.'

Jael shrugged. 'True. But if we stay here, we're dead. And so is everyone on Oss. Which is much worse, I think.'

Beorn sighed, knowing she was right.

'The Following wants to kill everyone in Osterland,' Jael reminded him. 'Everyone. We have to do what we can to stop them here. It's not enough, but we have to make a start. If we can free Tuura, we can free ourselves. We can't help anyone else until we do.'

***

'What do you think?' Gant wondered, pulling his horse to a stop just before the edge of the ridge. His eyes were focused on the tall, stone walls in the distance. Dusk was fast approaching, and he was relieved that they had made it to within a short ride of Tuura's gates.

'I think those walls are high, and unless they open the gates willingly, we're going to struggle to find a way inside,' Aleksander said with a frown. 'We need to send someone in. Tomorrow. Someone who isn't me. Perhaps they'll even know you, so, we need to send someone else.'

Gant nodded. 'I'll ask Oleg.'

'Good idea. He can go first thing in the morning. They should open the gates early.' Aleksander doubted that the Tuuran dreamers needed to see their men waiting outside the walls to know that they were there, though. He shook his head, wishing he could just ride straight down to the fort and find out if everyone was safe. Now. 'We've no idea what's happening in there,' he sighed in frustration.

'If anything is happening at all,' Gant countered.

Aleksander's stomach gurgled. 'Let's get back. We can give

Oleg the good news.'

'Well, as long as our new king agrees,' Gant grinned, turning his horse around, pleased to think that their new king wasn't Osbert.

***

Briga was a round woman with a pinched face that looked as though it had been scrubbed with a brush. Red-faced and angry, she glowered up at Kormac. 'That's it?'

Kormac glanced behind himself. They were standing around the back of the soldier's hall, and although the sky was darkening, it was still light enough to be seen. He could feel his heart throbbing loudly, wishing that Briga didn't have such a booming voice. 'Yes,' he whispered, trying to encourage her to do the same. 'Derwa said you need to add two cups to each cauldron. It will look like you're just adding water to the stew.'

Briga's scowl deepened as she took the water bags from Kormac and sniffed. 'Well, if you say. Just for the towers, then? I make a separate stew to be taken round to those men.'

'Yes, best you add it to that cauldron only, just to be safe.'

Briga grunted, turning to leave.

'Briga!' Kormac hissed, scurrying after her. 'You won't forget about the temple, will you? The kitchen door?'

Briga turned around, eyeing him moodily. 'Said I'd do it, didn't I? I'll be there.' And she waddled away before he could say another word.

Kormac's mouth hung open as he watched her disappear around the corner of the hall. The success of their plan relied almost solely on Briga now.

He could only hope she'd be true to her word.

***

Haaron surveyed the hall with barely concealed disappointment.

He'd been looking forward to the feast all day, but as he walked past the tables, there appeared to be nothing on offer that he hadn't eaten countless times before, and not even the company could put a smile on his weary face. His lords and their ladies pranced around the elaborately decorated hall, gossiping with merchants from Kalmera and Silura. Bayla flittered between them all looking as elegant as ever, but as she approached, Haaron could see the tension in her face as she scanned the guests.

Haegen was there with Irenna, talking to Nicolene.

But where were the others?

'You need to go and find your sons!' Bayla hissed as Haaron helped himself to a goblet of wine. She removed the goblet immediately, pointing him towards the stairs. 'Now!' she grumbled. 'Before I am asked one more time where they all are!'

Haaron was ready to put Bayla in her place, but one look at the panic in her eyes stopped him. She was upset; not wanting to say her goodbyes tomorrow; not wanting to let go of her sons at all. He was beginning to wonder if sending them away was such a good idea after all. If only he'd been able to convince her to get rid of Jaeger and keep one of the other three, who were almost as hopeless, but not as much trouble.

Sighing, Haaron took one last look at his goblet and navigated his way through the guests, ignoring their smiles and greetings as he headed for the stairs.

***

They had barely spoken during supper, but as Biddy cleared the table, everyone started to rouse themselves, realising that in a few hours they would have to begin.

'Make sure that you're only taking what you need,' Kormac reminded his sons. He glanced at Kayla, who, Branwyn liked to gossip, was a hoarder. 'Likely we'll have to leave in a hurry.'

Alaric, who was still finishing his second bowl of soup, seemed comfortable with that notion. He had nothing to take, but he was eager to leave; determined to go along with them, no matter what happened.

'How exactly *will* we leave?' Biddy wondered. 'If it unfolds as we hope?'

'Well, it depends on where Axl and Aleksander are, of course, but ideally, we all leave on *Sea Bear*,' Jael said, searching through her chest, looking for her arm guards. 'We'll sail to Andala, leave you there, and Fyn and I will head for Oss as quickly as we can.'

'*If* we can get out of here,' Gisila said quietly. She was as desperate to reach Andala as the rest of them, but she had much less faith in their ability to do so. 'I imagine that The Following will do anything they can to stop us. They will try all sorts of evil things, surely?'

'I imagine so, my dear,' Edela murmured, patting her arm. 'But we have our symbols. We have Jael. And we have Eydis too.'

Eydis' head swung around in surprise. She had not said a word all evening. Her mind was full of fears for their escape, and worry about what was happening on Oss. She hadn't been listening to their conversation much at all. 'Me?' she exclaimed.

'Yes,' Edela said. 'You know that book, Eydis. Gerod thinks we can't do anything to stop him now, but he doesn't know about you. That you can see the pages of that book in your mind.'

Eydis felt around for her cup of water. Her mouth had gone dry. 'Well, I will try,' she mumbled, embarrassed by the attention that she could feel but not see. 'If you need me to.'

'Hopefully, we won't,' Jael assured her. 'Hopefully, we'll be on the ship before morning. But until then, I have a very important job for you, Eydis. I want you to take care of the puppies. I don't want them disappearing just when we need to leave, as they have a habit of doing!' Jael smiled, but her eyes did not sparkle. She just wanted the night to hurry along.

Pulling her whetstone from her pouch, she sat down with the sword Kormac had given her.

Trying not to think about *Toothpick*.

Impatient to begin.

***

Meena wriggled her toes, trying to avoid tapping herself, not wanting to incur Jaeger's wrath. The voice in her head was loud. It rang in her ears, warning that she wasn't safe.

But what could she do?

She was trapped.

Jaeger had dragged her back to his chamber and thrown her on the bed; slapped her, forced himself inside her, then abandoned her to sit in front of the book for the rest of the day; silently stewing, fingering through its crackling pages, ignoring her completely.

Her face still burned where he'd hit her. Her eye had closed up, and it hurt to even blink. She had remained on the bed, not wanting him to notice her at all. Jaeger had calmed down as he listened to her frantic explanations of what she had done with Morana; of how she'd had no choice but to stay with her aunt. But only slightly. He still seemed on edge as he crouched over the book.

The knock on the door made them both jump.

Egil was not there, so Jaeger got up to open it himself.

'Your mother is waiting on you,' Haaron said crossly as he looked his son over with distaste. Jaeger was naked from the waist up, red-faced and angry. 'You appear to have forgotten that she is holding a farewell feast for your brothers tonight. It is important to her that you are there to say goodbye to them. They'll be leaving in the morning.' Haaron tried to look past his son, wondering who else was inside the chamber, but Jaeger held the door close to his head, with no intention of opening it any wider. 'They are leaving in the morning,' Haaron tried again, his enthusiasm waning with every breath. 'Everyone is down there, waiting.'

'Fine!' Jaeger spat, shutting the door in his father's face.

Turning around to the bed, he searched for the tunic he had slept in, not caring to find something fresh. It lay crumpled in a heap under the furs he had tossed off the bed. 'I'm going to the hall,' he said mutely. 'You are not. You will stay here. Morana will be coming for us before midnight. You will stay here.' And shrugging the tunic over his head, he strode towards the door.

Meena watched him go, listening as the key turned with a click.

Imprisoned again.

***

Hanna had spent the day in a muddled panic, trying to think of another way to approach Berard; convinced that all he needed was a small nudge in the right direction.

Discovering that the queen was hosting a feast in the castle, she had invited herself along, hoping to find Berard. She had tried to avoid talking with the guests in the hall, hugging the walls, hoping not to attract anyone's attention.

But she had been disappointed to find that Berard wasn't even there.

Turning to leave, her face lightened as she saw him enter the hall. But he was not alone, and so she slunk back towards the slaves, waiting for his mother to stop fussing over him.

Bayla was incensed. 'What were you *doing?*' she muttered between tight lips, growling at Karsten in particular. 'I have been here for hours. Hours! Where have you both been?'

Karsten smiled at his mother, holding up a hand. 'Calm down! Calm down! Berard and I were saying our goodbyes. We wanted to get it out of the way tonight.'

Bayla inhaled sharply. 'Well, your wife has been very upset,' she grumbled. 'Abandoned by her husband!' And grabbing Karsten's hand, she dragged him towards Nicolene, who looked barely bothered to see him at all.

Karsten turned, winking at his brother.

Berard felt sick. Worried for Meena. Unsure that there was any hope for what he and Karsten had planned. He looked around for a slave with a mead bucket or a goblet of wine. Anything to help him feel better.

'Hello again,' Hanna said shyly as she crept up behind him.

Berard jumped but quickly looked relieved as he turned around. 'You're still here,' he sighed.

'Yes, of course. I meant everything I said earlier.'

'Good,' Berard whispered. 'Because I'm going to do it.' He looked over his shoulder as Jaeger entered the hall, then leaned into Hanna. 'I'm going to steal the Book of Darkness.'

***

'My lord.'

One of Tuura's most experienced dreamers was waiting

at his door. Gerod, who had been eating his evening meal in peace, was annoyed, but instantly curious. 'You have news?'

'The Brekkan army is here, lord,' she said quickly.

Gerod's eyes widened in surprise. 'At the gates?'

'No, close by. Waiting. In the forest.'

'Waiting for what?' He frowned so intensely that his head ached.

'I saw them making camp, preparing food. They did not appear to be going anywhere. But they will come tomorrow.'

'And have you any word, any messages from Hest?'

The dreamer shook her head, knowing that it would displease him.

'Leave me now, Ada,' Gerod snapped, closing the door before she had even begun her farewell. His body was jerking with fury. He needed to think. Yorik and Morana had abandoned him. Not considered what was happening in Tuura important enough. Yet, he had Jael Furyck here.

Did they not care about her any longer?

His hands shook as he tried to steady them by his sides.

Glancing at his half-eaten plate of food, he turned instead to the back of the door, reaching for his cloak.

***

'And who do we have here?' Jaeger wondered, his amber eyes sparking with interest at the sight of Hanna.

Berard spluttered. 'This is...' He shook his head, trying to think as he glanced at Karsten, but Karsten appeared to be arguing with his wife again.

Hanna was ready to splutter herself, immediately intimidated by the sheer size of Jaeger Dragos. It had to be him. 'My name is Hanna,' she said faintly, attempting to meet his intense eyes. 'I met your brother today. In the markets. He invited me along tonight, which was very kind of him.' She slipped her arm through Berard's, smiling.

Jaeger was surprised. '*Berard*?' He peered at his brother. 'Well, you have been keeping yourself busy.' He turned back to Hanna. 'If only he wasn't leaving for Solt in the morning.'

Hanna could feel Berard shaking against her. 'I agree,' she said quickly. 'Although, I'm not staying in Hest for long.'

'No?' Jaeger was intrigued. 'And where are you from?'

'Helsabor,' Hanna said calmly. 'But I've always sought adventure. I've not stayed in one place since I was a child. I plan to travel to Silura as soon as I can find passage on a ship.'

'And who is this?' Karsten smiled, squeezing himself into their small group, having noticed Berard's panicked face and Jaeger's close proximity to him.

'This is Hanna,' Berard said quickly. 'The woman I met in the markets today. You remember, I told you about her?'

Karsten's eyes widened. Berard had not told him how pretty she was. 'Yes, you did,' he murmured, his eyes lingering on Hanna's small mouth as her lips pursed, uncomfortable with his attention. 'I'm Karsten. Perhaps Berard told you about me?'

Hanna shook her head. 'No.'

Karsten looked put out, then laughed. 'Well, he will, I'm sure.' He wanted to turn to his right and punch Jaeger in the stomach; hard enough to knock him flying. 'You look unwell, Brother,' he sneered instead. 'Not getting enough sleep?'

Berard didn't think that roiling Jaeger was the way to go, but he couldn't get Karsten's attention to convince him of that.

Jaeger turned to Karsten. There was so much he could say to wipe that smug smile off his brother's ruined face, but he didn't need the distraction. Not with the ritual approaching. He ignored him instead and nodded to Hanna. 'If you'll excuse me,' he muttered, turning away, looking for the wine.

Berard let all the air out of his lungs in a great, hissing rush, watching as Jaeger disappeared into the guests. He blinked at

Hanna and Karsten. 'We need to talk!'

***

Axl was alert as he sat propped up against a tree; disturbed by being so close to Tuura; anxious about what was happening inside the fort.

Aware that he was the king.

He leaned forward with interest as Gant, Aleksander, and Oleg discussed strategies, waiting for the right moment to speak, but it never arrived.

'The reason has to be plausible. We have to think of someone you could be there to visit,' Gant said, slapping his neck. Every flying bug in the forest seemed to be buzzing around him.

'But why don't we just march to the gates?' Oleg wondered. 'Axl is the king now. They would hardly turn him away.'

Axl was pleased to have been acknowledged, at last. 'I agree,' he said quickly. 'They would be more likely to listen to a king with an army. But I think Gant and Aleksander are right. We don't want to expose the men to more danger than we need to. Not yet. Aleksander's dreams might just have been dreams.'

Aleksander bit his tongue.

'But likely they weren't. After the ravens and wolves? Something is definitely wrong. And we're here for a reason. But we won't be able to help anyone if we reveal ourselves too early.'

Aleksander blinked in surprise.

'Well then, let's get some sleep. And maybe we'll think up a reason for Oleg's visit by the time the sun rises,' Gant sighed, ready to stretch out, even if it was on an unforgiving slab of earth. He slapped his neck again. 'If there's anything left of us by the time the sun rises!'

Aleksander smiled, watching as Gant and Oleg helped Axl to his feet.

Sleep was the last thing on his mind.

He couldn't stop worrying about Jael.

***

'We have to be as quiet as we can,' Jael murmured, holding Eydis' hand as she reached for the door handle.

Branwyn took a deep breath as she lined up next to Biddy.

'And if anyone stops you, say you're going to visit Aedan. That Edela had a dream that their baby was sick, remember?'

They all nodded: Branwyn and Biddy, Kormac and Alaric, Gisila and Eydis. And Edela. She was up and dressed too, feeling unsteady on her feet as she leaned into Kormac, who had an arm firmly around her shoulder.

They were going to meet in the secret room. It was the safest place that Jael could think of to hide everyone while they attacked the towers and the temple.

There was more nervous nodding; an impatience to leave.

'Remember, take your time. Stick to your route. I'll meet you there.' Jael pulled open the door, surprised by how still the night felt. How quiet. They had suffered through a relentless battering of rain and wind for days, but they had heard nothing all night.

It reminded Jael of the silence before the raven storm.

The hairs rose on the back of her neck.

She thought of Eadmund and Oss, and squeezing Eydis' small hand, Jael led them out into the moonless night.

PART SEVEN

The Shadow Moon

CHAPTER FORTY FOUR

'Go,' Karsten hissed at Berard. 'Jaeger's had a few cups of wine now. He's not going anywhere for a while. Trust me.'

They stood by the entrance to the hall, staring back at Jaeger who sat at the high table between Haegen and their father, his head drooping slightly, his eyes bleary, struggling to focus.

Berard gulped.

'Go!' Karsten urged again before turning to Hanna. 'You go too. As soon as Berard has Meena and the book, he'll head for your ship. You need to get those men ready to leave in a hurry. I'll stay with Jaeger and keep him down here.'

Berard's boots were stuck to the flagstones; his eyes as round as two full moons.

'Berard,' Hanna whispered. 'Your brother's right. We have to act now. I'll get to the ship. Please hurry!' And with a grateful smile at Karsten, who, despite his leery looks was being very helpful, she hurried to the castle doors.

Karsten watched her go, then shoved Berard in the direction of the stairs.

Berard stumbled nervously, trying to focus on what he had to do.

Get Meena. Get the book. Get to the ship.

'Don't worry,' Karsten whispered after him. 'I'll keep Jaeger busy.'

Karsten's eyes widened as he turned around. Jaeger was

struggling to his feet alongside Haegen, Irenna, and Nicolene, who all appeared to be leaving.

The guests had started dispersing much earlier than he'd anticipated.

He hurried towards them.

***

Morana was ready.

Her tiredness and hunger had given way to an all-encompassing sense of peace. She felt clean. Open. Her mind was in complete harmony with her body, as though she was not solid at all; not flesh nor bone, but mist and lightness.

Like smoke, she would drift into the night air.

Into the Dolma.

Morana shook out her hair, taking another drink of the ritual mead she had painstakingly prepared. It was bitter, but she kept drinking until her cup was drained.

Staring up at the window, she could feel the darkness, so heavy and powerful. Waiting for them. It would wrap the Followers in its shadowy embrace, hiding them from anyone who would try to follow them to the Crown of Stones.

Soon.

Morana felt neither hot nor cold as she let the fire slowly die.

She sat on the bed, pulling on her boots.

Soon.

***

Entorp had thought about his wife and children all day.

Their loss had caused a pain so great that he'd taught himself to pretend that it hadn't even happened. It was a black hole whose edges he'd skirted for many years. But now, as he thought about The Following and what they had taken from him, he opened up his heart and let that searing pain motivate him.

Standing before the door of the southern tower, he tried to still his body as he reached for the iron handle. He had waited there for some time, lurking in the shadows, listening. The moonless sky covered the night like a cloak, and he couldn't hear or see a soul. Just an annoying dog who kept creeping closer, wondering if he had any food to share.

Entorp hadn't heard any noises from inside the tower in a while. He knew that he had to open the door and begin. It was the only way to know if they stood a chance. Jael was waiting in the secret room, relying on him, he reminded himself.

They all were.

Patting his satchel, and feeling his tools through its soft leather flap, Entorp swallowed and turned the handle, pushing open the door.

***

Berard glanced behind himself every few steps, but he couldn't hear anyone coming. And then, just as he rounded the corner to Jaeger's chamber, he saw Egil.

Gulping, he pressed his boots onto the flagstones to stop himself, watching as Egil took a key from his pouch and unlocked the door. Thoughts flew through Berard's mind so quickly. He was not the biggest, nor the strongest, nor the most handsome of his brothers, but he had always been the cleverest.

So, taking a deep breath, he waited until Egil was pushing open the door before rushing at him, knocking him into the chamber and slamming the door shut behind them both.

Egil tripped into the room. 'Wh-wh-what are you doing?' he exclaimed, turning to Berard who immediately punched him hard, right on the very tip of his hooked nose.

Karsten had taught him that.

'Make them cry,' he'd said. 'You're small and weedy, but if you can make them cry, they won't be able to see a thing.'

And so, Berard did it again. His hand ached, and he cringed as Egil stumbled, toppling over, which was a feat, considering what a round, well-balanced man he was. Meena scrambled off the bed in surprise, hurrying to Berard.

'We have to tie him up!' Berard cried, grimacing, shaking his hand, looking around the chamber. He didn't see any rope and quickly changed his mind. 'We have to leave!'

Meena tapped her head, shuffling her feet, scared.

'Meena!' Berard yelled, gripping her arms. 'We're *leaving*! We're taking the book! It's evil. We have to get it away from Jaeger! Quickly! There's no time!'

Meena blinked and nodded.

Reaching down, she pulled the knife from Berard's scabbard and lunged at Egil, who was moaning loudly as he tried to sit up. She ran the blade across his fleshy throat, wiping it on her dress and handing it back to Berard before picking up the book, which Jaeger had left behind on the table.

Berard's mouth fell open, and he didn't move, staring at Egil's dying body as he gurgled wetly, falling backwards with a thump.

'We have to go!' Meena urged, wrapping her cloak around her shoulders and securing the book beneath it. 'Come on!' She hurried to the door, looking back for Berard.

He took one last look at Egil, whose throat was leaking all over the stone floor now, and shook his head, remembering that Hanna was waiting for them.

They had to hurry.

'And where do you think *you're* going?' Morana wondered, standing in the doorway. She could smell death approaching. She could feel that the book was in danger. Reaching out, she wrapped her long fingers around Meena's wrist. 'Where do you think *you're* going, little mouse?'

***

Entorp crept into the tower room.

It was cold and smelled of old farts. The fire had burned so low that there was barely any flame in the pit. He couldn't see where the guards were, but he could hear their guttural snoring.

Dipping his hand into his satchel, Entorp pulled out a soapstone lamp and tiptoed towards the fire, holding the wick to the last of the flames; holding his breath, for surely when there was light, the soldiers would wake?

***

Jaeger didn't think that he'd drunk much, but he could feel the effect of the wine. It was as though he had swallowed a barrel full. His head was spinning, and so was the room.

'You need to take your brother to his bed,' Bayla insisted, glaring at her sons.

Karsten rebuffed his mother at every turn, trying to ply Jaeger with even more wine.

Haegen knew that Bayla was right, but he frowned, not wanting to face the strain. His leg, though recovered, was not ready to have all of Jaeger's dead weight leaning on it. 'You'll need to help me, Brother,' he motioned to Karsten.

Karsten had sat down, trying to convince everyone to stay with him, and he had succeeded for a while. 'Already?' he said, with an easy grin. 'But this is the last time we'll all be together for who knows how long, and you want to go to bed now?' He held up his goblet of wine. 'Why leave so soon?'

Irenna sighed impatiently. 'Karsten, we all have to leave early in the morning.' She smiled at Bayla. 'I think I'll turn in. It's going to be a long day tomorrow.'

Bayla ignored her. 'Karsten,' she muttered, noticing that the hall was empty now, with only the slaves and servants milling about, clearing up after the guests. 'Help your brother, please. Your father is far too useless to do anything!' It had not escaped her notice that Haaron was avoiding her eyes.

But Karsten knew that he had to wait until he saw Berard and Meena slip down the stairs. He had to keep everyone in the hall until then. 'Irenna, Mother,' he smiled warmly. 'Just one more drink? A toast, perhaps? To the Dragos family! To rebuilding our reputation, our kingdom! To conquering all of Osterland!'

They all stared at Karsten without enthusiasm.

'Well, if you're not going to do anything to help your brother,' Haaron grumbled at Karsten, 'then I suppose I shall have to.' And sighing at the mere thought of it, he stood, glaring at his wife.

Karsten turned to the entranceway, trying to see up the stairs, but there was no sign of Berard and Meena.

He had to do something.

Jaeger couldn't go up there. Not yet.

***

Berard thought fast.

Rushing past Meena, he snatched at Morana's robe, yanking her into the chamber so hard that she stumbled, falling to her knees. Leaving her on the floor, he grabbed Meena's hand and pulled her through the door, slamming it shut behind them. Quickly realising that he didn't have the key, he burst back through the door just as Morana was struggling to her feet, knocking it into her, tipping her backwards.

Rushing to Egil's dead body, Berard saw the key lying in the spreading pool of blood.

'Aarrghh!' Morana scrambled to her feet, launching herself at Berard, wrapping her arms around his throat.

Berard spun quickly, throwing her off his back. She was so light that she flew towards the flagstones like a sack, and he scooped the bloody key into his hand, running back to the door, stopping as Morana charged him again. He turned and punched her on the nose as hard as he could, watching as she fell backwards, cracking her head on the flagstones.

She didn't move this time, and swallowing, Berard hurried through the door, slamming it after him, turning the key in the lock.

Grabbing Meena's shaking hand, they ran down the corridor.

***

His lamp was burning strongly now, and none of the soldiers had moved, so Entorp shook away his nerves and hurried to the barrels of ale, placing his lamp on the floor and pushing them away from the wall.

They scratched and creaked loudly across the wooden floor. He froze, turning around. Three men lay on the beds along the wall, haphazardly splayed across the furs. Two sat slumped over at the table, their heads on their plates. He couldn't hear any footsteps overhead. Hopefully, those men were asleep too.

Turning back around, Entorp brought the lamp down, looking along the wall for the symbol, but he couldn't see it.

Panic throbbed in his chest.

He couldn't see the symbol!

Aron had seen one in the northern tower. Aedan had seen one in the eastern tower, but Kormac had not had the opportunity to search the other two towers. There had been too many guards downstairs.

They had just assumed the symbols were there.

But what if they were wrong?

Entorp took a deep breath to calm his rising panic, pushing the barrels further away from the wall. But still nothing. He could feel his heart skipping with urgency. He thought of his wife and blinked.

He needed to think.

Picking up the lamp, Entorp brought it down across the wall to the floor, noticing some markings. Bending closer, he could see circular outlines where the barrels had obviously been at an earlier time. Crouching down, he ran his hand under a small stool, feeling the deep indentations in the stone wall.

The symbol!

***

Jaeger's head was up.

And suddenly clear.

He straightened his back, fighting off Haegen's attempts to help.

'Jaeger!' Karsten called as his youngest brother staggered

away from the table. 'Jaeger, wait!'

'Go after him!' Bayla urged, worried that Jaeger would topple down the stairs. 'Haaron!' she grumbled, pushing her husband forward. '*Do* something!'

Haaron was ready to argue that Jaeger was perfectly able to walk on his own, when he heard the blood-curdling cry.

'Nooooo!'

Haaron turned towards the entranceway, watching as Jaeger punched Berard in the face; watching as Berard fell back onto the stairs. He felt his right hand twitch, moving towards his sword.

'What is happening?' Bayla cried from behind him.

Karsten was running past his father, Haegen ahead of him.

***

Hanna stood on the path, waiting.

The sky was so dark that she couldn't see a thing.

Ulf and his crew had dragged the ship into the shallows and were now sitting at their oars, waiting.

All of them, waiting for Berard.

***

'Berard!' Meena screamed as Jaeger dragged her away.

'What are you doing?' he seethed, grabbing her chin, forcing her to look up at him, his emotions tumbling with the force of a waterfall. 'You were *leaving*? With *him*?'

Meena's face ached where he'd hit her, and she cringed

away from him. 'I, I want to leave,' she mumbled. 'I want to go!'

Jaeger looked as though she'd stabbed him. He raised his hand and slapped her hard across the face.

'Jaeger!' Haegen was there quickly, pulling back his brother's hand before he could touch Meena again. 'No!'

Jaeger elbowed Haegen in the eye and drew his sword, holding his brother at bay. Haegen shook his head, blinking as he stood shoulder to shoulder with Karsten, both of them hands out, trying to decide what to do.

Haaron quickly joined them, and then Berard, who had scrambled back to his feet, his eyes on Meena who cowered before Jaeger, her face a bruised mess of terror.

Berard drew his sword, rushing forward.

He'd already decided what to do.

***

Entorp, Kormac, Aedan, and Aron came back to the secret room, one by one.

If there had been any light, everyone would have seen the ghostly sheen on their faces, the shaking of their hands, the sweat drenching their tunics.

But each one of them had done it: carved the symbol into the tower walls, then cut through The Following's own symbol, hopefully breaking the binding spell.

And now it was time to go to the temple.

'Grandmother,' Jael murmured, tucking Edela's cloak tightly around her knees as she sat on the floor, leaning against the hay bales. 'Keep Eydis close. If we get in trouble, if you see anything, you'll need to guide Eydis.'

Edela nodded, her eyes alert, despite the hour. Her stomach was aching where Evaine had stabbed her, but that only spurred her on. She was never going to get back to Oss and see to that murderous little witch if they didn't get out of Tuura. 'I will. We'll sit quietly together and focus on what is happening. I'm sure there's something we can do. Don't worry.' She squeezed Jael's hand. 'Be careful. Be more careful than you normally would. Please.' It was too dark to see Jael's eyes, but she knew they would have been avoiding hers.

'You have the key?' Jael asked Branwyn.

Branwyn nodded, shaking all over.

'No one knows that you're in here, so just stay quiet. No light, no noise. Just wait. We'll come back soon,' Jael whispered to her aunt. 'We'll come back for you.'

Gisila, standing beside her sister, was struggling to breathe. It all felt impossible. Too dangerous. Jael had ridden off to many battles, and she had seen the scars now. She had always been so fearless and determined, just like Ranuf, but this... 'Jael.' She didn't know what to say. Her eyes filled with tears that her daughter couldn't see.

'Ready?' Jael asked Fyn, who she could feel jiggling nervously beside her.

'Ready,' he mumbled, readjusting his sword for the twentieth time.

'Right, then what are we waiting for?' Jael smiled. 'Let's go and pay The Following a visit.'

CHAPTER FORTY FIVE

'Berard!' Meena shrunk away, clutching her face as Jaeger turned to block Berard's blade with his own.

Haegen drew his sword.

'No!' Berard screamed. 'No! This is *my* fight!' He slashed his sword towards Jaeger's waist. 'Take her, Karsten!' he pleaded. 'Take Meena and go!'

Karsten felt torn.

Berard could not fight Jaeger and win, but Meena had the book. He could see her clasping her cloak awkwardly to her chest. She must have hidden it beneath there.

He was not inclined to do anything Jael Furyck said, but what Hanna had revealed about that book...

Drawing his sword, Karsten skirted Jaeger and Berard, attempting to reach Meena.

Jaeger sliced through Berard's tunic, drawing blood from his shoulder.

'Aarrghh!' Berard yelped, jerking away.

Bayla panicked. 'Stop this! What are you *doing*? Jaeger, stop this!'

'Put down your swords!' Haaron bellowed. 'Now!'

Jaeger and Berard eyed each other, swords poised, waiting to see who would make the next move. It was as though no one else was there.

'You thought to *take* her from me?' Jaeger snarled. 'Why?

Why would you do that, Berard? We were in this together! But now you *betray* me?'

Berard didn't want to talk at all. Meena had the book. Egil was dead. Morana...

He had to get Meena to safety.

Now.

He lunged, aiming for Jaeger's thigh. Jaeger jumped back, distracted, sensing movement out of the corner of his eye.

'The book! The book! She has the book!' Morana screeched, stumbling down the stairs, blood dripping down the back of her robe, pouring from her nose. She could barely hear with the clanging in her ears, but she knew that she had to stop them leaving with the book.

Jaeger spun around as Karsten grabbed Meena's hand. He snatched at her sleeve, pulling her back towards him.

Losing her balance, Meena stumbled, dropping the book.

Jaeger froze, watching as it fell to the floor.

Berard froze, watching as Jaeger turned to Meena, his face contorted with rage. Berard raised his sword, but not in time. Jaeger twisted back, blocking his blow, fury exploding from every part of him.

'He tried to kill me!' Morana screamed. 'Kill him!'

'You would take the *book* from me?' Jaeger roared, swinging back his blade and chopping it down, straight through Berard's arm.

Bayla gasped in horror as the arm fell to the flagstones.

Meena's eyes popped open as Karsten yanked her quickly towards him.

Jaeger bent down to scoop up the book, handing it to Morana, not troubled in the slightest as Berard collapsed to the ground, his mouth wrenched open in shock.

Haaron drew his sword. 'Haegen, Karsten, take your mother. Get Berard. Take the girl and go,' he said firmly.

Haegen rushed to help Berard up. His brother was whimpering. The stump where his arm used to be was gushing blood. 'Get me a cloth!' he cried to Irenna, who was already running back into the hall.

'No!' Bayla grabbed Haaron's arm as he turned to face Jaeger. 'You will not do this! It doesn't need to be like this! Jaeger, Jaeger! Stop this now! We are family! What are you doing? No!'

'My love,' Haaron said calmly, his eyes on Jaeger. 'You will go now. I am the king. This is *my* family. And *I* will defend it. You will leave the castle. Now. Our sons will keep you safe.'

Bayla could feel tears burning her eyes; panic blooming in her chest.

She took one last look at her husband before Karsten pushed her down the corridor, towards the doors.

*****

Gerod strode around the fort flanked by two rows of temple guards.

It was so dark that he could barely see one foot in front of the other. Burning lamps hung outside a few houses, but it was not enough to stop him from stepping in a lump of horse shit. He grimaced, lifting up his boot and shaking it in disgust.

Arriving at Branwyn and Kormac's house, he turned to the guards, lowering his voice. 'Four of you will fire this house. See that no one escapes and that nothing else catches. I don't want the whole fort going up. Four more of you will go to the stables where the Osslanders are housed. Burn it to the ground. Return to me in the temple once you're done. We need to start preparing. The Brekkans could attack at any time.'

Gerod motioned to one of his commanders. 'Take your men to the gates. I want reinforcements up on those ramparts. Wake up any soldier who is not already up there. Light your fires. Ready your weapons. They may come before dawn.' Satisfied with that as a beginning, Gerod turned back to the temple.

It was time to gather his dreamers together.

***

Haegen scooped Berard into his arms and hurried outside to where Karsten was waiting with Meena, Bayla, and Nicolene. Irenna followed them out with an armful of napkins which she quickly started packing around Berard's bleeding stump.

'We are not *leaving*!' Bayla insisted, too frantic to even look at Berard. 'Go back in there! Help your father! Stop your brother! You have to *do* something!'

'There is a ship, Mother,' Karsten said firmly, grabbing her shoulders. 'Jaeger has the book. The Following is there. We have to leave.'

'What book? *Leave*? What do you mean? What has any of this to do with The Following?' Bayla demanded. 'Go and help your Father! Please!'

Haegen ripped one of the linen napkins in half, tying it tightly around the stump, staring at Berard's face. It was dark, but he could tell that his brother was barely conscious. 'We have to get help. We have to find Sitha!' He stood and turned back to the castle.

'Haegen!' Karsten bellowed after him. 'You need to trust me! You all do! Berard was trying to take that book for a reason. We have to leave! There's a ship! We cannot stay here!'

Haegen was confused. He heard the panic in Karsten's voice, but he wasn't about to let his father be killed. He wasn't about to let Jaeger get away with what he had done to Berard. Drawing his sword, he ran back to the castle.

'Haegen!' Irenna called after him.

'We're not safe here... Hanna...' Berard breathed before

passing out.

But Haegen didn't hear him as he approached the castle steps, frowning. Rows of hooded men and women stood in front of the doors now, blocking his path. They didn't move or speak as they stared at him.

Swallowing, Haegen turned around, recognising some of the castle guards who were slowly approaching. 'Darius!' he bellowed. 'Get your men! Eron, with me!'

They didn't move.

Their swords were not drawn. Their arms remained by their sides as they stared at him too.

More guards arrived, but no one rushed to Haegen's side. He looked back to where Karsten was arguing with Nicolene; to where Irenna bent over Berard, trying to stop his bleeding; to where his mother was panicking.

He could hear his heart beating loudly in his ears. Sheathing his sword, he turned and ran back to his family.

'Haegen! No!' Bayla cried, grabbing his arm. 'What about your father? You have to go back! Save him!'

'The Following is there,' Haegen panted, his eyes up, checking for any sign that they were coming after them. 'The guards, they... we have to go, Mother! Karsten's right!'

'I am *not* leaving!' Nicolene insisted.

'Oh, yes you are,' Karsten growled, glaring at her. 'You may like fucking my brother, but you are *my* wife, and you're coming with me!' He grabbed Nicolene's hand. 'I am not leaving you behind!'

'But the children?' Irenna swallowed, glancing back at the castle. She could see the row of hooded figures blocking the doors now. Soldiers were moving into place in front of them. She panicked. 'We need to get the children!'

Karsten turned to Haegen. 'Take everyone to the ship. Follow the road away from the castle. It's waiting in Balder's Cove. She'll be there.'

Haegen looked confused. 'Who?'

'Her name is Hanna. She has a ship.' Karsten stared at his sister-in-law. She was smaller but more reliable than Nicolene. 'Irenna will come with me. We'll get the children and meet you there.' And before anyone could protest, he grasped Irenna's hand and together they ran to the edge of the square, disappearing around the side of the castle, heading for the kitchen door.

***

Haaron tightened his grip on the sword, watching Jaeger's every move, his body vibrating, his eyes never leaving his son.

He could sense Morana on the stairs, and as disturbing as her betrayal was, the more pressing concern he had was ending his son's life.

If that was even his son anymore.

'What are you *waiting* for?' Morana hissed, baring her teeth. 'We have to go! Kill him now!'

Jaeger smiled, all thoughts of Meena gone.

Morana had the book.

And now he had his father.

***

Haegen carried Berard away from the castle.

His brother felt limp, light; his head banging against his shoulder.

Bayla hurried along beside him. He could feel the tension in her, but his mind was back at the castle with his father. With

Irenna and Karsten.

With Jaeger.

He frowned, hoping he was making the right decision. Doubting himself. Changing his mind every few steps. But he knew, deep down inside he knew, that to go back would mean death for them all.

'The book,' Meena mumbled over and over again, slowing down, looking over her shoulder. 'The book.'

'Will you *shut up!*' Bayla growled furiously as she turned and snatched Meena's arm, dragging her along, pushing Haaron far out of her mind.

But not far enough.

Tears burst from her eyes again, streaming down her face.

It was dark.

There was no one to see.

***

'Aarrghh!' Haaron screamed as the tip of Jaeger's sword dug into his stomach. He staggered backwards, feeling old. Not sharp at all. His youth flashed past his eyes, and he saw the taunting image of the warrior he had once been: arms almost the size of Jaeger's; taut skin over well-worked muscle; shoulders that were broad and strong. He stepped back, swinging his sword again, reminding himself of who he was.

Haaron Dragos, King of Hest.

Old, but not dead yet.

'You will not rule here!' he bellowed, deflecting Jaeger's blade, feinting to the left, letting his son chase his shadow before stabbing his sword into Jaeger's side.

Jaeger growled and jerked away, grimacing.

It was time for the ritual, he knew. He could feel it.

'We have to leave!' Morana was urging behind him. 'Finish him! Hurry!'

But Haaron wasn't going anywhere.

He swung to the left, dipping, catching Jaeger's sword on the edge of his blade. Jaeger barrelled forward with his enormous bulk, swinging his sword from side to side and Haaron was quickly on the back foot, struggling for breath, trying to parry each heavy blow as they came faster and faster at him.

And eventually, he stumbled.

Lashing out with his foot, Jaeger kicked his father to the flagstones.

Haaron toppled over, feeling the painful crack of his back against the hard stone floor, and then Jaeger was over him. 'You will not rule here!' he repeated desperately, panting, staring into his son's vengeful eyes.

'Oh, Father, how right you are,' Jaeger snarled. 'I will rule *everywhere!*' And standing up, he took his sword in both hands, slamming the blade down into his father's chest.

Haaron's eyes burst open in horror.

He felt nothing but surprise, wanting more of an end than this, desperate to hold on, but then he saw the sudden explosion of darkness as death came to claim him.

Bayla, he thought fleetingly.

Bayla.

***

They were at the kitchen door.

Jael reached for the handle, hoping that Briga had indeed managed to hide away and open the bolts for them. She turned the large iron nob, cringing at the angry creak as it split the silence; breathing out in relief as the door gave way, creaking some more as she pushed it open.

Turning back to the Osslanders waiting behind her, Jael motioned for everyone to follow her, and one by one, they disappeared inside the temple.

***

Hanna was surprised to see so many shadowy figures rushing down the road towards her. She didn't know what to do. Her feet wouldn't move. She couldn't see Berard or Karsten.

There was no one she recognised at all.

'Are you Hanna?' came the breathless cry.

'Yes,' she answered tentatively.

'The book,' Berard moaned, his eyes flicking open. He felt the sharp, demanding pain in his arm and howled in agony.

'Berard?' Hanna recognised his voice. As they came closer, she saw that the man was carrying Berard in his arms. 'Berard!'

'Who are you?' Bayla wanted to know.

'Where is your ship?' Haegen demanded, panting. The climb up the gravel road with his brother in his arms had been a challenge.

Hanna nodded quickly, showing him to the path, but Bayla was reluctant to go. So was Nicolene.

Where were Karsten and Irenna?

***

Jaeger held the book against his chest, feeling his breathing slow.

629

'We don't have time to stand around!' Morana felt like vomiting. The noise in her head was as demanding as a hammer as she stalked around the body of Haaron Dragos, bleeding all over the entranceway. There was no time to enjoy such a sight, though. 'We don't have time!' she growled, hurrying towards the doors where Yorik and the Followers gathered, waiting impatiently.

'We must go!' Yorik called. 'Morana!'

Jaeger blinked, reminded suddenly of Meena. In all the noise and violence, she had disappeared, and he felt the loss of her mingling with the relief at being reunited with the book.

He frowned.

Where had she gone?

'Hurry!' Morana cried, turning back to Jaeger, imploring him forward. 'We must get to the stones! Now!'

'I'll meet you there,' Jaeger said mutely, walking past her. 'I have to get Meena.'

'*What*?' Morana was apoplectic, her teeth gnashing in fury. 'What for? No!'

But Jaeger strode towards the doors, past the row of murmuring, hooded figures, and out into the night.

***

The torches lighting the corridor made Jael feel exposed. She wanted to blow each one out as she crept around it. Her boots sounded loud on the flagstones. The silence was so absolute that she felt sure The Following would hear her breathing.

Turning back to Beorn, she motioned him to the right. Hopefully, Alaric was correct in his assumption that the corridor would lead her men to the guard's sleeping quarters. She turned to the left with Fyn and Aedan, hoping to find their way to the rear entrance of Marcus' chamber.

But when they rounded the corner, they found something better.

***

Meena stayed behind on the road.

She felt caught. Berard had come to save her. She had killed a man. They had hurt Morana. Maybe killed her too.

Berard had lost his arm.

But they didn't have the book.

She had heard Berard's faint pleas, begging his brother to go back to the castle, but Haegen wasn't listening. He had taken Berard down to the ship.

A ship to where?

Meena tapped her head with both hands, shuffling her feet. She wanted to escape with them, but if they left the book behind, Morana and The Following would raise that woman. She shuddered, knowing what that would mean; knowing that she couldn't leave with them. Not while the book was with Morana.

But what could she do?

'What are you *doing*?' Karsten bellowed, racing up to Meena; Irenna following behind him; both of them carrying sleepy-eyed children. 'Get down to the ship!'

Meena's mouth opened and closed. 'The book,' she mumbled.

'We have to leave it behind!' Karsten hurried past her, searching for the entrance to the path, trying to soothe his sons who were both whimpering over his shoulders. He disappeared down the rise. 'Hurry up!'

Irenna followed closely behind him, her youngest daughter

sobbing from her hip; her two other children too scared to say a word as they hurried behind their mother.

But Meena didn't move because she could hear someone else coming.

***

Marcus' mouth dropped open at the sight of Jael Furyck standing before him, sword drawn, two men behind her.

Jael sighed, relieved that he was still alive. It would hopefully make things easier. 'I need my sword. Gerod took it from me. He burned the book,' she whispered hoarsely.

Marcus' long face remained impassive, but he nodded and held a finger to his lips, then motioned for Jael and her men to follow him back down the corridor towards the scroll room, hoping that was where Gerod had stored her sword.

***

'Meena!'

He was just a shape. A black mass rushing towards her in the darkness, but she knew him, and her legs shook.

And her face ached.

But she didn't move.

Karsten stopped, ducking back down amongst the thorny shrubs. He had come back for Meena. Berard loved Meena, so Karsten had come back for her.

But when he got there, he could see that Jaeger had her.

He turned back down the hill, sliding, stumbling through

the undergrowth towards the ship. They had to leave. They had to get to Saala.

He shook his head, not believing that he was considering such a thing. But Berard would die if they did not get help. And there was no help to be found in Hest anymore. Not with The Following in control.

Meena shook all over as Jaeger held her in his arms.

'I thought you had gone!' he sighed, squeezing her. 'But you cannot leave, Meena. You are mine.'

Meena nodded against his chest, cringing as her face touched him. It hurt. Tears rolled down her cheeks as she thought of Berard, and they hurt too, stinging the cuts on her face where he had broken her skin.

She thought of Morana and the book. Of dead Egil and the ritual and The Following.

But mostly of Berard.

Jaeger took her hand, holding it so tightly that Meena thought her bones might shatter. 'Come!' he said loudly. 'We have to go. We need to get to the stones!' And dragging her away, they disappeared into the night.

***

They had waited for hours in the secret room at the back of the stables; jumping at every sound; worried by every rustle.

Edela kept Eydis close. Her body felt weak, but her mind was alert, and she knew that they were surrounded by danger. She could feel it approaching like a cloud in the distance. It was a black cloud, and it was low in the sky, and it threatened death and destruction, and so Edela remained alert, trying to calm her mind but awaken all of her senses.

She was determined to be ready.

They had come here for her. She had to help them leave safely.

But in the end, it was Eydis who called out. 'Fire!' she whispered hoarsely, gripping Edela's hand. 'Fire!'

CHAPTER FORTY SIX

Kormac and Aron were not in the temple.

They were not in the secret room, either.

They had been roaming the streets, waiting for the soldiers to wake up; desperate to see if the binding spell was broken; hoping they could convince those men to go with them to the temple and help Jael defeat The Following.

When the fire started, Kormac and Aron had seen flames rising over the buildings in the distance. They had raced to the house, quickly sliding into the shadows at the sight of the temple guards who were standing around, watching the thatch burn. Kormac could hear the frantic bleating of his goats, the panicked clucking of his chickens – all of them sensing the danger in the hot, smoking flames that were destroying his house. He turned to Aron. 'Go back to the gates. See if any of the soldiers are awake. Get help now!' And pushing his son away, he took a deep breath, stepping towards the guards.

There were four of them; only four, but he could feel the quickening thud of his heart in his chest. 'What are you doing?' Kormac bellowed.

The red-breasted men turned in unison, blinking in confusion, looking back to the house, surprised that Kormac wasn't in it.

'Get him!' one of the guards yelled, drawing his sword and charging.

Kormac turned and ran, the desperate pleas of his dying animals ringing in his ears as he slipped between the houses.

They were still bound! They were still bound!

***

'Where?' Entorp asked breathlessly, kneeling before Eydis. 'Where's the fire?'

He was sniffing the air, listening for any sound, but he couldn't smell or hear anything.

'Here!' Eydis cried, struggling to her feet, hands out. 'We must free the horses! We have to escape! The fire is *here*!'

'Tig!' Biddy grabbed Branwyn's arm. 'Give me the key!'

Edela was silent, visions of an old dream flashing past her eyes anew. She remembered seeing Jael and Aleksander fleeing Tuura.

It was in flames.

She couldn't breathe.

And then she smelled the smoke.

***

The door to the scroll room was the same as every other: wooden panels, iron handle. Nothing unusual, apart from the four big locks running down the right-hand side.

Jael frowned at Marcus, impatiently twitching her toes.

Marcus pulled his spare set of keys from his pouch and carefully inserted each key into each lock.

It took some time.

Jael kept glancing up and down the corridor. The only noise she could hear was the squeak and moan of Marcus' keys. What had happened to Beorn and the men? She would have expected to hear swords clashing by now.

Screams.

Anything.

Marcus finally pushed open the door, then lifted a torch out of its sconce and ushered Jael inside. The scrolls were tightly packed into thin shelves that rose from the floor to the ceiling. It was dark, musty, and tiny, with a passageway between the shelves that was barely wide enough for Marcus to squeeze through.

But squeeze through it he did.

Heart pounding, he walked quickly to the back of the room, to the chests where the elders secured items of great value.

Jael squeezed in behind him.

There were six chests. She tried a lid. They were locked as well.

Sighing impatiently, she turned to Marcus, who handed her the torch as he fiddled with his keys, bending over to unlock each one.

Jael stared into the flame, a sudden image of Aleksander bursting into view. He was sitting against a tree in a forest, his head flopped to one side, sleeping. A fire was burning low before him.

And lying all around him were men she knew.

The Brekkan army.

***

Aron started screaming as he raced across the face of the gates. 'Fire! Fire!' He didn't know who would respond; if anyone was even awake. Were the soldiers freed from their spell? Would they return to being the good men, the friends he had known?

Would they help him?

'Fire!' He ran on, screaming, trying to rouse the soldiers as he passed the hall. They were either going to chase him or help him. 'Fire!' he cried, opening the door to the northern tower. The smoke was drifting now, thirsty flames rising into the night sky.

'Fire!' one of the soldiers roared as he emerged from the tower, blinking. 'Quick!'

'Aron!' Another soldier stumbled outside, rubbing his eyes. 'Where is it?'

'My parent's house!'

The soldier frowned, pointing to flames which were coming from the opposite direction. 'That's not your parent's house,' he said slowly.

Aron's eyes widened in horror. 'The stables!' he shouted and ran.

***

Marcus closed the last chest and turned to Jael. 'It's not here,' he whispered, frowning.

Jael tried not to let the disappointment consume her.

'Well, maybe Gerod can tell me where it is,' she growled, remembering his sneering face as he ordered those men to murder her. 'Show me where he is.'

***

The stables were on fire.

Biddy and Entorp rushed in to release the frantic horses who were snorting and blowing, banging around their stalls, worried by the smoke; panicked by the quickly growing heat from the flames as they caught and spread.

'Tig!' Biddy cried. 'Tig!' The smoke tickled her throat and stung her eyes as she ran forward, not knowing which stall he was in.

She couldn't see.

Entorp hurried behind her, opening every stall he came across, trying his best to shoo the horses in the direction of the secret room, but they reared up on their hind-legs, charging around the burning stables, confused, getting in each other's way.

Panicking.

It was a complete mess.

Branwyn and Kayla raced in to help.

'Come on, come on,' Branwyn soothed, getting behind the horses, holding her arms out wide, Kayla on her opposite side. 'Go, go, go!' And they flapped their arms, trying to funnel the horses through the door to the room.

The stable doors were on fire. It was the only way out now.

Biddy reached the last stall and found Tig. He had shrunk back into the shadows, trying to escape the flames. 'Tig!' she croaked. 'Let's go, come on!'

Recognising Biddy's voice, he tentatively stepped forward as she opened the door to his stall.

'Come on! Come on, Tig! Let's go!' she pleaded, coughing uncontrollably now.

Entorp was by her side. 'Come on, Tig! Go!' He flapped his arms like Branwyn and Tig hurried off after the other horses who had finally all aimed in the same direction. They charged through the door in a line, Branwyn, Entorp, Kayla, and Biddy running after them as the flames chewed through the stable walls with ever-increasing hunger.

***

Kormac raced around the fort, trying to evade the temple guards until he came to the stables which he was horrified to see were on fire.

Soldiers he recognised were throwing water at the doors, trying to extinguish the flames. They looked him up and down but made no move towards him, so Kormac kept running until he reached the rear of the stables, looking for the door to the secret room.

The smoke was in his throat. He was struggling to breathe, not having run this much since he was a boy. But he didn't stop. He thought of Branwyn.

He didn't stop.

'Kormac!' Branwyn screamed as he ran past. 'Kormac!'

He skidded to a halt and rushed back to his wife, pulling her into his arms, inhaling the smoke in her hair, quickly looking around, checking who was there. They all were. And so was Aron, much to his relief. 'The horses?' he asked.

'They're all out,' Biddy croaked.

'We have to leave,' Edela said weakly. 'Tuura will burn.'

'You've seen this?' Gisila asked, her eyes watering.

Edela nodded.

'But Jael!'

'Don't you worry about Jael,' Edela promised. 'But we must open the gates. We need help!'

Kormac looked puzzled. 'Help?'

'Hurry!' Edela insisted, stumbling against Entorp. 'We must open the gates!'

***

'Fire!'

Aleksander's eyes sprung open.

***

'There was no one there,' Beorn said hoarsely as he caught up with Jael. 'Every room we tried was empty.'

Fyn gulped. He felt sick. His arms were shaking. Thankfully, it was too dark for anyone to notice.

Jael looked at Marcus. 'Do they know we're coming?' she whispered.

He shrugged. 'I'd say it makes little difference now.'

'How many guards in the temple?'

'I'm not sure. Maybe thirty? Forty?'

'We broke the binding spell tonight, so perhaps they won't be against us now?' Jael suggested hopefully.

Marcus shook his head, feeling his body tense. 'The temple guards are bound in a different way, I think. Most of them are Followers.'

Jael squeezed her fingers tightly around her shield grip, trying to force open her swollen eye. 'And the elders? The dreamers? What can they do?'

'It depends on what they might have been told. I honestly don't know anymore. But they will work together to stop you leaving. Know that.'

Jael turned to Beorn. 'We have to kill everyone we see. And quickly. We can't give them an opportunity to cause any trouble. Take your men and go for the guards. Aedan, Fyn, we'll go for the dreamers.' She smiled at the men whose eyes glowed eagerly back at her in the gloomy passageway; boots shuffling on flagstones; sweaty palms tightening around swords and axes.

They were eager to begin. Tired of feeling like prisoners.

'We kill them, we go home,' Jael growled. 'Think of Oss. They need us to get out of here. We can't help them until we do.' And turning back to Marcus, and thinking of Eadmund, she nodded. 'Let's go!'

***

The temple guards were going to be a problem.

There were more of them than Kormac had realised and they were lining up across the gates in a great red row, blocking their exit. He turned to Aron, feeling the heat from the flames as they edged closer, sensing the oppressive clouds of smoke drifting towards them.

It was getting hard to breathe.

They needed to open the gates.

Gisila was keeping the puppies close, wrapping their ropes around her wrist. Branwyn had Edela, and Edela had Eydis. Entorp had managed to secure Tig with a rope he had found, and Alaric was there too, cowering behind Kayla, who was jiggling her grizzling daughter.

But while the gates were blocked, there was no escape.

'Where have you been?' one of the temple guards yelled, turning to the straggling bunch of sleepy-eyed soldiers who emerged from the guard tower by the gates. 'Seize them!'

Horsa blinked, looking around at Aron and his family, then back to the row of guards. He turned back to his own men, searching for a commander, but he couldn't see one.

He felt as though he had woken from the longest dream.

And suddenly, everything was clear.

'Why?' Horsa wondered.

And Kormac drew his sword. 'They're all in The Following!'

he cried, pointing to the temple guards. 'The Following had you bound to them! We broke the spell! You're free now, but Tuura will burn! My mother-in-law, she's a dreamer, she's seen it! We must open the gates! Now!'

'Horsa, please!' Aron begged as more soldiers arrived. 'You have to help us!'

Horsa looked confused, his eyes widening as he caught sight of the flames sparking against the dark sky. He strode towards the guards. 'We need to open the gates,' he said simply. 'They're not our prisoners. Clear the way!' He saw people running towards them, trying to escape the fire, dragging their terrified children, clutching their possessions to their chests, pulling their animals behind them. Screaming, coughing, panicking people. He frowned, disturbed by the guards' reluctance to move. 'Clear the way!'

The guards didn't move.

Horsa drew his sword.

***

The grand chamber was full as Jael and her Osslanders strode into it.

Full of dead-eyed, red-breasted guards lining the walls and black-robed dreamers and elders surrounding the fires. And in the very centre of them all stood Gerod Gott.

'Ahhh, you've come!' he smiled, licking his red lips. 'I was growing impatient.'

He had no sword, but nor did he need one, flanked as he was by a shield of kneeling dreamers and a circle of guards.

'Impatient to die?' Jael wondered, quickly sweeping the room with her eyes. Marcus appeared right in his assessment. She guessed that there were about thirty guards and she had about thirty men. Those were better odds than she'd hoped for. 'I can help you with that. Kill them!' And raising her shield to her shoulder, she charged the circle of guards, Fyn and Aedan running behind her.

The Osslanders fanned out on either side of them, clashing against the temple guards who rushed up to meet them.

The cavernous temple was suddenly filled with noise.

And Marcus slunk away.

***

'Aron!' Branwyn screamed as her youngest son drew his sword, rushing to join his father and the melee of soldiers fighting against the guards.

'Branwyn, take everyone back!' Kormac cried. 'Get back!' His cry was muffled as he dropped his chin to his chest, ducking a sword blow.

Soldiers scattered; some rushing back into the tower for swords; others scrambling to defend themselves with what they had to hand.

Blood-curdling cries rose into the night.

Branwyn panicked, blinking through the smoke, glancing around at the burning buildings. Kayla looked terrified, trying to soothe her crying baby. Eydis was frozen, feeling the heat from the flames as they edged closer; the puppies' ropes tangling around her legs.

Everyone was petrified, desperate to escape the rapidly approaching fire.

With one last look at Kormac and Aron, Branwyn shepherded them all away, searching for a safe place to shelter.

***

Jael was confused.

As she fought her way to Gerod with Fyn and Aedan by her side, she was certain that she'd killed three guards, but each one was on his feet again, his wounds gone.

Jael spun, frowning and came face to face with Baccus.

She blinked in surprise.

'Thought you'd killed me?' he spat, gripping his enormous sword in both hands. There were no marks on his throat that she could see.

The fires were high. It felt unusually hot in the temple.

She smelled smoke.

'Well, lucky me,' Jael breathed, quickly realising how much trouble they were in. She backed away from him, glancing around. Gerod stood defiantly in the centre of the dreamers who had their eyes closed, their lips moving.

Chanting.

Jael's head felt hazy as she inhaled more of the smoke.

She knew that smoke.

Baccus charged, swinging, and Jael pushed back her foot, catching his sword on the edge of her blade. The vibration shot up her arm. She ducked his next blow, slicing across his waist. He jerked back, growling at her, shaking his head.

Lunging again, Jael slashed quickly from side to side, trying to keep Baccus busy while she thought of what to do. She had to stop the dreamers.

'Aarrghh!'

Jael's eyes darted to the right as one of her men fell, a sword through his middle. She looked back, swaying, avoiding Baccus' blow, dropping to the floor, sliding, slicing across the backs of his thighs. He stumbled, and she was up, kicking in his knees, knocking him to the ground, jumping onto his back, her sword through his neck.

She checked on Fyn who was struggling, grunting loudly with the effort of holding off the quick moving axe of a thick-necked guard Jael was certain she'd already killed.

They were all struggling. It was like fighting statues.

Men who would not die.

'Go for their heads!' she screamed. 'Take off their heads!'

Lunging to her right, she tried to do just that to a guard who was thankfully shorter than Baccus. He swayed away from her blade, snarling at her, spittle flying. Jael leaned to the side, taking all her weight on her left leg, snapping her right leg up, into his cheekbone, listening to the crack as the knife down her boot broke it.

The guard shrieked, falling to the ground, clutching his broken face. Jael was over him quickly, teeth gritted as she swung back her sword, hacking the blade down across his throat.

Taking off his head.

Wiping blood out of her eyes, Jael was up, ducking a whirling spear as another guard approached. She skidded across the floor, out of his reach, behind him, stabbing him in the back. His legs shook, and he staggered forward but not out of her reach. Jael kicked him in his gaping wound, and he tipped over, his face hitting the flagstones with a wet slap. She rushed to him, sword in both hands, cleaving his head from his neck.

Spinning around, she looked for Marcus, but he had gone, and all she could see was Gerod's shining face, confident in how it would all end.

Jael sucked in a breath as Baccus, back on his feet, lunged at her, chopping his blade down towards her head. She reached up with her sword, teeth gritted, anticipating the impact, pushing her boots onto the floor. 'Grrrrr!' she roared as Baccus' giant blade came down, cracking hers in two.

Jael quickly threw away the broken sword, unsheathing her knife.

Eydis, she begged. Eydis, help us!

CHAPTER FORTY SEVEN

Branwyn found a lean-to.

It was barely big enough to fit them all, but she squeezed everyone in beneath the thatched roof, waiting for the gates to open. Too anxious to speak, they huddled together. Kayla jiggling the baby over her shoulder; Gisila trying to calm the puppies; Branwyn checking on her mother and Eydis, her mind on Kormac and Aron.

Entorp stood outside, holding onto Tig, one eye on the rapidly approaching fire.

'They will not die,' Eydis said dreamily. 'They cannot die. We can't escape. They will not let us leave!'

Edela gasped at a sudden pain in her stomach. It was as though Evaine was stabbing her all over again. She groaned and adjusted herself, feeling light-headed, desperate for water. 'Eydis,' she croaked, patting her arm. 'Can you see the book? Close your eyes. Shut us all out now. Find the page, Eydis. Find the page!'

***

'Aarrghh!' Aron screamed, a blade nicking his cheek. He jerked back, his ears ringing. Gritting his teeth, he swung his sword up to meet the next blow.

The temple guard would not go down.

No matter how grievous their wounds, or how many times they fell, the guards would not die.

They could all see that now.

'Open the gates!' It was an urgent cry. 'Open the gates!'

Kormac shook his head, turning around. He knew that voice.

It was coming from the other side of the gates. He blinked, listening to the battering of swords on shields. Louder and louder. A furious roar was building in the distance.

'Open the gates for the King of Brekka!'

***

Jael threw her knife at Baccus' face.

It stuck into his cheek, but he didn't even sway.

He barely grunted before raising his sword above his head. Jael dropped to one side, slipping on blood, losing her balance, listening to the rhythmic hum from the dreamers echoing around the chamber.

And she remembered her dream about Gerod.

Scooping up an abandoned spear, Jael steadied herself, ducking Baccus' blow before charging at him, stabbing the spear into his stomach. Dragging it straight out, she plunged it into his chest as he stumbled backwards. He would get up, she knew, but if she could just get to the dreamers, maybe they wouldn't be able to control the guards. 'Kill the dreamers!' Jael roared, searching for a sword as she turned towards the circle of chanting, hooded women. 'Kill the dreamers!'

Gerod's smile twisted into an enraged scowl as the

Osslanders, those who could, abandoned their assault on the guards and ran after Jael. 'Stop them!' he screeched.

'You're going to die!' Jael taunted, watching Gerod's eyes twitch in fear as she found another spear and fought her way towards him. But just as she drew back the spear, she stopped and spun, ducking Baccus' blade as it swept towards her neck. 'Fuck! Won't you ever *die*?' she growled, turning to face him again.

'Aarrghh!' Fyn cried as a guard drove a spear straight through his armour, into his stomach. He staggered backwards, trying to keep to his feet as the guard kicked him, knocking him to the ground.

'Fyn!' Jael screamed, raising her spear as Baccus came for her again.

***

Eydis saw the book sitting on a table. A woman stood behind it.

Not her grandmother.

'Come closer, child,' the dark-haired woman urged. 'Come and see the book. Read the spell out loud. Draw the symbol in your blood. Hurry now!'

Eydis ran for the table, her ears buzzing. She swallowed, leaning forward, seeing the words. 'But, but...' and then suddenly her arguments fell away.

She could read them.

'Cut me, Entorp!' Eydis cried. 'I can see! Hurry!'

***

Aleksander was panicking, striding back and forth in front of the gates, but there was nothing he could do. He could smell the smoke, hear the clashing of swords, but there were no men on the ramparts.

And the gates were locked.

'Open the gates!' he bellowed until his voice broke. He turned to Gant. 'We have to get in there!'

Gant pulled on his beard, just as tense, but there was nothing they could do. Their men, who had marched so fast across the fields that they were almost running, were behind them now, but they were all waiting.

They had nothing that would open the gates.

No way to get inside.

***

'Fyn!' Jael spun away from Baccus, but he was quickly in her face again, knocking her off balance. She stumbled but kept to her feet, jumping out of reach as she tried to fend him off with her spear.

Baccus' strength never diminished, his arms never weakened as he threw his giant sword towards her over and over again until he broke her spear in half.

'Fyn!' He didn't answer, but Jael couldn't look around now. The smoke was dulling her senses, and she had to concentrate hard to keep Baccus' sword away from her stomach. Slipping past his blade, Jael punched him in the ribs, then dropped lower, stepped wide and punched him straight in the balls.

He groaned, curling forwards, spitting through his teeth as she skipped away, sweeping the room.

Fyn was back on his feet, but he didn't look like he would be for much longer with a broken spear hanging out of his middle.

The Osslanders were struggling to reach the dreamers at all as the guards pushed them back, creating a solid red wall in front of them.

Jael couldn't see Marcus anywhere.

She reached into her sock, pulled out a knife and ran at Baccus.

***

Entorp guided Eydis' finger to the thick, wooden post he had tied Tig's rope around. It was the only solid, clear surface he could find. 'Draw, Eydis!' he urged as she started chanting. 'Draw!'

'The fire!' Branwyn screamed as she turned, watching the flames jump from the nearest building to their shelter. 'We have to leave!'

Tig reared up, knocking his head onto the roof and Gisila got such a fright that she let go of the puppies, who got such a fright that they ran off into the smoke, trailing their ropes behind them.

***

Jael threw herself up onto Baccus. She needed to slow him down quickly and get to Fyn. Gritting her teeth, she clung to his neck with her left arm, digging her fingernails into his skin as he tried to peel her off him; bringing her knife around to stab him in the face.

Straight through an eye.

'Aarrghh!' he bellowed, roaring now, his head rearing up in agony as he tried to shake her loose.

Jael drew out her knife and stuck it back into his face.

Straight through his other eye.

'Aarrghh!'

Jael pulled out her knife as he stumbled and she slipped, running her blade across his throat. Dropping to the ground, she left Baccus to fall, anticipating his return as she rushed towards Fyn.

'Jael!'

Jael's head snapped to Marcus who stood in the doorway they had come through, holding *Toothpick* above his head. She ran towards him, weaving her way through the guards, taking her sword, watching it glint in the flames.

The dreamers' flinched.

'Get up!' Gerod seethed at Baccus who lay on the ground, blood draining from his face, his throat. 'Get up!'

But this time Baccus didn't get up, and Jael smiled.

Eydis.

***

The temple guards on the ground weren't moving now.

'Open the gates!' Kormac screamed at the soldiers, barely able to breathe. 'Horsa! Get them to open the gates!'

The guards who were still on their feet were backing away now, their wounds taking effect as the soldiers swarmed over them in greater numbers. The fire was encroaching on them all, and Kormac panicked, turning to Aron who was gripping his arm, his face contorted in pain. 'Find your mother! Hurry!'

***

'Jael!' Fyn pleaded, on his knees, clutching his belly, a guard towering over him.

Jael ran towards him, sweeping *Toothpick* across the guard's back, kicking him to the ground. Leaning forward, she drove her blade through his neck.

Fyn tried to speak, worried that he was about to vomit, then everything went black, and he collapsed onto his side.

'Jael! Jael!'

Jael spun around. '*Aleksander?*'

Marcus ran to the doors, hurrying to unlock them, stumbling out of the way as Aleksander and Gant burst in, swords drawn, Brekkan soldiers flooding into the temple around them.

'We have to leave!' Aleksander yelled as he rushed towards Jael. 'The fort is on fire!'

Fyn lay slumped on the flagstones, his stomach oozing, his eyes closed. 'Fyn!' Jael cried, sheathing *Toothpick* before bending down to him. 'Quick! Help me! We need to carry him out!' Aleksander quickly sheathed his own sword as he helped her lift Fyn up.

'No!' Gerod shrieked, watching Jael head for the doors. 'Stop her!' But his guards were too busy coping with the influx of Brekkans who were now fighting alongside the Osslanders.

Jael stopped, glancing around. 'Aedan! Come and help Fyn outside.' She leaned Fyn against Aedan, lifting his limp arm around her cousin's shoulders, before turning back. 'You?' Jael yelled, striding towards the fires, stepping over the bodies of the guards, and her men. 'Stop me? You tried to once before, didn't you? All those years ago, when you sent those men to kill me! But they didn't, and now *I'm* going to kill *you!*'

Gerod rose up before her, his eyes bursting out of his shining face.

'You think this is important? *This*?' he laughed hysterically. 'There's nothing you can do now! You may think that you've won, but this is all a distraction. She is coming! Tonight! You can't stop anything! Not now! Tonight they will raise her from the Dolma! And she will bring back Raemus!'

Jael shivered, knowing that he was right.

Knowing that Hanna had failed to get the book in time.

There was nothing she could do about it, though. Not while she was stuck here, with him; the one who had sent those men to rape her, to kill her cousin, to rape her mother.

She clenched her jaw and kicked Gerod in the chest, knocking him into the fire, watching as his robe caught, his gleaming face twisting in agony as it started to melt. 'And you forget that the prophecy says that *I* will defeat her!' she bellowed, wanting those to be the last words he heard before the flames took his life.

***

'The puppies!' Eydis sobbed, her eyes watering from the smoke as she panicked, unsure of what to do. She had promised Jael. She couldn't let anything happen to them. 'Where are the puppies?'

Gisila felt terrible, but they had to leave. She could feel the intense heat of the fire as the wind rose, fanning the flames ever higher. 'Eydis!' she insisted. 'We must go now! They'll have run out through the gates, I'm sure!' And wrapping her arm firmly around Eydis' shoulder, she moved her forward.

Biddy did not look convinced, knowing those puppies as she did. 'I'll go and find them, Eydis. They'll be hiding somewhere, big babies that they are.' She bent over, coughing. 'Don't you worry now, Gisila and Entorp will look after you.' And with one last look at everyone, she ran into the smoke, calling the puppies' names.

Branwyn sighed in relief as Kormac arrived with Aron. They looked terrible, though, both of their faces covered in blood.

'Come on!' Kormac called over the noise. 'The gates are open! Everyone's leaving!' He could hear the panicked screams now as the Tuurans fought to escape the rapidly burning fort. Animals were tearing past them, bleating and quacking. Children were wailing, falling over as they were knocked to the ground in the rush to leave.

'But where's Aedan?' Kayla sobbed. 'I'm not leaving without him! Take the baby, Kormac, I'll wait here for him!'

Kormac frowned, but he saw the stubborn set of her jaw and didn't argue. He recognised that determined look from his own wife. He would get everyone out then return to look for Aedan himself. His granddaughter coughed and cried over his shoulder as he wrapped his other arm around Branwyn and followed everyone towards the gates.

***

Jael, Aedan, and Aleksander hurried out of the temple towards Gant who had laid Fyn down on the steps. He hadn't opened his eyes, and even in the darkness, Gant could tell that his stomach wound was bad.

'Take Fyn to the pier!' Jael ordered, turning to another Brekkan who she recognised. 'Orm, help Gant. You'll need to carry him. *Sea Bear* is there. Get him on board now!' She caught sight of Beorn who had stumbled through the doors, hoping to catch a breath of fresh air only to be met with more suffocating smoke and flames. 'Is everyone out?' she asked.

Beorn looked back at the temple doors, then around at

his men who were coughing and panting, in desperate need of water. 'All that are left.' He was bruised, bleeding, ready to topple down the steps, but he shook himself awake. 'I need to get to *Sea Bear.*'

Jael looked at Marcus, who was beside her, coughing. 'We have to leave for Andala now. Will you come?'

'I need to find someone,' he said anxiously, his eyes not meeting hers.

'You mean Hanna?' Jael asked. 'She's not here.'

Aleksander turned to Jael in surprise.

Marcus looked confused. And worried. 'Where is she?'

'There's no time!' Jael insisted. 'She's not in Tuura. We can talk on the ship, but for now, we have to go!'

Marcus nodded, clutching a large satchel to his chest. 'I'm ready.'

'Good. Go with Beorn. I'll meet you at the pier.' She turned to Aleksander and Aedan as her men hobbled past them, following Beorn into the billowing clouds of smoke. 'We have to make sure everyone's out of the fort!' She glanced at the buildings which were mostly flames now.

Thinking about Tig. And the puppies.

'Let's go!' Aleksander ran down the steps, Jael and Aedan on either side of him, the ancient Temple of Tuura exploding into flames behind them.

***

'Ido! Vella!' Biddy called, her voice breaking as she bent over, trying to breathe. The smoke was too much. She couldn't see. She straightened up, grimacing. 'Ido! Vella!' she croaked, hurrying towards the flames as horses bolted out of crumbling buildings and mothers ran with their children, trying to find a way through.

And there they were.

'Ido! Vella!' Biddy sobbed with joy at the sight of those annoying puppies running through the smoke. 'Come on! Come on!' They raced for her, their paws up on her legs, whining, begging to be picked up, the ropes still tied around their necks.

They were too heavy, though, too big; not puppies anymore. Biddy scrambled around for their ropes, trying to keep them still long enough to gather them in her hands. Finally, wrapping the ropes around her wrist, she turned to leave, only to discover that there was nowhere to go.

Everywhere she looked, she saw nothing but flames.

***

Jael, Aleksander, and Aedan ran towards the gates.

'Kayla!' Aedan scooped his wife into his arms.

Kayla had been standing in the middle of the street, having rescued two children who were running in panicked circles in their sooty nightclothes, crying for their mother. She held the smallest child in her arms, gripping the other one's hand.

'Where's the baby?'

'Your father took her. I don't know where their mother is,' Kayla said sadly, glancing at the children. 'But we have to go now!'

'Aedan!' Branwyn and Kormac hurried towards them. Having seen everyone safely out of the fort, they had been desperate to go back for Kayla and Aedan. Aron had run off to try and rescue their horses.

'Where is everyone?' Jael asked urgently.

'Outside the gates.'

'Did you get my horse out? Tig?'

Kormac nodded. 'Entorp has him.'

'Then let's go!' Aleksander urged, pushing Jael forward.

Aron ran towards them, pulling his and Aedan's horses. He grinned in relief. 'I found them!' he cried.

Jael saw another child running towards them, his nightshirt on fire. She lunged, throwing him to the ground, rolling him in the dirt and mud until the flames were out. He was stunned, his sobbing ceasing instantly. 'Come on,' she smiled quickly. 'Let's get you out of here.' And standing up, Jael grabbed his hand, following everyone out of the fort.

There were people everywhere.

Animals rushed around their feet in a squawking, clucking panic. A chorus of frantic voices rose into the smoky night air as the Tuurans milled around watching their home burn, anxious for those people still trapped inside.

Jael forced her way through the crowd, trying to find her family.

She could hear Tig before she saw him, and perhaps he knew she was coming because he fought against the rope Entorp was hanging off. Jael didn't have time to feel relieved that he was alright, though, as she ran her eye over everyone. The orange glow from the fort helped her to see that they were all there, except...

'Where's Biddy?' Gisila panicked, running up to Jael. 'She went back for the puppies. I dropped their ropes. She went back for them!'

Jael's stomach clenched.

She turned and ran back into the fort, Aleksander behind her. 'Biddy!' she screamed, disappearing into the flames. 'Biddy!'

***

It was different than anything she had experienced before. But as Morana chanted, her head back, listening to the murmurs of The Followers echoing around her like supportive waves, she felt herself floating across the water. It was as though she was flying, faster than a bird, surging forward, the clouds rushing past her eyes in blurry streaks of pink and light-blue, grey, darker blue now and black and then nothing but darkness and suddenly there was no water, and she was nowhere.

She was in the Dolma.

CHAPTER FORTY EIGHT

Jael couldn't breathe. She was blinking so quickly to try and clear the smoke from her eyes that she could barely see either. 'Biddy!' she cried hoarsely. 'Ido! Vella!'

Aleksander was beside her, yelling into the smoke just as desperately. He peered around, but there were walls of flames everywhere they turned now. Flames that had leapt from building to building, consuming Tuura in one devastating, hot rush of destruction.

Part of him would have felt relieved to see such an end to Tuura, as though it were justice somehow, if only Biddy wasn't lost in there.

'I'm not leaving!' Jael screamed.

'Nor am I!' Aleksander screamed back, grabbing her hand. And they ran as far as they could until they reached another wall of searing flames.

'Ido! Vella! Biddy!' Jael tried to quell her panic as she listened. She closed her eyes, desperate to see something that wasn't despair.

She tried to shut out all the smoke, to just be in the darkness.

Opening her eyes, she ran to the right. 'This way! Biddy! Biddy!'

And then, through the flames, she saw a small, dark shape rushing towards her, another one following quickly behind.

The puppies. Both of them!

They were on fire.

Jael and Aleksander grabbed one each, rolling them on the ground until the flames were out. Jael snatched their ropes as Aleksander charged into the fire looking for Biddy.

'Biddy!' he yelled, shielding his eyes as a building crumbled beside him, burning debris, crackling and spitting at him. 'Biddy!' He saw her then, lying on the ground, not moving at all. Racing to her, Aleksander scooped her into his arms, trying not to inhale any more smoke as he turned and ran back through the flames.

***

Axl had not wanted to wait in the forest.

He had seen the fire burning against the sky, and he'd ordered two of his men to help him onto a horse, and with Amma beside him, they had ridden to the fort.

But when they arrived, the crowd of Tuurans standing outside the gates made it impossible to find anyone he recognised at all. Axl panicked, squinting in the darkness, trying to see his sister, his mother.

Anyone.

'And where have you been, King of Brekka?' Edela smiled wearily, so pleased to see her grandson as he sat upon his horse, not noticing her at all. 'Not hiding at the back like Lothar, I hope?'

'Grandmother!' Axl burst into tears. He couldn't believe it. She looked half dead, he was certain, but there she was, leaning against Entorp.

Alive.

Axl turned to slide off his horse, waiting for one of his men to help him limp to Edela, who quickly wrapped her arms around his waist. 'There, there,' she soothed, feeling him shudder against her. 'I'm not dead yet!'

'Edela!' Amma cried, sliding off her horse. 'I can't believe you're alive!'

'Yes, but not for long, I think, if I don't sit down,' Edela coughed.

Axl's eyes were up on the burning fort, then racing around the people before him. Some he knew. Some he thought he might know.

But not everyone was there.

Gisila hurried towards her son, throwing her arms around him.

'Where's Jael?' he asked over her head. 'Where's Aleksander?'

'Where's Biddy?' Amma wondered.

Gisila was beside herself, her eyes barely leaving the gates. 'They're inside. They're all inside the fort!' Hands to her face, she waited, holding her breath.

Kormac turned to her. 'I'll go and find them,' he said quickly.

'No!' Gisila gripped his arm, not wanting to think that she'd sent another person into those flames. 'No, please, don't go! Please, Kormac!'

He turned back to her, squeezing her hand, staring at her with a calm certainty that eased Gisila's shoulders away from her ears. 'I'll be right back, I promise.' And turning to the gates, he started walking, but before he could pace out two steps, Jael burst through the smoky entrance, nearly knocking him over, two singed dogs running behind her.

'Jael!' Gisila sobbed. 'Jael!' She looked past her daughter, who quickly dropped to her knees, desperate to breathe. And there, behind her, was Aleksander with Biddy in his arms.

'Biddy!' Entorp hurried to help Aleksander as he laid Biddy down on the grass.

Jael gave the puppies' ropes to Kormac and hurried to Biddy, bending over her still body. 'Biddy?'

Entorp dug into his leather satchel, pulling out a jar of salve. Uncorking it quickly, he lifted the jar to Biddy's nose, dipping his finger into it, rubbing the stinking paste under her nostrils.

Jael almost vomited.

Biddy sat bolt upright, coughing, retching, trying to breathe. She croaked, bending over, coughing some more, trying to talk. 'Where are the puppies?' she rasped anxiously, her eyes flicking to Jael. 'I had them!'

Jael couldn't take the smell anymore. Scrambling to her feet, she hurried away from them all and bent over, vomiting, her hands on her knees.

'The puppies are fine,' Kormac smiled, leading them towards Biddy as she sat on the ground.

Ido and Vella looked just as singed and sooty as she did. They lunged for her, paws on her chest, licking her face.

'Oh, get away from me!' Biddy spluttered, trying not to cry. 'Get away from me, you filthy creatures!'

Wiping her hand across her mouth, Jael hurried back to Biddy who still smelled terrible, but she wrapped her arms around her anyway. 'What were you doing?' she grumbled.

'Well, now you know what's it's like to watch *you* being brave!' Biddy grumbled back, pushing her off, trying to stand.

'Jael,' came Eydis' tiny voice, almost lost amongst the noise and the reunions and the relief and the coughing most of all. 'Jael, where's Fyn?'

***

Beorn was mute as he stood in the bow, thinking of the men burning in that temple. He dropped his head to his chest, sick of the smell of smoke.

Entorp was attending to Fyn's wounds inside the house.

He would live, Beorn was sure.

'You're sure?' Jael wondered anxiously, glancing at the entrance to the house. She wanted to go and see for herself.

'We don't have enough hands,' Beorn said flatly. 'Not anymore.'

'They're coming,' Jael assured him. 'My brother is coming. He's bringing enough of his men to get us to Andala quickly. We'll take those ships too,' she said, nodding at the three merchant ships that rolled against the pier behind them. 'We'll get as many people back to Andala as fast as we can so we can head for Oss.'

'If we're not too late.' Beorn felt a sense of exhaustion that was so deep he couldn't see hope anymore.

'We're not,' Jael assured them both. 'I promise you, Beorn, we're not. I've seen it. We'll save them. We'll save them all.'

THE END

EPILOGUE

When Thorgils closed his eyes, he imagined Isaura sleeping in that big bed all alone. No doubt not all alone, he smiled to himself. Mads was likely there, wriggling next to her, thumb in his mouth. Somehow, despite how much the little boy looked like Ivaar, Thorgils had developed quite a soft spot for him.

The feeling wasn't mutual.

He grinned as he walked to the edge of the mist-touched cliff, remembering Mads' furious face whenever he came near; turning away from him as quickly as he could.

Sipping from a water bag, Thorgils yawned, trying to blink himself into the morning. His was not a comfortable bed, and Torstan's snoring had been as ear-splitting as ever. No wonder he had never found himself a wife. Irritating, wifeless Torstan, who was snorting and spitting beside him. 'Do you mind?' Thorgils grumbled at his friend. 'I'm trying to enjoy the dawn chorus over here!'

'Oh, well forgive me!' Torstan snorted some more, scratching his head and yawning, trying to see past the thick bank of clouds in the distance. Squinting, he stepped forward, creeping his way carefully towards the edge of the cliff. 'Thorgils,' he said slowly, watching the long line of ships emerge from under the clouds. 'I think they're here.'

READD NEXT

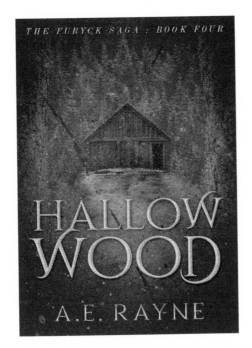

HALLOW WOOD

ABOUT A.E. RAYNE

I live in Auckland, New Zealand, with my husband, three kids and three dogs. When I'm not writing, you can find me editing, designing my book covers, and trying to fit in some sleep (though mostly I'm dreaming of what's coming next!).

I have a deep love of history and all things Viking. Growing up with a Swedish grandmother, her heritage had a great influence on me, so my fantasy tales lean heavily on Viking lore and culture. And also winter. I love the cold!

I like to immerse myself in my stories, experiencing everything through my characters. I don't write with a plan; I take cues from my characters, and follow where they naturally decide to go. I like different points of view because I see the story visually, with many dimensions, like a tv show or a movie. My job is to stand at the loom and weave the many coloured threads together into an exciting story.

I promise you characters that will quickly feel like friends, and villains that will make you wild, with plots that twist and turn to leave you wondering what's coming around the corner. And, like me, hopefully, you'll always end up a little surprised by how I weave everything together in the end!

To find out more about A.E. Rayne and her writing
visit her website: www.aerayne.com

Sign-up & get notified: www.aerayne.com/sign-up

Made in the USA
Columbia, SC
31 January 2021